Tales Alive in Turkey

Tales Alive in Turkey

Warren S. Walker
& Ahmet E. Uysal

TEXAS TECH UNIVERSITY PRESS
Lubbock, Texas   1990

This book was set in 10 on 12 Garamond
and printed on acid-free paper that meets the guidelines
for permanence and durability of the Committee
on Production Guidelines for Book Longevity
of the Council on Library Resources. ∞

Cover design by Cameron Poulter

Printed in the United States of America

Library of Congress Cataloging-in-Publication Data

Walker, Warren S.
    Tales alive in Turkey / Warren S. Walker & Ahmet E. Uysal.
      p. cm.
    Reprint. Originally published: Cambridge : Harvard University
Press, 1966.
    Includes bibliographical references.
    ISBN 0-89672-212-0 (alk. paper). — ISBN 0-89672-213-9 (pbk.)
    1. Tales—Turkey. I. Uysal, Ahmet Edip. II. Title.
GR280.W35 1990
398.2'09561—dc20

                                        89-27705
                                          CIP

Texas Tech University Press
Lubbock, Texas 79409-1037 USA

Bismillah

Acknowledgments

Every work of this type is inevitably the result of the collaboration of a great many people. Some of our informants we have cited with the tales selected for this volume; many others whose tales do not appear here contributed fully as much in helping us to approach an understanding of the whole range of Turkish folktales. To several colleagues of the Language and History–Geography Faculty of Ankara University we owe our thanks, especially to Hamit Dereli and Irfan Shahinbash of the English Department, to Faruk Sümer of the History Department, and to Orhan Ajipayamli of the Ethnology Department. To the Rector and the Faculty Senate of the University we are indebted for grants, made through the Research Institute for the Study of Western Literatures, which made it possible for us to continue field work during the summers of 1963 and 1964; to the President and Board of Directors of Texas Technological College we are similarly indebted for a research grant awarded during the academic year 1965–66. To the Turkish Ministry of Education and its Directors in several provinces we wish to express thanks for facilitating our travel and collecting. Appreciation is expressed for the assistance in collecting rendered by Muammer Birkan, Nebiye Birkan, Nuri Gench and his family, Neriman Hizir, Filiz Kiygi, the late Halil Temel, and Barbara K. Walker. For permission to reprint "Crazy Mehmet and the Three Priests" we are grateful to Moses Asch; the tale was first published in 1965 on Folkways Record Number FL 9922.

Contents

Contents

Contents

xii

Foreword

More than three centuries have elapsed since the Ottomans' defeat at the second siege of Vienna in 1683. It was that defeat, above all, that caused the Ottomans to question why the West was stronger than they and (with further indications of decline) led to their long and slow process of modernization or Westernization as it is often called. The Republic of Turkey is the final product of that process.

Officially imposed change in the Ottoman Empire came first in the military and technical arenas, but spread gradually to administrative and political institutions and to the higher echelons of education. Social and general cultural change was much slower to occur, but began to quicken its pace considerably after the middle of the nineteenth century when a small group of the intelligentsia started to create a modern Turkish literature. Strongly influenced by French literature and thought, this group of men began to substitute Western genres for the highly formalized poetry of the Islamic-inspired Arab-Persian tradition and the ornate (and often rhymed) prose of the Ottoman scholars and literati. Moreover, they initiated a language reform movement that eventually was to cleanse Turkish of most of the Arabic and Persian elements that had dominated it over the centuries and launched a movement that has culminated in this century in a vibrant and exciting Turkish literature. This literature, while producing works that are in full step with the literary directions followed by Europe and America, has turned also to the centuries-old heritage of Turkish folklore for inspiration.

It is no coincidence that modern Turkish literature has shown particular strength in the short story. The narrative medium in Ottoman literature was the *mesnevi*, a long verse genre with didactic, heroic, or romantic intent that served also as a vehicle for the very forceful current of mysticism existing among the Ottomans. Over the course of time, it became a highly stylized and precious art form. In contrast, the popular literature of the Turks—from its earliest days in Central Asia—demonstrated particular vitality in narrative prose. It is this oral prose tradition that is represented in *Tales Alive in Turkey*. First published in 1966, the book has been out of print for a number of years. The present reprint is to be welcomed, therefore, by teachers, who now can reinstate the title on their list of required readings for a wide variety of courses in the field of Turkish studies, and by anyone wanting to learn something about this very special aspect of the true national heritage of the Turk, which, as the title of the book implies, still flourishes in Turkey. The tales presented were collected, however, over the years 1961 to 1964, and the reader may well ask whether this implication still holds good as we approach the nineties, whether Professors Warren Walker and Ahmet Uysal can confirm the statement they make in their introduction that Turkey "is still dominated by an oral tradition." To answer such a question, we must look at conditions in Turkey today and record the more recent findings of the authors of *Tales Alive in Turkey* as they continue their work with the Turkish folktale.

Life in Turkey has undergone many striking changes since the sixties, both in the towns and cities and in rural areas. Urban populations have increased by leaps and bounds, and the expectations and lifestyles of those living in Turkish towns and cities today differ very little from those of urban populations in Europe and America. Villages that were remote in those days may now lie on or close to one of the newly constructed highways and take for granted such services as tap water and electricity that not long ago were regarded as luxuries. Many more village schools have been built, and literacy in general has experienced a huge increase, present forecasts being for total literacy by the year 2000, a notable contrast to the barely one-third rate at midcentury. The telephone, more radios, the television, and programs such as "Dallas" have become a part even of village life in many parts of Turkey. More and more Turks have had experience of town or big-city living. Some have spent long periods working in West Germany or other European countries, or at least know of these lands vicariously through friends and family members who come to visit or return to settle in their homeland once more, bringing with them their Mercedes and all the other accoutrements of a different world, a different lifestyle.

Such changes have had a deep influence on the habits, the tastes, and the cultural orientation of the Turks, especially on those groups linked traditionally to the folk rather than the Ottoman or, more recently, the Western mode of life. Over a large part of the country, especially in the more populated regions of central and western Anatolia, folklorists are finding fewer individuals who appreciate, let alone who are committed to, the folk traditions. Even in villages these days, people have less time and insufficient patience to sit listening to the long performances of the raconteurs. As for the raconteurs, a definite deterioration is noticeable in their repertories and performances as one generation succeeds another. The sons of well-known storytellers do not have the knowledge and skill of their fathers.

Yet in the eastern provinces, indeed as far west as areas such as Konya, the folktale *is* still alive. In recent fieldwork, Professors Walker and Uysal have found relatively young raconteurs, persons only in their forties or fifties, telling good tales in the old tradition, a tradition that continues to serve not only as an entertainment but also as a window opening onto the imaginative and moral world of the Turks. Moreover, they have come across rich veins previously not mined. They have collected, for example, very interesting material from among nomad groups in the Taurus Mountains (an area corresponding in some ways to America's Appalachia with its rich folklore), and plan to collect also from three villages in the Black Sea area near Trabzon said to have been settled by Scots who had taken part in the Second Crusade. As to categories and personages, a large corpus of religious tales has emerged: a number of tales dealing with figures who, though not part of the canon, are favorites of folklore; also, more long minstrel tales (represented only by Köroghlu in *Tales Alive*). Tales involving Hizir, the *deus ex machina* who appears mysteriously to save the main protagonist at moments of extreme danger, are still popular, as are Nasreddin Hoca anecdotes. Another comic figure previously documented only minimally but well covered by tales recently recorded is Behlül Dane—the wise simpleton depicted as the half brother of Harun al-Rashid and one of the Forty Saints.

All this is good news. Even better is the fact that a selection of this new material is now being prepared for publication under the title *More Tales Alive in Turkey*. Together, the volumes comprise a veritable treasury of Turkish tales to delight and inform present and future generations of English speakers who do not understand Turkish. Professors Walker and Uysal are to be congratulated and thanked for their painstaking research and fieldwork that made this possible.

Kathleen R. F. Burrill
Director of the Center of Turkish Studies
Columbia University

Introduction

From the tales of *Dede Korkut,* with their legends of the Oghuz Turks in Central Asia during the Dark Ages, through the *Arabian Nights* and the exempla of Jalal al-Din Rumi's *Masnavi* in the Middle Ages, to the countless court tales of the Ottoman era, there is a great wealth of narrative that could — on the basis of geography, politics, or culture — be considered in the realm of Turkish folktales. But for the scholar this way leads to madness. Because Anatolia, the bulk of the present homeland, has for centuries been the "loom of history" across which have been woven diverse cultural strands, and because the Ottoman Empire, at its height, incorporated so many peoples and so much territory, any general discussion or study of Turkish folktales is impossible. One must delimit narrowly and define closely if the rubric is to be at all meaningful.

As the title indicates, this volume is concerned only with living tales, tales current in the oral tradition in Turkey today. It is limited further in being restricted to narration in the Turkic language, the only reliable criterion of the Turkishness of anything. Excluded, therefore, are the tales of such sizable minorities in Anatolia as the Kurds, the Laz people, and the Armenians, except as they have been absorbed (as a great many undoubtedly have) by the Turks themselves.

Despite the giant strides it has made toward modernization during the past four decades, Turkey has remained unchanged in one respect: it is still dominated by an oral tradition. Formal education and the printed word have had relatively little direct impact on the masses of

1

people in a land where the illiteracy rate runs to almost 70 percent. In the 40,000 villages, where live the bulk of the population, newspaper deliveries are uncommon, regular mail service is nonexistent or minimal, and libraries are a rarity. Accordingly, the various kinds of lore governing the manifold activities of daily life, along with the accumulated wisdom of the people, are transmitted from father to son, from generation to generation, not so much by books as by spoken words.

Every vilayet or province boasts its own distinctive folk dances, performed locally, as they have been for centuries, and at national dance festivals promoted by the government since the formation of the Republic.[1] Every caza or county has its repertoire of folk songs and ballads, most of them fashioned for accompaniment on the saz, a popular three-stringed, lutelike instrument. Many cities have their own teams of riddlers — those from Konya and Antakya are especially well known — who participate in interurban competition, not on a regular schedule but in response to challenges. In every village lives at least one folk poet — poor, illiterate usually, but often inspired — who, like a medieval minstrel, earns his living by composing songs of adventure and love which he sings at weddings, entertainments, and other public occasions.[2] And raconteurs of folktales are ubiquitous. Seemingly every Turk can tell a number of folktales, and at least one person in every crowd not only knows a score but, what is more remarkable, can narrate them in an engaging and accomplished manner.

What are the social dynamics of such a strong narrative tradition? Pointing to the frequency of female protagonists, Boratav goes so far as to maintain that Turkish folktales were largely developed in and kept alive by the female community.[3] With this we cannot entirely agree, for our own experience indicates another institution, entirely male, which is of equal importance in the preservation of narrative forms, namely, the coffee house. It is there that the male villager customarily goes to meet his friends; it is there that the unemployed peasant whiles away time as he awaits day labor; and, most important for the propagation of folktales, it is there that men and boys often spend whole nights during Ramazan, the month-long religious observance that requires of the Moslem total fasting between sunrise and sunset but, mercifully, leaves the night free of such restriction. In the villages the precepts of Islam are still adhered to quite strictly, postsunset and predawn Ramazan meals are common, and the hours between are often spent socially. In the coffee houses the earlier part of the evening was, until recently, devoted to highly stylized puppet plays — Karagöz plays [4] they are called, after

2

the leading actor, Karagöz (Black Eye) — but the staple for the remainder of the night was, and is, the folktale. Raconteurs are rated by their performance during Ramazan. Throughout Hatay province,[5] for example, Kuru Abdu, one of our informants, is known by almost everyone for his ability to relate thirty long tales in a linked cycle (one for each night of Ramazan), with a "cliff-hanger" closing at the end of each in the best fashion of Scheherazade.

It would be of interest to know what percentage of the folktales familiar to the average Turk he first heard narrated in a coffee house during Ramazan. Many of the tales in our archive were collected in coffee houses, and of these, some of the best were recorded during Ramazan of 1962. For purposes of collecting, such places as old folks' homes and prisons are as likely locations in Turkey as they are anywhere else. Some of our more interesting tales, for example, were collected from men imprisoned for life in the Sinop Penitentiary, built within the towering walls of the medieval Genoese fortress that broods over that Black Sea port. But both these institutions are outside the main stream of life and cannot serve the same roles as the kitchen and the coffee house in the perpetuation of patterns of oral culture.

The selections in this volume were all recorded on tape between October 1961 and October 1964. Because electric power was often unavailable, most of the tales were collected with a portable, transistorized, battery-powered machine. No attempt was made to stage the performances recorded: background noises impinged upon the narration, interruptions were made by members of the audience, and questions were asked by the collectors. A few of these interpolations add enough to the stories so that we felt they should be retained in the printed version too — sometimes in the footnotes.

The translation is quite literal, and hence the style varies from narrator to narrator, from tale to tale. Such seemingly sophisticated flourishes as the opening and closing formulas for some of the tales are not uncommon elements in the art of folk narrative. Among these the most frequently employed is the *tekerleme*,[6] the nonsense jingle that introduces many a tale, including the first one in this volume. The material is entirely unexpurgated, except where noted. Generally speaking, we have chosen to omit completely tales scatological, perverse, or otherwise objectionable to English and American readers rather than bowdlerize them. It may logically be maintained that the extent of these omissions (8 to 10 percent of all tales collected) measures the degree to which we have distorted the perspective on Turkish folktales.

3

Almost every major section of Turkey is represented in this volume, and the entries in our larger archive are drawn from more than two hundred cities, towns, and villages, ranging from Antakya in the extreme south to Sinop in the north, from Edirne in the west to Erzurum in the east. Our itineraries extended over 10,000 kilometers of travel, most of it through rural Turkey. The precise location at which each tale was collected is indicated in the notes. Because relatively few villages are shown on ordinary maps, we have identified sites by listing after the village name that of the caza city (roughly, the county seat) to which it is attached for administrative purposes, and that of the vilayet in which it lies. A small map on page 252 shows all of the Turkish vilayets, and this will provide a guide for locating caza towns on more detailed maps. Beginning in January 1965 the difficulty of locating villages was doubled in many instances by the decision of the Ministry of Interior to rename all those which had indelicate names (Boklu Köy, dung-spattered village, for example) or names derived from non-Turkish words (Zir, Chorja). To folklorists it seems obvious that the illiterate peasants in such places will go on using the names that have stood for generations, and will, in most instances, be quite oblivious to the paper-shuffling efforts of bureaucrats in Ankara. Consequently, we have listed both names in order to avoid confusion.

The typing of folktales and the subsequent grouping of types are usually Procrustean procedures, and undoubtedly our classifications too have often been arbitrary. In identifying types we have used the standard general work, *The Types of the Folktale*, by Aarne and Thompson, and the specialized index for Turkish tales, *Typen Türkischer Volksmärchen*, compiled by Wolfram Eberhard and Pertev Naili Boratav. Many of the tales in our collection are represented, sometimes in widely variant forms, in one or both of these indexes; others do not appear in either. It should be understood that tales in this collection (and in any other, for that matter) are parallel in varying degrees to Aarne-Thompson, Eberhard-Boratav, and other types. In some cases the parallel may be quite close despite the presence of peculiar motifs; in other instances the similarities may be so tenuous that the reader may take exception to our typing. Motif numbers and captions are those found in Stith Thompson's *Motif-Index of Folk Literature*. We have made no attempt to list all of the motifs present but rather to cite those we consider pivotal in our particular versions of the tales.[7]

For the sake of simplicity we have reduced the major groupings of tales from the twenty-three listed by Eberhard and Boratav to seven.

4

Some of our headings may seem unduly comprehensive, but they do provide workable categories under which virtually all of our several hundred tales can be subsumed. Part I, for example, is devoted to tales based on supernatural elements, without regard to whether these tales demand credence on the part of the listeners. This includes the *märchen* as Thompson defines it: "A *Märchen* is a tale of some length involving a succession of motifs or episodes. It moves in an unreal world without definite locality or definite characters and is filled with the marvelous. In this never-never land humble heroes kill adversaries, succeed to kingdoms, and marry princesses."[8] It also incorporates the novella, the more literary tale of the *Arabian Nights* kind, which Thompson describes as closely related to the *märchen*. Thus Part I comprises seven of the first nine major groups in *Typen Türkischer Volksmärchen:* Helpful animals or spirits; Marriage to supernatural animal or spirit; Meetings with holy good spirits; The ways of destiny; Dreams; Meetings with evil spirits; People with magic powers. Similarly, Part VII is a broad category, but in this case almost entirely unrepresented in the Eberhard-Boratav index. We have labeled this section "Anecdotes" for want of a better word in English, though it does not parallel much of the material listed by Aarne and Thompson under that heading as Types 1200–1999. It includes the *fikra,* which relates a humorous or ironic incident, and the *nükte,* an anecdote that depends for its effect upon a witticism or a play on words. It is safe to say that there are literally thousands of these short tales current in Turkey today, most of them revolving around specific jesters or generic character types. Some of our other groupings are more restricted in scope.

An introduction is provided for each group, the level at which some generalizations can safely be made. To the notes have been relegated (1) analyses of types and motifs, (2) commentary on the content, form, and the ethnological background of individual tales, and (3) reference to scholarship in the field and to pertinent printed analogues. At the back of the volume can be found a selected bibliography of works used in the completion of this study.

PART I

Tales of the Supernatural

To draw together so many unrealistic tales under one heading, tales that in any way depart from the natural order of things, is obviously a gross oversimplification. This is especially true of Turkish folktales, a fairly high proportion of which still turn on some supernatural — or, to say the least, physically impossible — event. Over 25 percent of all the tales in our archive fall into this broad category; and in the Eberhard-Boratav index, of more restricted scope but often greater depth than the present work,[1] the proportion is even greater.[2] (We have excluded from this group legends and tall tales, which also contain physical impossibilities but clearly do not belong with *märchen* and fables.) Part I could readily be subdivided in many different ways. Indeed some of the major types that fall into this classification — the Cinderella–Cap o' Rushes story would be a good example — warrant separate studies of their own, so numerous and widely distributed are their variants in Turkey today. Such vertical research is not, however, in the province of a survey.

Boratav makes three generalizations about tales of this kind in Turkey: (1) that tales with supernatural elements are now almost exclusively urban; (2) that giants, dragons, monsters, and fairies are found in rural areas but in name only — they behave like human beings; and (3) that the Anatolian peasant has largely supplanted *märchen* with more realistic tales.[3] The material in our archive — collected largely in villages and towns rather than cities — denies completely his first contention and supports the second and third only after considerable qualification. Though some formerly monstrous creatures have indeed been

7

humanized by time — "The Keloghlan and the Köse" that follows provides a striking instance of such transformation — this is no more true in rural than in urban areas. Moreover, though our statistics show the proportion of *märchen* and related types to be now only 25 to 30 percent of all tales, there is no evidence whatever that there has been a greater shrinkage among the Anatolian peasants than among urbanites. We should hazard the guess that just the opposite is true: that in cosmopolitan jet-age Ankara, Istanbul, and Izmir, tales of the supernatural have less appeal even to children than they have to all age levels in villages, where life is often much the same as it was in Biblical times.

Character types peculiar to Turkish folklore appear in many of the tales in this volume. Such figures as Bekri Mustafa, the Bektashi, and the man from Kayseri are limited to a particular kind of tale, and so they are found in only one of the following sections. Other types are more general, more complex, more adaptable, functioning in numerous roles in a variety of tales. Of these, two are so versatile that they easily exceed all other folk characters in the parts they play, and so they merit special comment here. One is Keloghlan, and the other, Köse.

The word *kel-oghlan* means bald boy, but it is a particular kind of baldness referred to here, *kel* indicating hairlessness from disease. Among Turkish peasants, for whom cleanliness is not always next to godliness, a variety of ringworm is very common; this is a fungus infection, highly contagious, that sometimes leaves whole families bald or partly bald. More often, however, it will attack a younger child who, in a large family, may receive little care and who will be unable to attend to his personal hygiene. Although a sympathetic character, he is not, perhaps surprisingly, an object of pity; on the contrary, he is often thought to have become lucky by virtue of his malady. And so in folktales Keloghlan is usually the unpromising younger son whom fortune inevitably attends. Quite stupid or naïve sometimes, he blunders through one experience after another to win in the end. At other times he is endowed with a peasant shrewdness that enables him to earn his success, and here occasionally he assumes the role of trickster.

Frequently a person of high social status, the son or daughter of the padishah or ruler, will be or will pretend to be a keloghlan in order to pass undetected among peasants. The disguise is effected by means of shabby clothes and a sheep's stomach, cleaned, dried, and stretched to cover the head tightly and thus conceal one's hair.

Keloghlan is the Turkish Male Cinderella, Aladdin, Ali Baba, Brave

Little Tailor, and many another hero. A protean figure, he appears in a variety of tales — wherever, in fact, the protagonist is a young and sympathetic peasant boy. Frequently, in our field work, an informant would begin a tale about a nameless youth without mentioning any physical peculiarities, and then, halfway through the narration, would unconsciously refer to him as Keloghlan. Because his origin is usually lower-class, he is frequently viewed as a projection of peasant wish fulfillment, almost as much a state of mind as a character.[4]

Köse is a counterpart to Keloghlan, as consistently negative as the bald boy is positive. He is never a really sympathetic character, even when he is the protagonist of a tale, as he is in his trickster role (Part III). Like Keloghlan, he is a physical type to which have been attributed traits of personality and, as his function in Part I will demonstrate, a vague relationship with the nonhuman world.

The köse is a predatory creature who gains his livelihood by treachery of every imaginable kind. Avaricious, crafty, cruel, and vicious in all his actions, he lacks completely any human feeling for others, and he is accorded none. In the folktale his sole purpose seems to be to injure people, personally or materially, and then become the object of vengeance that usually culminates in his death. Although human in form — he is never young, much less a child, and so we do not know his origins — he is, in effect, an ogre, a monster, and many of the tales in which he appears are parallels of the Aarne-Thompson types involving the defeat of ogres (Types 1000–1199).

On the literal and simplest level, *köse* means a beardless man. Beardlessness, the result of glandular imbalance or of hormone deficiency, occurs among all peoples, but it is a condition that seems particularly noticeable in Turkey. Why this is so we do not know. Can it be shown statistically that there is a greater percentage of beardless men in Turkey than in countries of Western Europe? Probably not. Or, is the stigma attached to beardlessness so strong that it distorts the actual proportion?[5] Regardless, the köse is a familiar figure, and the word *köse* is number 270 on the army's frequency list for spoken Turkish.

The köse is not necessarily effeminate or impotent, and he is not necessarily a homosexual. In both real life and fiction, he ordinarily marries and rears a family. A heart-shaped face and short legs are thought to be secondary characteristics of the köse, though these are more matters of folk belief than fact. When one informant (Hasan Hazir of the village of Chamalan) was asked why the köse had short legs, he promptly replied, "Because all his strength goes to his head." In folk literature he is

9

often named Musa, probably for its near rhyming with köse and with
kisa, meaning short.

In only two of the following tales does a keloghlan appear named as
such, but it should be remembered that he is often the protagonist in
variants of tales 2, 3, 4, 5, 7, and 10, and his name could readily be
substituted for Mehmet or Hüsnügüzel or The Son of the Fisherman —
as it actually is in dozens of tales in both our archive and Boratav's. Tale
number 6 shows the keloghlan pitted against the köse in a sequence of
events which fairly well humanizes both types. The köse is still as vicious
as the ogre from which he evolved, and because of this evil origin, both
he and his entire family are exterminated by the keloghlan without the
slightest scruple. In a variant of this tale (collected in Ovajik village,
near Silifke) the keloghlan is not only named Ifrit (a non-Turkish
word that means demon or spirit — as it does in the *Arabian Nights*),
but he is also capable of transforming himself into many different forms,
and seems to be an agent of divine justice. Here, however, though he is
acutely perceptive, the keloghlan like the köse is merely human; the tale
was chosen to illustrate that tendency toward realism noted by Boratav
and commented upon above. In "The Blind Padishah with Three Sons"
there is no suggestion whatever that the protagonist is actually a keloghlan; he is named Keloghlan because of the association of the type
with the youngest son.

Variety was the chief criterion for the choice of the particular tales
included in this section. There occurs among them relatively little dupli-
cation of types and motifs except in tales 9 and 10, "The Caldron-
Headed, Ax-Toothed Sister" and "The Jeweled Cage and the Evil Sister." These are widely variant forms of the same basic tale, the first
stark, simple, childlike — and told to us by a ten-year-old boy; the latter intricately embroidered and more sophisticated, though no less dependent upon the marvelous for its action.

1.

The Blind Padishah with Three Sons [6]

Once there was and once there was not, a long time ago,
when God had many people but it was a sin to say so, when the camel
was a town crier and the cock was a barber, when the sieve was in the

straw and I was rocking my mother's cradle, "Tingir, mingir," [7] there was a padishah who had three sons, the youngest of whom was a keloghlan. After a time, the padishah became blind, and he was told in a dream that he could be cured only if someone could take a handful of dirt from some place on earth that had never been trodden by his horse's feet.

The eldest son said, "Father, I shall go and get a handful of dirt from a place where your horse has never walked." He mounted his horse, took along food enough for six months, and set out on his journey. He rode in a straight line for three months and then he said to himself, "Surely my father could not have come this far." So he took a handful of dirt from that place and started home with it. He arrived back at his father's palace at the end of another three months and said to the blind padishah, "Here is a handful of dirt from a place three months' distance from here."

His father smiled and said, "Son, I used to light a cigarette and reach the spot where you got this dirt before I had smoked it halfway down. My horse has walked on this soil many times."

The eldest son was humiliated at his failure and said nothing. Then the second son said, "Father, I shall get a handful of dirt never trodden by your horse's hoofs." He took enough food to last for a year — six months to go and six months to return — and then set out. After riding for six months he came to a high mountain covered with trees. He climbed to the top of this mountain and took from the very peak a handful of dirt. When he returned, at the end of a year, he said, "Try this earth, father, and see if it will do your eyes any good."

The padishah had traveled extensively, and he knew of every type of soil that existed anywhere. He pinched some of the dirt that the second son had brought and said, "Son, I used to light a cigarette and ride to the mountain where you got this soil before it was entirely smoked."

The second son was humiliated and said nothing. The youngest son, Keloghlan, said nothing also, but he decided that he would now go in search of the handful of earth that would cure his father's blindness. It was Friday and Keloghlan carried his blind father to the mosque on his back. Leaving the padishah there, Keloghlan rushed home and went immediately to his mother's room. "Where does my father keep his horse?" he asked.

"Why, in the stable with all of the other horses," she answered.

"No, that is not what I mean." He grabbed his mother and held the point of a knife to her throat. "You will tell me where he keeps his horse or I will kill you," he said.

"There is a lake in the courtyard," she said, "and the horse lives in that lake."

"How shall I take the horse from the lake?" asked Keloghlan.

"There is a special bridle hanging in the stable, apart from the others. If you take this bridle and strike the surface of the water with it, the horse will rise to the surface and come to you."

The keloghlan went to the lake in the courtyard and did as his mother had directed. When the magic horse came to the surface and swam over to him, Keloghlan slipped the bridle over his head. He led the horse from the lake and tied him to a nearby tree. By this time the service in the mosque was over, so Keloghlan went there and carried his father back home. Kissing his father's hands, he said, "Farewell, father. I am going to find the healing earth for your eyes."

"Your elder brothers have both tried and failed," said the padishah. "Why do you think that you can succeed?"

"If it is my kismet,[8] father, I shall be able to do it."

"Well, are you taking a good weapon with you? Go into that next room and take any of my swords that you can swing. They are all so heavy, you may not find one you can carry."

Keloghlan went into the next room, picked up a whole armful of swords, and dumped them down before his father with a great clatter. Greatly pleased, the padishah said, "I believe that you will succeed in this difficult undertaking."

After traveling for a day Keloghlan came to a house where he stopped and asked for lodging for the night. An old woman lived there with her daughter. "Where are you going, son?" asked the old woman.

"I am the son of the blind padishah, mother, and I am searching for a handful of dirt that will cure my father's blindness. It has to be dirt on which the hoofs of my father's horse have never trodden. I shall travel until I find this."

"But, young man, there is hardly a spot on the earth where the feet of your father's horse have not walked. There is just one spot that I know of, and that is beneath the head of a sleeping monster, a horrible dragon."

Before he left the house of the old woman he asked for the hand of her daughter for his eldest brother. The old woman agreed to this and they pledged the engagement by drinking sherbet together.[9] "I shall return later for her," he said the next morning, and then he left.

At the end of that day he came to another house and knocked on the door. An old woman came to the door and asked, "What do you want, son?"

"I should like to stay as a guest at your home tonight," he said.

"All right, son, come in. Where are you going?"

"I am the son of the blind padishah, mother, and I am searching for a handful of earth from a place never walked upon by my father's horse. This dirt will cure his blind eyes."

"I am afraid that you will never be able to do that. Your father has lived a long life and he has ridden all over this land on his horse."

They sat down and after a short time a beautiful girl brought them two cups of coffee on a tray. When Keloghlan saw the girl, he asked for her hand for his second brother. When the old woman agreed to this, they pledged the engagement by drinking their coffee.

The next morning Keloghlan left, saying that he would return for the girl. After riding for several hours, he came upon a plain, and in the center of the plain he saw a huge object dappled red and white. "Oh, my horse," he said, "what is that strange thing in the center of this plain?"

"That is the monster you have been seeking. My feet have touched every place on earth except the soil beneath his head. I have run around this monster a great many times as your father fought with it, but I have never walked on the spot where he lays his head, for your father could never defeat him. If he rears his head, the whole area may be engulfed in flames. I may be able to save myself by running, but you would be burned to death. It was these flames that damaged your father's eyes and eventually made him blind."

"You stay here," said the young man, "and I shall go alone to fight this dragon."

"Come along, young man," said the monster when he came close to it, "what do you want?"

"Dragon father," said Keloghlan, "with your permission I should like to take a handful of dirt from beneath your head. I have heard that my father often fought with you and that he became blind as a result. I want the soil to heal his blind eyes."

"Is it your turn to fight with me now? I shall give you the dirt on one condition."

"What is it?"

"Somewhere behind that farthest mountain lives a khoja girl.[10] If you will bring her to me, I shall let you have the earth you want."

13

Keloghlan went back to his horse, mounted it, and set out to search for the khoja girl. He rode past the mountain pointed at by the dragon and after several days found the khoja girl on a flat, grassy plain, performing her ablutions [11] and praying. The young man approached her as she was praying and shouted "Selamünaleyküm!" [12]

But the girl could not answer then, for she was in the middle of her prayer. The young man opened his mouth to speak again, but he was suddenly struck blind. After she had finished praying, the girl said to him, "Now, young man, speak!"

"What shall I speak? I came with eyes but now I am blind."

"You should know that everything has to be done according to its own rules. A prayer must never be interrupted."

"Well, I was an ignorant man and did not know this."

"I shall cure you then," replied the khoja girl and saying, "Bismillah!" [13] she drew her thumbs across the young man's eyes. Immediately he was able to see again, but there was no white in his eyes any longer. They were entirely black. "What is your purpose here, young man?" asked the khoja girl.

"My purpose here is to take you to a monster down in the valley so that he will give me a handful of dirt from beneath his head. This dirt will cure my father's blindness."

"I could cure his blindness," said the girl.

"But I have promised to bring the dirt from beneath the monster's head to cure him," said Keloghlan.

"Very well, then, I shall go with you to the monster, but I have one condition first."

"What is your condition?"

"There is a horse with six colts that lives in a river nearby. All of them come out to graze on an island in the center of the river. For years I have tried to catch that mare and her horses but I have always failed. If you can deliver them to me, I shall go with you to the monster."

The young man accepted this proposal and returned to his horse. He found his horse weeping. "Why are you crying?" he asked.

"Why shouldn't I cry? Those colts are my brothers and that mare is my mother. Once we all lived in a lake together. Your father built his palace by that lake. He caught me when I was very young and hid me. My mother looked for me everywhere but could not find me. Then she took my brothers and left, and now they live in the river."

"How can I catch them?"

"I shall try to lead my mother along the bank of the river. Take off

14

my bridle, and when she passes by, throw it over her head. If you can catch her, then the colts will follow after her." They went to the river bank and the young man took off the special bridle. Before the horse dived in he said to Keloghlan, "If you see a patch of red foam on the surface of the water after I jump in, do not wait for me. If you see a patch of white foam, it means that I am alive."

The young man waited on the bank for several minutes and then he saw a patch of white foam on the surface of the water. A few minutes later he saw his own horse swim by with the mare and her colts chasing it like a pack of dogs. As the mare swam past, Keloghlan threw the bridle over her head and in this way caught her. He returned to the khoja girl with the mare.

"At last I have caught you," said the girl.

"You did not catch me. I was taken unawares," said the mare.

Turning to the son of the blind padishah the girl said, "You have captured the mare that I could not capture. You must be more courageous than I am. I am ready now to go to the monster with you."

The khoja girl mounted the wild mare and Keloghlan mounted his own horse, and together they rode to the place where the monster lay on the plain. When they drew close to him, Keloghlan shouted, "Selamünaleyküm, dragon father!"

"Aleykümselam, son," said the monster. "You must be a very wise young man to be able to capture this khoja girl. I tried for many years to capture her but always failed. You are wiser than I am and you may take both the girl and the handful of dirt that you wish."

Keloghlan took the dirt and started toward home. The khoja girl rode alongside him and the six colts followed them. As soon as the dirt had been torn up from the ground and placed in the handkerchief of the young man, the eyes of his father were cured. The khoja girl knew this, and after they had ridden for a distance, she said to Keloghlan, "Beware of your two older brothers. They will set a trap for you at a crossroad where you will meet them. They will talk with you about your adventures and then they will leave you in the trap to die."

"I do not believe this," said Keloghlan.

"It is true, nevertheless. But do not worry about it. Here is a magic ring. When you have fallen into the trap, wait patiently until you hear the Friday ezan.[14] Then lick this ring and two rams will appear, one white and the other black. If you mount the white ram, he will carry you up out of the trap into which you have fallen, but if you mount the black one, he will carry you down to the seventh level of the earth."

15

They rode until they came to the cottage where the young man had pledged the engagement of a girl to his second brother. They placed this girl on a colt and then rode a whole day until they came to the house where Keloghlan had first stopped. There they took the girl pledged to his older brother and placed her on another of the colts of the wild mare, and together they all started toward the palace of Keloghlan's father.

As they approached a crossroad, Keloghlan saw his two brothers sitting before a tent waiting for him. "Remember what I told you," said the khoja girl. "After they leave you in the trap they will take me and the other two girls home with them. They will marry these girls, but I will refuse to marry either of them unless certain conditions are met. I shall ask for a dress that has not seen the sun, that has not been cut by scissors or sewn by the hand of man. No one will be able to provide this until you come, for there is only one dress like this in the world, and it is inside this hazelnut. When I see that dress, I shall then know that you have gotten out of the trap and returned." Saying this, she gave the young man a hazelnut. He put the nut in his pocket and smiled at her, but he still did not believe that his brothers would try to harm him. "After that I shall ask for a golden tray on which a golden dog is chasing a golden rabbit. There is only one of these wonderful objects in the world and it is inside this walnut. If I am presented with such a golden tray, I shall know it comes from you." Then she gave the keloghlan the walnut and he put this in his pocket too.

When the padishah's eyes were suddenly cured, he knew that his youngest son must have taken the handful of dirt from a spot never trodden upon by his horse's hoofs. He was very happy and arranged for a great celebration when Keloghlan returned. He sent his two older sons to meet Keloghlan and escort him home. The brothers went to a crossroad they knew he would pass and there they dug a deep well. They then covered this well with a fine rug and set up a tent over the rug. Letting their horses graze nearby, the brother waited near the tent for Keloghlan.

"Selamünaleyküm!" Keloghlan shouted to his brothers.

"Aleykümselam, brother! Welcome home!" they said. After the usual greetings and after some pleasant talk, the brothers asked Keloghlan to relate his adventures. He told them all that had happened since the day he had left home. When he had finished, the eldest brother said, "Come inside the tent and rest before we take you back to the palace." Keloghlan entered the tent and sat down on the rug, and, of course, he immediately fell into the deep well, where his brothers left him. The two brothers threatened the three girls with immediate death if any one of them should tell what they had done to Keloghlan, and then the five of them proceeded to the palace of the padishah.

The band was playing for their arrival, and the padishah welcomed them at the palace gate. But when he did not see Keloghlan with the others, he asked, "Where is my youngest son?"

"Father, we were attacked by wolves," said the eldest brother, "and Keloghlan was devoured partly by them and partly by the vultures that came down on us afterwards. Here is his bloody shirt that we brought home."

The padishah had to accept this explanation. What else could he do? Now let us leave these people and go back to Keloghlan, who is lying at the bottom of the well.

When Friday came and it was time for the main service, Keloghlan heard the ezan called. He licked the ring which the khoja girl had given him and two rams appeared by him in the well. One was white and the other black. He started to mount the white ram, but the black one jumped between his legs and carried him off. Before he knew what had happened, the black ram had carried him through a hole in the bottom of the well down to the seventh layer of the earth. There he looked around and discovered that he was in a land that he had never seen before. It had a sun and a moon and mountains, just like the world he had left.

Keloghlan started to walk and after a while he came to a small house where an old woman lived. "Grandmother, give me some water," he said. The old woman went inside, urinated in a pan, and brought the pan to Keloghlan. "This is foul water to give a guest, grandmother. Have you no fresh water?"

"O son," she said, "there is a seven-headed giant who owns the only well here. He allows us to draw water from this well only when we present him with a girl to eat. Otherwise we get no water at all."

"Where is this giant to be found?" asked Keloghlan.

"He lives over at the foot of that mountain, and today he is to eat the padishah's daughter. It is her turn."

Keloghlan walked toward the mountain, and on the way he saw a long procession of people. They were leading the padishah's daughter, dressed ceremonially, to the well, where the giant would eat her. She was walking along sadly carrying a pitcher of water and a plate of food. A short way from the well, the attendants left the padishah's daughter, and she walked on alone.

Keloghlan then stepped up to the girl and asked, "Where are you going?"

"I am going to the seven-headed giant to be eaten so that the people can have water."

"If I go along with you, will the giant eat me too?" asked the young man.

"Yes, he would, but you should not come with me. There is no need for you to die."

"I do not mind," said Keloghlan. "Let us go together."

When they came near the giant, he laughed and said, "Have you come to be eaten with your beloved, young man? Can't you stand being separated from her?" After saying this the giant exhaled a great breath at Keloghlan, and the young man was buried in earth up to his waist. Keloghlan stood up and the giant blew at him again, this time burying him up to his shoulders. He shook himself loose again. Then the giant blew at him a third time and buried him in the earth up to the top of his head. When Keloghlan struggled out of the earth alive again, the giant said, "My strength is at an end. I can harm you no more."

Hearing this, Keloghlan drew his sword and struck six times, cutting off six of the giant's heads. "O brave young man, strike once more!" said the giant.

"No, that is enough," [15] said Keloghlan.

When the giant had died, the girl dipped her hands in his blood and pressed them against the back of Keloghlan. Then she returned to the palace and said, "Father, a strange young man came and killed the giant. He saved my life and the lives of many others, for now we shall have all the water we want."

The padishah decided to give his daughter to the young man who had killed the giant and so he called together all his criers. He told them to announce that on the following day all the young men in the kingdom should march past the palace. The man at whom his daughter threw an apple would be her husband.

Many ordinary men [16] sold their fields and other properties in order to buy rich clothes to look handsome as they passed beneath the window of the padishah's daughter. But she did not throw her apple at any of the young men who passed. They counted the number of young men who had passed, and the number was correct. Apparently no one was hiding. Then there came to the palace the old woman at whose door the young man had first knocked, and she reported to the padishah that there was a brave young man hiding at her house. When Keloghlan was finally pulled from his hiding place and forced to march past the window of the padishah's daughter, the girl finally threw her apple at him.

"It is you, then," said the padishah, "who killed the seven-headed giant. You may have my daughter as your bride."

Keloghlan denied that he was the one who had killed the giant. The padishah's daughter then ordered that Keloghlan be seized and his shirt removed. "There are the prints of my hands made with the giant's blood, father," she said.

When Keloghlan still refused to marry the girl, he feared that the padishah might torture him. But the padishah forgave him and asked, "What is there that you would like?"

"My only wish now is to return to my own land, if I can find some means of getting there."

"You may have anything you wish in my kingdom," said the padishah.

Every day Keloghlan rode around the kingdom trying to find some way to return to the upper world. One day on his travels he stopped to rest and fell asleep in the shade of a large tree. After he had slept for a while he was awakened by a loud noise. When he looked around, he saw that the noise came from a nest of young birds who were being eaten by a huge snake that was coiled around one of the branches. Keloghlan drew his sword and killed the snake, which fell out of the tree onto the ground like a heap of pilaf.[17] Then he lay down and went back to sleep.

The nest in the tree belonged to the Emerald-Green Anka [18] whose brood of young was continually being eaten by this serpent. The brood now in the nest was the last that the Anka was destined to have, for after this it could produce no more. The young birds explained to her what had happened when she returned, and the mother bird spread her wings over Keloghlan so that no ray of sunlight touched him. When Keloghlan awakened again, he looked up and saw the huge wings spread above him, and he said, "O bird, are you here for good or for evil?"

"For good," said the bird. "What is your wish?"

"I am the son of the blind padishah and I wish to return to my country."

"That is not difficult. I shall take you there, but first you must get me forty kilos of meat and forty kilos of water for the trip," said the bird.

Keloghlan returned to the palace of the padishah and requested forty kilos of meat and forty kilos of water. All this was provided, and a number of attendants carried the meat and the water to the foot of the tree where Keloghlan directed them. They were very curious about what he would do there. Was the meat for a huge feast? Was the water to be poured on the roots of the tree? It was almost dark when they reached the tree, and the *yatsi* [19] service had already ended.

When the huge bird saw them approaching, she asked, "Is my meat ready?"

"Yes, it is," answered Keloghlan.

"Is my water ready?"

"Yes, it is."

"Well, then, load the water under my left wing and the meat under my right wing. Then climb on my back, and I shall carry you back to your own land. When I say 'Gok,' give me a piece of meat to eat, and when I say 'Guk,' give me some of the water to drink." [20]

Keloghlan did as he was directed, and the bird started flying. When she said "Gok," he gave her a piece of meat to eat, and when she said "Guk," he gave her some of the water to drink. He did this many times until both the meat and the water were gone. As they were approaching Keloghlan's land, the bird said, "Gok," once again, but there was no more meat to feed it. Then Keloghlan cut a small piece of flesh from the calf of his leg and fed that to the bird.

Finally the bird landed in Keloghlan's country and the young man climbed down from her back. After he had thanked her, the bird spat out the last piece of meat that Keloghlan had fed her and said, "Put that back on your leg and it will grow again. I knew that it was human flesh as soon as you gave it to me, and so I just held it in my mouth. I have now done all that I can for you. Farewell!"

After the bird had flown away, Keloghlan took from his pocket the magic ring that the khoja girl had given him. He licked the ring and at once a huge Arab appeared and asked, "What is your wish?"

"I have no way of getting home from here. Bring me a horse."

"Close your eyes, then," said the Arab.

Keloghlan did as he was directed, and when he opened his eyes, he saw before him a beautiful gray horse. It was a magic horse, three meters high, that would run until the rider let the reins fall on the saddle. Then it would disappear. Keloghlan rode all day toward his father's palace and dismounted at night to rest. As he did so, the reins touched the saddle, and at once the magic horse disappeared. Each day he got a new horse in this way, and at last he arrived home. There no one recognized him, for he was in very shabby condition. His beard had grown long and his clothes were tattered. He himself looked quite different, too, for now there were no whites in his eyes. Let us leave him for a while and see what was going on at the court of his father, the padishah.

A short time after Keloghlan's two brothers had brought the three girls back to the palace, the padishah began plans for a great wedding ceremony. As the time for the wedding drew near, he hired musicians to play on every street corner every day.[21] This continued for some time, for the wedding was delayed and delayed.

Keloghlan asked someone, "What is going on here?"

The man answered him, "The padishah had three sons but one was lost. The other two brothers want to marry all three of the girls that were to be the brides of the three sons before the youngest was killed. Two of the girls are ready to marry but the third will not even allow her hands to be hennaed." [22]

"Why does she not wish to marry?" asked Keloghlan.

"She has certain conditions. She wants a dress that has not seen the sun, that has not been cut with scissors, and that has not been sewn by the hand of man. She says that she will marry only the person who will bring this dress to her. All of the tailors in the land have been called, but they cannot make a dress without cutting or sewing it. The padishah has given them forty days to make such a dress, and if they do not bring one to him at the end of that time, then the oldest and most honored tailor will have his head chopped off."

"There is nothing very difficult about this," said Keloghlan.

"How could it be done?" asked the man, and then he took Keloghlan to the oldest and most honored tailor, who was sitting in his shop in deep meditation. "What are you thinking about so deeply, father?" Keloghlan asked.

"The padishah's sons are to marry, and I am to make a dress for one of the brides — but it is an impossibility. It is to be a dress that has never seen the sun, that has not been cut with scissors, and that has not been sewn by the hand of man. Because neither I nor any of the other tailors in the land can make such a thing, I probably have but a few days to live."

"Take me as your apprentice, and I shall make such a dress by morning."

The old tailor did not really believe Keloghlan, but he agreed to take him as his apprentice. Keloghlan spent the night in the shop and when the tailor came back in the morning, the young man handed him the hazelnut. "I wanted a dress from you, not a hazelnut," said the tailor angrily.

"But, tailor father, the dress is in the nut."

"Let me see it," said the old man. When he touched the button on the top of the nut, the shell split open and a dress unfolded from it, a dress that had never seen the sun, that had not been cut by scissors, and that had not been sewn by the hand of man. When he touched the button on the bottom, the dress folded back into the nut and the shell shut again. "It is a miracle," said the tailor.

"Take the good news to the padishah, collect your reward,[23] and give him the hazelnut," said Keloghlan.

The padishah rewarded the tailor generously, giving him money both for himself and for his apprentice. The dress was taken to the khoja girl, and as soon as she saw it, she knew that her young man was near.

That day there was to be a jirit game [24] as part of the wedding celebrations, and everyone was invited. The old tailor asked his apprentice to go with him, but Keloghlan said he preferred to remain at home. After the old man had gone, Keloghlan licked the ring, and the Arab appeared: "What is your wish, efendi?" [25]

"I wish a black suit and the blackest horse in the world," [26] said Keloghlan. When the Arab returned with these things, Keloghlan dressed himself in the black suit, mounted the blackest horse in the world, and rode to the field where the jirit game was being played. He entered the contest, and as soon as he had an opportunity, he threw his javelin at the older of his two brothers. He threw it with such force that it pierced his brother's body and then stuck into the ground so deep that fifteen men could not pull it out. Word of this was taken to the padishah, and immediately a search was made for the black horseman, but no trace of him could be found.

The eldest brother was buried, and three or five days [27] after the mourning ended, the padishah said, "One of my sons still lives. Let us continue the wedding celebrations now, and he will wed all three girls."

Two of the girls were willing, but the khoja girl now had another condition to be met: "I want a golden tray on which a golden dog is chasing a golden rabbit. Unless this is brought to me, I shall not marry."

All of the goldsmiths in the land were called together by the padishah, who said, "You have forty days in which to make a golden tray on which a golden dog is chasing a golden rabbit. If you do not bring it to me within that time, the oldest and most honored goldsmith among you will be beheaded."

At once all of the goldsmiths set to work to try to make the wonderful golden tray, but one after another, they all failed in their attempts.

As the days passed, the oldest and most honored goldsmith prepared himself for death. Then Keloghlan went to the old man and asked, "What are you thinking about so deeply, father?"

"Why shouldn't I think deeply? I am soon to die because neither I nor any of the other goldsmiths can construct for the padishah a golden tray upon which a golden dog is chasing a golden rabbit."

"That is not so very difficult," said Keloghlan. "Accept me as your apprentice and I shall make it for you overnight."

The master goldsmith did not believe that this strange young man could construct the tray, but he agreed to let him work in the shop that night, and he himself went home. In the morning he returned, and when he entered his shop, he saw Keloghlan staring at a walnut on the table. "Why are you not working on the golden tray for the padishah?" asked the old goldsmith.

"I have finished working on it, father goldsmith, and now I am admiring it."

"You are mad, young man. What you are looking at is a walnut."

"It is a very special walnut, father goldsmith." Saying this, Keloghlan touched a button on the top of the walnut. The shell split in half, and a small bright object inside it grew and grew until it was a golden tray. Around the edge of the tray a golden dog chased a golden rabbit. When Keloghlan pressed a button on the bottom of the walnut, the tray shrank back to its former size and the shell of the nut closed around it again. "Take the good news to the padishah, collect your reward, and give him the walnut."

The old goldsmith was overjoyed. He rushed to the padishah and said, "Your majesty, I have good news for you. Last night my apprentice completed the golden tray you ordered, and here it is." Then he showed the padishah how to open and close the walnut, and the padishah and all his vezirs marveled at this wonderful piece of art. The goldsmith was generously rewarded, and the golden tray was taken to the khoja girl who recognized it at once as the work of Keloghlan.

The next day another jirit game was announced. The master goldsmith was invited, and he asked the apprentice to go with him, but Keloghlan said he would rather stay at home. As soon as the old man had gone, Keloghlan licked the ring and the Arab appeared: "What is your wish, efendi?"

"I want a red horse and a suit so red that it seems to be dripping with blood." When these were brought to him, he dressed himself in the blood-red suit and mounted the red horse, and then he rode to the jirit field. At the first opportunity, he threw his javelin at his brother, who was among the players, and he struck him so hard that he killed him instantly.

The padishah was greatly grieved at the news, but the khoja girl went to him and said, "Your majesty, do not mourn. Your only worthy son has returned alive."

"How can that be?" asked the padishah. "How can dead men come to life?"

"How can a dress come from a hazelnut and a golden tray from a walnut?" Then, no longer fearing the two older brothers, she told the padishah all that had happened. The padishah cried when he saw Keloghlan's black eyeballs, but the young man said, "Do not weep, father. It was my kismet."

Then Keloghlan and the khoja girl were married in a wedding that lasted for forty days and forty nights,[28] and they lived happily after that.

2.

The Adventures of Mehmet the Mad [29]

There was once an Egyptian king [30] who was childless for many years, until, toward the end of his life, after visiting many khojas' convents and such places,[31] God gave him a son. He named his son Mehmet. As Mehmet grew up and was being educated in the palace, he became a very spoiled child, and he was soon known among the people as Mehmet the Mad.

Following the death of his father Mehmet inherited the throne, but as he was not popular, because of his strange behavior, he was deposed by his own people. He lived on, with his mother, in his father's old palace, but after a while he was reduced to poverty. One day his mother called Mehmet to her side and said to him, "What shall we do, son? We have lost everything, but we cannot starve. You must try to support us."

"Very well, mother," said Mehmet, "but what shall I do? This palace is too large for us. Why don't we get a small house with just two rooms and live there? Let us sell this palace."

His mother agreed to this proposal, and Mehmet sold the palace. The ready money went quickly, however, and soon Mehmet and his mother were again penniless. His mother said to him, "Mehmet, what shall we do now?"

"Mother, I should like to be a woodcutter," said Mehmet. "I like that job. Find enough money to buy me a donkey. Then I shall go to the forest, cut wood, bring it back on the donkey, and sell it in the market for money."

His mother gave him the last golden coin which she had in her necklace.[32] With that money, Mehmet bought a donkey, an axe, and some rope, and then he went to the forest to cut wood, along with several other men. He became separated from his companions, and after a while they feared that he might have got lost. They sent a search party after him, and when this group found him, they asked him why he had wandered so far from the other woodcutters.

"I couldn't find any dry wood," he answered, "and so I kept looking farther and farther."

One of the group said to him, "Why don't you just cut green wood, as all of us do?"

"No," said Mehmet the Mad, "I cannot cheat my customers and sell them green wood instead of dry. You can return to the city without me. I do not have to go back with you."

Mehmet spent that night up in a tree in the forest. During the night, wolves came and tore his donkey to pieces and ate it. When Mehmet climbed down from the tree in the morning and started to pick his way through the thick forest, he saw two monsters with human heads but the bodies of snakes.[33] They were fighting with each other. Mehmet watched them fighting from behind a large tree, and he noticed that one of the monsters had been badly caught by the other and was screaming. Deciding to help the one which was losing, he threw his axe at its opponent and cut off the head of that black monster. The other monster, which had thus been saved, spoke to Mehmet in human language and said, "What is your name?"

"My name is Mehmet the Mad," he said.

"You have done me a great service, Mehmet," it said. "I am the daughter of the king of the snakes. The snake you have just killed was a servant in my father's palace. He abducted me one day, and I have been in his possession now for two years, during which time I have continually fought with him, and I lost none of my chastity. But thank God that you came to my aid today. If you will now escort me to my father's palace, I shall do you some service in return."

Mehmet accepted this proposal and escorted the daughter of the king of the snakes to her father's palace. They went a great way but still went only a little way; they went over rivers and mountains and yet went straight; they went for six months and a summer, but when they looked back, they found that they had gone only the length of a grain of barley.[34] They told the first snake that they met near the palace to run along ahead and report their arrival to the king of the snakes. That little snake ran ahead and reported this at the palace, and the entire army of the king of the snakes came out to salute the long lost princess and her escort, Mehmet the Mad.

After the king had embraced his daughter and kissed her, she told him that the young man who had saved her from the wicked servant and had then escorted her to the palace was Mehmet the Mad. Mehmet was thereupon received into the palace as a guest.

The snake girl came to Mehmet and said to him, "My father may give you a present when it comes time for you to leave the palace. When he asks you what you want, do not show much excitement about it. Simply say, 'May your majesty live long. I want nothing more than that.'[35] He will never allow you to depart without giving you a gift. When he insists that you tell him what you want, say, 'Your majesty, I want your cap, your whistle, and your royal seal.' He will not want to give these things to you, but I shall be there, and I shall tell him that I will go away with you unless he gives you these three gifts. Then he will agree to give you the cap, the whistle, and the seal."

It happened as the girl had said. After Mehmet had been at the palace a few days, the king called him to his throne and said, "Mehmet the Mad, I am wealthy. I can give you anything that you wish."

"May your majesty live long. That is all I wish," said Mehmet.

"No, that is not enough," said the king. "My health is something that concerns only me. You must have something for yourself. Ask for something and I shall give it to you."

Unable to resist the king's invitation any longer, Mehmet then said, "Very well, then, your majesty, I should like your cap, your whistle, and your royal seal."

"I am sorry that you have asked for things that I cannot relinquish," said the king.

"It is all right, and may your majesty live long. I am leaving now," said Mehmet.

At that moment the king's daughter intervened and said, "Farewell, father, for I am going, too. Are the things Mehmet the Mad asked for so very valuable that you must refuse him? He is a man who saved me and my chastity as well as your honor."

26

Upon this, the king said, "Very well, Mehmet, follow me." He took Mehmet the Mad to his treasury, which was full of diamonds, pearls, and gold. There he gave Mehmet his cap, his whistle, and his royal seal. The young man did not know of what use these would be to him, but he took them and thanked the king.

After he had left the palace, Mehmet forgot about his experience there and thought only about his donkey which had been eaten by the wolves. He walked back to the same forest where he had formerly cut wood, but he saw there none of his friends. While he was wondering what he should do, it occurred to him that he might go and work as a night watchman in his village and thus make use of the whistle he had received from the king of the snakes.[36] He decided to try the whistle right there to see how it sounded, so he took it from his pocket and blew on it. Two immense ghosts appeared immediately who said, "Tell us, sir, shall we destroy or shall we restore?" Mehmet the Mad was terribly frightened by what he saw, but one of the ghosts said to him, "As long as you have your whistle, you need fear nothing. We are your slaves. You command and we shall carry out your orders."

Much relieved by this explanation, Mehmet the Mad said to them, "Take me to the city now." They took him up and a moment later set him down on the outskirts of his city. Then he commanded them, "Produce a donkey with a load of dry wood." Then he took the donkey home and said to his mother, "I am sorry to be so late, but I had to search long to get a load of dry wood."

In the morning he took the load of wood to the market and sold it. When he returned to his home, he said, "Mother, I am used to good living, and I don't think I can be a woodcutter any longer." He then shut himself in his room and blew his whistle. When the two ghosts appeared, he asked them to bring some money for him. In no time at all they returned with a pot of gold. Now Mehmet and his mother were wealthy again, and they began to lead the prosperous life they once had enjoyed.

In the meantime, Mehmet the Mad had forgotten all about the cap and the seal which the king of the snakes had given him. One day he said to his mother, "Mother, we had a cap and a seal, as well as this whistle."

"I put them in the chest," said his mother.

"Will you please bring them here. I want to see if I can become a king," he said.

When his mother brought the cap and the seal, Mehmet took the seal and after dipping it in water, tried to stamp pieces of paper with it. He was amazed to see that whatever he stamped with it turned into gold. Mehmet the Mad took the whistle and the seal and went out of the house. He forgot the cap, which his mother picked up and put back into the chest.

Mehmet went to the seashore, for this city was a port, and there he saw a ship anchored. He shouted at the crew, "Oh, sailors, who is your captain?"

"We have come from a foreign country," they shouted back.

"Will you sell me that ship?" he asked them.

"Yes," they answered, "but we want 300,000 gold pieces for it."

"I shall pay you 400,000 gold pieces for it," said Mehmet, "but I want the crew with the ship."

Mehmet the Mad bought the ship at the price he stated, and he also paid each member of the crew a thousand gold pieces, telling them to go ashore and have uniforms made for themselves, all of cloth of the same color. Quite impressed with their new employer, whom they called Mehmet Bey,[37] the crew members all went to the city and had very expensive uniforms made for themselves.

During the night Mehmet Bey was busy turning the most conspicuous parts of the ship into gold by stamping them with his seal. When the crew returned to the ship in the morning, they were amazed to see so many parts of their ship turned into gold and glittering in the sunlight. In fact, they hardly recognized their ship. When they asked Mehmet Bey how this had happened to their ship, he told them to mind their own business and not to ask him any more questions of that kind.

Mehmet Bey now returned to his mother, gave her some more money, and bade her farewell. He sailed away in his new ship, and after many days landed at a strange port. The king of this land was told of the arrival of a magnificent ship. He ordered his men to go and inquire whose ship it was, where it came from, and what its purpose was in coming to his land. He also sent an invitation for the ship's company to come and visit him in his palace.

When the king's men gave this invitation to Mehmet Bey, Mehmet Bey asked them, "Has your king a golden ship like this one?"

"No," they said.

"Well, then I cannot go to him. Let him come to me," said Mehmet Bey.

When this was reported to the king, he said, "He is right. A man who owns a golden ship is too important to pay me a visit. I must first go and visit him." Taking with him his vezirs and high-ranking officials, the king went to the pier where Mehmet Bey's ship was docked. Mehmet Bey watched the retinue coming as he stood on the bridge of the ship. When his guests came aboard, he introduced himself to the king as "Mehmet the Mad, the Noble Son of Unknown Lands." The king was very impressed by the reception given him on Mehmet Bey's ship, and, in return, he invited Mehmet Bey to his palace, where a big party in his honor was held that night. During the party the king could not help noticing Mehmet's peculiar behavior, his madness.

The next day the king said to Mehmet Bey, "I want you to stay in my palace as a guest for a week. I cannot let you go sooner." Very pleased, Mehmet Bey accepted this invitation.

One day the king invited Mehmet to a private dinner party at the palace. The queen, her daughter, Mehmet Bey, and the king were to dine together. Before the dinner, the king instructed his daughter to find out from Mehmet Bey the secret of his golden ship. The daughter used all her charms at the dinner table to win the heart of Mehmet Bey. She winked at him and looked at him in winning ways. When the king learned that Mehmet Bey was not married but a bachelor, he asked him whether he would like to marry his daughter.

"It is a great honor for me, your majesty," said Mehmet. Then he kissed the king's hand and formally asked for his daughter in marriage.

A secret wedding ceremony was held, and after the wedding feast, Mehmet went to his room with the daughter of the king. "Before I can sleep with you," she said, following her father's instructions, "I must know the secret of your golden ship."

"Just imagine that!" said Mehmet Bey. "What a thing to be concerned about at such a time as this. This whistle and this seal are responsible for all my wealth." Then he took the whistle from his pocket and blew it.

When the two ghosts appeared, they asked their usual question: "Shall we destroy or shall we restore?"

"Do neither," said Mehmet. "Just go away."

"Will these creatures obey me, too?" asked the girl.

"Yes," he said, "whoever blows the whistle will be able to command them."

"And what does the seal do?" she asked.

"It turns everything that it touches into gold," said Mehmet.

"Shall we try it?" asked the girl, and she brought her jewelry case. When she touched it with the seal, the case turned into gold.

Now the girl wanted to blow the whistle and see if the immense ghosts would really obey her command. She blew the whistle and the ghosts appeared.

"Shall we destroy or shall we restore?" they asked.

"Let everything stay in its place," she said, "except this dog beside me. Take him and carry him away for a distance of seven lands." [38]

The ghosts grabbed Mehmet by the arm and, carrying him over seven lands, dropped him in an unknown country. After many hardships and long journeys, he at last managed to return to his native city and to his mother, who was becoming very worried about him.

"What happened to your ship?" she asked him.

"It was caught in a storm at sea," he told her. "I lost all of my crew, but I managed to reach shore on a piece of plank."

After being home for a few days, Mehmet the Mad remembered the cap which he had left behind, and he asked his mother to get it for him from the chest. He tried to use the cap in every possible way. He made a whistle of it and blew on it, but nothing happened. He made a seal of it, soaked it in water, and stamped things with it, but nothing happened. He concluded that the king of the snakes had given him the wrong cap, for this one apparently had no magic powers. He thought that he might as well wear this cap if it was good for nothing else, but when he put the cap on his head, he immediately became invisible.

"Mehmet, where are you? I can't see you," his mother said.

"That is strange, mother. I am right in front of you," he said. He took the cap from his head and became visible once more, and then he knew the power that it had. After that, Mehmet the Mad gathered a quantity of money again by stealing from various houses while he was wearing the magic cap that made him invisible.

After a while he decided to leave home again. He went to the pier, and without being noticed by anyone, he boarded a ship and settled in the most luxurious cabin. Finally, after a long voyage, he reached again the land of the king whose daughter had cheated him. Unobserved, he entered the palace, where the king was holding an important meeting with his ministers. Mehmet sat in a chair in the corner and listened to their discussions, and then he joined them at the dinner table. He took food from the plate of each of the diners unnoticed, but when the food kept disappearing from the king's plate, the king turned to his vezir and asked, "Why do you take food from my plate when there is plenty on your own?"

"No, your majesty, I did not do such a thing," said the vezir.

When the king retired to sleep that night, he said to the queen, "I am worried about that son-in-law of mine, Mehmet the Mad. I had him searched for without success. I wonder what could have happened to him? I miss him very much." The king had, in fact, suspected that Mehmet had returned and was responsible for the strange things that had happened at the dinner table. And he also suspected that Mehmet might be present in his room and might hear him, and so he spoke in this kind way about his son-in-law. When Mehmet heard the king talk in this manner, he was happy, and so he took off his cap and became visible. The king pretended to be very pleased with Mehmet's return, and he sent word to his daughter, and when she came he said, "Your dear husband, Mehmet, is back."

The girl pretended great joy at seeing Mehmet again: "I have been ill all the time that you have been away. I was able to get up only now when I heard that you were back safe and sound."

By gestures and signs the king gave his daughter instructions to find out how Mehmet managed to become invisible. Mehmet said it was all done by his cap: "When I put it on my head, I become invisible." She asked Mehmet to see the cap, and when he gave it to her, she put it on her head, became invisible, and then blew the whistle.

"Shall we destroy or shall we restore?" asked the two ghosts when they appeared.

Pointing to Mehmet the Mad, she said to them, "Take this fool to a place so far away that he cannot return for fifteen years."

The ghosts carried Mehmet to a distant land and left him there in a dense forest. After wandering about for many miserable days, he came to an apple tree and, being very hungry, he ate some of the apples. Right away, two horns grew on his head. He hoped that these horns would be of some use to him sometime, somewhere, but as yet he did not see how they could help him. The horns kept growing. They grew so long that he could hardly walk between the trees of the forest without catching them in the branches. He came to a fig tree one day and decided to eat a fig, hoping that he might grow four arms and turn into a scorpion. But much to his delight, when he ate the fig, the horns disappeared, and he became his former self. He made a basket for himself, and in it he put some of the magic apples and some of the magic figs, and then he set out for the land of the king whose daughter had cheated him twice.

He went a little way, he went a great way; he went over hills and dales, and yet he went straight; he went for six months and a summer; and finally, a year after that, he one evening reached the palace of the king again.

31

In the morning, he walked round and round the palace shouting, "I am selling the fruit of paradise! I am selling the fruit of paradise!" The queen, her daughter, and the other women of the palace woke up to this nerve-wracking shouting, "The fruit of paradise! I am selling the fruit of paradise!" [39] The attendants looked out of the palace windows and saw that a shabbily dressed man was wandering about the streets, with a basket in his hand, shouting these words.

Just for fun, one of the palace women shouted, "Hey, Keloghlan,[40] what are you selling? And why are you dressed so shabbily?"

"I am selling the fruit of paradise," answered Mehmet. "Do you think you can eat it with that big mouth of yours?"

Finally the queen was told what a strange looking man it was nearby who was selling the fruit of paradise, and so she addressed him from her window: "What is it that you are selling?"

"I am selling fruit of paradise," he answered, "but you cannot afford to buy them. They are meant for palace people. Only wives and daughters of the kings can eat them."

"Well, that is what we are," she said.

"But there is a special way to be able to eat them," said Mehmet. "You have to buy them with money."

"How much are they?" asked the queen.

"They are one golden lira apiece," he answered.

They threw down two golden liras and asked for two pieces of the fruit. Mehmet instructed them then how to eat the apples which he had thrown up to them: "Peel one of them. Then divide it into three pieces, and each of you take one piece." The queen, her daughter, and the wife of the grand vezir did as the peddler told them. About fifteen minutes after each had eaten a piece of apple, she grew horns on her head. Mehmet, in the meantime, went away, changed from his keloghlan clothes, and hid himself.

The king was informed of the terrible condition of his wife, his daughter, and the wife of the grand vezir, and he was asked to come and see them at once. When he came and saw them, he was frightened by the large horns that grew out of their heads. He ordered his men to go and find all the soothsayers, pilgrims,[41] khojas, seers, and doctors — every sort of man with healing powers. Although many doctors and religious men came to the palace, none of them was able to cure the women of their condition. Then the king sent messages to foreign countries to ask that doctors be sent from those places, too, but none of them could cure the women.

Finally, Mehmet the Mad put on a gown, stuck an old book under his arm, and walked up and down the streets where the people would notice him. As the king's men had all been instructed to lead straight to the palace any healer from any part of the world, they also took Mehmet there and introduced him as the famous Doctor Lokman from Arabia.[42] He was shown into the room of the palace where the three ladies lay in bed with their heads covered with napkins. After examining them, he said, "These patients must be taken to a place where they will be completely alone. A bathhouse just outside the palace would be a most suitable place."

The king, thereupon, hired a nearby bathhouse, had it cleaned, and ordered that the patients be carried there. After they had been there for a day, Mehmet gave a piece of fig to the queen and another to the wife of the grand vezir, and in about five minutes' time their horns disappeared. The good news was carried at once to the palace, and a huge feast was arranged in honor of the famous doctor.

The third patient, the king's daughter, was still not cured, however. Mehmet visited her for forty days but pretended that he could not cure her. One day he said to the girl, "I happened to find the prescription in a book which I was reading today which, I think, will cure you. According to that prescription, you must first get married."

"All right, then," said the girl, "let my father find a husband for me."

"That will not be necessary," said Mehmet. "It need not be an official marriage. You can marry me."

Mehmet the Mad and the girl were married there in the bathhouse, and after a while the girl became pregnant. One day Mehmet said to her, "You may have something magical in your possession which makes all of my cures ineffective. It could be a magic whistle, or a magic seal, or a magic cap of some sort. As long as such things are in your possession, I cannot cure you."

"Yes, I think I have those very things," she said.

"Where are they?" asked Mehmet.

"In a drawer in a closet in my room," she said. She sent for these three things and had them brought to the bathhouse immediately.

As soon as he had recovered the whistle, the seal, and the cap, he gave her a piece of fig to eat, and shortly after that she lost her horns. Then Mehmet took off his mask and said to his wife, "Do you recognize me?"

"Yes, you are my doctor," she said.

"Yes, but try to remember where you saw me before," he said.

Then she struggled to think about him, and she was able to recall

33

him. Suddenly she said, "Why, you are my dear husband, Mehmet Bey!"

Then he said to her, "You have cheated me twice, and I have now taken my revenge upon you. I shall not stay with you." Saying this, Mehmet the Mad left the girl and returned to his own country. There he regained the throne and began to live happily thereafter. He enjoyed a very prosperous reign.

3.

Hüsnügüzel [43]

Once there was a padishah in Egypt who had been married for twelve years but still had no male heir. One day the padishah's wife said to him, "We have so much in this world, but we have no son. To whom shall we leave all this? We must try to find out what to do in order to have a son."

The padishah agreed with this and he consulted all of the wise men and doctors in his land to discover what he should do, but none of them could help him. He finally decided to travel to other lands to see if anywhere he could find the information he sought. He mounted his horse and rode away. After traveling for a month he came one day to a broad plain in the middle of which he met an old man with white hair who leaned upon a stick.

"Selamünaleyküm, father," he said.

"Aleykümselam, Padishah of Egypt," said the old man.

"How did you know that I was the Padishah of Egypt?"

"I just sensed it from your general appearance and from that of your horse," said the old man.

"Since you have understood this," said the padishah, "you probably also know my problem."

"Yes, your problem is that you have no male heir, and you are seeking a solution to this problem now. The mare that you are riding has never had a colt either. There is an old apple tree behind your palace. Do you know how many apples it yields each year?"

"Just one."

"What is done with that apple each year?"

"Oh, my vezirs pick it and eat it."

"Well, this year guard that apple tree, and when the apple is ripe, pick it yourself. Peel the apple and give the peeling to your horse. Then cut the apple in two, eat half of it, and give the other half to your wife to eat. Your horse will foal and your wife will bear you a male child, but you must promise not to name the child. I shall come at the appropriate time and name him."

"Very well," said the padishah, "I shall do exactly as you say." As he was reaching into his saddlebag for a handful of gold, the old man suddenly disappeared.

The padishah returned home and explained to his wife what had happened. He set men to guard the apple tree behind the palace, and when the fruit was ripe, he picked it himself, peeled it, gave the peelings to his horse, and then divided the apple. Half he ate and half he gave to his wife to eat. In a short time both the mare and his wife became pregnant, and in due time the horse foaled and his wife bore him a son.

As the old man had directed, the child remained for some time nameless. When he was still an infant this did not bother him, but when he was twelve, attending school, his namelessness embarrassed him. "Hey, Nameless!" his friends would call to him. One day after this had happened he returned home crying and he said to the padishah, "Father, I am the son of the padishah, but I have no name. All of my friends have names — Ali, Hasan, Ahmet, Mehmet. Why don't I have a name?"

The padishah and his wife talked with each other about this, and they finally decided that the boy should be named. The padishah called together all of the doctors, judges, and khojas in the land in order to get their advice on this, and they agreed that the child should be named. Long lists of names were drawn up, and from these names one was to be selected on a special holiday set aside for the occasion.

All of the people were gathered on the appointed day, and a huge feast was served. When everyone had eaten his fill, the ceremony of naming the child was about to begin, but at that moment there was a loud knocking on the palace door, "Tok! Tok! Tok!" When they opened the door they saw there the old man with the white hair and beard, leaning upon a stick. "Selamünaleyküm, O Padishah of Egypt," he said.

"Aleykümselam, father," answered the padishah.

"Didn't I tell you not to name the child, that I would come at the proper time and name him myself?"

"Yes, efendi, but we have waited so long. I beg your pardon, but we were only going to give him a temporary name at this time."

35

"Very well, then, I shall give him his permanent name. It will be Hüsnügüzel,[44] and the name of the colt born in the same year will be Altay." He then called the child to him and stroked his back. Taking a sword from his belt he said to Hüsnügüzel, "There is a sacred mystery about this sword that concerns your life. Take it. It is your sword, but guard it well. When you are in trouble, a drop of blood will appear on the tip. When you are in serious trouble, two drops of blood will fall from the tip. When three drops fall, you will have only forty minutes to live. You must not give the sword to anyone, not even to your own father."

The padishah ordered food brought for the old man, but when the food was brought, the old man had vanished. Everyone realized then that this must be Hizir.[45]

Hüsnügüzel returned to school where he studied from books, and he learned also how to shoot an arrow, how to handle a shield, how to use his sword, and how to wrestle. He was, in fact, the best student in his class in these sports. The other students now called him Hüsnür-Aghabey.[46]

One night in a dream Hüsnügüzel saw a very beautiful woman,[47] and then on the next two nights he saw her a second and a third time. She was the most beautiful woman in the world, he thought, and he fell in love with her. He thought of her all the time, neglecting everything else. After a while he even stopped eating and drinking, and he became pale and sickly. His father asked him, "What is the matter with you, son?"

"There is nothing the matter with me, father," said Hüsnügüzel. But the padishah saw that the boy was ill, and so he called together all of the khojas and learned men to examine his son. None of them could find anything wrong with the boy, however. "Perhaps he wants to marry," said the padishah, and he sent his vezir to find out what girl he wanted.

"Which daughter of which padishah do you want, Hüsnügüzel?" asked the vezir. "Your father will arrange for you to marry anyone you wish."

"No, there is no one I wish to marry," said Hüsnügüzel.

One day a witch [48] came to the palace and said to the padishah, "Your majesty, what is the difficulty here? You are calling here all of the doctors and khojas and wise men in the land. What is your problem?"

"I have a son who has a strange illness that nobody can understand," said the padishah.

"I think that I can discover his malady," said the witch. "You call

36

some of his school friends here. I shall prepare food for them and serve them coffee, and from them I can probably learn about his trouble. If I do, I shall tell you what it is."

Everything else had failed, and the padishah was willing to try anything that might help his ailing son. He called the boy's teacher and asked him to send to him the four closest friends of Hüsnügüzel. When the boys appeared before him, the padishah said, "You will go to Hüsnügüzel's room, talk with him, and take your meal with him there."

The four friends went to Hüsnügüzel's room and talked with him. After a while the old witch woman brought them food, and when they had eaten the food, she said to them, "Now I shall bring you coffee, but you must each, in turn, drink it in honor of your sweetheart." She brought in five cups of coffee and handed one to the first friend of Hüsnügüzel.

"Oh, for my Ayshe!" he said.

"Oh, for my Gülüzar!" said the second.

"In honor of my Feza!" said the third.

"In memory of my Fatma!" said the fourth.

Now it was Hüsnügüzel's turn. He sipped his coffee and groaned, "Oh, The Most Beautiful Girl in the World!"

When the old woman heard this, she ran to the padishah and said, "Your majesty, your son has fallen in love with The Most Beautiful Girl in the World. That is why he is sick."

The padishah was shocked to hear this. "It is impossible to find her," he said. "I searched for her for twelve years without success, and many other padishahs have also searched in vain. How could Hüsnügüzel ever find her?"

That night the padishah told his wife about Hüsnügüzel's hopeless love, and on the next morning she went to the boy and said, "My son, your father searched for twelve years for The Most Beautiful Girl in the World without finding her. Forget about her now, and we shall get forty girls for you instead."

"As this secret of mine is now revealed, I demand that you give me permission to go and search for her," said Hüsnügüzel. All that day both parents tried to dissuade him from this quest, but it was no use. He kissed his father's hands and beard and bade his parents farewell. After ordering that he be supplied with his horse and with provisions, the padishah came in tears to his son and said, "Take this sword of mine and remember me with it."

Hüsnügüzel set out upon his trip and rode a great distance. One day, after he had been riding for two months, he saw approaching a young horseman dressed like him and looking just as handsome. He came riding along raising a cloud of smoke and dust.[49]

"Selamünaleyküm, brother," said the young horseman.

"Aleykümselam," said Hüsnügüzel.

"I am the son of the Padishah of the Seas," said the stranger. "Where are you going?"

"I am the son of the Padishah of Egypt," said Hüsnügüzel. "I fell in love with The Most Beautiful Girl in the World, and I am now seeking for her."

"May I join you?"

"I was one, but now we are two," said Hüsnügüzel. "Let us seek her together. Whoever is destined to have her will have her."

The two young men rode along together, and after traveling for a way, they saw approaching a third horseman bearing a shield and a club and wearing a sword in his belt. When he drew near Hüsnügüzel and the son of the Padishah of the Seas, he shouted, "Selamünaleyküm, brothers."

"Aleykümselam," they both answered.

"I am the son of the Padishah of the Stars," said the stranger. "Where are you going?"

"I am the son of the Padishah of Egypt," said Hüsnügüzel, "and this is the son of the Padishah of the Seas. I fell in love with The Most Beautiful Girl in the World, and we are searching for her."

"May I join you?"

"I was one, then we became two, and now we are three," said Hüsnügüzel. "But let us search for the girl together. Whoever is destined to have her will have her."

The three young men rode along together, Hüsnügüzel in front and the other two behind him. Toward the end of the day, when they and their horses were tired, they came to a grassy area where they decided to rest and let their horses graze. After telling his companions to make them some coffee, Hüsnügüzel lay down in the grass and fell asleep.

Unknown to them, they had stopped in the land of the Padishah of Arabs, a ruler who guarded his territory so closely that not even a bird flew over it.[50] Three of the padishah's watchmen saw the three strange horses grazing in his pasture, and when they rode up to the place, they saw also the three horsemen there. One was sleeping in the grass, and the other two were making coffee.

"Don't you know that you are trespassing on the territory of the

Padishah of Arabs? Don't you know that not even birds fly over this territory? Come, pack up, and we shall take you to the presence of our padishah."

All during this meeting Hüsnügüzel was asleep. Now he woke up and asked, "What is the matter?"

"It seems that we are in the territory of the Padishah of Arabs," said the son of the Padishah of the Seas.

"I do not care whose territory this is," said Hüsnügüzel. "Do you have the coffee ready yet?"

Two of the guards went toward Hüsnügüzel now and one of them said to him, "Get up on your feet!"

When Hüsnügüzel heard this, he jumped up, cut off the ears of the two guards and hung them around his neck on a string. To the third guard he said, "Go and tell your padishah that I am a visitor here. I shall leave his territory in a few hours' time. If he wants to see me, he should come here with all of his men."

The soldier rode in haste to the padishah and said, "Your majesty, three strangers have entered your territory with their horses. One of them cut off the ears of two of us and hung them around his neck. He sent me to tell you not to disturb him, for he will stay for a few hours only. If you want to see him he said that you should go to where he is with all your troops."

The Padishah of Arabs was furious when he heard this, and he said to the guard, "Go and tell my vezir to take two hundred men and bring those fellows to me alive."

The two hundred horsemen approached the pasture raising a cloud of smoke and dust as they rode. The son of the Padishah of the Seas and the son of the Padishah of the Stars were terrified and they called out to Hüsnügüzel, who had fallen asleep again.

"What is the matter?" he asked them as he woke up.

"Look," they said, "we are being attacked by a large force of men."

"Are you going to search for The Most Beautiful Girl in the World with such frail hearts?" asked Hüsnügüzel. "You go and drink your coffee and don't interfere with me."

When the troops of the padishah reached the pasture, one of them asked, "Who cut off the ears of our padishah's men?"

Hüsnügüzel jumped up and asked, "Where is your padishah?"

"What do you want with our padishah?" asked the same soldier.

At that, Hüsnügüzel rushed upon these men like a wolf attacking a flock of sheep. He scattered them about this way and that way, and

39

when they were completely routed, he cut off the ears of three of them and hung these ears around his neck with the others. "Now go back and tell your padishah that he shouldn't disturb me. I have only half an hour left here in his land. If he wants to see me, he should come here with all his army. If he wants to fight, let them bring all their weapons."

When the padishah received this message, he thought about it in silence for several minutes. He decided that it might be better to have such a man as his ally than to maintain a huge army. He ordered his vezir to bring him a flag of truce. Then he mounted his horse, gathered two thousand of his men around him, and rode toward the pasture where the strangers were.

The three young men were drinking coffee when they saw the huge body of troops riding toward them. The son of the Padishah of the Seas said, "Agha-bey, this time they are coming in numbers too great for us to fight. Let us run away."

"Didn't I tell you not to interfere in anything?" said Hüsnügüzel. He looked and saw the two thousand troops coming with the padishah riding in front waving a flag of truce. "Make more coffee," he said, "for the Padishah of Arabs is coming."

Ordering his men to halt and dismount, the padishah, still holding the flag of truce, marched up to a distance of seven paces from Hüsnügüzel, and saluted him.

Hüsnügüzel got up, walked the seven paces to the padishah, took his hand and shook it, saying, "Come, efendi, and join us here."

"What is your name?" asked the padishah.

"Hüsnügüzel."

"I am sorry to have disturbed you, Hüsnügüzel, but I did not understand the situation. Come to my palace with your friends as my guests."

"We have no time to stop on our travels," said Hüsnügüzel.

"But you can surely spend the night with us," said the padishah. And so, after drinking coffee, they all rode to the palace of the Padishah of Arabs.

That evening at dinner the Padishah of Arabs said to Hüsnügüzel, "I have three daughters so beautiful that they have been sought by many padishahs. I will marry these three girls to you and your two companions if you will stay here and live with us. You can become the padishah of this land, your friends can become vezirs, and I shall serve as your grand vezir."

"I started this journey I am on to find The Most Beautiful Girl in the World," said Hüsnügüzel, "but I shall discuss your offer with my friends and let you know our decision in the morning."

That night the three friends talked about this, and after some time, the son of the Padishah of the Stars said to Hüsnügüzel, "We shall do as you wish in this matter."

"Yes," said Hüsnügüzel, "but I see that you really wish to stay here."

The next morning Hüsnügüzel sent word to the Padishah of Arabs that his proposal had been accepted, and immediately the padishah started a wedding celebration that lasted for forty days and forty nights. At the end of that time, Hüsnügüzel was married to the youngest and fairest of the padishah's daughters, the son of the Padishah of Stars was married to the second of the daughters, and the son of the Padishah of the Seas was married to the eldest.

When Hüsnügüzel went to the nuptial chamber, he found the youngest daughter standing against a wall waiting for her bridegroom. Without looking at her Hüsnügüzel went and sat on a cushion on the floor. "Come here, sister," he said. "I shall call you sister for the present. Those two men who married your sisters are my friends, and for their sake I could not refuse your father's offer. But I am really searching for The Most Beautiful Girl in the World, and tomorrow I am going to continue my search. If I return without finding her, then you will be mine."

The girl cried when she heard this, but Hüsnügüzel would not change his mind. When they lay down to sleep, Hüsnügüzel placed his sword in the bed between them. "I am going to sleep now," he said, "but I wish that you would do certain things for me. First prepare food and other provisions for my departure tomorrow. Then, after I leave, I want you to guard constantly this sword that I shall leave with you. Don't touch the sword, and don't let anyone else even see it — not even your father. Keep it locked in this room at all times. Several times each day and several times each night look closely at it. If you see a drop of blood clinging to the tip, you will know that I am in trouble. When two drops of blood drip from it, I shall be in serious trouble. And when three drops of blood fall from the tip, I shall then have only forty minutes to live. If you see three drops, go immediately and inform the sons of the Padishah of Stars and the Padishah of the Seas of this, and they will come and help me."

The girl spent the night preparing provisions for Hüsnügüzel's trip, and when the morning came, she went and stood over him and admired him. As she cried, looking at him, a tear fell upon his face and he awoke. Saying farewell to the girl, Hüsnügüzel left the palace of the Padishah of Arabs, mounted his horse, and rode away.

After riding for a week, Hüsnügüzel stopped one evening at about the time of the evening prayer. Letting his horse graze, he said his prayers and prepared to sleep there for the night. It was becoming dark as Hüsnügüzel unbuckled the sword that his father had given him. Just then, however, he saw a light in the forest opposite him, and he decided to go there to spend the night, thinking there must be a village where he could get lodging. He rode until he came to the forest, and then he walked, leading the horse behind him. At last he came to the house from which the light was coming, but when he looked inside, he could see no one there. "Is anybody at home?" he shouted.

"Come in, Hüsnügüzel," said a voice.

Hüsnügüzel was greatly surprised. "How does this person know my name?" he wondered.

An old man with a long white beard appeared in the door and said, "Come in, son."

"How did you know my name, father?"

"Come in, son."

When Hüsnügüzel went into the house he saw a dining table set with a feast. It had on it all the kinds of food that a man could wish to eat. After they had eaten, the old man said to Hüsnügüzel, "I see that you have left somewhere the magic sword that I once gave you." Hüsnügüzel then knew that the old man was Hizir, and he kissed his beard and his feet and he begged his forgiveness. "It was I who caused you to fall in love with The Most Beautiful Girl in the World, just as I once caused your father to fall in love with her. But she is also in love with you and she is looking for you. She lives in a palace by the sea and no one can open the door of that palace. You have a week's journey left to reach that palace. Now let us retire, and in the morning I shall tell you how to reach that palace and enter it."

At dawn the old man awakened Hüsnügüzel and said to him, "Come now, son, and tell me what you see off in that direction."

Hüsnügüzel looked toward the dawn, in the direction that the old man pointed, but he said, "I cannot see anything."

"Look carefully. You should be able to see the palace of The Most Beautiful Girl in the World."

"I think I see it now," said the young man, "for that must be the red glimmer that I see in the east."

Hizir looked hard and said, "No, that glow that you see is only the light given off by a hair in the head of The Most Beautiful Girl. She is sleeping at a window on the top floor of the palace, and one hair of her head is hanging out the window. That is the glimmer that you see, and now you know where the palace is located. It will take you a week to get there. Now leave the sword of your father here and take instead this magic sword from me."

Hüsnügüzel took the sword, and then the old man gave him further directions. "When you reach the palace of The Most Beautiful Girl in the World, mark the point on the wall that you come to first, and then go around the walls three times reading this prayer as you go." Here he handed Hüsnügüzel a prayer written on a paper. "After you have gone around the third time, stop at the spot you have marked on the wall, strike that spot with your sword, saying 'Ya Allah!' [51] and a door will open there to let you in."

Taking leave of the old man, Hüsnügüzel mounted his horse and rode off in the direction of the palace of The Most Beautiful Girl in the World. After a week he reached the wall of the palace, marked the spot, rode around the wall three times, reading the prayer as he rode, and then struck the spot as he shouted, "Ya Allah!" Just as Hizir had said, a door in the wall opened at the spot and Hüsnügüzel entered.

The Most Beautiful Girl in the World had awakened at the noise, and now she came down to the second floor of the palace and looked down on Hüsnügüzel. She knew at once that this was the man with whom she had fallen in love in her dreams. She immediately ran downstairs to him, embraced him, and led him by the hand up to the top floor. There they ate and drank and made love to each other for a whole week. The palace had everything in it that one could wish, but after a week's time, Hüsnügüzel became restless. Noticing this, The Most Beautiful Girl said to him, "Darling, what is it that you would like to do?"

"I have seen many partridges over there on that plain. I should like to take a bow and arrows and go to hunt those birds. Those that I shoot you can cook for our dinner."

"Very well," she said, "but don't go too far away. When you opened a door in the wall of the palace, you dissolved all of my magic power, and I now have no way of defending myself. There are many other padishahs searching for me, and you may lose me while you are gone."

"Don't worry," said Hüsnügüzel, "for only God, your Creator, could take you from me now. Besides, no one could ever find you here."

When he was out hunting Hüsnügüzel came upon a flock of partridges, but when he aimed at one of them, the image of The Most Beautiful Girl in the World came before his eyes so that he could not see the bird. This happened every time that day that he tried to shoot a partridge. At night, after he had returned to the palace, he told the girl about this.

43

"I shall give you something to change this," she said, "though it could also be something that will cause you to lose me."

"Don't worry about that. I won't lose you."

"Take this hair from my head, then, and wrap it around your bow. When you aim at a bird, my image will be drawn to this hair, and you will then be able to see past it to shoot the bird."

Hüsnügüzel took the hair and did as she instructed. That day he shot three partridges. In the evening he brought them home to the palace where The Most Beautiful Girl in the World cooked them for their dinner. For many days he went hunting and came back each night with partridges for their dinner. One day when he was out hunting, the hair on his bow came loose, and as he was riding back toward the palace, the hair slipped off the bow and flew away in the wind. He rode after it, trying to catch it, but it disappeared before he could reach it.

Now let us see what happened to that strand of hair. It flew on in the wind for a long time and finally it came to rest in the garden of the Padishah of Giants, who lived by the sea. That padishah had remained a bachelor for thirty years, during which time he had searched constantly for The Most Beautiful Girl in the World. As his guards were patrolling the garden on that day, they saw something glimmering in the grass. They picked up the hair and took it at once to the padishah. "Your majesty," one of them said, "we have found this strange thing in your garden, but we do not know what it is." The padishah could not understand what it was either, nor could any of his wise men, so he wrapped it carefully in a handkerchief and put it in his pocket.

Now let us go back and see what Hüsnügüzel and his beloved are doing. They were both deeply concerned over the loss of the hair. That day Hüsnügüzel did not go hunting but stayed with The Most Beautiful Girl all day. In the afternoon they went bathing in the sea near the palace. As they were about to leave, a large wave came along and carried away one of the golden sandals worn by The Most Beautiful Girl in the World. Hüsnügüzel dived into the sea many times searching for this sandal, but he was unable to find it.

The waves carried the sandal to the seashore alongside the garden of the Padishah of Giants. The guards patrolling the garden noticed the glittering object on the beach and took it at once to their padishah.

"Where did you find this sandal?" he asked one of the guards.

"On the beach, your majesty, not far from the place where we found the gleaming hair before."

"What a strange business this is," said the padishah. He called to-

44

gether all of his wise men, but they could not tell him anything about the golden sandal. As they were puzzling over the sandal, a witch came along and asked, "What are you thinking about, my padishah?"

"I am thinking about this golden sandal."

"I have good news for you," she said, "but I don't suppose you would reward me for it."

"What is your news?"

"That is one of the golden sandals worn by The Most Beautiful Girl in the World."

"Since you know what this is, perhaps you can also tell me what it is that is wrapped here in my handkerchief," and he took from his pocket the handkerchief containing the gleaming hair.

"Of course I can. That is a hair from the head of the girl who has kept you a bachelor for thirty years," said the witch.

"Since you know what these things are," said the Padishah of Giants, "then perhaps you also know how their owner can be found."

"Of course I do," answered the witch, "and if you will give me a pot of gold, I shall help you find her."

"I shall give you five pots of gold if you can locate her, but if you fail, I shall have you executed."

"The task will be done, but first you must get me a large clay pot,[52] a goat skin, and a whip. Then I can find her."

The padishah ordered that these objects be brought to her. The witch placed the skin on the clay pot and sat astride it. Then she took the whip and, beating the pot with it, flew away through the air in the direction of the palace of The Most Beautiful Girl in the World. She landed in the garden of the palace, and because the wall had been broken by Hüsnügüzel and his magic sword, she was able to walk right into the courtyard. Just inside the wall door, right near the threshold, she dug a hole and buried her clay pot. Then she bent her back as if she were a hunchback and groaned, "Oh! Oh!" [53] as if she were ill.

When The Most Beautiful Girl heard this, she looked out her window and saw the old woman walking about below. "Are you fairy or jinn?" she asked.

"Neither, but a human being like you. I am a sick old woman and I have no one in the world to care for me. Have you a place here for me to sleep?"

"My husband is away hunting," said the girl, "and I cannot accept anyone into the palace when he is gone."

"Which way did your husband go?" asked the old woman.

"He went over on those plains, toward the distant forest."

The old woman started in that direction, hobbling slowly at first, but walking rapidly once she was out of the girl's sight. She met Hüsnügüzel on his way home from hunting, and as soon as she saw him she bent over again like a hunchback, crying, "Oh! Oh!"

"What are you doing here, mother?" he asked.

"I am a lonely old woman, son. I am sick and I have nobody in the world to care for me. I have neither son nor daughter, father nor mother nor brother. I have lost my way, and I have no place to spend the night. Can you give me a place to sleep tonight?"

"If you have no place to live, why don't you live with us? My wife is The Most Beautiful Girl in the World, but she feels very lonely when I am away hunting. If you would stay with us you could keep her company."

"I would like that," said the witch.

"Very well, then," said Hüsnügüzel, "climb up on the back of my horse." But when the old woman tried to mount the horse, the animal kicked at her and reared up on its hind legs.[54] No matter what Hüsnügüzel did to it, the horse would not let the evil woman come near it.

"It looks as if your horse won't let me ride," she said, "but it doesn't matter. You ride and I shall walk along behind."

When Hüsnügüzel reached the palace he went upstairs to his beloved's room and said to her, "I have found an old woman who is willing to live with us. When I am out hunting, she will be company for you."

The girl looked at the old woman and said, "She was here earlier, but I did not let her in. I am glad, however, to have her here."

"What a perfect pair you two are," said the witch. "I shall pray for your happiness."

Now let us go back for a moment to the Padishah of Arabs and see what is happening at his palace. The friends of Hüsnügüzel had been living in the palace with their wives since he had left. The son of the Padishah of Stars had become padishah and the son of the Padishah of the Seas had become his secretary. The former Padishah of Arabs had become the grand vezir, just as he had promised he would. Each of Hüsnügüzel's friends had a son now, and they were very happy with their wives. The youngest princess who was married to Hüsnügüzel remained always in her room guarding the sword he had left with her. She stayed there alone and she would not let anyone enter the room. Because her father, like everyone else, was afraid of Hüsnügüzel, he respected his daughter's wishes and did not force her to open the door.

Now let us leave these people where they are and go back to the palace of The Most Beautiful Girl in the World. It was near the end of the month that the Padishah of Giants had allowed to the witch for getting The Most Beautiful Girl. One day when Hüsnügüzel was out hunting, as usual, the old woman said to her, "Your husband leaves you alone here so often. It is quite all right while I am here to keep you company, but, as you can see, I am old and unhealthy, and I shall die someday. Then you will be very lonely. This young man of yours seems to have a secret charm of some kind, for without one, he could not have found you here. Many padishahs searched years for you and failed, but he succeeded. He will tell you about his secret charm, and then when I am gone you will have something living to enjoy."

That night when Hüsnügüzel and The Most Beautiful Girl in the World were in bed, she said to him, "Hüsnügüzel, how did you find me here? You must have a secret charm of some kind. Why don't you tell me of it? The old woman in our palace will one day die, and then I shall be very lonely, for I am used to having her company. If you will tell me of your charm, then when she is gone, I shall have something living here with which to entertain myself."

"You have never asked me this before," said Hüsnügüzel, "and so why do you ask me now? My secret charm is that mirror on the wall. If that mirror should be broken by someone, I should have only an hour to live. Don't ever take any chance of breaking it, but while I am away, you can play with it and enjoy yourself in that way."

When Hüsnügüzel had gone hunting again next day, the old woman asked the girl, "Did you ask him about his secret charm?"

"Yes, I did, mother. His secret is that mirror on the wall, but don't ever touch it, for if it should be broken, he would have only an hour to live."

"All right, my girl." But when The Most Beautiful Girl in the World was in the next room, the old woman took the mirror from the wall, broke it into many pieces, and threw the pieces into the sea. She thought that she had killed Hüsnügüzel and she was surprised when he returned that night unharmed.

"I think that your man has not really told you his secret," she said to the girl. "A mirror cannot contain the secret of someone's life. It must be something else. Ask him again."

When the girl asked Hüsnügüzel again, he said, "Why do you keep asking me about this? I have told you once already, but if you insist, I shall let you know my secret charm. It is in that broom behind the door. If that broom is lost or burned, then I am lost too. So don't ever take any chance of losing that broom."

The next day when the old woman asked the girl about Hüsnügüzel's charm, The Most Beautiful Girl in the World said, "It is in that broom behind the door. We must never lose the broom, however, for if it is lost then Hüsnügüzel will be lost too."

"Very well, my girl," said the witch, but when she was alone in the room, she took the broom from the corner and threw it out the window into the sea. That evening she was again amazed to see Hüsnügüzel come home in good health. She now pretended that her illness had become much worse. "Dear girl, my health is getting much worse, and I may die in a day or two. You will then be very lonely. Try to learn your man's secret — won't you?" She cried as she said this.

After eating dinner and going to bed, the girl said to Hüsnügüzel, "Why do you keep your secret from me? I am The Most Beautiful Girl in the World. Many men searched for me without success, but you found me, and I am yours. Why, then, don't you tell me where your secret charm is located?"

"Very well, then," said Hüsnügüzel, "I shall tell you. My life force is really in this sword that I keep here in our bedroom. If anyone even touches it, I become ill. If anyone draws it halfway out of its sheath, I become seriously ill. If anyone should draw it completely from the sheath, I would then have only forty minutes to live. You may go close to the sword and enjoy it from a distance, but don't ever touch it."

When the young man went hunting again next morning, the old witch went to the girl, groaning, "Oh! Oh!" pretending to be very ill. "Did you ask him?" she inquired.

"Yes, I did, mother."

"Well, what is it?"

"His life force is in his sword. If anyone touches it, Hüsnügüzel becomes ill. If anyone draws it halfway from its sheath, he becomes seriously ill. And if anyone should draw it all the way out, then he would have only forty minutes to live. So we must leave this sword alone."

"Very well, my girl. My own trouble is too great for me to bother about that sword. I had a dream last night in which I saw myself very, very ill. I may be much worse tonight. Will you leave your bedroom door open so that you may hear me if I cry out for help? If I need water you can bring me some."

"Yes, and I shall explain this to Hüsnügüzel," said the girl.

While the young couple slept that night, the old woman crept slowly and quietly into the room, went over to their bed, and very gently slipped the sword from beneath Hüsnügüzel's pillow, where he always kept it at night. She immediately drew the sword from its sheath and threw it out a window into the sea.

Immediately after this Hüsnügüzel got up out of bed and began to roll around the room like a millstone. The girl awakened and shouted, "Hüsnügüzül! Hüsnügüzül!" but he did not answer at all. The Most Beautiful Girl in the World began to cry aloud, "Hüsnügüzel is dying! Come, let us help him, mother."

"Quick, my girl," said the witch, "let us go down to the garden and pick some mint leaves. If he smells these, he may be revived." They went downstairs to the garden, but in the dark the girl could not find any mint. "It was here or over there," said the old woman. "No, it was right here. Dig in this spot quickly!"

As The Most Beautiful Girl in the World dug, she uncovered the mouth of a large pot. The witch pushed the girl into the pot, sat on the skin, whipped the pot, and away they flew through the air straight to the palace of the Padishah of Giants.

Now let us see what the youngest daughter of the Padishah of Arabs is doing. When she looked at the sword of Hüsnügüzel, about midnight, she saw that three drops of blood had dripped from its tip. She grew very agitated at this and rushed to tell the son of the Padishah of Stars and the son of the Padishah of the Seas that Hüsnügüzel was dying. "Find him at once and help him!" she ordered.

The son of the Padishah of Stars looked at the sky and studied the stars. After a minute he pointed and said, "We must go that way." They went in the direction he indicated, and they reached the palace of The Most Beautiful Girl in the World just three minutes before Hüsnügüzel was to die.

The son of the Padishah of the Seas saw the empty sheath on the floor near Hüsnügüzel, and then, looking out the window, he saw the sword gleaming on the bottom of the sea. He immediately jumped into the sea and brought back Hüsnügüzel's sword. When the sword was put back in its sheath, Hüsnügüzel opened his eyes and looked around. Seeing his friends, he jumped up and embraced them. He wanted to order coffee for the son of the Padishah of Stars and the son of the Padishah of the Seas, but he could find neither the old witch nor The Most Beautiful Girl in the World. Explaining to his friends what had happened to him and how the witch had deceived him, Hüsnügüzel thanked them for saving his life and bade them farewell: "You go back to the palace of the Padishah of Arabs, and I shall search once more for The Most Beautiful Girl in the World."

As soon as they had gone, Hüsnügüzel began to look for the girl. After traveling for several hours, he met a shepherd along the way and he said to him, "Selamünaleyküm."

"Aleykümselam," returned the shepherd.

"Have you some bread, friend?" he asked the shepherd.

"Yes, I have, my padishah," answered the shepherd.

"How did you know I was a padishah?"

"There are no horses like yours in this kingdom, nor does anyone but a padishah carry a sword like yours." Saying this, the shepherd gave Hüsnügüzel some bread and cheese.

As they were eating, Hüsnügüzel heard a drum and pipes playing somewhere. "What is this music for?" he asked the shepherd.

"The Padishah of Giants, who rules this land, is getting married. He has been a bachelor for thirty years, but at last he has found The Most Beautiful Girl in the World, and they are getting married."

"Here is a handful of gold for you. I want to exchange clothes with you, and while I am gone, I want you to take care of my horse." Hüsnügüzel dressed himself in the shepherd's tattered clothes, stuck his sword in his belt, and started down the road toward the town. He saw an old hag near the town. Although she did not recognize him, dressed like a keloghlan, Hüsnügüzel thought that this must be the witch who had taken The Most Beautiful Girl in the World from him. Lifting her veil to be sure it was the witch, he shouted at her, "What did you do with my girl? Tell me at once or I shall kill you."

"She is sitting at the window in the palace of the Padishah of Giants, watching for you. The padishah gave me a great quantity of gold for bringing her to him, but my bargain with him is now complete, and I can get her back for you."

"Very well, then," said Hüsnügüzel, "take this ring and give it to her. Tell her not to worry and tell her that tonight I shall come beneath her window where we can talk."

The old woman went to the palace and asked the padishah for permission to talk with the girl. When she went to the girl's room and knocked on the door, The Most Beautiful Girl in the World would not let her in. "Go away, you filthy hag. You have brought me here and now you want to come near me."

"Don't misunderstand me. I simply want to show you something, and then I shall go away."

The girl opened the door a crack and saw Hüsnügüzel's ring in the hand of the witch. "Where is he?" she asked.

"Don't worry, daughter. He will rescue you. He sent greetings to you and said that tonight he will come beneath your window, in the garden, to talk with you. Watch for him." Saying this, the witch left her.

In the evening when Hüsnügüzel came to the garden of the palace, the vezir saw him and called out, "What are you doing there, you son of a donkey [55] Keloghlan? Get out of this garden and go back to your sheep."

"All I want is to have one glimpse of our padishah and The Most Beautiful Girl in the World, and then I shall return to my flock. A friend is tending it now."

The padishah heard this discussion from his room. He came out and asked the vezir, "What is going on here?"

"Your majesty, this filthy, stinking shepherd has come into your garden, and he won't go away."

"Perhaps he is hungry," said the padishah. "Give him something to eat from the leftover food and from the scrapings of dinner, and then get him out of here."

When they brought the food to Hüsnügüzel, he said, "Take this back to your padishah. I don't eat such filthy food."

"Catch that scoundrel," the vezir ordered his men, but Hüsnügüzel ran away and hid in the garden.

The Most Beautiful Girl in the World was waiting for Hüsnügüzel at her window, and she saw all this, but she did not speak to him for fear this would reveal his identity. Later in the evening, she signaled to him, when no one was nearby, and he came beneath her window.

"Ask the padishah to give you a basket and a rope," Hüsnügüzel said to her. "Tell him you wish to buy vegetables from passing sellers and pull them up to your apartment. Then you can lower the basket on the rope and pull me up to you."

The Most Beautiful Girl in the World called her attendants and told them to go to the padishah to ask for a large basket and enough rope to reach to the ground. "Tell him that I wish to buy things from passing hawkers." The padishah sent the basket, some money with which to buy things, and three times as much rope as she had requested.

When everyone else was in bed that night, the girl lowered the basket and pulled Hüsnügüzel up into her room. It was the last night of the wedding period, and the nuptial day was to follow.

"I'll hide in this wardrobe," said Hüsnügüzel. "When the padishah comes into the room, you praise me and say, 'He is such a brave man. If he came here now, what would you do?' Let us see what he will say about me."

When the wedding ceremonies were complete and the nuptial night was approaching, the padishah prepared to enter the girl's room. Hüsnügüzel hid himself in the wardrobe and waited. The Most Beautiful Girl in the World simply sat by the window, looking out, and didn't pay any attention to the padishah when he entered. "My beloved," he said, "I have searched for you for thirty years. I am the Padishah of Giants and no one can defeat me in battle. I have finally got you. Why don't you stand up so that I can have a full view of you?"

"Pooh!" said the girl, despising the padishah. "You should have seen my own lover, Hüsnügüzel. He would have held you in the air on the tip of his sword."

"Who is this fellow you call Hüsnügüzel?"

"He is the son of the Padishah of Egypt," said the girl.

"I don't care whose son he is. Even if all of the padishahs of men in the world should come, I would not be afraid. They would tremble before me, for I am the Padishah of Giants." He went over to The Most Beautiful Girl in the World and started to fondle her shoulder. Then Hüsnügüzel came out of the wardrobe.

"Oh, Padishah of Giants, I was the shepherd to whom you sent the leftover food, but I am actually Hüsnügüzel."

The giant was speechless with amazement. "Oh, Padishah of Giants," said the girl, "before Hüsnügüzel came, you were bragging about your courage. If you have anything to say to him, say it now that he is here." But the giant was struck dumb. Hüsnügüzel drew his sword, struck the giant dead with it, and, cutting his body into four parts, stuffed him into the wardrobe. Then he and the girl ate and drank the food that had been prepared for the nuptials and went to bed.

Toward morning they arose and went to the baths. Maidservants led The Most Beautiful Girl in the World to a bath for women, and Hüsnügüzel went to another. When he came out of the bath, the members of the court said to each other, "How young our padishah has become after sleeping for just one night with The Most Beautiful Girl in the World."

Coffee was served to the padishah, and then the grand vezir came in and asked, "What is your wish today, your majesty?"

"Call the town criers together and have them announce that there will be no further wedding celebrations today." The vezir did as Hüsnügüzel had ordered, and when the people heard this, many of them concluded that the padishah had grown proud after sleeping one night with The Most Beautiful Girl in the World. Hüsnügüzel said to the grand vezir, "We are going on a journey and we shall be away for a long time. You will be in charge while I am gone. Here are the keys to the palace, but do not open that wardrobe door in the nuptial chamber while I am gone."

"Very well, your majesty."

Hüsnügüzel and the girl left the palace that morning, and all of the people who saw them again commented upon the unbelievable youthfulness and health of their padishah. They still could not understand why he had canceled the wedding celebrations.

As the two lovers were crossing a bridge, they met the old witch. "Why did you commit such treachery against me?" asked Hüsnügüzel. "We took care of you all that long time, and in return you sold my wife to the Padishah of Giants." Without even waiting for the witch to answer, he drew his sword, cut her body into four pieces, and threw the pieces in the river. Then they went to the shepherd and Hüsnügüzel said, "Take this gold and give me back my padishah's clothes and my horse."

After Hüsnügüzel had put on his own clothes again, the two mounted his horse and set out along the road. After riding all day, they were tired, and so they stopped by a fountain near a poplar tree. They ate and drank and then sat by the fountain where Hüsnügüzel fell asleep with his head in the girl's lap. They slept there that way all night, but when morning came, the girl was awakened suddenly by the noise of many horses' hoofs.

We must go back to the palace of the Padishah of Giants to learn about these horses. After Hüsnügüzel had left, the grand vezir smelled something strange, and he noticed many flies around the forbidden door. "The padishah warned me not to open that door," he said, "but something must be done about this. Let us open the door for just a moment and see if perhaps a cat or dog died in that closet."

When they opened the door of the wardrobe, they found the body of the Padishah of Giants, covered with flies, and near it a heap of the shabby clothes Hüsnügüzel had worn as a disguise when he entered the garden. One of the palace attendants recognized the body and said, "*This is our own padishah.* That keloghlan must have killed him and taken on his identity, wearing our padishah's clothes. How could a man have grown so young in just one night?" The grand vezir then gathered some troops around him and set out in pursuit of Hüsnügüzel and The Most Beautiful Girl in the World. It was the noise caused by these troops that had awakened the girl.

When the girl saw the approaching troops, she slipped the saddlebag under Hüsnügüzel's head, without awakening him, drew her sword, and advanced to meet the troops. While she fought with them, Hüsnügüzel's horse neighed several times until the young man awoke. He joined his wife in the battle against the palace troops, and between them they killed many soldiers. Finally, Hüsnügüzel captured the grand vezir and said, "What a fool you have been! Don't you realize that I am Hüsnügüzel? I took back my own girl, killed your padishah, and left you in charge. Go back to the palace and live comfortably. Go and let me not kill you."

After the vezir had left, Hüsnügüzel and the girl mounted his horse and rode to her palace. They lived there for some time, and then one day Hüsnügüzel said, "Now let us go to the palace of the Padishah of Arabs. I have friends there who saved my life once. After visiting them, we can go back to Egypt, the land where my father is the padishah. I have missed my parents."

"As you wish, Hüsnügüzel," said The Most Beautiful Girl in the World.

They rode to the palace of the Padishah of Arabs and stayed there a few days. There Hüsnügüzel married the youngest daughter of the padishah, the girl who all this time had been guarding his sword that once dripped blood. Hüsnügüzel then asked his friends to permit him to leave. To the Padishah of Arabs he said, "You should return to the position of padishah, for I shall return to Egypt. The son of the Padishah of the Seas shall be your vezir and the son of the Padishah of Stars shall be your secretary. All I want is a horse for The Most Beautiful Girl in the World and a horse for my new bride."

The Padishah of Arabs was saddened when he learned that Hüsnügüzel was determined to leave. He granted him the two horses that he wished, and when Hüsnügüzel left, the padishah and his attendants rode along with them toward Egypt for a week. Drums and pipes were played as they rode along.

After the Padishah of Arabs left them, Hüsnügüzel and his two wives rode for a whole month and finally arrived at Egypt. There his parents rejoiced at his return, and they arranged another wedding for him and his two wives that lasted for forty days and forty nights. They lived happily thereafter, and may God give happiness to us all. And may you remember me, Mehmet Anli, of Samsun, by this tale.

4.

The Son of the Fisherman [56]

There was once a fisherman named Tüljül who died leaving one son. The boy's mother used to work in the household of a rich pasha [57] as a maid, and each night she would bring home bread and other food for her son to eat.

One day the boy said to his mother, "What was my father's business?"

"He did not have much of a business," said his mother. "All he had was a net with which he used to fish. He was a fisherman."

"All right, then, I shall be a fisherman like my father," he said.

The next day he took his father's net and went down to the seashore. Although he tried very hard to catch a fish, on that first day he caught nothing but a tortoise shell. When he returned home, he put the tortoise shell on a shelf in the kitchen and said to his mother, "This is our kismet for today."

After that the boy was known as the Son of the Fisherman, and he became a good fisherman himself. The normal routine of their lives continued much the same but there was one difference. When the mother and son returned home from work, they discovered that the house was always swept, the dishes were washed, and the food was prepared, cooked, and set on the table ready for them. The son thought that his mother had done these things, and the mother thought that the son had done them. The boy said, "Mother, what is the meaning of this? You never used to bring such fine things to eat. We managed to survive with the scraps of food which you brought home. What is all this now?"

"I didn't bring home anything, son," she said. "Who could have done this?" After she had thought for a while she said, "I wonder if this is somehow the work of that tortoise shell which you brought home on the first day that you went fishing?"

One day shortly after that, the Son of the Fisherman decided to remain at home during the day and watch what happened in the house after he and his mother had supposedly left. He hid himself behind some furniture, and after a while he saw come from the tortoise shell a girl as beautiful as the fourteenth of the moon. [58] She swept the house, washed the dishes, and cooked a number of dishes of food, and then she walked back to the place where the tortoise shell was. But before she reached it, the young man ran ahead of her, took the tortoise shell, and smashed it into pieces. Then he asked the girl to stay with them and to marry him. She agreed to this, and very soon after that they were married, and the Son of the Fisherman, his new wife, and his mother lived very happily for a while.

One day the king of that city decided to go on a tour of inspection. Before he started out to examine all the houses, he called his grand vezir to him and ordered that the city be darkened for his visit, that all the lights be turned off. The grand vezir sent messengers to all parts of the city to tell the people to put out all lamps that evening.

As the king was making his tour of the city, however, he noticed a light coming from one house. "Didn't I ask you to have all the lights put out?" he asked his vezir angrily. When they came to the cottage from which the light was shining, they found that the light was not coming from a lamp. In that house there was a very beautiful woman sleeping by the window. Her arm hung out of the window, and that arm was so beautiful that it gleamed brightly, and it was this that they had thought was a lamp.

The king took one look at this girl with the bright arm, and he fell in love with her at once. He ordered the doors of that cottage sealed [59] and the next morning he directed that the seals be broken and the girl brought to him. But his vezir reasoned with him, saying, "Your majesty, that woman has a husband who is a fisherman and a poor man. We cannot just take his wife away from him like that. Let us impose some task upon him which he cannot possibly fulfill, and tell him that if he fails to perform the task successfully, we shall take his wife from him as punishment."

"Very well," said the king, "what shall we tell him to do?"

"You have twelve fierce lions, your majesty," said the vezir. "Let us tell him he must produce twelve lions of his own to fight with your lions. If he fails to produce the lions or if his lions are defeated by your lions, we shall then take his wife from him."

The king agreed to this, and a messenger was sent to the house of the Son of the Fisherman to tell him that he was wanted at the palace. Just before the Son of the Fisherman left his home for the palace, his wife said to him, "Whatever the king tells you to do, you just say, 'All right, your majesty.'"

When the young man was shown into the presence of the king, he was told, "You will catch twelve lions to fight with my twelve lions. If you fail to catch twelve lions or if my lions beat those which you manage to catch, I shall take your wife from you as punishment. Go and get your lions."

"All right, your majesty," said the Son of the Fisherman and departed.

When he told his wife about the task which had been given him, she said, "Take this seal and go with it to the place where you were standing on the beach the day that you caught the tortoise shell in your net. Stamp this seal on the large stone there and an Arab will appear. Give him my greetings and tell him to provide you with twelve lions fiercer than those of the king."

The Son of the Fisherman did as his wife directed him. When he pressed the seal against the large stone, the Arab appeared and said, "What do you want with me?"

"The girl from the tortoise shell sends you her greetings and orders that you provide me with twelve lions fiercer than those of the king," said the Son of the Fisherman.

The lions were produced in a short time, and the next morning the young man took them to the palace saying, "Here are my lions." In the fight that followed, his lions tore apart the lions of the king and threw about the pieces of their bodies.

A few days later, the king began to think again of the girl with the gleaming arm. He called his vezir to him and said, "I want that girl for myself."

"Well, your majesty, let us set another task for her husband. If he performs the task, very well. But if he does not perform it, we shall have reason to take his wife from him."

"What difficult task can we set for him this time?" asked the king.

"This fisherman is very poor," said the vezir. "We can ask him to feed the entire population of this city for a whole day. He will not possibly be able to do this, and so we shall have reason to punish him by taking his wife."

"A very good proposal," said the king.

A messenger was sent to tell the Son of the Fisherman that he was wanted at the palace. Again his wife said to him as he was leaving, "Whatever the king tells you to do, you just say, 'All right, your majesty.' Then everything will be all right."

When the young man arrived before the king, he was told, "Tomorrow you must feed the entire population of this city."

"All right, your majesty," the young man answered.

When he returned home, his wife asked him, "What did the king ask you to do this time?"

"He said that I must feed the entire population of this city tomorrow," replied the young man.

"Very well," she said. "Take this seal again and stamp it on the same stone on the beach. When the Arab comes, give him my greetings and then he will do whatever you wish. Tell him that the girl from the tortoise shell wants him to provide the food you need."

The Son of the Fisherman went to the beach and stamped the seal against the stone, and again the Arab appeared. "The girl from the tortoise shell sends you her greetings. She wants you to provide me with enough food to feed the entire population of the city tomorrow." The Arab handed him a hazelnut and nothing more. Not knowing what to do with one hazelnut, the young man threw it on the ground.

"Go and pick it up," the Arab told him, "for it is full of food. Whenever you need food, just crack the shell and say, 'Open, my food store, and let hundreds of different kinds of foods be scattered about, and let all the dishes be of gold.' When you do this, you will suddenly have tons of food brought to you in golden dishes." [60]

In the meantime, the king had sent criers around the city announcing that everyone should come to the public square tomorrow for a huge feast. The next morning, thousands of people began to gather in the square to await the feast. When they were all assembled, the Son of the Fisherman took the hazelnut from his pocket, cracked the shell, and said, "Open, my food store, and let hundreds of different kinds of food be scattered about, and let all the dishes be of gold."

As soon as he had said this, the entire city square was simply filled with food of all kinds. Everyone ate and drank as much as he could. Just before the feast was over, the Son of the Fisherman had criers go among the crowd and announce, "All guests may take their golden dishes home with them if they wish to do so." When the people heard this, they all took some of the golden dishes home with them. Even the king took a few with him. [61]

The king then forgot about the wife of the fisherman for a while, but then she came into his mind again and he desired her. He called his vezir to him and said, "I want that girl from you. Deliver her to me!"

"Please, your majesty," said the vezir. "You have seen that the Son of the Fisherman is a person who can perform miracles. He has had your lions killed and he has fed the entire population of this city. How can we take his wife from him without cause? He might put a curse upon your head."

"But I want that girl!" shouted the king.

"Then let us require of him an even more difficult task," said the vezir. "Let us require him to build a wall around the city, with four iron gates in it, all within twenty-four hours. Of course, he will not be able to do it, and as punishment we shall kill him and take his wife."

"An excellent idea," said the king.

The next morning a messenger was sent to the Son of the Fisherman to tell him that he was wanted again at the palace. "You must build a wall around the city, with four iron gates in it, within twenty-four hours, or I shall have your head cut off," said the king.

The young man returned to his home and told his wife what the king had demanded this time. She gave him the magic seal again and told him that the Arab would do the work for him and have the wall built within the required twenty-four hours.

The Son of the Fisherman went to the beach, struck the seal on the stone, and when the Arab appeared, he said, "The girl from the tortoise shell sends you her greetings and says that you are to build at once a wall around our city, and in that wall you are to place four iron gates." When he walked back to the city, the young man was amazed to see that the wall with the iron gates had already been built by the Arab.

When a short time had passed after the wall had been built, the king again started thinking about the girl and desiring her. He called his vezir and this time said to him angrily, "Don't you understand that I really want that girl? You must get her for me!"

The vezir knew now that the Son of the Fisherman had been assisted by magic power of some kind, and so he said to the king, "Please, your majesty, do not try again to take this woman from her husband. He is a man who has performed miracles. He may curse us or he may bring about some great calamity to the city."

"I don't care. I must have her," said the king.

"Then we must impose an even more difficult task upon him," said the vezir. "Let us ask him to capture the wild mare with the forty colts which lives in the mountains." [62]

When the messenger had summoned the Son of the Fisherman to the palace, and when the young man had arrived there, the king said to him, "You must capture and bring to me the wild mare who eats everyone who comes near her. You will bring her and her forty colts here. You will fight the mare and thus save your wife and yourself. If you lose the fight, the mare will eat you, anyway."

The Son of the Fisherman went home and told his wife what he had been ordered to do. She said to him, "First get a horse, and ride it to the beach. There strike the stone twice with the seal, and you will find a set of reins. Take those reins and go to the mountain. There you will find a fountain with a large pond full of water before it. Drain this pond and fill the hollow space with wine. At noon the mare with the forty colts will come to drink from the pond, and when they drink their fill of the wine, they will become intoxicated. Then you will be able to fight the mare and capture her, and when you have done this, put the magic reins on her at once. After that, you will be able to control her."

The Son of the Fisherman did all the things which his wife had told him to do. When the mare had drunk from the wine in the pond, she attacked the young man's horse. The Son of the Fisherman defeated the mare, however, and putting the reins on her head, led her into the city with the forty colts following their mother. The news spread all over the city that the Son of the Fisherman had captured the mare with the forty colts and was leading her into the city. Everyone was amazed.

Again the king forgot for a while about the wife of the Son of the Fisherman, but again he began to think about her after a few days had passed. Once more she came back into his mind.[63] He called his vezir to him and said, "For the last time, I am ordering you to get that girl for me. Do not fail this time!"

The vezir was afraid again and said once more to the king, "Your majesty, won't you please forget about this girl? We have seen the great power of this fisherman many times. Sooner or later he will surely avenge himself upon you."

"It makes no difference. I want the girl anyway," said the king, "and this time *I* shall set the task for him. Tell him to go and bring back the sister of the seven giants who live in such-and-such a place. Tell him that she is even more beautiful than his wife. If he brings her, he can have her; if he fails — well, he will be killed anyway by her seven brothers."

A messenger was sent again to the home of the Son of the Fisherman to invite him to the palace. When he arrived at the palace, the vezir said to him, "In such-and-such a place there live seven giants with a sister. You must go and bring their sister back here, and if you do, you shall have her. She is even more beautiful than your wife. If you do not bring her back with you, I shall have you executed."

When the Son of the Fisherman returned home this time and told his wife about the new task, she said to him, "Alas! I cannot help you in this matter. You will have to perform this task by yourself."

The Son of the Fisherman set out on his journey to such-and-such a

place in search of the sister of the seven giants. On the way, he came
to a mill where seven millstones were all grinding wheat. A large man
was eating the flour as fast as the seven millstones could grind it, and
this man still complained to the miller that he was hungry.

The Son of the Fisherman approached this man and said to him, "You
must be a very powerful man to be able to eat so much flour and still be
hungry."

"What I do is nothing compared with the achievements of a man
called the Son of the Fisherman," said the Big Eater. "I wish I were like
him."

"Would you like to be a friend of this person?" asked the young man.

"Of course I would," replied the Big Eater.

"Well, I am he," said the Son of the Fisherman.

The two became friends, and the Big Eater, who was almost as strong
as a giant himself, decided to go along with the Son of the Fisherman.
After the two had traveled along together for a while, they came to a
river. There they saw a huge man who was stopping the water of the
river with one hand while he scooped it up into his mouth with his other
hand. Between swallows, he kept complaining, "Oh, I am thirsty! I
cannot quench my thirst!"

"What a powerful man you are to be able to drink so much water,"
said the Son of the Fisherman.

"It is nothing compared with the things that the Son of the Fisherman
can do," answered the Big Drinker.

"Would you like to be a friend of this person?" asked the young man.

"Of course I would," replied the Big Drinker.

"Well, I am he," said the Son of the Fisherman.

The Big Drinker and the Son of the Fisherman became friends, and
the Big Drinker joined the young man and the Big Eater. The three of
them walked along for a way when they came upon a man playing a
flute so beautifully that rocks and streams and even the hills were dancing to the tune.[64]

"What a marvelous art!" said the young man to the Flute Player.

"It is nothing compared with the ability of the man known as the Son
of the Fisherman," replied the Flute Player.

"If you met this person, would you be a friend to him?" asked the
young man.

"Yes, I would," replied the Flute Player.

"Well, I am he," said the Son of the Fisherman.

The Flute Player joined the three and all four of them walked along until they came to another river. There they saw a man kneeling on the bank with his ear to the ground.

"What are you doing there?" asked the Son of the Fisherman.

"Oh, I am just listening to the tinkling of a needle that my mother dropped here seven years ago," replied the man, who was a Seer. (He could do all sorts of things like find articles that had been lost.) The Seer joined the group without any comment.

After they had walked a way, the Son of the Fisherman asked the Seer, "Do you know where we are going?"

"Yes," he said, "we are going to see the sister of the seven giants. These giants have two chairs. If we sit on the one on the right-hand side, it will mean that we have come to ask for the hand of their sister. If we sit on the chair on the left-hand side, it will mean that we have come for war.[65] We should go and sit at once on the right-hand chair. If they should say, 'Get up from there and sit on the other chair,' we should refuse to do so."

They proceeded on their journey and eventually came to the home of the giants. As soon as they entered the house, they all went immediately and sat in the chair on the right. "You cannot sit there," said one of the giants. "Get up and go over and sit in that other chair," he said, pointing to the chair on the left. But their visitors refused.

At this, the giants all looked each other in the eye, and then one of them made the following proposition to the Son of the Fisherman and his friends: "We are seven brothers. We cook and eat seven caldrons of meat a day. If one of you can eat all this meat, he can have our sister."

They arose and killed a few water buffaloes and cooked seven caldrons of water buffalo meat. The Big Eater, who could not be satisfied with the flour ground by seven millstones, swallowed up all the meat, some of it before it was even properly cooked. As he ate it, he kept saying, "I am starving! I am so hungry!"

When the giants saw this, they all looked at each other again, and one of them said, "There is still another requirement before we will give our sister away. Here are seven skins full of water. If one of you can drink all of this water, he can have our sister."

The Big Drinker took up the seven skinfuls of water and went, "Luk, luk, luk," and emptied them one after another.

The seven giants now realized that they could not defeat these men by ordinary trials, and so they went aside and decided among themselves to poison them. They ordered bread to be baked and poison to be put in some of the loaves. They would serve poisoned bread to the guests and themselves eat the pure bread.

The Seer, the man who had been listening to the tinkling of a needle dropped seven years before, said to the Son of he Fisherman, "The loaves of bread given to us are all poisoned."

When the Flute Player heard this, he said, "You need not worry. When the dishes are brought, I shall play my flute and make all the dishes dance. Then I shall have them change places so that the poisoned dishes go to the giants."

The poisoned food was brought in dishes and placed in front of the guests, and pure food was served to the giants. The Flute Player then spoke: "This is a fine feast. We must have music on such an occasion." He began to play his flute, and to the tune of the music he made, all the dishes began to dance. The giants were so amazed at the beautiful music that they were not looking at their dishes but at the Flute Player. They did not see that the dishes were dancing about, and so when the music stopped, the giants ate the poisoned food and they all died.

The Son of the Fisherman took the sister of the seven giants. The Big Eater went back to his mill. The Big Drinker went back to the bank of the river. The Flute Player returned to the forest, and the Seer again listened for the beautiful tinkling of the needle his mother had dropped seven years before.

As the Son of the Fisherman was leading the sister of the giants home, she said to him, "Where are you taking me?"

The Son of the Fisherman then explained to the giantess: "The king of my land has been causing me trouble for a long while now. He wants my wife, and to deprive me of her, he has given me very difficult tasks to perform. If I should fail to perform any of these, he will take my wife. He ordered me to deliver you to him. If I had failed, either your seven brothers or the king would have killed me, and thus he would have taken my wife."

As they neared the city, the sister of the seven giants said, "I shall help you. Pitch your tent here, and when the king's army comes, we shall fight them. I am a wrestler, and I could destroy the entire population of this town in twenty-four hours if I wanted to do so." The Son of the Fisherman did as she directed.

In the meantime, the king was informed that the Son of the Fisherman had arrived with the sister of the seven giants and was camped outside the walls of the city. He sent a large army to capture the Son of the Fisherman and the giantess, but she routed the entire army. Later, when the king led forth another army, she defeated it, too, and in the battle she killed the king himself. After that, the Son of the Fisherman sat on the throne and no one tried again to take his beautiful wife from him.

5.

The Young Lord and the Cucumber Girl [66]

Once upon a time, there was a young lord who had a horse. One day when he took his horse to the fountain to water it, the animal accidentally stepped on the foot of a witch who had come to the fountain to fill her pitcher. Becoming angry with the young lord, the witch put a curse upon him: "May you become pale and thin," she said, "and may you fall in love with a cucumber girl." [67]

After a time it happened just as the witch had said: the young man grew pale and thin, he looked quite yellow, and he began to yearn for a cucumber girl. [68] This young lord was the only son of his father, a bey, and the father, greatly worried, kept asking him, "Son, what is the matter with you?"

The young lord kept quiet each time he was asked such a question, and finally the bey called the young friends of his son to ask them to discover what it was that was ailing his son. These friends went to the young lord and asked him, "What is the matter with you, anyway?"

The young man tried to answer his friends. "My problem is of a kind that no one else can really understand. I don't know what happened to me, but one day when I was at the fountain my horse accidentally stepped on the foot of an old woman there. She said to me, 'May you become pale and thin, and may you fall in love with a cucumber girl.' Maybe she was a witch, for right after that I did start to become pale and thin, as you see me now, and I do yearn for a girl somehow associated with cucumbers."

The young friends reported this conversation exactly to the bey, and after hearing their account, the bey called his son to him. "Son," he said, "I know now what your problem is. Here are forty mules and here are forty saddlebags of gold for you. Take these and go in search of your cucumber girl, and when you find her, bring her here."

The young lord took the forty mules and the forty saddlebags of gold and he went in search of the cucumber girl. He went little and he went far, and yet he had gone only the length of a grain of barley. In the evening he stopped at a house owned by an old man with a long beard, and this old man had a daughter. After they had eaten their supper, they all went to bed, but the daughter did not fall asleep right away, and so she asked her father, "Father, what is this young man doing here?"

The old man, thinking that the young lord was asleep, said to his daughter, "He is in great trouble because he fell in love with a cucumber girl, and unless he finds her, he will never be happy again." [69] The young lord was awake and listening to this conversation.

"Well, father, how can the young man go about finding this cucumber girl?"

"It is rather difficult, my girl, but may God help him!"

"Yes, but how is he going to find her?" asked his daughter.

"Well, on his travels he is going to find a lion for whom he must buy milk; he is going to meet a tiger for whom he must buy meat; and finally, he will meet a witch for whom he must buy six kilos of chewing gum. [70] Then he will go on and reach a fountain which has two pipes flowing from it, one pouring out blood and the other, pus. He must say to the fountain, 'What nice water you have,' and as he says this, he must scoop up three handfuls and drink it. [71] After this he will go on, and then he will come to a large pine tree from which he will knock a chip with his axe. This chip he must take to the giants he will meet next. When he comes to the giants he must wait until they are asleep. If their eyes are closed, that will mean that they are awake; but if their eyes are open, then they will be asleep. When he is sure that they are asleep, he must go past the giants to a giantess who guards three cucumbers. To her he must give the pine chip and all the gold that he has in his saddlebags, and for this, he will receive the three cucumbers. If he cuts open these cucumbers in a waterless place, three girls will jump from them but they will soon die of thirst. If he cuts them in a place where water is available, the three young girls will live, and then this young man will be saved from his trouble."

The young man listened to this carefully, and the next morning he arose early. He went to the market and bought milk for the lion, meat for the tiger, and six kilos of chewing gum for the witch. Then he set out on his journey. When he came to the lion, he gave it milk; when he came to the tiger, he gave it meat; and when he came to the old witch, he gave her the six kilos of chewing gum. Soon after that he came to the fountain with two pipes, one pouring out blood and the other pus. Saying, "What nice water you have!" he stooped down and drank three handfuls. When he came to the large pine tree, he took his axe and knocked off a chip, as the old man with the beard had said to do. When he came to the giants, he saw that their eyes were open, and he knew that they were asleep, and so he entered their cave where he found a giantess guarding three cucumbers. Giving her the pine chip and the forty saddlebags of gold, he took the three cucumbers and prepared to leave the place, but as he was mounting his horse, the giants closed their eyes and woke up.

"Stop him, you witch!" they called to the witch.

"No, I won't stop him, for he brought me six kilos of chewing gum," she said.

"Stop him, you tiger!" they called to the tiger.

"No, I won't stop him, for he brought me meat," said the tiger.

"Then you stop him, you lion!" they called.

"No, I won't stop him either, for he brought me fresh milk," said the lion.

And so the young lord escaped from the giants, and he proceeded on his journey toward home. After a while he came to a plain where he decided to cut open one of the cucumbers to see if it really contained a girl. He cut open one cucumber, and a very beautiful girl jumped out crying, "Oh, young lord, give me water, give me water!" He looked everywhere for water, but there was no water to give her, and she soon died. The young lord went a little farther and then he cut open the second cucumber, and from this came another beautiful girl who soon died begging for water. The young man then decided not to cut open the third cucumber until he reached the fountain that stood at the edge of his own town.

When he finally arrived at the fountain at the edge of his own town, he cut open the third cucumber. A girl came from it who was as beautiful as the fourteenth day of the moon, and when she cried, "Water! Water! Water!" the young man dipped her head into the trough.

The girl said to the young lord, "You go to your village and hold a wedding ceremony for forty days and forty nights, and then come back for me. I shall stay in the top of that poplar tree until you come." The girl then said, "Bend down, poplar tree!" and the poplar bent down. The girl sat on its top branches and then commanded, "Now straighten up, poplar tree!" and the poplar immediately straightened up again.

The young lord then proceeded to his own village, but while he was gone, an ugly woman came to the fountain, so ugly that she looked like a witch. While this ugly woman was filling her pitchers at the fountain, she saw reflected in the trough the face of the Cucumber Girl who was sitting above in the poplar tree. She was greatly taken by what she thought was her own beauty, and she said to herself, "I am more beautiful than my sisters, and my sisters are more beautiful than the people I work for, and so why should I work for these people any longer?"

After saying this, the ugly woman knocked the two pitchers together and broke them. When she reached home, they asked her what had happened. She said, "I am more beautiful than you. Why should I work as your servant?" Her employers laughed at her, and the next day they sent her to draw water again. This time when she approached the fountain she saw the beautiful girl sitting in the top of the poplar tree. The ugly woman said to her, "Please, beautiful girl, let me be your mother, and you be my daughter. Take me up there where you are, or tell me how you climbed there."

"By putting one egg on top of another I made an egg ladder for myself, and that is how I climbed up here."

The ugly woman piled egg on egg on egg, but when she tried to climb up on this egg ladder, the eggs collapsed and she fell back down. The woman started begging the girl to help her climb to the top of the tree, and finally the girl asked the poplar tree to bend down for her. The tree obeyed, the woman sat on the top of the tree, and when the girl ordered the tree to straighten up, it stood erect with the woman sitting beside the girl. The woman said, "Now I am your mother and you are my daughter."

After sitting there for some time with nothing to do, the woman said to the girl, "Will you please search in my hair for lice?" The girl complied with this request and she killed the lice that she found in the woman's hair. A few days later, the woman suggested that this time she delouse the girl's hair, and the girl agreed to this. As the woman was examining the young girl's hair for lice, she said to her, "My daughter, where is your vital spot?" [72]

"My vital spot is one white hair in my head. If it should be pulled out, I would die."

The ugly woman kept searching for this hair until she had found it, and then she immediately pulled it out. Upon this, the girl fell, senseless, to the foot of the tree, and where she fell a sesame plant sprang up. The ugly woman observed this plant and was suspicious about it.

When the forty days and forty nights had elapsed, the young lord returned to the poplar tree, and he was very surprised to see that the beautiful girl he had left on the top of the tree had become so ugly. He asked the woman, "How did you become like this?"

"Well, I was burnt by the sun on the right side and bitten by the frost on the left, and finally I became what you see me now," she said.

"Well, why don't you come down, anyway?" asked the young man.

"I got up here all right, but I can't get down," said the ugly woman.

The young lord sent several of his men up the tree, and they tied her with a rope and lowered her in that way from the tree top. Just as they were about to ride away, the young lord saw the sesame plant growing at the foot of the poplar, and he bent down and broke off the stalk and stuck it in his hat. Then they rode away toward his home, and when they arrived there they were married.

One day the wife, who was now pregnant, said to the young lord, "I don't like that sesame plant sticking on your hat. Throw it away!"

He threw the stalk into the fire, but when it burned, two pigeons sprang from the flames and flew away. These pigeons began to frequent the garden in front of the young man's home each morning at dawn. They would sing, "Sleep, sleep, oh young lord, and when you get up, may you not attain your wish."

Hearing them sing this song every day, the ugly wife became suspicious, and she thought that they might have something to do with the sesame plant and with the beautiful girl. She said to her husband, "If you will catch those two pigeons and let me eat them, I shall stay with you. Otherwise, I shall leave you."

"What harm do these innocent pigeons do to you, oh my wife? They come here every day and sing, and then they fly away."

"No, no," she said, "you must kill them."

"How are we going to kill them?" he asked.

"Just spray some tar on the branches of that tree where they alight. When they come there they will get their wings stuck with tar and will fall to the ground unable to fly."

The young lord did as his ugly wife suggested. When the pigeons came the following morning, they alighted on the tarred branch and sang, "Sleep, sleep, oh young lord, and when you get up, may you not attain your wish." Then they tried to fly away, but their wings were stuck up with tar, and they fell to the ground trying to fly. They were caught and their throats were cut near the threshold of the house, and where their blood trickled to the ground a poplar tree grew.

When the poplar tree had grown tall, it began each night to lean down and rap on the top of the house. Fearing that it would knock down the roof upon them, the ugly wife asked her husband to cut it down. She suspected that it had something to do with the pigeons, with the sesame plant, and with the beautiful girl. "Cut it down," she said, "and from the wood make a crib for our child that is to be born soon."

The young lord had the tree cut down, and he had a carpenter make a crib from its wood. One of the chips, however, was picked up by an old woman who came each day to the young lord's house to work and returned to her own house at night. She put the pretty chip on her mantelpiece in the kitchen. Now this chip held the spirit of the beautiful girl, and when the old woman had left the house each morning, the chip quivered, and the girl came to life again. She would clean the old woman's house, bring in wood for the fireplace, and cook a meal for the old woman. Then she would climb up to the mantelpiece and change back into a chip before the old woman returned from her daily work. The old woman was amazed at this, and could not understand who could be doing her housework. One day as she was about to leave for the house of the young lord, she opened the door and shut it several times and then stood perfectly still behind a curtain. The chip quivered and became a beautiful girl. The old woman rushed to her, grabbed her by the arm, and said, "Oh, beautiful girl, let me become your mother and you be my daughter." The girl accepted this suggestion and they lived there together.

One day the girl said to the old woman, "Don't go to work any more in the house of the young lord. Just tell him that you are tired of working in his house and that you no longer wish to work for him." The old woman agreed to this and told the young lord that she would not work for him any longer.

"All right," he said, "please yourself."

After a while it happened that there was a famine in the land. It was so great that people ate the food of the horses and so there was no food even for the horses. The young lord wanted to distribute his many horses among the people to have them fed until the famine passed away. A crier was sent around the streets announcing this: "The young lord wants to farm out his horses among his neighbors. Anyone who wants a horse may go and choose one from his stable."

The girl said, "Mother, you go and choose a horse for us."

The old woman went to the young lord and asked, "Will you give me a horse?"

"Go away, old woman," said the young man. "How are you going to look after a horse at your age?"

"Well, I have a daughter who wants to have a horse," said the old woman. So the young lord sent four men to pick up a horse so weak from hunger that it could not walk or even stand. They carried this horse to the stable of the old woman and left it there. When the girl saw the horse, she walked before it forward and she walked before it backward, and green grass grew up where she walked. The horse was able to eat this grass without even moving, and after it had eaten grass for many days, it became a fine fat horse.

After forty days the famine was over and the young lord sent a crier around announcing that he wanted his horses back again. But it was found that all of the horses had died of starvation except the one that was fed by the old woman and the beautiful girl. The girl said to her mother, "Go and tell the young lord to come and get his horse."

The old woman went to the young lord and said, "Come and get your horse."

"What are you saying, old woman?" he asked. "All of the good and healthy horses have died. How could the horse that had to be carried to your stable by four men survive? It must be dead, too."

"No, no, it is living," she said.

When the young man heard this, he sent a man to find out whether that horse was still alive yet. When the man who was sent for this purpose saw the horse he was greatly surprised, for this horse had grown into a very fine animal. When he left the old woman's stable to report to the young lord what he had seen, the beautiful girl came to the horse and said, "Kick anyone who comes behind you and bite anyone who comes in front of you, and don't let anybody untie you except me." [73]

When the young lord came to the stable to take away the horse, the horse jumped at him and started to bite him. In fear for his life, he asked the old woman to come and untie the horse for him. When the old woman came to him at his command, she suggested that he join them in a meal first. "Let us first eat and have a cup of coffee in our humble dwelling, and then we shall see about the horse."

The girl had cleaned the house carefully and she had also cooked many dishes. They had a good meal, and then they drank coffee. When the young man asked them, after this, to untie his horse, the young girl said to him, "If you will unroll your turban and stretch it from the kitchen to the stable, I shall untie your horse. Otherwise, I won't."

He did as he was directed, and the girl walked over the turban as it lay stretched out on the floor. The girl untied the horse and delivered it to the young lord. As he mounted the horse, the girl slapped it on the rump, saying, "We have derived much benefit from your master, and let us hope that we do the same from you."

This remark by the girl puzzled the young lord, and after he reached home, he kept thinking about what she had said. What did she mean, he asked himself, by saying such a thing: "We have derived much benefit from your master, and let us hope that we do the same from you"? He made up his mind to go back and ask the girl what she meant by such a remark. He went back to her house and said to her, "What did you mean by the remark that you made as I was leaving your house with the horse?"

"You did not marry the cucumber girl, for I am that girl. You married a woman ugly enough to be a witch. I became a sesame plant and you burned me; I became a pair of birds and you killed me; I became a poplar tree and you cut me down to make a crib out of me for your child. But I was the girl who was your betrothed."

Without saying a word the young lord left the girl and returned to his own home. He went to his wife and said to her, "Would you rather have a horse to return home with or a sword?"

"What would I do with a sword?" she asked. "A sword is for cutting the throat of enemies. I should rather have a horse."

The young lord then had the ugly woman and her children mounted on the back of the powerful horse that had been fed by the cucumber girl. The horse took her and her children to the mountains, where he dashed them to pieces on the rocks.[74] Then he returned to the stable of the young lord.

In the meantime, the young lord had arranged a wedding celebration for himself and the cucumber girl. It lasted for forty days and forty nights, and then they were married, and they lived happily ever after.

6.

The Keloghlan and the Köse[75]

A man had three sons but no money, and so it was necessary for his sons to work. The eldest son hired himself out to a farmer who was a köse. The agreement between them was that neither the employer nor his worker was to become angry with the other, no matter what happened. If either lost his temper over something that the other did, the angry man was to forfeit enough skin from his back to make the other a pair of sandals.[76]

Right from the beginning the köse teased the boy in order to make him lose his temper, for he was a very mean köse. He soon succeeded in his purpose, and he took from the young man's back enough skin for a pair of sandals. The young man quit his job in anger and the next oldest brother accepted it.

"I shall hire you," said the köse to the second brother, "but I have certain conditions under which you must work."

"What are they?" asked the second brother.

"You must not disturb the cream on the top of the yogurt [77] that I give you to eat, and you must not break the edges of the yufka [78] bread. You must never say, 'I am hungry.' If you break any of these conditions, I shall cut a piece of hide off your back large enough to make myself a pair of sandals. On the other hand, if you can make me admit that I am angry, then you can cut a piece of hide off *my* back large enough to make a pair of sandals."

The young man agreed to this and several days passed as he worked on the farm. Every day he became more and more hungry, however, for he found it impossible to eat. He could not get at the yogurt to eat it without disturbing the skin of cream on the top of the jar, and he could not eat the yufka without breaking its edges. As a result, he was very hungry and started to grow weak. Three days and five days passed in this manner, and the young man ate nothing at all. Finally he fell ill and lay down. The köse came to him and asked, "What is the matter?"

"Nothing," said the young man, "except that I am starving to death."

"All right," answered the köse, "lie still there, and I shall take a strip of hide from your back." The köse took enough skin from the second son's back to make himself a pair of sandals.

The second son returned home and the youngest son, who was a keloghlan, went to the köse and asked for his job. "Very well," said the köse, "but you must meet my conditions. Your brothers were not good workers, for the one became angry, which is forbidden on my farm, and the other complained of hunger, which is also forbidden here."

"Are these the conditions?" asked the keloghlan.

"Yes," said the köse, "you must never become angry with me, for if you do I shall cut enough skin from your back to make a pair of sandals. And you must never say you are hungry or I shall punish you in the same way. I shall provide plenty of food, but you must never break the skin of the yogurt or tear the edges of the yufka. On the other hand, if you can upset me and make me angry, you can take enough skin from my back to make yourself a pair of sandals."

"Very well," said the keloghlan, "it is a bargain."

The keloghlan began to work for the köse. He ate the yufka by cutting a large piece from the center of it with his knife, leaving the edges intact. He ate the yogurt by breaking a hole into the bottom of the jar and sucking the yogurt through that hole. In this way, he left undisturbed the skin of cream on the top of the jar. After a week he took to the köse the heap of broken yogurt jars and asked, "Köse, are you angry with me?"

"Of course not," answered the köse.

At the beginning of the next week the köse said to the keloghlan, "Today you will do some plowing. Take these oxen and this hound and go to that big field yonder. Plow wherever this hound lies down."

So the keloghlan went to the field with the oxen and the hound. He spent a long while following the hound around the field, but it did not lie down anywhere. Finally it climbed up on top of a rocky mound and fell asleep there. The keloghlan climbed up to the top of the mound and kicked the dog to death. Then he returned to the köse without having done any plowing at all. He told the köse what had happened and asked him, "Are you angry with me?"

"Oh, no, of course not."

The young man took the oxen to the stable and then went back to the köse for his next orders. "Take the oxen to the fountain to water them, but lead them out of the stable through that little window high on the back wall."

The keloghlan went to the stable, cut the heads off the oxen, and threw the heads through the little window in the back wall. He took these heads to the fountain where he dipped them into the watering trough, whistling all the while they were there. He whistled all the while they were supposed to be drinking, just as if they had been alive.[79] Then he lifted the heads of the oxen from the trough and carried them back to the stable where he poured a bagful of hay before them. After that, he went to the köse, told him that he had watered the oxen, and invited him to come to the stable to see for himself. When the köse entered the stable, he was astonished at what he saw. He asked the keloghlan, "What did you do, boy?"

"Well," said the keloghlan, "you asked me to take the oxen through the little window in the barn to the fountain to water them, and that is what I did. Are you angry with me for what I have done?"

"No, no — nothing of the sort," answered the köse.

The next day the köse asked the young man to take a leg of one of the slaughtered oxen to the home of his married daughter who lived in the neighborhood. When the keloghlan appeared at the door, carrying the huge leg, the daughter feared that her father had lost an ox, and she lay down on the floor and cried. "You must be hungry," said the keloghlan. "Here is some meat for you." And with that, he threw the quarter of an ox on top of the woman, breaking her neck and killing her. When he returned to the köse and told him what had happened, he asked, "Are you cross with me?"

"No, not at all," said the köse, but in fact he was gravely concerned now about what job he could safely give the keloghlan to do. "Can you tend sheep?" he asked the boy.

"Yes, of course I can," said the keloghlan.

So the next day the keloghlan went to the pasture with the köse's flock of sheep. After a few hours, he made a large fire in the field and put several skewers into the coals. When they were red hot, he took them out and stuck them into the bellies of the sheep. In this way he killed five or six hundred of them by the end of the day. When the köse came to the field where the sheep were all lying dead, he asked, "What is the matter with them?"

"They are tired and they are just resting. Isn't that all right? Are you angry at me?"

"No, I am not angry. Why should I be?" But, of course, the köse was angry and he wanted to find a way to be able to cut a piece from the back of the keloghlan. Again he tried to think of some safe job for the boy to do. "Can you garden and care for fruit trees?" he asked.

"There is nothing I can do better," said the keloghlan.

The köse gave him a forty-acre orchard to tend, but the keloghlan cut down all the trees during the first night. When the köse went to the orchard next morning, he was amazed. "What happened?" he asked.

"Why, nothing," said the boy.

"But why are all the trees down?"

"Well, köse father, do you sleep standing up or lying down?"

"Lying down, of course."

"So do the trees," said the keloghlan. "They were very tired and they slept this way almost all night. When they have had enough sleep, they will awaken and stand up again."

The next day there was a wedding in the village and the köse was invited. Before he went he asked the keloghlan to watch the front door of the house. "Watch the front door, and be on guard against thieves," he said. But a short time after the köse had gone, the keloghlan tore the door off its hinges, strapped it to his back, and went to the wedding himself. When the köse saw him, he was surprised and asked, "What is this?"

"Well, don't you remember? You asked me to watch the front door to guard it against thieves. I brought it with me so that I could be sure thieves did not steal it. Are you angry with me, master?"

"No, no — nothing of the sort," said the köse, but he was by now deeply disturbed about the keloghlan's behavior. After the wedding, he said to his wife, "Sooner or later, this young man is going to kill me. Let us run away before he does so. Bake a large bagful of chörek,[80] and let us escape secretly tonight."

But the young man had overheard their conversation, and he thus discovered the köse's plan. He got into the bag which the wife had placed by the oven for the chörek and he hid himself in the bottom. The bag was then filled with freshly baked chörek and loaded on a cart by the köse and his wife, who departed quietly at midnight.

After the cart had gone for some distance, the keloghlan had to urinate, and he couldn't wait any longer. When the köse noticed the wet spot in the cart, he said to his wife. "You must have put a great amount of butter in those chörek. It is oozing out."

"Of course I did," she said. "I didn't want to leave any of the butter for that keloghlan."

A little farther on they were beset by a number of fierce dogs which surrounded their cart and barked loudly at them. The köse's children cried, and the köse himself was quite frightened. "Now I wish that the keloghlan were here, for he would protect us from these beasts."

Overhearing this, the keloghlan cried out, "I am here, Uncle Köse." They helped him out of the bag in which he had been hiding, and in a short time he drove off the dogs.

After a while they came to a river bank where they decided to spend the night. After they had eaten their dinner, one of the children had to urinate. The köse's wife said to the keloghlan, "Keloghlan, take this child and 'burst'[81] him."

The keloghlan took the child into the nearby woods and dropped a large rock on him, thus bursting him. He returned to the river bank without the child and told the köse and his wife what he had done. While they went to look for the child's body, the keloghlan took from their chest one of the wife's gowns and hid it. After everyone else had fallen asleep, the keloghlan got up and put on the woman's gown. He carefully lifted the sleeping wife over into his bed, and then he crawled into her bed. Imitating the woman's voice, he said quietly, "Köse! Wake up! Let us pick up that damned keloghlan and throw him into the river, bed and all. Then we shall be rid of him."

Half asleep, the köse got up, and he and the keloghlan threw the

75

woman into the river in the keloghlan's bed. It was only after his wife was lost in the water that the köse realized what had happened. He began crying.

"Why are you crying?" asked the keloghlan. "Are you angry with me?"

"Of course I am angry with you. You have killed my oxen. You have ruined my flock and cut down my orchard. And now you have destroyed my family. Why shouldn't I be angry with you?"

Hearing this, the keloghlan cut a piece of skin from the köse's back and made a pair of sandals with the skin. In the morning, he put on the new sandals and started walking toward a nearby town. But the köse had reached the town first, and he had hired several men to kill the keloghlan. They began to chase the keloghlan. The boy fled until he came to a shepherd with his flock of sheep. "Why are you running away from those men?" asked the shepherd.

"I refused to marry the padishah's daughter, and they are trying to catch me to force me to marry her."

"Why should anyone run away from that?" asked the shepherd. "I should be happy to marry the padishah's daughter."

"Well, if you put on my clothes and let me put on your shepherd's clothes and heavy felt coat,[82] they may catch you and and force you to marry her." The shepherd agreed to this and they exchanged clothes. The shepherd pretended to be running away and the keloghlan pretended to be herding the sheep.

Shortly after this the köse and his hired men arrived at this spot. They thought that the shepherd was the keloghlan, and so they grabbed him, beat him severely, and threw him into the river. After resting for a while, they started back to the town. On the way they came upon the keloghlan dressed in shepherd's clothes. They were amazed to see him alive and even more amazed to see him with a flock of about forty sheep. "Where did you get these sheep?" asked the köse.

"I found this flock in the river where you dumped me. If you would throw your men into the river, they could each get forty sheep in the same way I did."

When the köse heard this, he threw his men, one after another, into the river. As they were drowning, they made a gurgling noise in their throats, "Kirk! Kirk! Kirk!"[83]

"You see!" said the keloghlan. "Your friends are shouting 'Forty! Forty! Forty!' to you. Why don't you jump in and help them pull all those sheep out of the water?"

After the köse had been drowned with his men, the keloghlan gathered his flock and started to drive them toward his father's home.

7.

The Sultan's Forty Sons [84]

Once upon a time there was a sultan who had forty sons. One day these sons all held a meeting in a meadow near the palace. The youngest of them had now reached the age of fifteen, and so the eldest called them all together in this meeting. He said to his brothers, "You all know that our youngest brother has now reached the age of fifteen. Let us go now to our father and ask him to find wives for all of us."

They debated this question and tried to decide who should go to ask their father, the sultan, about this. While they were discussing this, the youngest jumped up and said, "I shall go — but what exactly should I say to our father?"

"You don't have to say anything," said the eldest brother. "Only watch that you don't sit on just any chair that he offers you as a seat. Refuse each chair until he pulls out the green chair for you. When he does that, sit on it, and he will know that you have come to ask him to let us marry." [85]

The youngest brother then proceeded to the palace. He refused to sit on the first two chairs that his father offered to him, but then when his father offered the green chair, he accepted it and sat down. Immediately after he had sat down, his father said, "I shall give the forty of you forty horses and forty saddlebags filled with gold, and it will be up to you then to find forty suitable girls to marry. I shall have all forty of you married on the same night, and I shall pay all the expenses of the wedding myself." The youngest son bowed and left without having said a word.

He returned to the meadow where all his brothers were waiting. "What did our father say?" asked the eldest brother.

"Our father said that he would give us forty horses and forty saddlebags of gold but that we must find our own wives," said the youngest brother. "He will marry us all in one night, and he will pay all the expenses of the wedding himself."

Very pleased with this news, they all went to the palace and took their horses loaded with saddlebags of gold. They mounted their horses and set out in search of their future wives. They went for a spring and they went for an autumn, but they found that they had gone only the length of a grain of barley. One evening they reached a ruin into which they pulled their horses, dismounted, and prepared to sleep. They all fell asleep except the youngest, and he drew his sword and stood behind the door.

In the middle of the night, a seven-headed female giant entered the ruin. She was so large that the forty of them would not have made forty mouthfuls for her, but the youngest brother managed to drive her off. She went away but soon she returned with her children, forty sons and forty daughters, all of them giants. The youngest son stood at the doorway, and as each giant stepped through it, he killed him. Finally he had killed them all except their mother, the seven-headed giant, and there was a huge mound of bodies heaped inside the entrance of the ruin. She ran away, and the youngest son chased her. She jumped into a well, where she lived, and the boy went after her. At the bottom of the well, she said to him, "I have lost forty sons and forty daughters. Don't kill me. Here are forty keys to forty rooms in which you will find forty girls to marry. Take these and spare my life."

The boy agreed to this, and, taking the keys, he began to unlock the doors of the forty rooms. After he had opened them all and taken the forty girls from the forty rooms, he divided them among his brothers. He told each girl which brother she was to marry.

Having done this, the boy went back to the ruin with the girls. He discovered that his brothers were all up. They were surprised to see the bodies of so many dead giants heaped up inside the entrance of the ruin. They all asked, "Who has done this?" Every brother except the youngest swore that he was not responsible for the massacre, and they then knew that it was he who had done it. He then related to them what had happened.

"While you were all asleep, a seven-headed female giant tried to enter the ruin. When I drove her off, she returned with forty sons and forty daughters. All of these sons and daughters I killed, one by one, as they tried to enter the ruin. Their mother then ran away and went down the well where she lives. I chased her down to the bottom, and there she said, 'I have lost forty sons and forty daughters. Don't kill me. Here are forty keys to forty rooms in which you will find forty girls to marry. Take these and spare my life.' I agreed to this, and then I took the forty keys and opened the forty rooms and found in them the forty girls. They shall be our wives."

The brothers were all pleased at this, and they went to the mouth of the well. The youngest brother went down into the well and released thirty-nine of the girls. He took them up to the surface of the earth, and he took the first girl and said to his eldest brother, "This one is for you." And he took the second girl and presented her to his next oldest brother and said, "This one is for you." And after he had in this fashion distributed all the thirty-nine girls among his thirty-nine brothers, he went back down the well for the one whom he had saved for himself. Before he took her from this underground prison, he was addressed by the female giant: "Please take me with you," she said. "There is nothing here for me now. I shall be your slave, your sweeper." He agreed to this proposal.

They all mounted their horses, and each took his girl up behind him on his horse. They started toward home, and the giantess followed them. When they came to a marble column lying beside the road, the giantess addressed it, saying, "Oh, Father-in-law, why are you lying there like that? I have lost forty sons and forty daughters." Upon this, the horsemen were all surrounded by a high stone wall, and the King of the Giants, who was also seven-headed, came up out of the earth and said to them, "Come here! Which of you has slaughtered the children of this giantess?" Each of them except the youngest brother swore that he had not done it, but he was unable to swear. He admitted the deed and said farewell to his brothers. He said to them, "If I reach home safely, I shall marry my sweetheart. If I do not reach home, one of you can marry her." Then his thirty-nine brothers and the forty girls were allowed to proceed on their journey.

After the brothers were gone, the King of the Giants said to the boy, "I have a proposal to make to you. If you can do what I tell you to do, I shall let you go free. If you cannot, I'll eat you." The boy accepted the proposal, and the giant said to him, "You will burn me in a large oven; then you will sweep together my ashes, put them in a bag, and sprinkle them on that distant mountain."

The youngest brother pushed the giant into his oven, and when he was completely burned up, he gathered his ashes together, put them in a bag, and took them to the distant mountain, where he sprinkled them. Having finished this task, he prepared to mount his horse to follow his brothers, but at that moment he heard a cry, "Oh, gallant young man, are you leaving? Where are you going?" It was the voice of the King of the Giants, who had come back to life again. "Now do you see what I am capable of doing?" he asked.

79

"Yes, I do," answered the young man.

"I have another proposition," said the giant. "If you can accomplish this task, I shall let you go free; if you can't, I shall eat you. I have been at war with a neighboring king for forty years. The object of our quarrel is his daughter, whom I want to marry. If you can get this girl for me, I shall let you go."

The young man accepted this proposition and, mounting his horse, rode to the apartment [86] of that king. He knocked at the door of the apartment and told the king that the purpose of his visit was to ask for the hand of his daughter in marriage. Before reaching a decision, the king said to the young man, "You go out and walk around the palace once and then return." The young man did not know that this king killed all those who came to ask for his daughter but failed to fulfill the difficult tasks that the king set for them. He had actually made a huge mound of the skulls of the men who had come and failed. [87]

When the young man returned, the king told him that he was going to be given a difficult task that he had to accomplish in one night. "I shall give you my daughter if you can plow a field of a hundred acres, sow it, and gather the harvest all in one night. But if you fail to finish this work in one night, I shall kill you."

The youngest brother accepted the challenge and started to work, but before he had finished the plowing, he fell asleep. Toward morning he was told in a dream that an ant was coming to help him, and that he should burn the grain of wheat that the ant brought to him. He awoke, saw the ant with the grain of wheat, and when he had burned this grain of wheat, all the ants in the world came to his aid. They finished plowing the field; then they sowed it; and as morning approached, they gathered the harvest. It was all done in a very little time.

When the king came to the field to see whether the work had all been done, he was amazed at what he saw, but he quickly set another task for the boy. "I shall have forty caldrons of food brought for you," he said, "and if you can eat them all before tomorrow at this time, you shall have my daughter. If you can't eat them, I shall have you killed." The boy accepted the challenge, and the forty caldrons of food were brought and set before him. He took a mouthful from each caldron, but soon he fell asleep. Toward the next morning, he heard a voice in a dream which said to him, "Why don't you burn that hair that was given to you as a child by the black Arab?" He woke up, burned the hair that had been given to him by the black Arab, and lo! half of the black men in the world appeared outside the room, breaking the windows and the doors to get in. In no time, they had gobbled up all of the food in the forty caldrons. A lame Arab, who came late, said, "Isn't there any food left for me?" They said, "No." At that, the lame man scraped the bottoms of the caldrons, and he scraped so hard that he made holes in them. Having eaten all the food, the Arabs disappeared.

When the king came in the morning, he was again amazed. "Let alone the food in the caldrons, this young man has almost eaten up the caldrons themselves." But the youngest son could not yet have the daughter, for the king set still one more task. "I want one more task to be performed. If you can do this, you may have my daughter. You must wrestle with her tomorrow morning. If you defeat her, she will be yours; if you do not, I shall send you to the executioner."

An announcement was made throughout the land that on the next day the king's daughter would wrestle with a young man. And at the scheduled time on the following day, there were thousands of people waiting to see the contest. It was a very exciting wrestling match, for the two were good wrestlers. They wrestled for a long while, but toward midday the young man seemed to be weakening. He was having great difficulty with the king's daughter, who was very powerful. Panting hard, he called for a rest period; he said that he wanted to smoke tobacco. His real purpose, however, was to burn another of the Arab's hairs, for he knew now that he could not defeat the girl without help. He burned the hair with the tobacco, and out of nowhere the Arab appeared.

"Disappear from sight again," he said, "but stay here and help me defeat this powerful girl in this wrestling contest." The Arab did as he was commanded, and when the two wrestlers fell to the ground, he pulled the girl so that she was beneath the sultan's son.

When the king saw that his daughter was defeated, he ordered that the wedding be held at once. Since there had been no preparation for their marriage, the two were not actually united after this ceremony but lived apart for the first three months. After this time had elapsed, the young man went to the king and said, "Your majesty, I am the son of a ruler, too, a sultan. If you will let me, I should like to return now to the land of my father."

"You may go, my son," said the king, "but first tell me what you wish from me."

"I have nothing to wish for except that God may give you good health," said the young man.

"There must be something that I can give you as a farewell gift," said the king.

"You can give me a bed and a cart with horses, then, that I can use in traveling home." [88]

The bed and horses and cart were provided, as he had requested, and the young man took his wife and started for home. The girl did not know that in fact the young man was taking her to the giant in accordance with the bargain he had made. When he finally told her this, near the giant's house, she threw herself down out of the cart, and she tried to escape. But the giant had heard them coming and he had come out to welcome them, and he quickly caught the girl and held her fast.

"Well, my son," said the giant, "you have done well. You may go now, and good luck to you."

But the young man was very sorry for what he had done. He could not keep his eyes off the girl. He did not go far from the giant's house, for he had now decided to try to rescue the girl. He noticed that each day the giant went hunting and did not return until evening, and so one morning after the giant had left, he went into the house and said to the girl, "I am sorry for what I have done, but if you will help me, we can kill the giant and escape. When he comes back this evening, don't give him any food and don't speak to him. Pretend that you are angry with him. When he asks, 'What is the matter?' say, 'You leave me alone in this house all day while you go and enjoy yourself.' "

The girl did as she was instructed, and when the giant heard this complaint, he went to the forest and pulled up a large tree and brought it to his house. He stood it against the door of her room and said to her, "Look, there are bird nests in this tree, and there are young birds in the nests. They will sing to you and keep you company."

Next morning, as usual, he went hunting, and while he was gone, the young man came to the house again. When he saw the tree full of birds that the giant had brought to entertain his wife, he said to her, "When the giant comes home this evening, tell him that the twittering of the birds made you sick and nervous. Say to him, 'If you want me to enjoy myself, tell me where you keep your source of life so that I may have its company.' "

When the giant came home that night, the girl again looked moody and sullen. When the giant asked her what was the matter, she said, "I am angry with you because you brought that tree with the noisy birds. They drive me mad all day long. I am quite sick of them."

"Well, what shall I do to please you, then?" asked the giant.

"Show me where you keep your life source so that I may have its company," said the girl.

"When it rains," said the giant, "three deer will come to drink water from a ditch in the forest. In the belly of the yellow deer that will stand toward the south I have three naked lives hidden in three boxes. Take them and enjoy yourself with them."

The next morning the giant went to hunt again, and after he had gone, the sultan's son came and asked his wife, "Did the giant tell you where he keeps his life source?"

"Yes," she said, "but there are three of them. When its rains, three deer will come to drink water from a ditch in the forest. In the belly of the yellow deer that will stand toward the south he has three naked lives hidden in three boxes. He said I should take these and enjoy myself with them."

Upon hearing all this from his wife, the young man went and kept watch for the deer. When they finally came to drink water, he aimed an arrow at the yellow deer standing toward the south and killed it. He cut open its belly and took out the three boxes containing the three naked lives of the giant and put his feet on them. As he was about to crush the three boxes, the giant appeared in a great rush, sweeping along a whole cloud of dust and stones in his haste. He stopped before he reached the young man and begged him, "Spare my naked lives, oh gallant young man."

"May they be carried to hell!" said the sultan's son, and he crushed the three boxes. Thus the giant was killed and could not be restored to life again.

The sultan's son returned to the giant's house and released his wife. They then started for the young man's home country, but first they took as many valuable objects as they could carry from the giant's house. They proceeded to the young man's country, and when they arrived there, they went immediately to the meadow which the forty sons had always used as a meeting place. When he reached this place, he found his thirty-nine brothers arguing over the fortieth girl, the one whom he had taken for himself from the well of the seven-headed giantess.

When news reached the sultan that his fortieth son had arrived home, he announced the weddings of all his sons. The youngest son married both his sweethearts, and the festivities lasted for forty days and forty nights. And when they were concluded, the forty sons of the sultan lived happily all the rest of their lives.

8.

Troubles in Youth Rather Than in Old Age [89]

Once there was and once there wasn't, when God had so many people, but it was a sin to say so, in that time when the camel was a barber and the owl was a judge, there were a farmer and his wife. This farmer used to go and plow his fields each day, and one day while he was doing this, he heard someone shout at him from the top of a rocky mound, "Oh, farmer! Something terrible is going to happen to you. Would you rather have it happen in your youth or your old age?"

When he went home that night, he said to his wife, "A strange thing happened to me today. While I was plowing, a voice called from high on the rocks. It said to me, 'Oh, farmer! Something terrible is going to happen to you. Would you rather have it happen in your youth or your old age?' What should I answer if this happens again?"

His wife said, "Better have it in youth. Whatever is to happen to you, let it come while you are still young."

The next day the voice from the rock asked the farmer the same question. This time the farmer shouted back, "Oh, son of man! Whatever is to happen to me, let it happen in my youth."

That evening when the farmer came home from work, he saw that his house was going up in flames. He was able to save only his wife and his two small sons from the flaming house. Having no reason to stay there any longer, he went to another village, and there he became a shepherd for someone.

On the second day of new employment, while he was away from home with flocks, he suffered another disaster. A bezirgan [90] who had stopped for a while in the area sent someone to his house for some eau de cologne [91] with which to have his back rubbed. The shepherd's wife was a kind woman, and she gave the bezirgan a bottle of eau de cologne. The bezirgan concluded that the woman was interested in him, and so he abducted her, locked her up in his chest, and had her carried away.

When the shepherd returned home that night, he found his two small sons crying and his wife gone. All that the boys could tell him was that their mother had been put in a chest and carried away.

The shepherd now felt that he could remain in that place no longer. He packed up his few belongings, took his two sons, and departed for still another village. On the way he had to cross a river. He left the one child on the bank and taking the other on his back started to wade across the river. When he was about halfway across, he heard the child on the bank call, and he turned around in time to see a wolf carrying off the child. In his effort to rescue the child, he rushed back toward the bank, but in the process he dropped the first child from his back, and it was swept downstream by the current. Thus he lost both his sons.

He continued his walking, and after a while he came to a village. There he saw a large crowd gathered, and he went among the people in this crowd. The people of the village were busy electing a padishah [92] for themselves, and to do this they kept releasing a tame bird until it landed on someone. That person would be the new padishah.

The first person on whom the bird landed was the shepherd. Many of the people of the village objected. "Leave that keloghlan [93] out of this. He cannot possibly be our padishah. Try the bird again." But once again the bird landed on the shepherd's head, and so this time he was declared padishah.

The new padishah ruled for many years. During this time his two sons that he thought had died grew up, and both became gendarmes. [94] They did not recognize each other, but it happened that they were both stationed at a gendarme post near the village. One day a bezirgan came along and left his chest at their post to be guarded while he went to pay a visit to the padishah.

One of the gendarmes said to the other, "To make the time pass faster, tell me about your life. What happened in it?"

The other gendarme told him this. "I had a father once who was a farmer. One day when he was plowing his field, a voice from a rock addressed him and said, 'Something terrible is going to happen to you. Would you rather have it happen in your youth or your old age?' My father answered that he would rather have it happen in his youth, and then he had many troubles. Our home burned down. Our mother was carried off in a chest. A wolf carried me away, and my brother was drowned in a river."

"I am your brother, and I wasn't drowned. A woodcutter pulled me out of the river, and I lived with him until I became a man." As the brothers embraced each other, they heard a crying sound from inside the bezirgan's chest. When they pried it open, they found a woman inside, and she said to them, "I am your mother who was carried away in this very chest."

The two gendarmes were embracing their mother when the bezirgan returned. The bezirgan was furious and went back immediately to the padishah and complained about the behavior of the gendarmes. The padishah ordered that the gendarmes and the woman be brought before him. He then asked them to explain their behavior. Each of the gendarmes told his life story, and when they were finished, he said to them, "These are strange stories, but they are really stranger than you know, for I am your father, and this woman is my wife."

The padishah had the bezirgan arrested. He then had him tied to the tail of a horse, and then he had the horse whipped. The bezirgan was dashed to pieces against the rocks as the horse ran, and so ends our tale.

9.

The Caldron-Headed, Ax-Toothed Sister [95]

Once there was, and once there was not, when it was a long time ago, there were a husband and wife. They had three sons and a lot of sheep, but they had no daughter. One day the mother prayed to God, "O, God, let me have a daughter, even if her head is as big as a caldron and her teeth are like axes." It happened that after a while they did in fact have a daughter whose head was as big as a caldron and whose teeth were like axes.

They noticed after a while that a sheep was missing from their flock every day. To find out who it was that was carrying off the sheep, the sons were put on guard at night, each taking his turn. The first night it was the turn of the eldest son. While he was watching he became sleepy, and did not see that his caldron-headed and ax-toothed baby sister got up from her bed and went to the flock and there ate the sheep. The next night it was the turn of the middle brother to be on guard, but he also fell asleep toward the middle of the night, and again the caldron-headed, ax-toothed sister got up, killed another sheep, and ate it.

When it was the turn of the youngest brother to watch, he managed to stay awake, and he saw their baby sister get out of her bed, go to the flock of sheep and kill one, and then eat its flesh. In the morning he told his parents about this. He said to them, "The sheep are being eaten by your caldron-headed, ax-toothed daughter."

The parents were very angry with what the youngest son told them about their daughter. They said to him, "How could a little baby like that possibly do such a thing?"

Very much offended at the attitude taken by his parents, the youngest son left home. He mounted his horse and rode away. As he left home he was eating dates along the way and throwing the pits on the side of the road. Finally, after riding for some time, he saw a light in the distance and went toward it. When he arrived at the cottage where the light was burning, he discovered that an old woman lived there. He asked her whether she could use him as a shepherd. She hired the young man as a shepherd, but she warned him never to take the sheep near the three nearby mountains because they were filled with monsters.

The next day the young man began his job as a shepherd for the old woman. He took his gun and his flock and he went to the first of the mountains about which he had been warned. There he came face to face with a lion. When the young man aimed his gun at the creature, the lion said to him, "Stop — have pity on me. Spare me. I have two cubs in a cave, and I will give you one of them if you will spare me." The lion went back and got one of the cubs and gave it to the young man. The young man returned that night to the cottage of the old woman. He took the cub with him, and told the old woman to take care of it for him.

The next day he took his flock to the second mountain. This time a bear approached him, and when he was about to shoot the bear, the animal said, "Stop — have pity on me. I shall give you one of my cubs if you do not shoot me." He got the cub from the bear, and that evening he took it home and told the old woman to take care of his bear also.

The next day the young man went with his flock to the third mountain, where he met a tiger. He was about to shoot the tiger when the tiger said to him, "Stop — have pity on me. If you do not shoot me, I shall give you one of my cubs." The tiger gave him the cub, and he took it home and gave it to the old lady to take care of, along with the lion cub and the bear cub.

The young man lived this way for a long time with the old woman, taking care of her sheep. One day, however, the old woman noticed that the young man sat by the side of the cottage during the evening, and was stabbing the ground with a stick and thinking. The old woman asked him, "What are you thinking about so deeply?"

"Well," said the young man, "I am thinking about my parents. I want to go and see them."

"Very well," said the old woman, "why don't you go and visit with them?"

Before he left, the young man said to the old woman, "Take care of my three cubs. Feed them with milk. If they should vomit blood, you will know that a disaster has befallen me. Then you are to release them and let them come to help me."

During the time that the young man had been away from home, his caldron-headed and ax-toothed sister had been harassing the neighboring villages by eating everything that she could lay her hands on. When the youngest brother returned to his village, he was greeted immediately by his sister. She said, "Welcome, brother. Shall I take your horse to water?"

"All right, you may take my horse to water," said the young man.

While she was away with the horse, taking it to water, she ate off one of its legs. When she returned with the horse she asked her youngest brother, "How many legs had your horse? Had he three legs?"

"Yes, he had three legs."

"Shall I take your horse to eat now?" asked the caldron-headed, ax-toothed girl.

"All right, sister, you may take him to eat."

While she was away with the horse taking him to eat, she ate off another one of its legs. When she returned with the horse she asked her brother, "Had your horse two legs?"

"Yes, it had two legs."

"Shall I take your horse to water again?" asked the caldron-headed, ax-toothed girl.

"All right, sister."

This time she ate a third leg off the horse. When she brought it back, she asked her brother, "Had your horse one leg?"

"Yes, it had only one leg."

"Shall I take it to eat again?"

"All right, you may take it to eat again."

This time she ate the fourth leg off the horse. When she returned to her brother without the horse, she asked him, "Did you come on horseback or did you come on foot?"

"I came here on foot," answered her brother.

The caldron-headed, ax-toothed sister then asked her youngest brother, "Shall I delouse your head?"

"All right," said the youngest brother, "you may delouse my head."

When the caldron-headed, ax-toothed sister was delousing her brother's head, she opened her mouth and was prepared to bite his head off. He realized this and said to her, "Stop! Do not eat me in this way. You go and stand in the fireplace, and I shall go to the top of the roof and jump down the chimney into your mouth. You can eat all of me better in that way."

He went out and left his monster sister standing in the fireplace. He locked the door of the room and climbed up on top of the roof. There he took the heavy roller [96] from the roof and dropped it down the chimney into the mouth of the caldron-headed, ax-toothed sister. The young man then escaped, running down the road.

Very soon, however, he saw that his caldron-headed, ax-toothed sister was chasing him. He climbed up a date tree, which had grown from one of the pits he had thrown there when he first left home. When the caldron-headed, ax-toothed sister came to the tree, she simply gnawed it at the base and cut it down. Before the tree fell, the young man jumped to the next tree. Then the caldron-headed, ax-toothed sister gnawed that tree down too. He jumped from one tree to another, all along the line of date trees which had grown up from the pits that he had thrown there, until he came to the last tree. He realized then that there would be no more trees to which he could jump.[97]

"Stop, sister," said the young man. "You will eat me, all right, but before you do, let me play a few sad tunes on my flute." He then played several tunes, and after a while the three cubs came running from the cottage of the old woman. The lion cub came first, and then the bear cub, and then the tiger cub.

"I am afraid of these creatures," said the sister.

"You need not be afraid of them," said the brother. "They are coming to you as your prey."

But when the cubs came close enough, he said to them, "O, lion, catch her! O, tiger, swallow her! O, bear, split her ax-toothed jaws!"

Just before the cubs killed her, the caldron-headed, ax-toothed sister said, "You will kill me, all right, but before I die, will you please cut out my tongue and put it in your pocket? You may need it in the future."

The young man cut out her tongue and put it in his pocket. On the way home, he met a man with a long caravan loaded with goods. This man took a stick from his pocket and showed it to the young man and said, "If you know what this stick is, you can have the caravan that I have. If you cannot guess what it is, you will give me those cubs."

The young man said, "All right, I shall guess what the stick is." At that moment the sister's tongue, which he had in his pocket, spoke to him and said, "The stick is called the magic staff."

The young man won the caravan of goods in that way, and he became very rich. He ate and drank and lived happily ever afterwards, and so may we all.

10.

The Jeweled Cage and the Evil Sister [98]

Once there was a ruler who had a son, and then, many years later, he had a daughter. From the time that she was born there was something strange about this girl that was known only to the padishah. When she was three years old, the padishah called his son to him and said, "Take your sister to the mountains, kill her there, and bring me a cup of her blood to drink." The son could not understand this, for he had waited many years for a sister. He stood there speechless, and so his father said, "If you are my son, go and kill this girl. If you do not, she will surely be a source of trouble to you later."

The young man took his sister to the mountains to kill her, but he was unable to bring himself to carry out his father's order. He walked along with her until he came to a small house in which lived an old woman all alone. The old woman had only a cow to support her.

"Selamünaleyküm, grandmother," said the young man.

"Aleykümselam, my son," she said.

"I shall make you very rich, grandmother, upon one condition. You will take this infant girl, feed her, care for her, and rear her. You will have to do nothing else, and for this service I shall give you this saddle-bag full of gold."

The old woman agreed to this proposal, and the young man left his sister with her. He then shot a rabbit, cut its throat, and caught a cupful of its blood. He took this back to the palace and said to his father, "I have done what you ordered. I have killed my sister and brought you this cup of her blood to drink."

As soon as the padishah tasted it he said, "But this is not her blood, and I suspect that you have not killed her. Remember what I told you: you will be sorry for this, for she will bring trouble to you."

"No, no, father," he said, "I have killed her, and this is her blood."

Twice a week the young man visited the old woman and his sister, taking them food and money. When the girl had reached the age of eighteen, her father, the padishah, suddenly went blind for no apparent reason. Many doctors and healers were called, but none of them could restore his sight. One night in a dream the padishah was told of a Jeweled Cage that was kept in fairyland, a magic cage which would cure his blindness if it were rubbed against his eyes.

In the morning his son found the padishah crying. "Why are you crying, father?" he asked.

"Why shouldn't I cry? I was once a mighty ruler, and now I am blind. No cure can be found for my blindness, but in a dream last night I was told of a Jeweled Cage [99] in fairyland, a magic cage that would cure my eyes if it were rubbed against them while I recited the Kulhuvallahi [100] three times. Otherwise I shall remain blind all the rest of my life."

"Father, you have reared me, and I am grateful for this," said the young man, "but until now I have rendered you no service. This is my opportunity to serve you, and I shall go and find the magic cage."

The next morning the young man went to his father's treasury and filled his carpet saddlebag with a great quantity of money. Then he set out. First he went to visit the old woman and his sister before searching for the cage.

"Selamünaleyküm, grandmother," he said.

"Aleykümselam, my son."

"Grandmother, I am going on a long journey, and I do not know whether I shall return. I have three requests to make of you. You will not let my sister be moneyless but will give her generously of the money I shall leave you. You will permit her to join in the festivities on religious holidays and at weddings. My third request is that when my sister falls in love with some man, you will allow her to marry him, and you yourself will complete the wedding arrangements. I am going now, so give me your hand."

He kissed the old woman's hand and pressed it to his head,[101] and then he kissed his sister. But the girl said, "Brother, I do not want to be separated from you. I shall go wherever you go."

"No, you cannot go with me. I am going on a long journey, and I do not know whether I shall return. You stay here and live comfortably."

When the young man left the old woman's house, he noticed that his sister was following him at a distance. He thought to himself, "My

91

father told me to kill this girl but I didn't. Now I am going on a dangerous mission, and if she goes with me, it may mean my death or hers." After she had continued following him a long way, he took her up on his horse, and the two traveled together.

At last they came to a town, but nowhere in the town could they find a single living person, nor could they find cattle, or donkeys, or even a dog. All of the shops and stores were open, but there was not a living creature anywhere, and this puzzled the young man greatly. He forgot about the cage he had set out to find, so great was his curiosity about this strange town. He left his sister in one of the deserted houses and started looking through the town, hoping that somewhere he could find a human being who could tell him why the town was deserted. But he lived there for six months without seeing a single person.

Then one morning when he was walking down a street that he had never seen before, he met a giant, a huge, horrible black Arab.[102] This giant was so horrible that it was impossible not to be frightened by him.

"Where did you come from?" asked the giant Arab. "I have eaten all of the people in this town, and I have left no living creatures anywhere. How fortunate I am in finding you at a time when my appetite is so great. I shall eat you too."[103]

"I have been wandering through this deserted town for six months hoping to find someone with whom to talk. But I shall not talk with you. You have eaten so many Moslems and so many good people that I challenge you to a fight instead."

(There were no rifles or artillery in those days and Moslems could fight only with swords and their religious fervor. Warriors carried only swords, and sometimes they preferred to fight without even these weapons, trusting to their arms and fists. There were many wrestlers in those days, even more than now.)

The young man fought with the giant all that day, but neither could defeat the other. They agreed to cease fighting until the next morning when they would meet again at the same place. This went on for three days, but at the end of the third day the young man finally knocked the giant down and tied him, hand and foot. "I shall not kill you right away," said the young man, "for then your suffering would be too brief. You have tortured many people and do not deserve to die easily, and so I shall hang you in that poplar tree and let you die slowly, in agony." Then the young man hung the giant in the poplar tree and left him there.

92

The young man had completely forgotten about the cage which was the purpose of his journey. He now gave himself to hunting, going into the nearby mountains every day with bow and arrows. One day he came upon a very fertile spot watered by a fountain, and there he planted three young cypress trees. Every day he shot partridges and rabbits, and these he took home at night to his sister who cooked them for their meals. This went on for some time.

The young man's sister became bored after a while with living alone in the deserted house all day long while her brother hunted in the mountains. She began to spend some of her time walking about the deserted town. One day, as she walked along a street that she had never seen before, she came upon a poplar tree with a giant black Arab hanging from its branches. "Isn't there a soul to help me? I suffer greatly here."

The girl looked up at the Arab and asked, "What are you doing up there? Who tied you there?"

"A young man did this to me, tied me here hand and foot. For God's sake, save me!"

"That young man was probably my brother," she said. "What offense have you committed?"

"He thought I was too ugly. That is why he hung me here."

"I shall save you, then," said the girl.

(I am sorry to have to say this, but women have long hair and short brains.)

When the girl loosened the chains that held the giant, he made love to her. She liked this Arab giant and so she said to him, "Let us become companions. We can meet here every day and enjoy ourselves."

"That will be good," he said.

From that day on, the girl would take to the giant a large part of the game that her brother had killed and that she had cooked. Slowly the giant grew stronger, and after a while he became twice as powerful as he had ever been before. The girl said to him one day, "Our life cannot go on forever like this. Let us kill my brother and live together. If you do not kill my brother, I shall tell him about you and have you killed instead."

The giant said, "I fought with your brother for three whole days and could not kill him. He is the most powerful man I have ever seen. I ate all of the people in this town, but I never met anyone like him. He defeated me and tied me up in the poplar tree. I cannot fight with him, but I shall send him along the road of death from which he cannot turn. One day you will tell your brother that you are sick and that to be cured you must have some of the black grapes and some of the white grapes that grow in the land of the giants. Ask him to go to the land of the giants and bring some of these grapes to you. There are nine giants and their mother — ten in all. They are my brothers from whom I parted many years ago. If your brother goes among them he will certainly be killed."

The next day the girl pretended to be ill and lay in bed groaning. "What is the matter with you?" her brother asked. "Are you sick?"

"I am so ill that I fear I shall die," she said.

"There is no doctor in this town to help us. How terrible to live in such a strange land!" That night the young man could not sleep, thinking of his sister's illness. Toward morning he heard his sister cry out. "Why are you crying?" he asked her.

"I dreamed of black grapes and white grapes that grow in the land of the giants. I was told that these would cure me. If I eat these, I shall get well; otherwise, I shall die."

The young man immediately promised his sister that he would go and find some of these grapes for her. When morning came, he mounted his horse and rode away to look for the land of the giants.

As soon as he had gone, his sister went to the Arab giant and brought him back to the house with her. There they began to live a life of pleasure.

The poor young man tried and tried to find the land of the giants. One day he came to a mountain with a large flat top — about a thousand acres. There was a spring nearby, and he decided to stop there, to eat and pray and rest his horse. He took ablution and prayed. Then, after saying "Bismillah," he laid his food on the ground and began to eat. As he was eating, a fox came along and walked very close to the young man. The young man looked at the fox and said to himself, "Although it is a wild animal, this fox is not afraid to come near me. Surely it must be hungry. Let me give it some bread to eat." And he threw a piece of his bread to the fox.

"Oh, young man," said the fox, "you did not condescend to invite me to your side to eat but instead threw me a piece of bread."

Surprised, the young man said, "Come, then, and sit by me." And the two of them ate together.

When they had finished eating, the fox asked, "Friend, why did you come here? What are you looking for in this land?"

94

"I have a sister who fell ill. I am supposed to find the black and white grapes that grow in the land of the giants and take them to her. She thinks that she will be cured when she eats them. If I do not find them, she will not live."

"But do you know this land of the giants?"

"No, I don't."

"Then let us be friends," said the fox, "and the rest will be easy." When the young man had agreed to this, the fox said, "Friend, the land of the giants is very far away. You cannot reach there today. Wait until tomorrow to leave and I shall tell you many things about that land."

They slept that night in the mountains, and in the morning the fox addressed the young man: "Do you see that hill over there? Well, the land of the giants lies beyond that hill. There is a large and tall apartment there in which live nine giant brothers and their mother, all of them greatly feared. Each morning the sons leave to hunt for food, and their mother remains at home to crush forty camel loads of wheat for their daily caldron of soup. Her breasts are as large as pitchers, and when she works, she throws one over each shoulder to keep them out of the way. When you approach their home, listen to hear the millstones grinding wheat, and if you hear that noise, you will know that you are at the right house. Then enter the house, sneak up to her from behind, grab one of her breasts, and suck it. Then she will say to you, 'Ah, you have sucked my milk and so I shall take you as my child.' [104] Then you will walk around in front of her and kiss her hands. If you do not do just as I say, you will be discovered and torn to pieces for a meal for these giants."

The young man mounted his horse and rode away toward the land of the giants. He found the tall apartment, and when he came closer to it, he heard the noise of millstones grinding. "This must be the mother of the giants crushing bulgur," [105] he said, and he began to stalk her from behind. Her breasts, each weighing a hundred kilos, were thrown over her shoulders, and one of these the young man caught and began to suck.

"Hah! Who are you? Come around in front of me. No harm will come to you. What is your wish?"

The young man came before the mother of the giants and kissed her hands. She pressed him to her bosom and asked, "Why did you come here?"

"Mother, I have a sick sister who needs black grapes and white grapes or she will die. I heard that those grapes grow here, and that is why I have come."

"It will be easy to get those grapes. Sit down and wait for your brothers, who will return soon and pick the grapes that you need."

After an hour or so had passed, the nine giants came home. They rushed at the young man to eat him, but their mother said, "Stop! He sucked from my breast and thus became your brother. Ask him how he is and what he wants."

The giant sons all began to say, "Welcome, brother! Welcome, brother!" and then later one of them asked, "Brother, what is it you wish?"

"A basket full of white grapes and a basket full of black grapes."

After they had picked him these grapes, the young man thanked them and left, going back to where the fox was awaiting him. The fox tasted some of the white grapes and some of the black grapes. "Take them to your sister now and let her eat them. And when you are in trouble again, come to me."

Taking the grapes, he returned to the deserted house where he and his sister had been living. She lay in bed during the day and pretended to be sick, but when night came, and she thought her brother would not return, she would invite the Arab giant to spend the time with her. When the young man walked in, she said, from her bed, "Welcome, brother. Have you brought the grapes?"

"Yes, I have," he said, and leaving the grapes with his sister, the young man went hunting again.

When the giant came and saw the grapes, he said, "Yes, these are black grapes and white grapes from the land of the giants. A man who can take these grapes from the nine giants could beat me easily. I cannot fight against him."

The Arab giant ate the grapes, and each day he ate the food that the brother brought home and the sister cooked. He was growing stronger all the time. The girl noticed his size and his strength, and it annoyed her that he did not kill her brother so that they could live together uninterrupted in their pleasure. One day she threatened him again, saying, "If you do not kill my brother, I shall tell him about you."

"I cannot kill your brother, for he is much stronger than I, but there is another way of getting rid of him. I have a task so difficult that he will surely be killed in trying to accomplish it. Pretend to become ill again, and when your brother asks you what is the matter, say, 'Brother, I was told in a dream last night that there is a mountain where many lions live. You must go there, milk a lioness, put the milk in a lion's skin, load this skin on the back of another lion, and bring it to me to drink. That milk will make me well.' "

The girl did as the Arab giant had directed, and when her brother came home at night, he found her lying in bed groaning. "What is the matter, sister?" he asked.

She vomited and then said, "Oh, brother, this time I am so ill that I think I shall die."

The young man looked at his sister and he feared that she might actually die. He lay awake all night worrying, and in the middle of the night, he heard her cry out. "What is it, sister?" he asked.

"I just had a dream in which I was told that the only cure for me was lion's milk. You are to go to the mountain of lions, milk a lioness, put the milk in a lion's skin, put this skin on the back of another lion, and then bring that milk to me to drink."

"Sister, do not give up hope. I shall set out tomorrow, and, God willing, I shall find the mountain of lions and bring you that milk."

Along the way the young man met the fox again, and the fox asked him, "Where are you going?"

"I am going to the mountain of lions to get some lion's milk to cure my sister's illness. I must milk a lioness, put the milk in a lion's skin, put the skin on another lion, and take the milk to my sister to drink. Otherwise, she will die. How can I do these things? Can a man cope with lions?"

The fox replied, "I know a way to do these things, but it is too late for you to reach the mountain of lions tonight. Let us spend the night here, and I shall tell you about it tomorrow."

They ate dinner and then spent the night there. In the morning the fox said, "Oh, brother, listen to me carefully. It is that distant mountain over there that is the mountain of lions. Nothing else can live there, and you will have to reach the mountain tomorrow morning before sunrise. You will find a fountain with forty spouts flowing into a pool filled with slime and moss that no one ever cleans out. You will clean out the pool and clean the spouts so that the water flows freely. There is a dead tree near the fountain, and in this tree you will make a hiding place for yourself. Get inside this dead tree and hide until noon, when all of the lions will come to drink. Last will come the mother of these lions, limping, for she has a foot that has been infected by a thorn for the past seven years. It is filled with pus and it is very painful to her, but no one can pull out the thorn. When she comes, roaring with

97

pain, the other lions will run away, and she will be left there alone. She will drink from the fountain and rest her sore foot in a fork of the dead tree where you are hiding. You must then reach out quickly and cut off her infected foot. She will faint in pain, but when she revives, she will say to you, 'My sons have done nothing to ease my pain for seven years, but you have ended my suffering. What can I do for you?' Then you will come out from hiding, bandage her foot, and tell her what it is that you want there. But if you fail in this undertaking and you are seen by the lions, then there is nothing that you can do to save yourself."

The young man traveled all of that day and he reached the mountain before sunrise of the next day. He cleaned the fountain and the spouts, and he hid in the dead tree. The lions came and left at the approach of their mother, who drank from the pool and then rested her swollen foot in a fork of the dead tree. The young man cut off the foot and then bandaged it up, as he had been told to do.

"Who is it that has saved me from all this suffering? Ask what you will, young man, and I shall fulfill your request."

"My sister is ill, and I should like some lion's milk for her. I should like it put in a lion's skin and carried on the back of another lion to my sister, who must drink it to be cured."

"All of these lions are my children," said the lioness, "and I could not bear to see one killed and skinned. But over by those rocks are some young cubs. Go over there where I cannot see you, kill one, skin it, and bring the skin here. Fill it with milk from my teats, and I shall order two of my sons to bear it to your sister."

The young man did as he was directed, being careful not to let the lioness see him kill and skin the cub. When he had filled the skin with milk, the lioness called two of her sons to her and said, "This young man will be both father and mother to you. You must never desert him even if he beats or kills you. If you leave him and return here before he sends you back, I shall kill you. Now take this skin of milk to the place where he directs."

On the way back to his sister, the young man stopped to visit with the fox. The fox tasted the milk and said, "Take this milk to your sister, and take good care of these two lions, for they will be your most valuable friends from now on."

When he reached the deserted house in which he and his sister lived, she said to him, "Welcome, brother! Have you brought me the lion's milk?"

"Yes, I have, sister. Here it is," said her brother, and then after chaining the two lions, he took his bow and arrows and went hunting as was his custom.

The girl took the skin of milk to her giant lover. When the giant Arab saw the milk, he said, "Don't you see that he managed to bring this milk from the land of the lions? How could a giant like me fight with such a strong and brave man? Bring me that milk and let me drink it."

When the giant Arab had drunk the lion's milk he became even stronger. "What else did your brother bring from the mountain of lions?" he asked.

"He brought back two of the lions with him." ·

"Ah," said the giant Arab, "then you must melt some lead and pour it into their ears right away."

"Why?" asked the girl.

"You wouldn't understand, but just do as I tell you."

The girl melted a ladle full of lead and poured the molten metal into the ears of the two lions. But after she had done this, one of the lions shook his head violently, and the lead fell out of one ear. The other lion was completely deaf in both ears.

The young man still went hunting every day, and often on these trips, he went to the spot where he had planted the three cypress trees and tended them. They were almost fully grown trees by this time.

While he was away hunting, his sister still entertained the Arab giant, and all the time she grew more and more indignant that her lover could not kill her brother and then come and live with her all the time. Once again she said to him, "This cannot go on. Either you kill my brother or I shall tell him to kill you."

"I cannot kill your brother alone," said the Arab giant, "but together we may be able to do it. While I attack him, you sneak up behind and hit him on the head with this ax, and perhaps in that way we can get rid of him."

The next day the young man went hunting, and at noontime he stopped by the fountain and the cypress trees to eat his lunch. He made his ablutions and started to pray, coming to the part of the prayer where he looked first to his right and then to his left.[106] As he looked to the left, he saw the Arab giant and his sister coming toward him, and then again he remembered his father's warning about his sister, and he said to himself, "My father cautioned me against this girl and ordered me to kill her. Now I wish I had obeyed him. I have neither taken my father's advice nor fulfilled his wish to bring him the jeweled cage

99

to cure his blindness. I have been an unworthy son, and I have wasted my time in this land. What shall I do now? I am not afraid of this giant, for I could cope with ten like him, but I fear that my sister will in some way betray me." Then, turning to the cypress trees, he said, "Oh, cypress trees, for seven years I have tended you and taken care of you. Bend down, one of you, now and take me up, for this giant and my treacherous sister want to kill me." The first tree bent down, and after the young man had climbed into its top, it straightened up again.

The Arab giant looked up at the young man in the cypress tree and said, "Let us see what you will do now. I am coming, with your sister, to get you. We shall chop down that tree and catch you that way."

The giant took the ax from the girl and began to chop. When only a small section of the trunk remained to be cut through, the young man said to the next cypress tree, "Bend over to your sister." When the tree bent over, the young man climbed into the top of the second tree. The Arab giant then began to chop at the bottom of the second tree, and when he had cut it almost through, the young man said to the third cypress tree, "Bend over here to your sister tree so that I may climb into your branches or this Arab giant and my evil sister will kill me." And the third cypress tree bent over and took the young man into its branches.

The giant said, "I have cut two trees already, and this is the last. Let me rest a while and then I shall cut this last one."

While the giant was resting, the young man was thinking of how to save himself. He remembered at last the two lions that he had brought from the mountain of lions and, cupping his hands against his mouth, he called them. He shouted once, but the lions could not hear him, for their ears had been stopped. He shouted a second time and they still did not hear. When he shouted a third time, the lion with one good ear heard his call, nudged his brother lion, and started running in the direction of the cypress trees.

When the Arab saw the lions approaching, he asked the girl, "Didn't you pour molten lead into the ears of these creatures?"

"Yes, I did," she said.

"It will not be easy to fight these lions," he said.

From his perch in the tree the young man shouted at the lions, "Don't touch my sister, for I shall deal with her. You are to tear this Arab giant to pieces." After they had done this, the young man climbed down, killed his sister, cut her into tiny pieces, and then he hung these pieces on the branches of a thorn tree. Turning then to the lions, he said, "I am now setting you free. Go back to your mother and take to her my greetings. Tell her that I do not need your services any longer."

After the lions had gone, the young man mounted his horse and rode to where he usually met the fox. "Greetings, brother," he said to the fox.

"Welcome, brother," said the fox, "and I am glad that your troubles here are all past."

"How did you know that I had just escaped from troubles?"

"I have known everything that has troubled you here from the beginning, but I did not think it proper to tell you so, for a gallant man should solve his own problems. But from now on, we shall do everything together. Now tell me why you came to this land."

"My father is a padishah. One day he became blind and the doctors could not restore his sight. In a dream he was told that in fairyland there was a jeweled cage that could cure him. If he rubs this cage against his eyes while he recites the Kulhuvallahi three times, his blindness will disappear. Otherwise he will remain blind forever. I started out to find that cage, but when I came to the deserted town, I forgot all about it. Now that the Arab giant and my sister are dead, I can begin my search again."

"We shall search together for this cage, but it is too late to start today. Let us spend the night here and start in the morning." So they ate and drank and spent the night there, and in the morning the young man left his horse there and set out on foot with the fox for the land of the fairies. After they had come to a strange land, the fox pointed out a tall apartment house and said, "That is where the fairies live. When you enter this apartment, it will seem to be completely empty. You will see a cage hanging in a corner, and you should take this immediately and start to leave. When you do so, a thousand hands will thrust handkerchiefs into your bosom. As fast as they put them there you must throw them out again, and be sure that they are all out when you leave the apartment, for if even one remains with you, the cage will be wrenched out of your hands and stuck to the wall. If that happens, do not go back into the apartment again but come back to me."

The young man entered the apartment, found the cage on the opposite wall, took it down, and started to leave with it. At once a thousand hands went into his bosom, each leaving a handkerchief there. The young man tried hard to get rid of all these, but as he was leaving, there was still one handkerchief left in his bosom. Just as the fox had said, the cage flew out of his hands and stuck to the wall.

"What happened?" asked the fox when the young man came out of the apartment.

"Just what you said would happen," answered the young man. "Just one handkerchief was left in my bosom, but the cage flew out of my hands and stuck to the wall."

"Go back into the apartment and shout, 'O Fairies! Give me the cage!' You will not see any of them, but you will hear a voice. Listen to what it answers and come and tell me this."

The young man entered the fairy apartment again and shouted, "O Fairies! Give me the cage!"

"Yes, we shall give you the cage," a voice answered, "but first you must get for us a sword stolen by the giants and kept by them in their land."

The young man told the fox what the voice had said, and the fox ordered, "Well, then, go and get that sword."

"Yes, but where is it?"

"Don't you remember the giant mother whose breast you sucked? It is there in that land. You must go and greet her and ask her for this sword. She is bound to give it to you."

The young man traveled to the land of the giants, and when he came to their apartment, he entered and greeted the giantess.

"Welcome, my son," she said, "I hope that all of your troubles are over."

"How did you know that I had had adventures?" he asked.

"Why shouldn't I know? That Arab giant used to be my son, but he left us and went to the town where you found him, and there he ate all of the people. You two fought, and you proved to be superior to him. You sucked my breast and you are my son too. What can I do for you?"

"I want the sword that was once taken from the land of the fairies," he said.

"We have that sword here, but it has now rusted in its sheath for seven years. If you can pull it from its sheath in one attempt, you may take this sword with you. If you cannot draw it, then you must leave it here."

The young man said, "Bismillah!" and then he recited the Kulhu-vallahi three times. Gripping the sword, he pulled it out in one attempt and thus was permitted to keep it.

When the young man took the sword back to the fox, the fox said to him, "Now don't really give the sword to the fairies. Ask for the cage, and when they have given it to you, extend the sword, blade first, to them. Start backing out of their apartment, and when you are at the threshold, pull the sword. They will fear that the blade will cut their hands, and so they will let go. Then hook the handle of the cage over the blade of this magic sword, as you leave the apartment, and they will then not be able to take it away from you."

The young man proceeded to do as the fox had directed him, and this time he managed to keep the Jeweled Cage. When he returned, the fox said to him, "O young man! We have been brothers to one another for some time, and we have succeeded in everything we have undertaken. Now I have a request to make of you. Will you grant it?"

"Of course I will. What is it?"

"Will you recite the Kulhuvallahi three times and wave this sword over my head?" [107]

The young man did as he was requested, and suddenly the fox turned into a youth of matchless beauty — even greater than that of the padishah's son. The fox-boy then said, "There is just one more thing that I want. You may keep the cage, but give me the sword. It was mine once, and the fairies stole it from me, and then the giants stole it from the fairies. When you turn that sword upside down over someone, he will become whatever you wish him to become. That is how the fairies turned me into a fox, after they had stolen the sword. The land beyond those distant mountains belongs to me. Let me go there in peace with the sword, and you return to your father with the Jeweled Cage."

They embraced and parted, the fox-boy going toward the distant mountains. The padishah's son looked about until he found his horse, and then he started on the long journey back to his father's home. His father had been waiting for him for a long time, thinking that every knock on the door must be that of his son.

At last, after traveling for many days, the young man reached home. He kissed his father's hands and then he gave him the Jeweled Cage. Rubbing the cage against his eyes, the padishah recited the Kulhuvallahi three times, and suddenly he could see again — better than he had ever seen before. I have dedicated this tale to our distinguished visitors, to our dear teachers, and to the director of this prison. [108]

II.

Shemsi Bani,[109] Padishah of Pigeons

Once there was a padishah whose only child was a daughter. When the infant had grown to a girl, she used to spend her time sitting in the harem section of the palace, crocheting. One day a bird flew into the palace and carried away her needle before she could stop it. The girl became so upset by this event that she grew ill, and she weakened and began to fade away. A few days later, while she was sitting in the palace garden, the bird came again and this time flew away with her thimble. After this her health grew much worse, until finally she had to be taken to the hospital.[110]

Her father called all of the famous doctors in the land to try to cure his daughter's illness, but none of them could help her. One of the wise men advised the padishah: "Let us build a large bath in town which anyone might use for the price of a story. Everyone who uses the bath will tell a story to your daughter, and perhaps one of these tales will cure her." The padishah accepted this suggestion, and within a short time a bath was built. In one corner was built an apartment where his daughter lay, and it was there that bathers went to pay their admission price of a story. These stories meant little to the girl, and her health did not improve as a result of hearing them.

At this same time, in another country far away, there was an old woman traveling about, begging for her food. One day when this old woman was resting by the side of the sea, she saw moving into the water several mules and camels loaded with all kinds of merchandise and foods. She followed them, holding one of these animals by the tail as it slipped into the water and sank to the bottom of the sea. After traveling some distance under water, they came to a beautiful building on the bottom of the sea. The old woman entered the building with the camel whose tail she was holding and there she came to a great chamber containing a large pool around which were tables containing all sorts of fine food. The old woman was very hungry, but as she reached for a ladle to serve herself from one of the bowls, a voice said, "You may not eat of that food!"

Upon hearing that voice, she looked around, but she saw no one but the camels all standing over in the corner of the room. She went over and sat down among them. At that moment a pigeon flew into the room, circled around the pool several times, and then dipped its wings into the water. As soon as it did this, it turned into a handsome young man. Soon another pigeon entered the room and in the same way circled the pool, dipped into the water, and turned into a handsome young man. To make a long story short, within a short time between two and three hundred young men gathered there, all of them entering as pigeons. Apparently they were going to have a dinner party, but they waited for some time, and then one of them said, "Our padishah is late today." All this time, the old woman sat silently among the camels watching them and observing everything that took place. Finally another pigeon flew into the room and dived into the water, whereupon all of the young men stood up and shouted, "Here is our padishah!"

When the padishah of pigeons came from the water, they all sat down and ate the rich feast spread out upon the many tables. After dinner, they talked among themselves for a while, and then, one by one, they all left except the last comer, the padishah, who was finally left there all alone. As soon as he was alone, he went to a table, pulled open a drawer, and took a needle from it. Addressing himself to this object, he said, "O crocheting needle, how fine you are and how delicate must be the hands that sew with you. Let everywhere weep!" Everything in the building wept except the camels standing in the corner; they and their stable laughed aloud. Then he took from the drawer a thimble, and holding it up to the light, he said, "O thimble, how fine you are! I wonder how delicate must be the hands which wear you. Let all things cry!" All things did cry except the camels and their stable, and these things laughed aloud. Then the padishah of pigeons put these back into the drawer and walked out of the room.

The old woman noticed that now the camels, all unloaded, were beginning to leave, and so she caught hold of the tail of one of them and moved along with the group. Traveling along on the bottom of the sea, they finally arrived at a land which the old woman had never seen before. Although she had but scant clothing, she slept that night among the bushes and thorns, for it was summer and quite warm. On the following morning, when she woke up, she saw a man walking along, and she asked him, "Son, will you please take me to town with you?" The man placed her upon his donkey and took her along with him toward the nearest town. As they went along, he said to her, "Mother, you are very dirty from traveling. In the town which we are approaching there is a free bath. Why don't you go there and wash?" The old woman was very pleased with this suggestion, for she had, in fact, been traveling for many days and was very dirty.

When they reached the town, she thanked the young man and left him, proceeding to the bath. At the entrance of the building she was told that according to the custom of the land all could use the bath without paying any charge but that all bathers had to tell a story to the sick daughter of the padishah, who resided there. She entered the bath, went to the place where the sick girl was sitting, and told the following story:

"An old woman was traveling, and one day as she sat to rest along the seashore, she saw a train of camels coming along, and when they came to the sea, they continued walking right into the water. The old woman caught hold of the tail of one of these animals and traveled along with them on the bottom of the sea. They reached a large house, after a while, and when they entered, they came to a large chamber with a pool in it. Soon pigeons began to fly into the room, and as each dipped into the water, he turned into a handsome young man."

The daughter of the padishah took more interest in this story than she had in most others, and so she said to the old woman, "Come a little closer, mother, so that I may hear you better." The old woman moved closer to the girl, and then she went on:

"Soon the padishah of pigeons arrived, and then all of the handsome young men sat down and spent much time eating a great feast that had been prepared there for them. After all the rest had left, the padishah of pigeons went to a table and took from a drawer a needle. Holding it up, he said, 'O crocheting needle, how fine you are, and how delicate must be the hands that sew with you! Let everywhere weep.' Everything except the camels and their stable wept, and these laughed aloud." Then the old woman started to leave, saying, "I am going for my bath now."

"No, no, stay, mother, and tell me the rest of the story. You can take your bath afterwards," said the daughter of the padishah.

"Well," the old woman continued, "the padishah then took from the drawer a small thimble and holding it up to the light said to it, 'O thimble, how fine you are and how delicate must be the hand that wears you. Let all things cry!' Then everything wept except the camels and their stable, and these laughed. At this, the young man left the room. Then the old woman noticed that the camels were about to leave, so she grabbed the tail of the animal nearest her and so followed them until they returned again to dry land. That is my story."

"It is a wonderful story," said the girl, "but tell me, mother, who the old woman was."

"It was I, daughter," she said.

When the daughter of the padishah heard this, she embraced the old woman and ordered her attendants to bathe her and dress her in fine clothes. When all this had been done, the old woman looked like a very respectable lady. Every day for a week the old woman told the sick daughter of the padishah the same story, and then the girl said, "Mother, let us go together and find these camels again."

The old woman said, "First get permission from the padishah to leave. Then we shall go."

The girl went to the padishah and said, "Father, we wish to walk down to the seaside with the old woman."

"Very well, daughter. I place the old woman in your command. But I shall order a coach to carry you to the sea."

The girl and the old woman rode to the seashore in the coach, and when they reached the water, the old woman said to the driver, "If we do not come back to you within an hour's time, then go on back to the palace without us." After the two women disappeared, the coach driver waited one, three, and five hours, and then when they did not return, he went back to the padishah and told him what had happened.

"Never mind," said the padishah. "Everyone will recognize them, and whoever finds them will bring them back safely." But after three or five days, the padishah gave up hope of their returning, and he regretted having allowed his daughter to leave the palace. Now let us leave him crying and go back to the seashore.

A large number of camels with their loads of food — rice, and lentils, and other things — again came along and walked right into the sea. Each woman took hold of a camel's tail, and after traveling along on the bottom of the sea for a long way, they came to the building that the old woman had visited before. There the camels were unloaded by invisible attendants, and the two women entered the large hall and came to the pool surrounded by tables filled with all kinds of food. They were very hungry after their trip, and so the daughter of the padishah reached for a plate of the food, but, just as before, a voice said, "You may not eat that food."

Then the women went and sat among the camels in the stable at a place where they could see the pool and the dining tables. As each pigeon flew into the chamber, the old woman asked the girl, "Is that the bird that stole your needle and thimble?"

"No," the girl said each time until, at last, the padishah of pigeons flew in. "That's the one!" she said.

Once again the padishah of pigeons remained after the others had left. Going to a table, he pulled open a drawer, took from it a needle, and said, "O crocheting needle, how fine you are, and how delicate must be the hands that sew with you. Let everywhere weep!" Everything wept but the camels and the stable, which laughed. Then he took the thimble again from the drawer and, holding it up to the light to look at it, said, "O thimble, how fine you are, and how delicate must be the hands that use you. Let all things cry!" Again everything wept except the camels and their stable, which laughed aloud. This time the padishah of pigeons was annoyed and walking over to the stable said, "Why are you so disrespectful?" There was no answer, and then the young man saw the two women among the camels and asked, "Are you fairies or jinns?"

The old woman stood up and said, "Neither. We are God's creatures."

Then the sick daughter of the padishah stood up and said, "You cruel thief! You stole my needle and thimble and you have reduced me to this condition!"

The old woman grabbed the tail of a camel as the animals were leaving the stable, but the girl remained there and married the padishah of pigeons, with the will of God. At the end of nine months the girl was about to give birth to a child. Then the padishah of pigeons said to her, "It is not safe for you to remain here any longer, for it will be impossible to hide both you and the child. If the other pigeons should discover you here, they would immediately kill both of us. I shall direct you to a place where you will be quite safe. I am actually the son of a human padishah, and my father and mother are both alive. My name is Shemsi Bani.[111] When you reach our palace, knock on the door and say to the person who opens it, 'Let me in for the sake of your lost son, Shemsi Bani.'"

The girl followed the directions Shemsi Bani had given her, and after traveling for some time she came to the palace of his parents. When she knocked on the door, a maid opened it and asked, "Whom do you want, young lady?"

"Call the lady of the house here," she said. When the wife of the padishah came to the door, the girl said to her, "Accept me as a guest in your house for the sake of your lost son, Shemsi Bani."

"How did you know that we had a lost son?"

"I just know it. If I didn't, I shouldn't be here," said the girl.

The wife of the padishah admitted to the house the young woman who, in a few days, gave birth to a child that cried, "Vyah, vyah, vyah."

A short while later Shemsi Bani came in bird form to the window of the palace and pecked at the glass with his beak. The young woman opened the window, and the bird sang:[112]

> "O soul of my soul, and sultan of my soul,
> Did my mother recognize you when she let you in?
> And did she embrace the child of her child?"

The young woman answered:

> "O soul of my soul, and sultan of my soul,
> Your mother didn't recognize me when she let me in,
> And she didn't embrace the child of her child."

After the bird had flown away, one of the servants who had overheard this conversation went to the wife of the padishah and reported to her that the young woman talked out the window to some secret lover. "How could this be?" asked the lady.

"I do not know," said the servant, "but I heard it."

"The next time this happens, call me so that I may hear it too," said the wife of the padishah.

The next day Shemsi Bani again came in the form of a pigeon and sang:

> "O soul of my soul, and sultan of my soul,
> Has my mother recognized you yet?
> And has she yet embraced the child of her child?"

And again the girl answered:

> "O soul of my soul, and sultan of my soul,
> Your mother has not recognized me yet,
> And she has not yet embraced the child of her child."

But this time the wife of the padishah had been called, and she had listened outside the door of the girl's room to this conversation. After the bird had flown away, she knocked on the door, and when she was admitted to the room, she asked, "Who was the person to whom you were just talking?"

"O lady, that is a hard question to answer. Actually, he is somehow your son, and I shall tell you what I know about him." And then she told Shemsi Bani's mother all that had happened.

"How can I see my son again?" asked the mother.

"Cut a small hole in the door and look through that tomorrow when he comes to visit me again."

The woman agreed to this, and the next day when it was time for Shemsi Bani to return, both she and the padishah were watching through the hole in the door. The girl placed a large bowl of water near the open window and then hid herself. The bird came and sat on the window sill and sang:

"O soul of my soul, and sultan of my soul,
Has my mother recognized you yet?
And has she yet embraced the child of her child?"

From her hiding place the girl answered:

"O soul of my soul, and sultan of my soul,
Your mother has recognized me now
And she has embraced the child of her child."

The bird could not see the girl, and so he entered the room, looking for her. When he saw the bowl of water, he dived into it and at once turned into a handsome young man. The mother and father, watching through the hole in the door, were amazed to see their son come to life in this way. But soon he turned back into a pigeon and flew away.

As soon as he had left, both his parents rushed into the room and asked, "Isn't there something that you can do to make our son stay here?"

"I do not know of anything," she said, "but let me ask Shemsi Bani about this." The next day Shemsi Bani again flew into the window, dipped his wings in the bowl of water, and became himself once more. "Your parents have seen you through the hole in the door," his wife said, "and they want you to come home again. Is there anything that we can do to keep you here? Why must you fly away?"

"When I was seven days old I was stolen from my home by fairies. I lived with them until I grew up, and then they made me their padishah. If I try to stay here, my suit of feathers must first be destroyed, for the spell on me is in those feathers. As long as they exist, I shall go mad trying to find them. Tell my parents to build a bath one hundred meters from the palace and place a large pile of firewood near it. Then tomorrow night, when I shall come and spend the time with you, have the feathers burned while I am asleep. But make sure that the bath is a hundred meters away, for if I sense that the feathers are being burned, I shall rush madly to them and perhaps be burned to death in the fire."

The girl reported all this to the padishah, who had a bath built and supplied with a great pile of pitch pine wood. The furnace was then fired until it was red hot with burning pitch pine. When Shemsi Bani came to his wife's room, she gave his pigeon feathers to his father, who ran with them to the furnace of the bath and threw them into the flames. When the smell of burning feathers came to Shemsi Bani as he lay in bed with his wife, he jumped up and started running wildly in the direction of the fire. But the padishah had taken measures against this and he had placed three rings of soldiers around the bath. As Shemsi Bani rushed toward the bath, they grabbed him and held him until the feathers were consumed in the flames.

"What a terrible thing you have done to me," he shouted. "What shall I do now? When the fairies find out, they will come and kill me."

But when the feathers were completely burned, the spell was broken, and after that, Shemsi Bani remained at the palace with his father and mother, his wife, and his son. The pigeon fairies waited three and five days, and then they knew that their padishah would never return.

After a while, the padishah said, "We must have a wedding ceremony for our son." Then there was a wedding that lasted for forty days and forty nights, and when it was over, the girl said, "My father was a padishah, too. Let us go and visit him." So they traveled to her kingdom, and there they had another wedding that lasted forty days and forty nights. In the end, Shemsi Bani came to rule over both kingdoms, and they and their children lived happily ever after that.

PART II

Perplexities and Ingenious Deductions

Aconsiderable proportion of Turkish folktales involve deduction in one form or another. It may be solutions based on acute observation, as in "The Auspicious Dream"; it may be shrewd guesswork; or it may be only the *appearance* of deduction — mistaken conclusions that seem correct or sheer bluff that cannot be gainsaid. The most common vehicle for such apparent deduction is the Aarne-Thompson Type 924 B, Sign Language Misunderstood,[1] exemplified by the climactic episode of tale number 3 below, "Stuck to Some Great Door." (This is a humorous story about a noodlehead, a silly keloghlan, and as such it would fit as readily into Part III as it does here.)

The "Guessing Children" of our second tale have appeared so frequently in Turkish stories as invincible detectives that there is a tendency to make them superhuman. Without any real clues on which to base deduction, they determine who has committed a crime, apprehend the culprit, and return the stolen property, even though the case may be a month old and both criminal and plunder may be removed a thousand miles from the scene. However improbable our tale may seem, in some parts, it is one of the more realistic versions of "The Guessing Children."

Audience response is sometimes elicited to solve the perplexities and knotty problems of these tales. This occurred during the taping of "The Guessing Children" and "The Many Dilemmas of the Padishah's Three

Sons." When this happens, there may be heated discussion about the resolution of a dilemma, for often there are several acceptable answers, one of which is supposedly the best. In such cases, where the narration may be held in abeyance until the puzzle has been solved, there would seem to exist a hybrid form of oral art, a crossing of the folktale and the riddle.[2] "Caliph Ali and the Three Sons' Inheritance," perhaps the best-known tale in this section, is also related to the riddle, and it often ends with a question about how to solve the dilemma rather than with the solution.

The theme of "The Daughters of the Broom Thief" is one of the most common in folktales: the peasant girl weds the king. Here piquancy is added to this variation on the theme by the use of symbolic language that seems silly to all save the initiate.

1.

Caliph Ali and the Three Sons' Inheritance [3]

A man died and left his three sons much property, including seventeen camels. In his will he stated that his oldest son should have half of his estate, the second son one third of his estate, and his youngest son one ninth of it. Most of the properties were easily divided according to the provisions of the will, but the sons could find no way of dividing the seventeen camels into three parts, one of which would be one half, one of which would be one third, and the remaining part one ninth.

They went to wise man after wise man to ask for advice about how to accomplish this division. Finally they went to the Caliph Ali,[4] the wisest of all men alive. He said, "This is very simple. Here is the way to do it," and he proceeded to explain his plan to them. "I shall give you a camel for one day. Then you will have eighteen camels. The oldest son will now get nine camels, one half of this number; the second son will receive six camels, one third of this number; and the youngest son will receive two camels, one ninth of this number. This will total seventeen camels, the number your father left to you. Then you will bring me back my camel, and we shall all be satisfied, including your father."

2.

The Guessing Children [5]

Once there was a man who had three sons. He called them to him one day and told them that he would soon die. "I want to distribute my property among you," he said, "but I fear that I shall not be able to do it justly. Before your mother died, she said that one of you was not my son and should not inherit any of my lands but only some money. But she would not tell me which of you it was, and I cannot decide. When I die, you are to go to the kadi [6] of the next village and have him divide the property fairly. He is a wise man and will know which of you to dispossess from my lands." A short while after talking thus with his sons, the man died and was buried.

The three brothers packed some food and set out for the neighboring village where the kadi lived. On the way they came across the footprints of a camel. The eldest brother said, "A camel has passed this way."

The second brother said, "But the camel had only one eye."

The youngest brother then added, "And, besides, this camel had one tooth missing."

The eldest brother said, "This camel was probably stolen from its owner." They walked on a little farther, and when they came to a place where the camel had lain on the ground, the eldest brother spoke again. "The camel's load consisted of butter on one side and honey on the other."

The second brother said, "The camel's tail was cut off; it had only a stump for a tail."

The youngest brother looked about the spot carefully and then said this: "There was a pregnant woman riding on the camel's back."

Then, having rested for a while, they continued on their journey. A little farther along the way they met a Yürük [7] carrying his heavy felt overcoat over his shoulder. This Yürük asked the three brothers whether they had seen a camel.

"Was the camel blind in one eye?" they asked.

"Yes," said the Yürük, "he was."

"Is the camel you are looking for missing one tooth?"

"Yes."

"Was it stolen from its owner?"

"Yes."

"Was it loaded with butter and honey?"

"Yes."

"Was there a pregnant woman riding on the camel?"

"Yes, yes. Now tell me where I can find my camel, good men."

"We don't know where it is," they all answered at once.

The Yürük could not believe this, and he said to the brothers, "You know all about my camel, and yet you say that you do not know where it is. Tell me, at least, where you saw it."

"We have not seen it, efendi," answered the eldest brother.

The Yürük then became very angry with the three brothers, and he got up and left them where they were sitting by the road. He went to the nearby village and went to the very judge the three brothers were seeking, and he complained to the judge about their suspicious behavior.

While he was still talking to the judge, the three brothers arrived, and when all four were present before him, the judge addressed the brothers:

"This man has made a complaint against you. You described his camel accurately for him, but then you told him that you had never seen this camel. How can this be?"

"Efendi, we didn't see the camel, but we knew what it looked like from various signs," said the eldest brother.

"How did you know it was blind in one eye?" asked the judge.

The second brother said to the judge, "Efendi, there was corn growing on both sides of the road, but the camel ate from only one side. I concluded that it must have been blind and didn't see the corn on the other side."

"That was a reasonable guess," said the judge, "but how did you know that it had a tooth missing?"

"When the camel cropped grass," said the youngest, "there was always a small tuft of grass left where it had bitten. That is how I knew it must have a tooth missing."

"Very well," said the judge, "but how did you know that the camel had a bobbed tail?"

"Efendi," said the second brother, "wherever the camel left droppings along the trail they were always in a single heap. If the camel had a long tail, it would be swishing off flies in this hot weather. If it were swishing off flies, it would scatter the droppings, and they would not then fall in one heap."

"How did you know that one saddlebag was loaded with honey and the other with butter?"

"I saw," said the eldest brother, "that all along the road there were bees on one side where some drops of honey had oozed down, and on the other side were ants where melted butter had dripped."

"How did you know that the woman who was riding on the camel's back was pregnant?" asked the judge.

"Because she dismounted often to urinate," said the youngest, "and in order to get up each time she pressed her hands heavily upon the earth."

"That may be," agreed the judge, but he was still not satisfied with the innocence of the brothers, and he decided upon one more test. He had a chest with a locked drawer, and when the brothers went to drink water, he opened this drawer, put an orange in it, and then he locked the drawer again. When the brothers returned, he placed the chest in front of them and said, "If you can tell me what is in that locked drawer, I shall acquit you at once."

The eldest brother shook the chest and said, "The object in this box is a round one."

The second brother said, "If it is round, then it is yellow."

And the youngest brother said, "If it is yellow, then it is an orange."

The judge then opened the locked drawer, and to the surprise of all those standing about the place, they saw that it was an orange inside. Then the judge said to the Yürük, "Go and search for your own camel. These men have not seen it."

The judge then went to his wife and said to her, "Cook a good meal for three men who are visiting me. Buy a lamb and make kebab,[8] and have fresh bread baked, and buy some pekmez."[9] And later, when all this food was prepared, he had it placed before the three brothers. But he did not sit down to eat with them. Instead, he hid behind the door to overhear their conversation.

The eldest of the brothers took a piece of meat, and immediately after biting it, said, "What a pity! This was a good lamb, but it was fed with dog's milk."

The second brother took a piece of bread, dipped it into the gravy, and said, "This was good bread, but unfortunately the woman who baked it was menstruating."

The youngest said, "This judge is a good judge, but unfortunately he was a bastard."

When the meal was finished, the pekmez was served, and the eldest brother tasted it and then said, "This is good pekmez, but unfortunately the root of the vine which produced the grapes for it grew in a grave."

The judge had been behind the door all during the meal, and after the plates were taken away by his servants, the judge left the house quietly and went immediately to the house of his mother. He said to her, "Mother, tell me the truth. Whose son am I?" And he drew his dagger and held it against her breast.

"The man you have always called your father was very rich," said his mother, "but he had a partner who was an infidel. When we did not have any sons, I was afraid that the infidel would outlive my husband and thus inherit all his wealth for himself and his son. To prevent this, I bought you from the infidel at a very high price."

When his mother had finished her story, and when he was satisfied with her explanation, he took his dagger from her breast and sheathed it. Then he went to the shepherd from whom his wife had bought the lamb, and he asked the shepherd, "On what did you feed the lamb which you sold to my wife?"

"Efendi," replied the shepherd, "I had a female dog with pups. I used to carry the lamb and the pups together. The lamb's mother had died, and therefore it sucked milk from the pups' mother."

Then the judge returned to his own house and asked his wife, "Was the woman who baked the bread today menstruating?"

"Yes," his wife said, "she was."

Having heard this, the judge went back to the three brothers. He told them that he had overheard what they had said while they ate their meal, and he said that he had verified most of their comments.

"How did you know that the lamb was fed with dog's milk?" he asked.

The eldest brother replied, "When we chewed bread with the meat, it turned into little lumps. That's how I knew."

"How did you know that the woman who baked the bread was menstruating?"

"When fresh and pure bread is dipped into gravy, it absorbs the gravy. But this bread hardly soaked up the gravy at all. That's how I knew that the woman who baked it was unclean," said the second brother.

"How did you know that the grapes for the pekmez came from a vine that had roots in a grave?"

"It was good pekmez, efendi," said the eldest brother, "but when we ate it, we had the taste of human flesh on our palates."

Finally, the judge turned to the youngest brother and said to him, "How could you tell that I was an illegitimate son?"

"Efendi, forgive my words. If you had been a legitimate son, you would have sat beside strangers while they ate and talked with them, even if you did not wish food for yourself."

The judge was surprised but satisfied with these answers. After a few minutes he said, "Young men, now tell me what it is that brings you here to me."

The eldest brother said to the judge, "Efendi, my father, who is now dead, sent you his greetings before he died and asked that you divide his property among us, for you would be able to decide which of us is not a true heir and should therefore be dispossessed of lands."

The judge looked from one son to another and thought about this problem. He said nothing for some time, and being unable to offer any solution, he said, "Let me go home and think about this and look in my books."

At home the judge had a very difficult time. He found nothing at all in his books that would help in the solving of such a problem. He was sweating as if he were in a Turkish bath. This judge had a beautiful daughter who noticed that her father looked perplexed. "What is the matter with you, father? You seem to be upset by something."

"I am trying to divide the property of a friend of mine, now dead, among his children. He has three sons and one of them is to be excluded from the inheritance of lands for he is not a legitimate heir, but which it is I cannot discover."

"Father, will you let me go near these young men? If they are sons of your friend, they will not harm me."

The judge hesitated, but then he said, "All right. After all, you are not a pear that they can eat. You go and try to solve the problem."

The girl put on her finest dress, and she put on her jewelry, and she decorated herself the best she could. She went to where the young men were and said, "Welcome, friends," and they accepted her greeting.

"Since you are my father's guests," she said, "I am going to tell you a story to make the time pass. Once my father gave my hand to the son of a rich man. I was engaged to him for over a year, and we were together all of the time. One day our fathers quarreled. My father broke off the engagement, and I was separated from my fiancé.

"My father then engaged me to the son of another rich man. Just as I was being taken to the house of my husband, after we were married, my old lover turned up and said to me, 'You have given me your word. What are you doing now?'

" 'Well, what can I do?' I asked. 'My father has given me to another man in marriage, but I shall keep my word to you. I shall meet you at the corner of the coppersmith's house at midnight tonight before I go to bed with my husband.'

"When I got to my husband's house, I told him that I had had a former fiancé whom I had agreed to meet and that I had given my word to do this. 'I want to go and see him at midnight. Will you let me go? I shall be back as soon as possible.'

"My husband was an honest man and very religious, and when he heard that I had given my word to see my former fiancé, he permitted me to go and speak with this man."

The judge's daughter now turned to the eldest of the three brothers and said, "Suppose that you were my former fiancé. What would you have done when I met you at midnight by the coppersmith's house?"

"I should have talked with you for a while," said the eldest brother, "and then I should have let you go."

Then she turned to the second brother and asked him the same question. "I should have done the same as my elder brother," he said.

Finally, she asked the youngest brother, "What would you have done?"

The youngest brother glared at her and said, "I should have stripped you of all your clothes and jewelry and done every conceivable offense to you. I should have robbed you and raped you and then sent you back to your husband."

"Very well," said the judge's daughter, "your problem is solved. You two elder brothers should inherit your father's lands, and the youngest should be dispossessed." [10]

Upon hearing this, the youngest brother said, "Your father may have been a bastard, but you are certainly your father's daughter!"

3.

Stuck to Some Great Door [11]

Once there was and once there wasn't in the olden days, when the sieve was in the hay, when the camel was an auctioneer, and when I was rocking my father's cradle *tingir mingir,* there was a keloghlan.

One night Keloghlan saw a saint in his dream, and the saint said, "You, fellow, can't be any good this way. Tomorrow morning, as soon as you get up, go and get yourself stuck to some great door [12] and your life's work will be there. You'll earn your living there."

The next morning as soon as he got up he got on his way. He went

119

and went, and looked at many doors. But none of them seemed to please him. Finally he came to the gates of the palace in Istanbul.[13] "Well," he said, "I've found my door." He got some tar on the back of his clothes and got himself stuck on the door by his robe.

In the morning the gardener of the palace came to the gate. He opened the gate, and when he saw Keloghlan stuck on the gate he became frightened and began to shout. "What is this stuck on the door?" said he.

Keloghlan began to laugh, and he said, "Oh, I have been able to frighten somebody."

The gardener said, "What is this that you do here?"

And Keloghlan said, "Well, I got stuck on the door, and I'll never get away from here."

"You must go away from here," said the gardener.

And Keloghlan said, "No, I won't go anywhere else. This is a palace and I can work here, and you can't make me go away."

All this noise was heard inside the palace, and the padishah said, "What's all this noise? Bring this keloghlan to me, and let's see what's ailing him."

Keloghlan slipped out of his robe and went to the padishah. The padishah asked, "What's your name?"

Keloghlan answered, "My name is Ahmet, but they don't call me that. They call me Keloghlan."

"Well, then, what do you want, Keloghlan?"

Keloghlan said, "I had a dream, and in it a saint told me what to do, to get myself stuck to some great door, and there I would find my life's work. That's how I came to your door, and this is how I'm going to earn my living."

"All right," said the padishah. "Can you work in the kitchen and help the cook?"

"Certainly I can," said Keloghlan. And Keloghlan went down to the kitchen, and the cook showed him here and there little things to be done. So Keloghlan went to work in the kitchen.

One day the cook said to Keloghlan, "Now, look here. Whatever I tell you to do, you always do the opposite. This time be careful, or else I'll have to chase you out of my kitchen. I am going out to the market for some vegetables. While I am gone, you wash the dishes and arrange them nicely without breaking a single one." And the cook went out to market.

What Keloghlan did was to take the plates one by one and break them. Then he piled the pieces neatly in the cooking pot.[14]

When the cook came back, he said, "Have you done what I told you to do?"

Keloghlan said, "Certainly I did, and they are all arranged neatly in the pot."

When the cook looked, he found that all the plates were broken. "What have you done?" he shouted. "I won't keep you here any more. Get out!" And he chased Keloghlan out of the kitchen.

When the padishah heard the noise, he said, "What is it all about?"

The cook said, "I have had enough of him. Take him away from me."

"All right," said the padishah. "Bring him to me."

The padishah said to Keloghlan, "Now listen to me, son. You are going to stay with me. Only when I go to sleep, you'll make no noise, and you'll see to it that nobody else makes any noise, either."

"All right," said Keloghlan.

"Fine," said the padishah. "Now go and bring me a glass of water."

Keloghlan went and filled a glass with water and ran back. On the way back, he came up the stairs, and right across from the stairs there was a mirror. Keloghlan saw himself in the mirror. When he saw himself in the mirror, he thought it was someone else, and he said, "It was from *me* the padishah asked for a glass of water. Why do you hurry before me?" When he saw his image repeating his own actions, he began to quarrel with it. He shouted and shouted at his image. Finally he became so angry that he threw the glass at him, and of course the mirror broke.

When the padishah heard the noise, he came out and said, "What's all this noise about?"

Keloghlan said, "I was bringing you the glass of water. Why did he try to do it before I did?"

"Oh," said the padishah. "Haven't you ever seen a mirror before?"

"A mirror? What is a mirror?" asked Keloghlan.

The padishah took him to a mirror and showed him his own image. "When you saw him bringing the water, it was only you," he explained.

"Oh," said Keloghlan. "Now I know. I won't do it again."

"Now," said the padishah, "I'll go to sleep. See to it that nobody makes any noise and nobody wakes me up." And the padishah went to sleep.

While the padishah slept, everything was quiet except the clock on the wall, which ticked away. Tick-tock-tick-tock, it said. Keloghlan began to give orders to the clock. "Be quiet," he said. "Don't you know the padishah is trying to sleep? Stop that noise! Don't you hear me?" he shouted. "And the more I say, the more you tick-tock!" Finally Keloghlan became so angry that he took the clock down off the wall and smashed it on the floor.

The padishah jumped up in his sleep, frightened by the noise.

"Sir," Keloghlan explained, "you told me to keep everything quiet, but that clock wouldn't listen to me. That's why I gave it what it deserved!"

And the padishah said, "Oh, son, it cannot stop. That's its duty, to show what time it is — to tell the night and day."

"All right," said Keloghlan, "I won't do it again."

After a few days, a representative came from a foreign country which intended to declare war on the padishah's country. The representa-tive said to the padishah, "I will ask some questions in signs, and if these questions are answered correctly, then we won't wage war against you.[15] The opposite party will answer in signs, too, and we must be apart from each other. I will be on one minaret, and your representative will be on another minaret. Remember, if the answers aren't correct, then we're at war."

The padishah said, "What sort of thing is this? I must think about this before I answer. What shall I do about this? If I ask a clever man, he won't see any sense in this. He'll think it's stupid. If I put a dumb one there, his answers won't be of any use. What should I do?" And finally he thought of Keloghlan. "Well, *he'll* lay some eggs about it.[16] Let's see what he'll say about it." The padishah called Keloghlan and told him all about it. "You'll be on one minaret and he'll be on the other. You'll answer him in signs without saying a word."

"All right," said Keloghlan. "What's easier than that?"

The two representatives got up on the minarets. For the first sign, the foreign minister held up one finger. In answer Keloghlan held up two fingers. For the second sign, the minister held his arms out before his waist in a flat circle. In answer, Keloghlan bent his left arm at the elbow and put his right hand under his left elbow, to show one half of his arm. For the third sign, the minister held his right hand out with the fingers and thumb hanging down. Keloghlan answered by holding his right hand out with the fingers and thumb pointing up. "Well done," said the minister, and they got down from the minarets.

The padishah said to the minister, "Could you tell me, please, what the questions were?"

The minister answered, "First I said, 'There is one God.' And Keloghlan answered, 'Oh, but the Prophet makes two.' And then I said, 'The world is round.' And he answered, 'But half of it is water and half is land.' And last I said, 'The rains come from above.' And he answered, 'But the plants grow from the bottom up.' Keloghlan answered the questions correctly, so there will not be war between your country and mine." The foreign minister left to return to his own land.

Then the padishah asked Keloghlan what the questions and the answers were. "Well, sir," said Keloghlan, "first he said, '*I* am the mighty one around here.' And I answered, 'Behind me there are two.' He wanted to frighten me, and I showed him there were some to help me. Then he said, 'Here is a tray full of pilaf.' I answered, 'We shall provide the meat to go on top.' Then he said, 'We have five generals who will drop down on your land.' And to this I said, 'We have already planted in the ground five sharpened stakes on which to impale them.' "

Whether Keloghlan's answers were right or wrong, the padishah was pleased, for the boy had saved the country from a war. He said to Keloghlan, "You will always stay in this palace, but there must be no fighting, and you must always be good to others."

And Keloghlan replied, "Well, the saint was right, after all. This is what I dreamed, and this is where I shall stay all my life."

4.

The Many Dilemmas of the Padishah's Three Sons [17]

There was once an old padishah who was about to die. He called his oldest son to his bedside and said to him, "According to our tradition, you will inherit the throne when I am gone."

Not long after this, the padishah died, and, as it had been willed by him, his eldest son became the new padishah, and with the approval of his two brothers and his mother he sat upon the throne. One night shortly after he had become padishah, the young ruler had a dream in which he was told that he would go on a most adventurous journey and see many miracles before he returned home. When this dream was repeated for three nights, he left the throne temporarily to the older of his two brothers, filled a saddlebag with gold, mounted his horse, and set out on his journey.

He went a short way; he went a long way. He went over hills and dales, but he went straight, too, stirring up dust from the road like flour that is borrowed. [18] And when he looked back, he saw that he had gone only the length of a grain of barley. He finally reached a place where three roads branched off. One of these roads was marked with a sign that read, "Whoever goes will probably return." The second was marked, "Whoever goes will probably not return." And the sign on the third road read, "Nobody returns."

After reading these three signs, the boy talked to himself. "Anyone," he said, "can complete an easy journey. It is the task of the brave to choose the difficult." And so he took the road labeled "Nobody returns."

He traveled for a few days along this road and then he saw in the distance a high hill, but this hill was somewhat different from all the hills he had ever seen before. As he drew nearer to it, he realized that the hill was made entirely of human skulls.[19] Near this hill there was a city which he entered. Tying his horse in the courtyard of an inn, he took his saddlebag of gold with him and went to a barbershop. As he was leaving the shop he asked the barber, "Will you keep an eye on this saddlebag until I return?"

"Yes, of course," said the barber.

"May I ask you a question?" inquired the young man.

"Certainly," answered the barber.

"Where did that hill of skulls come from? How did it get there?"

Sighing deeply, the barber said, "Please don't ask me this question, for if I answer it, then, in the end, you too may leave your skull there. Don't make me be the cause of this."

But the young man insisted that he be told how the mound of skulls came to be there, and after a while, the barber gave in and told him the facts of the matter. "Our padishah has a daughter who became mute as a result of some strange disease. The padishah said that whoever could make his daughter talk again would receive her in marriage, along with a large dowry. Anyone who tried to cure her and failed would have his head cut off. Many have tried and failed, as you can see from the hill of skulls."

When the young man heard this explanation, he realized that what he had dreamed about now looked as if it might come true. Whatever was written on his forehead [20] was apparently now about to take place, for he decided to try to cure the girl himself. He wrote a petition to the padishah requesting that he be permitted to try to cure his daughter of her inability to talk. The padishah advised him not to take such a chance, and he said to him, "You look like a noble young man. I should be very sorry for you if you should fail."

"My blood is no redder than any other's," said the young man. "I shall try my luck and discover what is written on my forehead."

A khoja was called in and a wedding contract [21] was drawn up and signed, and then the young man began to do his utmost to make the girl talk. He had three days and three nights in which to do this, but although he spent all this time trying, he was unable to make her utter a single sound. Consequently, he was brought to the public square to be executed. When the executioners were about to chop off his head, they noticed that the young man was wearing a leather band on his upper arm, an indication of royalty. When it was discovered that he was the son of a ruler, the padishah stopped the execution and ordered that the young man be thrown in jail instead.

At home on the throne, the next oldest brother wondered why his eldest brother stayed away so long, and after wondering thus for some time, he decided to go and search for him. This middle brother called the youngest of the three to him and said, "I am giving the throne to you temporarily. I am going to search for our brother, and I shall not return without him."

After a long journey, he too came to the place where the three roads branched off, one marked "Whoever goes will probably return"; one marked "Whoever goes will probably not return"; and the third, "Nobody returns." Like his brother before him, he was a young man who preferred to undertake the difficult, and so he chose the road with the sign "Nobody returns."

Traveling along this road for a few days, he at last saw the huge hill of skulls in the distance, and he too was curious about it. He came to the inn where his brother had left his horse, and when he saw the animal he was glad, for he knew that he had indeed traced his elder brother. He left his horse at the same inn and then went to the barbershop, where he saw his brother's saddlebag hanging on the wall.

"What is the meaning of that huge hill of skulls that I saw as I entered the city?" he asked the barber.

"Young man, I cannot answer this question, for I do not want to be the cause of your death. A couple of months ago another young man, exactly like you, came and asked me the same question. You and he are like two halves of the same apple. His head was not chopped off because he was discovered to be the son of a padishah; they threw him in jail instead. I fear that the same thing, or worse, may befall you, and so I will not answer your question."

"But I came here to save my brother," the young man said, and he insisted so long that finally the barber told him the story of the padishah's daughter and the skulls of the young men who had failed to cure her.

The middle brother sent a petition to the padishah saying that he would like to try his luck in curing the speechless girl. The petition was granted, a khoja was called, a marriage contract signed, and the young man started to work. He tried for three nights in succession to make the padishah's daughter talk, but it was no use. As a result, he was also condemned to death, but his arm band was also discovered by the executioners. He too was recognized as the son of a ruler, and his sentence was changed to imprisonment, and he was thrown in jail with his elder brother.

When the youngest son of the padishah saw that the second brother failed to return too, he decided to go and search for his two brothers. His mother cried night and day when she heard this, with a handkerchief in each hand and her two eyes running like fountains.

The boy said to her, "Mother, I shall go and find my brothers."

"Your elder brothers are gone," she said, "and while I am burning with the grief of their loss, I do not want to risk losing you too. Please do not go."

But the youngest son was determined to search for his brothers, and so he said, "Mother, I am turning the throne over to you temporarily. You will rule the land while I am gone, and now, farewell." [22]

He took a saddlebag full of gold, mounted his horse, and set out in search of his brothers. Like them, he too came to the roads marked "Whoever goes will probably return," "Whoever goes will probably not return," and "Nobody returns." He chose the same road taken by his two brothers before him, and after he had ridden on and on, he at last saw in the distance the strange hill made of human skulls. He reined in at the same inn where his brothers had stopped, saw their horses in the courtyard, and tied his alongside theirs. Leaving his horse there, he took his saddlebag and went to the barbershop nearby. When he saw there the two saddlebags of his brothers, he hung his beside theirs, and then he sat down in the barber's chair for a haircut. While he was having his hair cut, he questioned the barber about the hill of skulls that he had seen upon entering the city.

"Two other young men have recently asked me that question," the barber said, "and their lot has been unfortunate."

"What was their lot?" asked the youngest brother.

At first the barber refused to say more, but when the young man insisted on learning about the lot of the two others who had come before him, the barber told him the story. "The daughter of our padishah has been unable to talk for many years. The padishah has promised both the girl and great wealth to anyone who can restore her ability to speak. Those who try and fail have their heads cut off and added to the hill of skulls."

"And were the two young men who recently tried to cure the girl executed?" asked the youngest brother.

"No, they were thrown in jail instead when it was discovered that they were the sons of rulers. The executioners saw that they were wearing the leather arm bands of royalty."

The young man said to the barber, "In all this city there must be someone who knows the remedy for the disability of the padishah's daughter. If you know of such a person, tell me where he may be found, and the three saddlebags of gold will be yours."

"I know of such a person," said the barber, "but he is a wise man with such great power that I am afraid to show you where he lives. If I tell you where he lives, my tongue will be cut out. If I show you by a look or a gesture, my eyes will be poked out. If I point at his house with my finger, my arm will be chopped off. So please don't ask me."

But the young man pleaded so hard that the barber could not resist forever, and so he said to the youngest brother, "This learned man lives on such-and-such a street, and I shall show you where he lives. I shall walk along that street and you follow me at a distance. When I come before his house, my foot will slip and I shall fall down. You will know then which house is his."

They went to that street, the barber ahead of the young man, and when he came to the house of the learned man, who was called Ahmet Efendi, he fell down. He got up immediately, brushed off his clothes, and went on his way. The young man went up to the door of this house and knocked and was admitted. When shown into the parlor of that house, he saw an old man sitting on a rug on the floor. He went to the old man, kissed his hand, and then touched it to his forehead. Kneeling before the old man, he said, "Efendi, I am in trouble. I am the son of a padishah, and I have come here to save my two brothers, who are in jail, by curing the daughter of the padishah of her inability to speak. I have heard that you are a very learned man. Will you teach me how to cure the girl?"

"All right, my son," said the old man; "since you have come to consult me, I consider it my duty to show the truth to those who seek my advice. Take this box. It is a talking box. As soon as you have entered the girl's room, hide this box somewhere. Then greet the place where you have hidden it, and it will answer you. After that, you can carry on a conversation with that place."

After leaving the wise man's house with the box, the youngest brother wrote a petition to the padishah requesting permission to try his hand at curing the girl. The petition was granted, the khoja was called, a marriage contract was signed, and the young man was led to the room of the padishah's daughter. Many of the palace women were secretly listening through a door to see whether or not the girl would at last talk.

When the young man entered the girl's room, he immediately slipped the box he had brought into a bookcase near the door. "Selamünaleyküm, O Bookcase," he said.

"Aleykümselam, my young guest," answered the bookcase. "Come in and sit down."

The young man sat down and then he said to the bookcase, "Dear Bookcase, the nights are very long. Let us tell stories to one another to pass the time away."

"But you are my guest here," said the bookcase, "and it is not proper to tire guests by making them tell stories. Let me tell you a story."

"All right, let us hear it, then," said the young man, and the bookcase told the following story.

"Once there were three friends, a tailor, a carpenter, and a khoja. They became acquainted with each other while they were on a journey. One day they walked until dark, and then, since there was no village in sight, they decided to spend the night in a cave by the roadside. They entered the cave, covered the mouth of the cave with a large stone, and built a fire to keep themselves warm. One of them suggested that they take turns staying awake to keep guard while the others slept, and they agreed to this.

"The carpenter was the first to be on watch, and while his two friends slept he stayed awake. For something to do to while away the time, he took his adze from his belt and started to carve a log which lay in the cave. By the time his watch was over, he had carved from that log a statue of a girl. When the time came for the tailor to be on guard, the carpenter woke him up and then went to sleep himself.

"When the tailor saw the wooden statue of the girl, he said to himself, 'Look at what the carpenter has made! If he has done this, then I, in my turn, should make a dress for the statue.' He cut a piece from the lining of his overcoat and with it made a pretty dress for the girl. He put the dress on the statue and then stood it against the wall of the cave. When the khoja's turn came to watch, the tailor awoke him and then went to sleep himself.

"When the khoja saw that the carpenter had carved a statue of a girl and that the tailor had made a dress for her, he thought it his duty to try

128

to give life to this wooden girl. He immediately made ablutions [23] and then prayed to God to endow the statue with life. All at once, the girl became alive and started to walk around the cave talking like a nightingale.[24] In the morning when the khoja's two friends got up they were surprised to see a living girl. She was, of course, the product of all three of them."

Having finished its story, the bookcase addressed itself to the young man again: "My dear guest, here is a dilemma. To which of the three friends would you have given this girl?"

"I would give her to the carpenter," said the young man, "for it was he who laid the foundation for what they made."

"True," said the bookcase, "but it would be very awkward to travel with a nude girl. I would give her to the tailor."

When the padishah's daughter heard these answers to the dilemma, she jumped up and said, "Nonsense! I would give her to the khoja. What would be the use of a piece of dead wood covered with a piece of cloth? It was the khoja who gave her life, and he should have her."

This was the first time in many years that the padishah's daughter had said anything. The palace women who were listening outside the door clapped their hands and raised a cry, shouting, "The padishah's daughter has spoken! The padishah's daughter has spoken!"

When the padishah heard their outcry, he rushed to the room and asked, "Did she really talk?" He did not believe that she had spoken, and so he examined his daughter to see whether she could talk. "Did you really talk, my dear?" But the girl would not say a single word.

"It doesn't matter, sir," said the young man. "I still have two nights more in which to try."

As the young man left the girl's room, he quietly took the talking box from the bookcase and put it in his pocket. After he had gone, the padishah's daughter took an ax and smashed the bookcase into pieces. When the young man came to the room next day, he saw what she had done to the bookcase, and so this time he put the talking box on a table and then greeted the table as if it were a person: "Selamünaleyküm, O Table!"

"Aleykümselam, O young man!" said the table.

After talking with each other for a few minutes, the young man said, "Oh, Brother Table, the nights are very long. Let us tell tales to one another to pass away the time."

"You are a guest here," said the table, "and so it is my duty to entertain you with a story."

129

"All right, then, go ahead," he said, and the table told the following story.

"There were three cousins once, and one of their uncles had a beautiful daughter. Each of the cousins wanted to marry the beautiful girl, and the father did not know what to do. If he gave her to any one of the cousins, the other two would certainly be offended. He thought to test them to decide which would get the girl, and so he said, 'Whichever of you can bring me 500 pieces of gold will receive my daughter.'

"The three cousins set out for different parts of the country in search of work which would pay them the necessary money. All three worked hard and each earned 500 pieces of gold. When the first cousin was about to return to his village, he heard a town crier announcing the sale of a wonderful device which, when placed on the ground, would tell the news from all over the world. The price of this device was exactly 500 pieces of gold, and so the young man spent all his money for it.

"In the town where the second cousin was working, there was a rug being sold. When anyone stood on this rug and touched it with a magic stick that came with it, the rug would fly into the air and carry him to any place that he wished. All he would have to do was close his eyes, touch the stick to the rug, wish where he wanted to go, and he would find himself there when he opened his eyes again. This rug cost 500 pieces of gold, and the second cousin used all his money to buy it.

"The third cousin heard that there was a magical bead to be sold in the town where he was working. He asked what power the bead had, and he was told that it would cure any disease when placed on the forehead of the patient. The third cousin thought this a very valuable object to have, and so he bought it with the 500 pieces of gold which he had earned.

"The three started home, and along the way, they met, and so traveled along together. The one who had the device for getting news from all over the world was asked by the others to try it and see what the daughter of their uncle was doing. He placed it on the ground and put his ear to it. It said to him, 'By God, the girl is very sad, for your uncle is gravely ill. One doctor leaves and another comes, and your uncle is about to give out his last breath.'

"The cousin who had the magic rug was asked to carry them all back to their own village. 'All right,' he said, 'climb on the rug and close your eyes.' He hit the rug with the magic stick. It left the ground and immediately afterwards it landed right near their uncle's front door.

"They walked in and saw at once that their uncle was near death.

The cousin with the magic bead placed it on his uncle's head, saying, 'In the name of God, be well,' and the sick man began at once to recover."

Having finished this story, the table addressed itself to the young man again and said, "Now, my young guest, here is a dilemma. If you had been the uncle, to whom would you have given the girl?"

Without hesitating, the young man answered, "I should have given her to the cousin who had the device for getting news from all over the world, for if they hadn't heard of the uncle's illness, they would not have gone so quickly to cure him."

"No," said the table, "I should have given her to the cousin with the magic rug. What would have been the use of getting the news if they had been unable to reach the uncle until after his funeral?"

When the padishah's daughter heard them arguing in this way, she said, "You are both wrong! You are both wrong! Suppose they did get the news of their uncle's illness, and suppose that they did reach his bedside before he died. Of what use would that have been if they had not had the magic bead with which to cure him? I should have given her to the third cousin." [25]

When the girl started to talk, the palace women listening at the door called the padishah at once, and he reached the spot while she was still speaking. He agreed that the girl had been cured of her inability to speak, and so he gave her to the youngest son and freed his two older brothers from prison.

On the way back to their own kingdom, the brothers discovered that the girl's inability to talk had recurred. She would not say a word. The three brothers were so annoyed at her that they drew their swords and were going to cut her throat. They noticed, however, that she was choking and straining in an attempt to do something. Finally a large rat jumped out of her throat, and they killed this rat, and then she began to talk like a nightingale.

They then proceeded on their journey home, and at last they reached their palace, where they were greeted by their mother. They were all very happy, but they were faced with a dilemma: Which of them should have the girl? They had all contributed to curing her and bringing her here, and there began a great discussion among all the people at the palace as to which should have the girl. But their mother said, "I shall settle this dilemma at once. The youngest shall have her, for he not only cured the girl but he saved my other two sons as well." Everyone agreed to the justice of this decision, and so a gorgeous wedding was held for the girl and the youngest son, after which they all lived happily forever.

5.

The Auspicious Dream [26]

Once there was a man who had a son. In order to educate his son, this man could afford a private tutor, and so he hired one. The teacher said to the boy one day, "When you dream, don't tell it to anybody unless he says first, 'May your dream be an auspicious one.' " [27] This lesson constituted one of the most important subjects that the tutor suggested to the student, and he repeated this lesson to him every day for several days.

Later, after the child had completed his training with this tutor, he had a dream one night. He told his mother in the morning, "I had a dream last night."

"Let us hear it," said the mother.

"No, I cannot tell you."

"Let us hear it," insisted the mother.

"No, I can't tell you," said the boy. Since the boy refused to tell the dream he had, in spite of his mother's insistence, she gave him a good beating.

The boy went to his father crying. The father asked the child, "What is the matter? Why are you crying?"

"I had a dream last night and Mother beat me because I wouldn't tell her."

"Well," said the father, "let us hear about the dream."

When the boy refused to answer, the father insisted, "Tell me what the dream was!"

The boy refused again and he got a good beating from his father this time. The boy then went to his teacher crying. "Why are you crying, son?"

"I am crying because I had a dream last night and I refused to tell it to my mother and she beat me. Then I refused to tell it to my father, and he beat me too."

The teacher had by this time forgotten what he had taught his pupil about telling dreams. He also said to the boy, "Well, let us hear what sort of dream it was." Because the teacher did not say, "May it be an auspicious one," the boy refused to tell the dream to him. Once again he got a good beating for this refusal. Crying, the boy went by himself to the public square, where there was a large crowd gathered.

In the crowd the boy saw the padishah of Turkey and his wise men sitting. The padishah of Turkey had received a stick from a foreign padishah with a message that war would be declared on Turkey if the Turkish padishah could not determine which end of the stick came from the base of the tree from which it was cut and which end of the stick came from the higher part of the tree from which it was cut. "If you can answer this riddle," said the foreign padishah's messenger, "there will be no difficulty between our countries. If you cannot answer, then there will be war." The padishah of Turkey and all his vezirs were trying to determine which end of the stick came from the base of the tree. The boy watched them for a while. Nobody in the crowd was able to guess which end of the stick was from the base.

Finally the boy said, "I can tell which end of the stick is from the base of the tree."

Thinking that the child might perhaps have an answer, they permitted him to try. The boy asked that a pool be built there. When the pool was built and filled with water, the boy threw the stick into the pool and said, "The end which sinks is the end closest to the base of the tree from which it was cut. The end which stands up in the water will be from the tip of the tree."

After this solution was arrived at, the padishah of Turkey marked the stick accordingly, and sent it back to the foreign padishah saying that the problem had been solved. Upon this, the foreign padishah sent another puzzle. He sent two mares. "Which of these horses is the mother?" The horses looked exactly alike, and there was no way to distinguish their age. Many people tried to solve the problem about which was the mother, but all of them failed. Then the boy volunteered and said that he could tell which was which. Again the padishah permitted him to try.

The boy mixed some barley with some gravel. He divided the mixture into two parts and he gave it to the two horses to eat. He then asked everybody to go to bed for the night and come the next day to see the results of this experiment. As it turned out, the older horse ate the complete mixture in the feedbag, gravel and all. The younger horse, with better teeth, had been able to pick out only the barley and leave the gravel there. Again the Turkish padishah, who was very happy, sent the answer to this problem to the foreign padishah.

Finally another letter came from the foreign padishah with one more problem to solve. The foreign padishah ordered the Turkish padishah to have made for his troops a set of marble uniforms. The Turkish padishah started thinking deeply as to how he could perform this task. He and his vezirs thought for a long while but could not arrive at a way of making marble uniforms. Desperate, at last, he thought about the wise boy again and he wondered if he could solve this problem too. He had him called to his presence for this purpose.

When the boy arrived he asked the padishah, "Efendi, why are you thinking so deeply?"

The padishah answered, "Well, they want me to make marble uniforms for my troops. I do not know how marble uniforms can be made."

The boy took a pen and paper from the hands of one of the padishah's vezirs, and he wrote on the paper this message to the foreign padishah, "Your majesty, we have cut the cloth for the marble uniforms, but we do not have the right thread to sew them. Will you please send us the right kind of waxed thread for sewing marble uniforms?"

When this letter reached the court of the foreign padishah, the learned men there thought that there must be a very great genius indeed in the Turkish court, and they decided to invite him to their country in order to learn some of his scientific knowledge. One of them wrote a letter to the Turkish padishah asking him to let whoever that genius was come to the country as their guest.

When the boy was informed of the invitation, he said that he would go, but only on the condition that he be given a camel, a goat, and a cat. A camel, a goat, and a cat were found for the boy. He placed the cat and the goat on the back of the camel and strapped them there. Then he set out to journey to the land of the foreign padishah. When he arrived in the strange country, great crowds were waiting for him in the city streets. People lined the streets because they wanted to have a glimpse of the Turkish genius. When they saw, however, that he was only a child, they were disappointed. To the man who said, "You are very small to be a genius," the boy responded, pointing to the camel, "He is very large. You could ask him."

To the man who said to him, "You have no mustache," he pointed to the cat and said, "He has a mustache. You can ask him."

To the man who said, "But this genius has no beard," the boy pointed at the goat and said, "He has a beard. Ask him what you want to know!" In this manner he passed through the huge crowd in the city and finally reached the presence of the foreign padishah.

This padishah had had his wise men design a contraption which would automatically send flying through the air into the chair next to him anybody who stepped on the machine. When the boy stepped on this spring contraption, he suddenly found himself sitting next to the padishah, but he said nothing at all about the ingenious gadget. A little later, a mechanical girl brought coffee to the padishah and to his young Turkish visitor. After taking a cup of coffee from the tray in the hand of the mechanical girl, the young man commented, "She is a beautiful girl, but it is a pity that she has no life!"

The foreign padishah, observing the calm manner of the young man, began to realize how intelligent he was. The padishah decided to give his own daughter to him in marriage. There was a long wedding, after which the young man stayed a year in the court of the foreign padishah. He then asked his father-in-law to let him and his wife go to Turkey. Permission was granted. When he returned to Turkey he visited the Turkish padishah, who gave him his own daughter.

The boy said to the Turkish padishah, "But I already have a wife."

The Turkish padishah answered, "That doesn't matter. One wife can pour water on your hands, and the other can hold the towel for you." [28]

The young man laughed when he heard this proposal. "Why did you laugh? Did I say something funny?" asked the Turkish padishah.

"No, not really. But once I had a dream, and what you said reminded me of it."

When the Turkish padishah heard the boy say that he had had a dream, the padishah said, "May it be an auspicious one." Then the young man proceeded to tell him what the dream was.

"Once I dreamed that the moon came up and entered my bed from the right-hand side. Then a short while afterwards the sun came up and entered my bed from the left-hand side. Perhaps that is why my foreign bride is named Ay and why my new Turkish bride is named Günesh." [29]

When the girls heard him tell about this dream, they both jumped up and embraced him.

6.

The Daughters of the Broom Thief [30]

Once there was and once there wasn't, a man had three daughters whom he was unable to support. In order to feed them, he went to the palace of the padishah each day and stole three brooms; he sold the brooms, and with the money he bought food. After a while this became a regular practice with him, and he ceased doing any other work at all.

The palace attendants noticed that each day three brooms were missing, and finally one of them reported this to the padishah: "Your majesty, three brooms disappear each day from the palace, but we cannot discover who takes them."

"We shall set a trap to catch the man," said the padishah. Then he ordered his vezir to hide a soldier near every broom in the palace in order to catch the thief. In this way the man was finally caught and brought to the presence of the padishah.

"Your majesty, this is the man who has stolen all the brooms," the attendants said.

Looking at the man, the padishah said, "You are a fine, strong man. Why do you steal?"

"Your majesty, I have three daughters whom I cannot support. I sold the brooms that I stole from the palace in order to buy food for them. I could not help this."

"Only if your daughters are in an advanced state of pregnancy could this kind of theft be pardoned. If you do not bring them to me in that condition within three days, I shall have you hanged."

The man went home, sat down, held his head between his hands, and thought about what he should do. As he sat there pondering, his oldest daughter came to him and asked, "Father, why are you thinking so deeply?"

"Unless I take you and your two sisters in a state of pregnancy before the padishah within three days, I shall be hanged."

"Oh, is that it?" said the girl. "I thought perhaps the butcher had sent a matchmaker to ask for my hand."

After a while the second daughter came and asked, "Father, why are you thinking so deeply?"

"Go away, you dog! You will say the same sort of thing as your sister did."

"No, I won't, father. Why are you thinking so deeply?"

"Unless I take you and your two sisters in a state of pregnancy before the padishah within three days, I shall be hanged."

"Oh, is that it?" said the girl. "I thought perhaps the son of the boatmaker had sent a matchmaker to ask for me in marriage." (He was a boatmaker at whom the second daughter had once winked.)

The second daughter went away, and finally the youngest daughter came to her father and asked, "What are you thinking about, father?"

"Get out of here! You will act in the same thoughtless way your two sisters have. Go away!"

"No, I won't, father. Tell me your trouble and perhaps I can help you."

"Unless I take you and your two sisters in a state of pregnancy before the padishah within three days, I shall be hanged."

"Don't worry about that, father. It is easy," said the youngest daughter. "Go and buy three kilos of cotton wool."

The man went out and bought three kilos of cotton wool. The girl then stuffed a kilo of this under the shirt of her older sister and a kilo under the shirt of her second sister, and finally she shoved a kilo under her own shirt. "Now we have become pregnant," she said. "Take us before the padishah."

When the man presented himself at the palace, the padishah asked, "Have you brought your daughters along?"

"Yes, I have, your majesty."

"Then call in the oldest daughter." The oldest daughter was brought in, her belly almost touching her chin, and she stood before the padishah. "What wish can I grant you, my girl?" he asked.

"I want to marry the butcher," she said.

"Take her out," said the padishah to his attendants, "find out which butcher she wants to marry, and see that she is married to him."

When the second daughter was brought in, the padishah asked her, "What wish can I grant you, my girl?"

"I want to marry the son of the boatmaker," she said.

"Take her out," said the padishah, "find out which boatmaker she wishes to marry, and see that she is married to him."

Then it was the turn of the youngest daughter. She came into the room with her belly up to her nose. Just as before, the padishah asked, "What wish can I grant you, my girl?"

"You cannot give me what I want," answered the youngest daughter.

"Why don't you speak your wish? You are the daughter of a broom thief and I am the padishah. It would be a shame upon me if I could not give you what you want."

"But you would not be able to find it, your majesty."

"You just name it," said the padishah.

"Very well, then. I want watercress from the sea, lemons from a poplar tree, and oranges in the winter. Those are the things I wish."

"Why don't you wish for something sensible? Is it possible to have watercress in the sea, lemons from a poplar tree, or oranges in winter?"

137

"Your majesty, is it possible to bring three girls here nine months pregnant in three days?" asked the youngest daughter.

The padishah thought about this. Then he ordered that the broom thief be given a job at the palace and the girl be sent home. A little while later the padishah sent two of his attendants to the youngest daughter with two parcels. "Take these to the girl and report to me everything that she says," said the padishah.

The two attendants went to the home of the former broom thief and knocked on the door. The youngest daughter called through the door, "Who is it?"

"Tell your father to come out," said one attendant.

"My father is in the roses," she said.

"Let your older sister come out, then," they said.

"My older sister has gone to make one thing two," she answered.

"Well, then, let your second sister come out," they said.

"She has gone to make the ugly beautiful," answered the girl.

"What have you been doing?"

"Well, I have just finished cooking up and down," she said.

"What are you doing now?"

"I have a four-footed horse and horseshoes but I have no nails to fasten them and no way to get nails."

One of the attendants said to the girl, "We have left the things you wanted on the steps, from where you can get them after we leave." They left the parcels on the doorstep and started to leave.

The girl opened the door quickly, took the parcels, and unwrapped them quickly. Then she raised the window and shouted after the attendants, "Come back! Come back!"

"What are you saying, madam?" they asked her.

"Take greetings from the hawk to the falcon. From time to time things are revealed to the dung-spattered crow. Our time was twelve years, and has it now been reduced to ten?"

The attendants asked each other if they had heard all of this correctly. Then they went to the padishah to report what she had said. "We have delivered the parcels, your majesty."

"What did she say?" asked the padishah.

"When we asked her to send her father out, she said that he was in the roses."

"Ah," said the padishah, "he must be working in my rose garden."

"Then we said, 'Let your older sister come out,' but she said, 'My older sister has gone to make one thing two.' "

"I see," said the padishah. "She has gone as midwife to deliver a child."

"Then we asked her to send out her second sister, and she said, 'She has gone to make the ugly beautiful.' "

"She had probably gone to have the hair taken from her face, then," said the padishah, for he knew that this was an expression used when hair is pulled out with resin patches.

"We asked her what she was doing, and she answered, 'I have just finished cooking up and down.' "

"Ah, that means that she had been cooking lentil soup," said the padishah.

"Then we asked, 'What are you doing now?' and she answered, 'I have a four-footed horse and horseshoes but I have no nails to fasten them and no way to get nails.' "

"Ah, I see," said the padishah. "She was embroidering. The four-footed horse was the embroidery board; the horseshoes were sequins; and the nails were the silver threads used for sewing on sequins. Did she say anything else to you?"

"As we were leaving, she called us back and said, 'Take greetings from the hawk to the falcon. From time to time things are revealed to the dung-spattered crow. Our time was twelve years, and has it now been reduced to ten?' "

"You scoundrels!" said the padishah to his two attendants. "She is the hawk, I am the falcon, and you are the filthy scavengers. The twelve years represent the twelve pieces of gold which I sent to her, but you delivered only ten. Return the other two pieces of gold to her. Then buy silver thread so that she can sew sequins on her wedding gown." [31] A wedding was then held for forty days and forty nights, and the daughter of the broom thief became the wife of the padishah, and the two lived happily ever after.

PART III

Humorous Tales

Apparently no culture is without its humor, and that of the Turks has its full share, for folk laughter flows from every coffee house door. Clearly humor is a contributing factor in a number of tales listed under other headings in this collection — under Anecdotes, under Moralistic Tales, and, to a lesser degree, under Perplexities and Ingenious Deductions — but here it exists entirely for itself. It will be noted that after the first two tales in this section, the rest are about clever, stupid, and naïve people, about tricksters, *dummkopfs* or sillies, and rustics.

The cleverest of the clever people come from the city of Kayseri,[1] and in Turkey "Kayseri Man" is an epithet for a sharp dealer. "He can't read or write, but he comes from Kayseri" is a proverbial warning. There are various accounts about why there are no Jews in Kayseri, each involving a battle of wits in which a Jew is bested by a resident of this city. There is even a tale — it is similar to one told in England and America about Wicked John and the Devil — in which Satan is beaten by a Kayseri merchant.[2] Just before World War I when Hugo Winckler and his crew were triangulating on the site of Hattushash (modern Boghazköy), the lost and long-sought capital of the ancient Hittite Empire, they discovered first the craftiness of Kayseri. According to legend, a cache of Assyrian records at nearby Kanesh (modern Kültepe) had long been known to local residents. One of these clay tablets, sold to the expedition, provided valuable data about Hittite settlements, and the archaeologists were eager to locate the source of the tile for what it might further reveal. But the citizens of Kayseri, knowing a good thing when they saw it, refused to divulge the desired information, and, instead, sold the records to the scientists, one at a time, for a good price. (In some versions of this story the victim is Friedrich Hrozny, who later used data on such plates to decipher the Hittite language and establish its Indo-European origin.) It is said to be an ill-starred day that begins with the sight of a Kayseri man.

Among the most popular of the naïve and unsophisticated figures who make up Turkey's roster of comic characters are Keloghlan (discussed briefly in Part I) and Karagöz (Black Eye). Karagöz did not originate in the folktale but rather in the shadow puppet play named after him.[3] The various dramatic episodes in which he appears have been the creations of his stage masters, the old-time coffee-house puppeteers, now almost extinct. A rough-and-ready country type, Karagöz is always pitted against the "city slicker" Hajivad. Although baffled in the play of wits with Hajivad, Karagöz wins in the end with a display of physical force, usually driving his opponent from the scene in a flurry of fisticuffs. For centuries he has been the delight of folk audiences both for his earthy slapstick and for his flamboyant dramatization of the victorious peasant. It was inevitable that Karagöz would not be restricted to one genre, and so, passing from the coffee-house stage into the general oral tradition, he has reappeared in the folktale.[4] "You Shouldn't Say That, Karagöz" illustrates some of the interplay between different forms of the oral tradition. The slight story is built upon a folktale type much older than the puppet play, but the high proportion of dialogue and slapstick, along with the recognizable characters, clearly derives from the Karagöz theater.

Although exaggeration is certainly not lacking from Turkish humor, it is rarely the primary element in a folktale. Among the few tall tales in our collection a pattern that recurs several times is well illustrated in the last tale of this section. It is a series of imaginary adventures that befall a soldier on his way home from a war, commonly, as here, the War of Independence of the early 1920's.[5] As is often the case with tall tales, this one is told in the first person, usually by someone regarded as a wag.

How the Three Itching Peasants Won Their Rewards [6]

One day the padishah became bored with all of the entertainment provided for him. He called the grand vezir and said to him, "Today I want you to provide me with some different sort of entertainment."

After some thought, the grand vezir went to a peasant's hut where there lived three brothers, each with an itch in a different place. The oldest had a dripping nose which itched and which he continually wiped with his sleeve. The second had a mangy scalp which he scratched. And the youngest had a similar infection on his back which he scratched. The grand vezir said to the three brothers, "If you will come before the padishah and stand for a whole hour without scratching your itches, I shall give each of you a piece of gold." After a brief consultation among themselves, the peasants agreed to this offer.

The grand vezir went to the padishah and informed him of the trial of endurance to which he was going to put the three brothers with the itch, and the padishah was curious to witness this spectacle. When the three brothers appeared, they were at ease at first. Then as the desire to scratch became greater, they started to squirm in discomfort. The hour was almost up when the three could bear it no longer, but they refused to lose the gold by relieving themselves in such a way that they could be accused of scratching.

The eldest brother pointed out to sea and said, "Look! There is a fine new boat." As he said this, he pointed in the direction of the boat, running his sleeve past his nose as he did so.

"Yes," said the second brother, "and they are playing a drum on board," and he imitated the drummer by beating on his head with his fists.

The youngest then said, "Yes, and see how fast they are rowing it!" working his arms back and forth and hunching up his back as if he were pulling an oar.

The padishah laughed at the cleverness of the three brothers and told the grand vezir that he had enjoyed their performance. The grand vezir gave them each a piece of gold.

IB.

How the Three Itching Peasants Won Their Rewards⁷

There was once a padishah with a very peculiar temperament. Frequently he demanded strange things from his subjects, and from time to time he requested peculiar entertainment. One day he said to his grand vezir, "I feel like enjoying something funny today. See that I am amused."

"How can I entertain you, your majesty, while the palace is already filled with all sorts of entertainment? What would you like?"

"Something original," said the padishah, "something that I've never seen before."

"Very well, your majesty," said the grand vezir, "I shall see what I can do."

He went to the marketplace of the town where he saw a young man whose head was bald from one ear to the other. He was a *kel*.

"Come here, young man," said he.

"What do you want with me?" asked the bald young man.

"I am going to take you to the padishah," said the grand vezir. "You are going to receive many gifts and money there. What else do you want?"

"All right," said the young man, "I shall come with you."

The grand vezir continued to look through the marketplace and at last he came upon a man who had a mangy back. He scratched his back continuously because it itched him. The grand vezir said to this young man, "I am going to take you to the padishah. You are going to receive many gifts and money there. What else do you want?"

"Very well," said this mangy man, "I shall come with you."

The grand vezir looked still longer in the marketplace and eventually found a lip-licker.⁸ He said to the lip-licker, "I'm going to take you to the padishah. You are going to receive many gifts and money there. What else do you want?"

"Nothing else," said the lip-licker. "I shall come with you."

As they were walking to the palace, the three asked the grand vezir what it was that they had to do in order to receive the money and gifts. "You will have to stand and do nothing," said the grand vezir. "In fact, to earn the money and the gifts you must guarantee that you will do nothing."

143

"How can this be?" asked the *kel*. "Are people paid so well for doing nothing?"

"Yes," said the grand vezir. "You will stand before the padishah for an hour and do absolutely nothing. And that is your task."

The men were amazed that jobs for the padishah were so easy. They followed the grand vezir to the palace.

When they arrived at the palace, the grand vezir whispered to the padishah, "Your majesty, one of these men is a *kel,* one of them has a mangy back, and one of them is a lip-licker. Let us see how long they can stand before you without relieving themselves." The padishah was pleased with this entertainment and observed the men standing in front of him.

The room was very warm, and the three men soon began to be extremely uncomfortable. The *kel* wanted very desperately to scratch his head. The man with the mangy back wanted to scratch his back, and the lip-licker wanted to lick his lips to moisten them. They knew, however, that they would not win the reward offered to them if they moved at all during the time that they were supposed to be standing there. Finally, the *kel* could stand it no longer, and so he began talking.

"Your majesty," he said, "I'm going to tell you something very important. When I was in the marketplace, a charitable man bought me a new fez. I tried on the fez. I pressed it like this and then I turned it like this, and then I turned it this way, and then I pressed it that way, and finally I got it to fit on my head." In this manner, by imitating his moving the fez, he was able to scratch his head and stop the itching for awhile.

The man with the mangy back was encouraged by what he had heard from the bald man, and so he, too, addressed the padishah. "Your majesty," he said, "a charitable person bought me something, too. He bought me a jacket today, and I tried it on. I pulled it this way and pulled it that way. I stretched it over this shoulder and I stretched it over that shoulder, and, finally, after working on it for awhile, I made it fit me." By going through these gestures, as if he were trying on a coat, the man with the mangy back had been able to relieve the itching of his back.

Now it was the lip-licker's turn. He was standing between the *kel* and the man with the mangy back. He said to the padishah, "Your majesty, this man on my left is lying," and as he said this, he pointed to the man on his left with his tongue, thus wetting the left side of his mouth. Then he said, "And that man on my right is lying, too." As he did that he stuck out his tongue to point at the man on his right, thus licking the right side of his mouth.

The padishah was quite impressed with their cleverness and he was also pleased with the entertainment which the grand vezir had provided for him. He gave the three peasants the gifts and the money which the grand vezir had promised them as rewards for their cleverness.

2.

The Persistent Creditor and the Dishonest Debtor [9]

There was a man in a village who became known as the Persistent Creditor because he had hounded his neighbor for months for the payment of one kurus [10] which this neighbor had borrowed from him. The neighbor was determined not to pay the one kurus, and so he was called the Dishonest Debtor. The Persistent Creditor grew more and more determined to collect the debt, and he demanded payment of the kurus.

One night the Dishonest Debtor went home and said to his wife, "That bastard will never leave me in peace. There is no getting away from him. I am going to pretend that I have died. Put me in the coffin and take me to the mosque. We may perhaps be able to get away from him in this way."

The Dishonest Debtor "died," according to plan, and his wife grieved for him. She called in the neighbors and said, "My husband has died." The neighbors came to her house and prepared for the funeral. They washed the husband's body [11] and put him in the coffin, [12] and took him to the mosque. Before he was taken to the mosque, his wife said to the khoja, "Before my husband died, he willed that his corpse should be kept in the mosque one night before he was buried."

"All right," said the khoja, "we shall leave him in the mosque tonight." And so they left him there after the funeral service.

Now the Persistent Creditor was suspicious about the sudden death of the Dishonest Debtor, and when he saw that his neighbor was not buried but left in the mosque, he was sure that there was some trick. He went to the mosque and hid in the mimber, [13] and from there he quietly watched the coffin of the Dishonest Debtor to see whether he was really dead or was only pretending.

The mosque in that village was a gathering place for all the thieves in the province, and that night, around midnight, the thieves met there to divide the booty they had stolen. They divided into equal portions all the food that they had stolen, and then they divided the money, but there was also a very valuable sword in their booty and they could not agree on who was to receive this weapon. They quarreled for some time over the sword, and then one of the thieves suggested, "Let us give the sword to the one who can drive it through that corpse with one blow."

"All right!" said all the thieves, and they lined up to take turns stabbing the corpse.

"Wait! Wait!" shouted the Persistent Creditor from the mimber. "He still owes me one kurus!"

When the thieves heard his voice, they were frightened and they ran out of the mosque leaving behind all the food, all the money, and the sword. The Persistent Creditor came from the mimber and the Dishonest Debtor came from the coffin, and they started to divide the booty.

In the meantime, the thieves had gone about a kilometer down the road when one of them said, "Why are we running away? We are forty and they are but one man and a corpse. We can surely handle them. Let us go back and get our booty." But to make sure that the booty was still there, they sent one of their members back to the mosque to see what the situation was.

When this thief, who was to act as scout for the rest, got back to the mosque, he stuck his head in the open window and watched the Persistent Creditor and the Dishonest Debtor divide the booty. They had it divided exactly evenly, but the Persistent Creditor said, "Where is that one kurus that you owe me?" They started quarreling about the one kurus, but then the Dishonest Debtor saw the thief's head sticking through the mosque window. He walked over to the window, snatched the cap off the thief's head, and said to the Persistent Creditor, "Here, take this. It is worth a kurus. Now our accounts are settled." The Persistent Creditor was satisfied, and they started to pack up their unexpected wealth.

The thief ran back to his companions and said, "Damn that booty! There is a curse on it. Let us not go back for it. Even two people cannot divide it satisfactorily. They had to add my cap to it in order to make their shares balance!" And so the thieves left all that booty to the Persistent Creditor and the Dishonest Debtor, and these two were now wealthy. They lived happily ever after.

146

3.

The Professor and the Man from Kayseri[14]

A professor visited Kayseri one day. He was a man famous for his knowledge of all subjects. But a Kayseri man said that he doubted the reported wisdom of this professor. "I shall ask you a question," he said to the professor, "and if you cannot answer it, you will pay me ten liras. Then you will ask me a question, and if I cannot answer it, I shall pay you one lira — for, after all, I am an uneducated man and not a professor."

The professor agreed to the arrangement, and the Kayseri man proceeded to ask him this question: "What creature is it that has three legs?"

After thinking about this for a while, the professor finally said, "I don't know what it is," and he paid the Kayseri man the ten liras. The people standing around watching also began to puzzle about the question, but none of them could answer it either.

The professor said to the Kayseri man, "Now I shall ask you a question: What *is* the creature that has three legs?"

"I don't know," said the man from Kayseri, and he gave the professor one lira back and walked away pocketing the other nine.

4.

Three Kayseri Men in a Restaurant[15]

Three men from Kayseri went to Istanbul, and while they were there they ran out of money. On their last day there they did not have even enough money to buy a meal, but they went into a restaurant anyway and ordered dinners. They did not sit together in the restaurant, but separately, at different tables, as if they were strangers to one another.

When they had finished their meal, the first Kayseri man started to leave the restaurant. The waiter rushed up to him and reminded him that he had not yet paid for his meal. "I paid for it before," he said. When the waiter started to argue with the man, the second Kayseri man went up to him and said, "The man is right. When you were bringing me back my change, I saw this man at the cashier's desk paying for his meal."

Just then they heard a loud crying, and they saw that the third Kayseri man was weeping. "What's the matter?" asked the confused waiter.

"I'm afraid that you will try to charge me twice for my meal too," he said.

The waiter assured him that he would not do such a thing, and so the three men from Kayseri left the restaurant with dirty looks at the poor waiter.

5.

The Two Bankrupts and the Merchant of Kayseri [16]

There was a merchant in Kayseri who was very rich. One day he was visited by two of the friends of his youth from another city. Both of these friends had suffered bad fortune and they were both penniless. The Kayseri man fed them well and they left his house, but every day thereafter they came back again, together or separately, to accept his hospitality.

The Kayseri man soon tired of their unwelcome presence, and he thought of some way of ridding himself of them. When one of the friends came alone to his house, the merchant said to him, "Here are 1000 liras with which you can return to your town and start life all over again. Will you sell me three whiskers from your beard for this amount of money?" After thinking about this proposal for a few minutes, the friend agreed to the bargain, gave the merchant the three whiskers, and left with the 1000 liras. He went immediately to the other bankrupt and told him that the merchant had given him 1000 liras for three whiskers from his beard.

The second friend now went to the merchant's house and waited for the same largesse to be offered to him. Tired of his presence, the merchant held out 1000 liras to him and said, "Will you sell me three whiskers from your beard for this amount of money?"

The second friend said, "Efendi, for that amount of money I'd give you as much of my beard as you wished," and he pulled out a whole handful of hair and offered it to the merchant.

The merchant thought for a minute, and then he put the 1000 liras back in his pocket. "No," he said, "I have changed my mind. A man like you would probably squander my money and become penniless again."

6.

Three Friends and the Innkeeper of Kayseri [17]

Three friends were digging a well when they found a chest full of treasure. They were happy at first, but then they were worried, for they did not trust one another, and each feared that one of the others would try to steal the whole chest for himself. They made an agreement, therefore, that wherever the treasure went, all three of them would accompany it together.

They started toward their village, stopping for the night at an inn in Kayseri. They gave the chest to the owner of the inn for safekeeping for the night, telling him that he was to give it to no one, not even one of them unless the other two were with him. The innkeeper agreed to this and at their insistence wrote out a statement to that effect and gave it to them.

The three friends went upstairs and went to bed. It grew colder in the night, and after a while they woke up shivering. "We need more blankets," one of them said. "Let's draw lots to see which of us will go down and get more blankets from the innkeeper." They did this, and the oldest of them was the one who went after the extra blankets. But when he arrived at the innkeeper's room, he said, "Give me the chest which we left with you."

"I can't," said the innkeeper, "for I have agreed to give it not to one of you alone but only to all three of you."

"But my two friends sent me down for it," said the oldest. "There are some things in it that we want."

The innkeeper shouted upstairs to the other two men, "Shall I give him what he is asking for?"

"Yes," they shouted back down, and so the innkeeper gave the man the chest and went back to bed. Instead of going back upstairs, the man took the chest and left the inn.

After waiting for a while for the blankets and their friend, the two men upstairs became suspicious, and they went downstairs to see what was keeping their companion. They awakened the innkeeper again and asked him where their friend was. "I don't know," he said. "I gave him the chest and went back to bed again."

"You gave him the chest?" they both shouted. "You agreed to give it only to the three of us together, and not just to one of us."

"But," protested the innkeeper, "when I shouted up the stairs and asked you if I should give him what he asked for, you said 'Yes.' "

"He came down for extra blankets, and we thought you were talking about the blankets!" The two friends were very angry with the innkeeper, and the next morning they had the innkeeper arrested and taken before a judge. The two friends stated their case, and produced the written statement that the innkeeper had given them.

"Did you make this agreement with these men?" the judge asked the innkeeper. "Did you agree to return the chest to these men only when all three called for it together?"

"Yes, efendi," said the innkeeper, "I did. I still have the chest, and when these two men come to me with the third man, I shall return their chest to them."

The judge, thereupon, dismissed the case against the innkeeper.[18]

7.

The Köse and the Sultan [19]

Once upon a time when there wasn't such a time, and it was sinful to speak too much, there was a köse in a village who did not get along very well with his neighbors. One day one of the villagers said, "Let us all go and defecate down the chimney of that köse." And that night they actually did this.

When the köse got up the next morning, he found his fireplace completely filled with excrement. Without appearing at all disturbed, he got two sacks, filled them with the excrement, and loaded them on his mule. Then he left the village with his loaded mule. On the way he saw a traveling peddler with two mule loads of merchandise.

"Selamünaleyküm," said the peddler.

"Aleykümselam," said the köse. "Where are you going, my fellow countryman?"

The peddler answered, "I am going to such-and-such a place."

"What does your merchandise consist of?" asked the köse.

"Oh, clothes and small items of various kinds. What have you in your packs?"

"I have pearls and corals in mine," answered the köse.

"How about exchanging your load for one of my mule loads of merchandise?"

"All right," said the köse, "but only on the condition that you will not open my sacks until you reach your destination."

"Very well," said the peddler, "I won't open them until I reach such-and-such a town."

Later the köse returned home with his new load, and he called his wife. "Come here, wife. Look at this. Don't think that those cuckolds did us any harm by defecating down our chimney."

"What are you talking about?" asked his wife.

"Well, I exchanged the two sacks of excrement for a mule load of fancy goods. Will you stretch a rope from our house to our neighbor's so that I can hang all these fancy things on it?"

The villagers saw that he had acquired some very colorful and pretty things, and they admired these on the rope that stretched between his house and that of his neighbor. They asked him, "How did you get such fine things?"

"Did you think that you did me a bad turn by defecating down my chimney?" asked the köse. "Well, you didn't, for the sultan of Ankara [20] is having an apartment built of excrement, and he is paying high prices for building material. I took my mule load of excrement to him and he paid me a lot of money, and with this money I bought all these pretty things that you see hanging here."

As soon as the villagers heard this, a crier was sent around in all the streets announcing, "One man from each house must report to the oda [21] tonight at sunset." When the meeting was held, it was explained to all the villagers that the sultan of Ankara was having an apartment built of excrement and that he was paying high prices for his building material. The muhtar [22] said to them, "Why don't we all use this opportunity to earn some money? We can all sell excrement to the sultan."

The villagers all thought this a good idea, and so on the following morning they all set to work immediately to bag all the excrement from their outhouses. They loaded this on their donkeys and took it to Ankara. There they discovered, to their delight, that the sultan was indeed having an apartment built, and so they went to his home. After the customary greetings, they asked, "Where is the sultan?"

"He is in his room," the servants told them.

News was brought to the sultan that there were some peasants who were looking for him. He received them and asked them, "What is the matter, my sons?"

"Well, your majesty, we have heard that you were having an apartment built of excrement," said the muhtar. "We have brought many loads of excrement for you."

"Who told you to do this?" asked the sultan.

"A köse in our village did," they all said.

Explaining in a kind way to the villagers that he really did not need any excrement, the sultan called two gendarmes. He told the gendarmes to go to the village and bring this köse to him.

The köse was brought, and after the customary greetings, the sultan said to him, "How did you trick the villagers into bringing all that excrement to me?" After the köse had explained all that had happened, the sultan said, "You tricked the villagers, but do you think that you could trick me too? Let us see if you can."

The köse said, "Well, your majesty, I can do that all right, but unfortunately I left my tricking stick back in the village."

"Well, let us have that stick sent for, then," said the sultan.

"It will not allow itself to be brought here unless I go for it in person," said the köse. "But if you will lend me a cart and two oxen [23] I can go home and carry this heavy stick here to your apartment."

The sultan loaned him the two oxen and the cart, and he asked, "How long will it take you to get the tricking stick and return?"

"I shall be back by the end of a week," said the köse, and he started for his village. When he got there, he called to his wife, "Bring me a knife at once." He took the knife, cut the oxen's throats, and skinned them. With the hides he made many pairs of sandals and he sold them. When he was asked by the villagers what had become of the sultan's two oxen, he told them that he had killed them for their hides. "In the village of Chubuk [24] there is a great shortage of sandals, and the people there are paying many times the usual price for sandals."

Hearing this, the villagers called a meeting that night in the oda, and the muhtar addressed them again. "This is an opportunity for us all to become rich," he said, "for we all have oxen that will provide hide enough for many pairs of sandals." And so the villagers went to their stables next morning early and killed all their oxen. From the hides they made many pairs of sandals, and they packed these on their donkeys and took them to Chubuk. When they got there, however, they found that no one was interested in buying their sandals.

152

It was now time for the köse to return to the sultan, but instead of going to Ankara he stayed in his village. Finally, the sultan sent men to fetch the köse, but when they arrived at the köse's house, they could not find him there. The köse had put on woman's clothes, and when the men came to the door, he answered their calls, appearing in the form of a beautiful young woman.[25] He told them that he was the köse's daughter.

When news of this was brought to the sultan, he ordered that the young lady be brought to him instead. When she arrived in his presence, he asked her, "Where is your father, young lady?"

"My father killed the oxen that you loaned him," she said, "and he has gone to another town to sell the sandals which he made from the ox hides."

The sultan was greatly taken with the köse's daughter, and he ordered a wedding ceremony to be held at once, and he married the köse's daughter. But, you know, she wasn't a girl at all, and the sultan had married the köse himself. He did not say anything about the trick he had played on the sultan, but after the feasting and the music were finished, it was the wedding night. And it was then that the sultan discovered that he had married the köse.

"Well, köse, now I understand what you mean by your tricking stick," said the sultan. "You tricked me just as completely as you did the villagers."

8.

The Clever Son and the Confused Lovers[26]

There was once a khoja in a village who became very friendly with a woman whose husband was away on business. This woman had a clever son who observed what was going on between his mother and the khoja. One day he said to his mother, "Mother, doesn't this khoja come to our home very often?"

"Well, son," said the woman, "he is a close friend of your father, and that is why he comes to visit us."

The next day the khoja came to call again, and while he was there, the woman said to him, "Tomorrow I am going to bake a goose for you. Tell me in what field you will be plowing so that I can bring it to you."

"I will be in the far field to the south," said the khoja.

"Very well, I shall bring it there when it is cooked."

The next day the woman killed the goose, but before she could finish preparing it, her husband came home from his trip. He returned earlier than she had expected. When he saw that his wife was cooking a goose, he said, "What is the matter? What are you cooking that for?"

"The whole flock of geese crowded around the front door. I threw a stick at them to drive them away, and the stick broke the leg of this goose. That is the bird that I am cooking now."

"Well, that is good. Cook it well and bring it down to me in the south field where I shall be plowing."

"All right," said the woman.

It happened that the field that was being plowed by the khoja was right next to the field that the husband was plowing. The woman was afraid that she would not be able to distinguish between her husband and her lover when she went to deliver the goose. So she sent a servant to the khoja to ask him how she was to identify him from a distance. The khoja sent back this message: "One of my oxen is white; you can tell which is my team from that." But the clever son overheard this before he went to join his father in the field.

The father and son were plowing in their field, and when it was noon, they decided to rest. While they were resting, the clever son covered one of his father's oxen with a white sheet. From a distance the husband's team looked just like that of the khoja, and so when the woman started to the fields with the goose, she could not tell which was which. "The khoja's must be that one over there," she said to herself, but when she reached that place, she discovered that it was the team of her husband. It was too late to change her direction now, for the husband and the son had seen her coming.

"What do you want?" called the husband.

"Well," she said, "I have brought the goose." There was nothing she could do but give it to her husband and son. While they were eating the goose, however, she said to them, "You should be ashamed of yourselves. You never think of your neighbors. Look at that poor khoja who has been plowing in the next field all day. Shouldn't you give some goose to him, too? When you die, the very first question that will be put to you as you lie on the funeral altar [27] will be whether or not you were considerate to your neighbors. Is it right that you should be eating goose while that poor khoja is not having any of it?"

"Well, what shall we do?" asked the husband.

"Go and invite him to join you in your meal," said the wife.

The son was sent to invite the khoja to come and join the meal, but when the clever boy reached the khoja, he said to him, "Oh, Uncle Khoja, my father has heard of your visits to my mother, and he is going to kill you."

Hearing this, the khoja was quite frightened, and he prepared to run away. The clever son returned and told his father that the khoja had refused to come and join them in their meal. Upon this, the husband said to his wife, "Apparently our son has not been able to explain the invitation clearly to the khoja. Why don't you go and invite him yourself?"

The wife was gone for a long time, and finally the man asked his son, "What do you suppose is keeping your mother?"

Disgusted by his father's stupidity, the clever son said, "Oh, she has probably gone to the police station to make a report about you, because she has heard that you were having a love affair with a donkey."

The husband was frightened at this news and he asked, "Oh, son, where should I hide from the police?"

"There is a cave over at the edge of the field. Why don't you go and hide yourself in it?"

The man went and hid in the cave, and while he was there, two hunters came along. When the clever son saw them, he shouted, "Come here, oh, my hunter uncles!"

The hunters came to the place where the boy was standing and asked him, "What is the matter?"

"A male fox just ran into that cave at the edge of the field," he said. "Why don't you drive it out and shoot it?"

To drive the fox from its hiding place, the hunters built a large fire at the mouth of the cave. Smoke poured into the cave, and after a while, the man could stand it no longer. He came out gasping for fresh air, and when he saw the two men with guns, he shouted at them. "What if I did have a love affair with a donkey? It was my own donkey — so what is that to you?" Saying this, he returned to his house and left the two hunters speechless with amazement.[28]

9.

The Köse Who Became Muhtar [29]

There was once a large village which had no muhtar. The people of the village searched and searched to find a suitable person for this job, but they never found a really satisfactory candidate. Finally they decided to elect a köse muhtar, thinking that he would make the village prosper. So they elected him.

Soon after the köse became muhtar, he ordered that every day an ox should be slaughtered and its meat sold cheaply to the villagers. Each day somebody's ox was slaughtered and its meat sold. Those who lost their oxen in this way became very angry, and finally they banded together and went to the köse's barn and slaughtered his pair of oxen in retaliation. When the köse discovered his dead oxen, he did not show any anger. He just skinned the animals and decided to barter the skins for some other goods.

That evening he went to a neighboring village and knocked on the door of the first house he came to. When a woman came to the door, the köse said to her, "I have some fine hide here for making sandals. Would you like to buy some?"

"My husband is at the mill and so not home now, and I do not wear sandals."

The köse saw that the woman was quite pretty and he said many flattering things to her. Finally she agreed to buy some hide for sandals. She did not pay for the hide with money but with wheat. As the woman was pouring the wheat into the köse's bag, he deliberately jerked the bag aside and allowed some of the wheat to fall on the floor. He did this to stall for time. Slowly he started to pick the wheat up, one grain at a time.

"Leave it there on the floor," said the woman. "I'll pour some other wheat into your bag."

"No, no, it was my fault that it was spilled," said the köse, "and so it is my duty to pick it up for you."

By the time that the köse had finished picking up the wheat it had become quite late, and darkness had fallen. The woman felt obliged to make up a bed for the köse in one of the rooms of the house, and then she went to her own room and went to bed, propping something against her door.

156

Shortly after this, the woman's lover came to call on her. She got up and visited with him, and after a while she decided to cook some eggs for him. She put some fat in a frying pan and placed it on the stove, and as there were no eggs in the house, she went out to the henhouse to get some. Her lover was lying in bed in the meantime, half asleep. The köse got up quietly when the woman went out, and he took the frying pan of hot fat and poured it down the throat of the unsuspecting lover. The lover died choking, "Kuk! Kuk! Kuk!" Then the köse went back to bed.

When the woman returned and saw the empty frying pan, she thought that the cat had tipped over the fat. She put more fat in the pan and broke eggs into it. When they were ready, she said, "Come! Get up and eat!"

Her lover did not come, and so she went to the bedroom and there discovered that he was dead. She called out to the köse to come and see what had happened. "Please do come and see what has happened. There is a dead man in my room."

"No, no!" said the köse, "I did not come here to see dead men. My own troubles are enough for me." But when the woman continued to plead with him to come and help her, he said, "I'll come and help you get rid of the dead body only if you will pay me a thousand liras."

The woman was afraid that her husband would come home and find the dead lover in her bed, and so she agreed to pay the köse this amount if he would help her. He took the corpse and started to dump it into the latrine, but before he could finish this job, the husband arrived home, and so the köse rushed back to his own bed.

The husband said to his wife, "Here, hold my donkey. I must go to the latrine." When he went into the latrine, he stumbled over the corpse and shouted, "What are you doing here? If you were a decent fellow, you wouldn't be found here!" Saying this, he clubbed the corpse.

The husband returned to the house and said to his wife, "I think I have killed a man that I found in our latrine. What shall we do with the body?"

"Let us go and consult the guest who is sleeping next door," suggested his wife.

When they told the köse their problem, he said, "I do not want anything to do with a dead body." But the woman understood the köse, and she went and got some more money and gave it to him, and the köse agreed to dispose of the body.

Before sunrise he loaded the corpse on his donkey and left that village. Along the way he stopped at a field of watermelons and allowed his donkey to graze among the watermelons. When the owner of the field saw this, he shouted at the köse, "Hey! Stop that donkey from eating my watermelon vines!"

But the köse did nothing but sit delousing his shirt. He did not heed the warning at all. The owner of the field got a gun and fired it at the donkey. When the köse heard the shot, he jumped up and started crying, "You have killed my dear brother! You have killed my dear brother! He was ill and I was taking him to a doctor."

The farmer came and begged the köse's pardon and said it was an accident. But the köse said, "No! No! I do not want to hear such nonsense. I am going to court to sue you." As they walked toward the nearest town, they reached an agreement. The farmer paid the köse a thousand liras, and the köse forgave him. Later he threw the dead body into the sea.

After making a great amount of money in these ways, the köse returned to the village where he was muhtar. He built a fine house for himself and a good coffee house for the village. He gave a generous amount of pocket money to his children, and so everyone knew that he was rich. The villagers asked him, "Where did you get all this money, muhtar?"

"Oh, if I had only split my ox hides into thinner layers, I could have made even more money," he answered.

"What do you mean?" they asked.

"There is a great shortage of sandals in the village by the sea," the köse said. "If everyone kills his ox, splits the hide thin enough to make many sandals he can become rich too."

The people were all very excited when they heard this, and they went home at once and killed their oxen for their skins. They split these skins until they were very thin and then they made sandals from them. But when they took the sandals to the village the köse told them about, they could not sell any of them there.

Returning home with their loads of sandals, the men decided to get rid of that terrible köse by putting him in a box and throwing him into the sea. They made a box of wood and put the köse in it. They put a cover on it and nailed it down, and at night they carried the box to the seaside. But as they were about to throw the box into the sea, one of the men said, "Let us wait until the morning to throw him in so that we can have the pleasure of watching him drown." They all agreed to this, and so they left the box by the sea that night.

Early the next morning a shepherd came along the shore with his flock. When he saw the box on the beach, he approached it and kicked it. The köse inside cried out loudly.

"What are you doing in there?" asked the shepherd.

"Oh, friend, do you know what trouble I am in?" asked the köse.

"No," said the shepherd. "What is the matter?"

"They wanted to give me to the daughter of the padishah. When I refused to marry her, they put me in this box to carry me to her."

"Why did you refuse her?" asked the shepherd. "I'd have married her if I had been you. Could there be anything better than that?"

"Well, if you would really like that," said the köse, "just trade places with me."

The shepherd quickly took the cover off the box and let the köse out. Then he climbed inside, and the köse closed the lid again. The köse then took the flock of sheep and started for the village in a very roundabout way.

The men of the village, in the meantime, went to the shore and threw the box into the water. After it had sunk, they started back to the village, but on the way they encountered the köse with his flock of sheep. They were amazed to see him, and they said to him, "How did you get those sheep?"

"You thought you did me a disservice when you threw me into the sea," he answered, "but you can see with your own eyes what I got. If I had only known how to swim better, I should have been able to pull out forty sheep every time I dived. *Kirk! Kirk!*"

The villagers rushed back to the seashore and they all jumped in at the place where they had thrown the box. All of them drowned, and as they sank, the last noises that they made were gurgling sounds that said, *"Kirk! Kirk! Kirk!"* [30]

10.

You Shouldn't Say That, Karagöz! [31]

Once there was and was not, a long time ago — back then, Hajivad went to visit his friend Karagöz. It was during Ramazan, and they ate only after sundown, but the time of fasting was almost over. When Hajivad knocked on the door, Karagöz opened it and said, "Welcome, Hajivad!"

"I feel welcome! And, friend, Karagöz, let us talk quietly and peaceably tonight, like gentlemen."

"Very well," said Karagöz. He ordered some tea and some pide,[32] and then he asked, "What shall we talk about?"

"Oh, let us talk about my trip to the bazaar yesterday. The holiday [33] is not far off, you know, and so I went to the bazaar to buy new clothes and shoes for my children to wear during the visiting. You should see how fine they look in them!"

"What do I care?" said Karagöz.

"Oh, Karagöz, is that the way to talk?"

"Well, what should I say?" asked Karagöz.

"You should say, 'Let them wear their clothes with smiles. Let their things go to pieces on them.' [34] That is what you should say."

"All right," said Karagöz. "Let them wear their clothes with smiles. Let them go to pieces on them."

"That is well done, my Karagöz! You know, while I was in the market I thought about winter coming on, and so I went to a wood seller and bought five hundred measures of coal and two loads of wood. Now my family will all be warm."

"Let them wear them with smiles," said Karagöz, "and let them fall to pieces on them."

"Oh, brother, I am talking about wood and coal!"

"All right! All right! Let them fall to pieces!"

"You shouldn't say that, Karagöz. You should say, 'Let them burn it with smiles. And let the children be heated before its fire.' "

"All right! Let them burn it with smiles, and let the children be heated before its fire."

"Thank you, Karagöz! That is ery kind of you. You know, last winter the roof of our house leaked. I hired a man to rearrange the tiles, and while he was there, I had him whitewash the house all over. You should see it. It is almost like a new house."

"Good! Good! Burn it with smiles, and let the children heat themselves before it."

"Oh, Karagöz! What are you saying?"

"But you taught me to say that, didn't you?"

"Yes, but this is different! You should say, 'Live in it happily with your children.' "

"All right," said Karagöz. "You live there happily with your children."

"Well, Karagöz, we needed some food yesterday to break the fast after sunset, and so I went out to buy some. On the street I saw two people quarreling. I said to them, 'Shame on you! On a holy day you should not be quarreling!' But right then two policemen came along and thought that I was one of the people quarreling. They grabbed me by the arms and led me to the prison."

"Oh, may you live there happily with your children, Hajivad."

"No, no, you shouldn't say that, Karagöz! You should say, 'Don't be unhappy. You have many friends. Surely one of them will come and take you out.'"

"All right," said Karagöz. "Don't be unhappy. You have many friends. Surely one of them will come and take you out."

"Well, when they discovered that I was not guilty, they let me out of prison. On the way home I stopped at a bakery to buy some pide. The pide smelled so good that I looked into the oven at it, but just then the baker swung back his big wooden shovel and it almost knocked out my eye."

"Oh, don't be unhappy," said Karagöz. "You have many friends. Surely one of them will take it out."

"Oh, my Karagöz, that is not what you should say. You should say to the baker, 'Are you blind! Why don't you look before and behind you? You shameless person!'"

"You shameless person!" shouted Karagöz, and then he hit Hajivad on the head with his hand several times.

"Oh, brother," said Hajivad, "what are you doing?"

"I'm beating that baker so that he will be more careful from now on," said Karagöz.

11.

The Keloghlan Who Would Not Tell [35]

Once there was a stupid keloghlan who lived with two older brothers. They made their living by hauling wood from the forest on their donkey and selling it in the village. One day Keloghlan said to his brothers, "Let me take the donkey and bring back the wood today."

"No," said the oldest brother, "you would probably leave the donkey in the forest, and then we would have nothing."

"No, I wouldn't," insisted Keloghlan, and after some discussion, they decided to let him take the donkey to haul the wood that day.

As Keloghlan entered the forest, he discovered a bag of gold under a tree. He started to pick it up when some crows in the tree began to shout, "Ga! Ga! Ga!" Keloghlan thought they were saying, "We'll give you the bag of gold for your donkey."

"All right," he said, "I shall sell him to you, although my brothers may be angry with me." After the crows had led the donkey away, Keloghlan dug a hole and buried the gold. Then he went home and told his brothers what he had done.

His brothers beat Keloghlan for losing their donkey, as they had feared he would. But Keloghlan insisted that he had received a bag of gold in exchange, and finally the brothers decided to go and see if there were really a bag of gold buried in the forest.

As they were digging up the gold that night, the village bekchi [36] came along and asked them what they were doing. The brothers were afraid to be caught with so much gold, and so they knocked down the bekchi and left him there, thinking they had killed him.

On the way home with the gold, the brothers passed a flock of goats. Being hungry from their work, they decided to steal a large goat, a kechi. They stole a kechi, and cut off a hind leg to roast. Then before anyone could discover what they had done, they threw the rest of the carcass down a well and went on home.

When they got home, they started to roast the leg of the kechi and to count their money. "Let us weigh the gold, too," said the eldest brother. "Keloghlan, you go to our neighbor and borrow his scales, but do not tell him we want to use it to weigh gold."

Keloghlan went to the home of their neighbor and asked to borrow the scales. "What do you want to weigh with them?" asked the neighbor.

"We do not want to weigh gold," answered Keloghlan. When the neighbor heard this, he became suspicious and put some thick grape syrup on the bottom of the balance pan. Later, when Keloghlan brought the scales back, the man found a piece of gold stuck to the grape syrup, and so he notified the gendarmes at once of his discovery.

When the gendarmes arrived to arrest the two older brothers, they knocked several times on the door. As they were knocking, the oldest brother said to Keloghlan, "No matter what happens, remember this carefully: You didn't sell the donkey for a bag of gold. We didn't knock down the bekchi or throw the kechi in the well."

"Yes, I'll remember that," said Keloghlan, and he repeated to himself several times, "I didn't sell the donkey for a bag of gold. My brothers didn't knock down the bekchi or throw the kechi in the well."

The gendarmes arrested the two older brothers and took them to the village jail. Then they came back and started to question Keloghlan. At first Keloghlan did not know what to say to them, for he was badly frightened, but he remembered then the instructions of his older brother. "I didn't sell the donkey for a bag of gold," he said, in confusion. "My brothers didn't knock down the kechi or throw the bekchi in the well."

"Throw the bekchi in the well?" shouted the gendarmes.

"No, no, I didn't mean that," Keloghlan tried to explain, but the gendarmes refused to listen to him. They called for the bekchi, and when he did not answer, they ran to the well, dragging Keloghlan with them. When they arrived at the well with a crowd of people following them, the gendarme captain said to Keloghlan, "We are going to lower you into the well on a rope so that you can pull out our bekchi."

"All right," said Keloghlan.

When they had lowered Keloghlan to the bottom of the well, the captain called down to him, "Have you found our bekchi yet?"

Keloghlan's hand rested on the ear of the goat. "Did your bekchi have an ear?" he shouted up to them.

"Yes, he did," they all shouted back.

Keloghlan's hand then moved to the goat's woolly back. "Was your bekchi wearing a fur coat?" he asked them.

"Yes, he was," they shouted back.

Now by this time the bekchi, who had been knocked down by the brothers, had regained consciousness and was performing his duties again. When he saw the crowd of people gathered, all looking into the mouth of the well, he called to them, "What are you looking for?"

Everyone looked up in amazement, and everyone said, "You!"

12.

The Stubborn Keloghlan [37]

Once upon a time there was a keloghlan who lived with his grandmother. Because they were very poor, Keloghlan used to go about barefooted. One day when he was walking around the village barefooted, a thorn stuck into the sole of his foot. He came limping home and asked his grandmother to remove the thorn. The old lady took a needle, removed the thorn from Keloghlan's foot, and then she put the thorn on the corner of the stove.

One day when she was sweeping the house, she knocked the thorn into the stove and it burned. A few days later, when some winds were blowing in his head,[38] Keloghlan remembered the thorn that had been taken from his foot. He came running home and he asked his grandmother for the thorn. She told him that it had fallen into the stove and been burned. Now it happened that that day was one on which Keloghlan felt obstinate. He had his baldness about him.[39] So he continued to request the thorn from his grandmother. He said, "You will either give me the thorn or I shall take the stove, *tingir, tingir, tis!*"[40] This teasing went on for days, Keloghlan always saying, "*Tingir, tingir, tis!*" Finally his grandmother's head was swollen.[41] She had no more patience, and so she said, "Well, then, take the stove and get out of here!"

Keloghlan took the stove from the house and went with it into the street. Then he began to wonder what he would do with such a large thing. He went to the home of a neighbor and asked, "May I leave my stove for a while in your house?"

"Very well," said the neighbor, "put it over there in the corner where it will not be in the way."

But the stove did get in the way, and when Keloghlan did not return for it, after many days, the neighbor moved it to the cow shed. One day an ox kicked the stove and broke it to pieces. Keloghlan finally returned for the stove, and it happened that he came on one of his stubborn days. When he heard what had happened to his stove, he said to the neighbor, "You will either give me back my stove in perfect condition or you will give me your ox, *tingir, tingir, tis.*" His baldness was upon him again, and he repeated his threat day after day after day until finally the neighbor shouted, "Curses be upon you! Take the ox and get out of here!"

Keloghlan took the ox and went his way. Along the road he noticed a wedding going on at a large house. He tied his ox in a corner of the courtyard of that house and went inside the house to join the wedding party. It was a long wedding celebration that lasted many days, and a great amount of food was eaten by the guests. Seeing the ox tied in the courtyard for several days, the owner of the house thought that it must be a wedding gift. So he killed the ox and used the meat to make a large meal for all his guests.

When Keloghlan was ready to leave the wedding, he looked for his ox but couldn't find it where he had left it. He asked the owner of the house if he had seen the ox. "Yes, we saw an ox tied in the corner of the courtyard," said the owner, "but we thought that it was a wedding gift, and so we slaughtered it and fed its meat to the guests. I shall give you another ox in its place."

But Keloghlan replied, "I do not want any other ox. I want my own ox. You will either give me my own ox or you will give me the sister of the bride, *tingir, tingir, tis.*" He continued saying this day after day after day as his stubbornness continued. Finally the father of the bride realized that there was no escaping Keloghlan.

"Take my younger daughter and go!" he said. The girl was as beautiful as the fourteenth day of the moon, and Keloghlan was very happy to leave with her.

13.

My Return from the War of Independence [42]

When the War of Independence was over, I was in Izmir. I was discharged and wanted to return to my village, and so I started walking. I decided to work along the way in order to feed myself, and so, along the way, I stopped at a village and asked for a job as a farm hand.

The villager to whom I applied asked me, "Where are you from?"

"Haymana," [43] I said.

"What do you do?" he asked.

"I am a farmer," I said.

"How much pay do you want?"

"One hundred and fifty liras a month," I said.

"All right," said the villager, "I hire you."

They gave me a stick with a point, a belt, and a piece of iron. [44] "Take these and go to bed. We shall show you which field to plow in the morning." They had a comfortable house, and I could hear the villager and his family laughing and enjoying themselves.

The next day they gave me the oxen and showed me the field to be plowed. I plowed for a while, and then I lay down in the field and fell asleep. While I slept, the oxen, with the yoke still on their shoulders, entered somebody else's field of wheat. The next thing I knew, somebody was kicking me and shouting, "What are you doing here?"

When I woke up, I said, "I am plowing this field."

"Where are your oxen?" he asked me.

I looked around and saw that the oxen were in the next field eating wheat. The man grabbed my goad with one hand and my ear with the other hand, and then he started leading both me and the oxen to the village. As we were getting close to the village, the man slackened his grip a little. I pulled my head aside and got away from him and ran into a nearby forest.

After a while I saw a horseman approaching, and so I stepped out to the path and said to him, "Selamünaleyküm!"

"Aleykümselam," he said. "Where are you from?"

"Haymana," I said.

"What are you doing here?" he asked.

"Oh, I am just trying my luck," I said.

"Would you like to work for me?" he asked.

"Yes, I would," I said.

"Very well," he said, "take this hound, this fur coat, and my sword to my house in the next village. When you get there, just ask for the house of Ali Bey. I shall see you there tonight."

I took the man's hound, his fur coat, and his sword and started for the village. I had just one more hill to climb before I got there when I saw three flocks of sheep. With them were nine dogs, three for each flock. I was afraid these dogs might knock me down and hurt me, so I gathered up some stones to throw at them.[45] But they were attracted instead to the hound. I had put the horseman's fur coat around the hound, tying it there with my belt, in order to avoid having to carry it myself. The sheep dogs chased the hound until they caught him, and then they tore that fur coat all to pieces. The hound ran on to the village, and some time later I reached it too and went to Ali Bey's house, where I found two women baking bread. After the customary greetings, they asked me to sit down. They placed a dish of pekmez[46] before me on the floor and gave me bread to dip into it. I must have eaten more than I realized, for after a while my belly was quite swollen.

When Ali Bey finally arrived home, after dark, he asked me, "What is your name?"

"Sorsavush,"[47] I told him.

"Sorsavush," he said, "walk my horse for a while. It is sweaty and I do not want it to get stiff." After I had walked the horse and then put it in the stable, Ali Bey gave me two partridges that he had shot. "Go and pluck their feathers," he said, "and clean them in the spillway of water near the mill."

Singing a song, I took the two partridges to where he had directed me. Putting one of the partridges on the ground, I started plucking the other one. Just then a dog came along and snatched that other bird from the ground and ran off with it. When I took off my shoe and threw it at the dog, the partridge I was plucking fell from my hand into the deep water. As it was now quite dark, I could not find the shoe I had thrown at the dog, and so I returned to the house with just one shoe and no partridges. The women laughed at me and thought it was all very funny, but Ali Bey looked at me and asked, "Have you lost your mind?" I explained to him what had happened, and he said angrily, "Go to bed!"

I went to bed on a pallet in the stable. After I had slept for a short while, I heard someone knocking on the stable door. I thought it must be Ali Bey, but when I opened the door I discovered it was his wife's lover. He used to meet her there, and he was angry at finding me there instead. We started to fight, and I chased him around the stable wildly. When I threw my sword at him, I missed the man and the sword stuck into a cow's belly. The animal cried, "Augh!" and died. When I threw it at him again, it hit the leg of a horse, severing its tendons. By this time Ali Bey had heard the noise and had come to the stable, but his wife's lover had escaped.

"What is going on here?" he asked. When I explained to him what had happened, he asked, "Why didn't you call me?"

"Well, sir, I am new here," I said, "and I didn't know what to do."

"All right. Go back to bed."

In the morning Ali Bey's camel driver was ill. Ali Bey called me to him and said, "Today you will drive the camels. Load these six bags of wheat on my three camels and go to the mill with them. Have the wheat ground and bring it back as soon as possible. You may ride on my horse."

To reach the mill I had to cross the mill stream. When I saw the miller watching me, I called to him, "Where can I safely cross this stream?"

"Wade through over there where it is shallow," he said, pointing downstream a little.

As I led the camels through the part of the stream where the miller had pointed, one of them slipped and fell. The two bags of wheat from its back started floating down the stream. First I tried to save the camel from drowning, but the other two camels became frightened in the confusion. Unable to save the camel which had fallen, I tied my horse's reins to the two camels standing in the middle of the stream and then

I swam after the two bags of wheat. By the time I had dragged the bags of wheat ashore, the two camels had climbed out on the opposite bank. When they stood up on dry land they were so much taller than the horse that they lifted his front feet right off the ground. By the time I could cut the reins to release the horse, he had been strangled to death.

"Where are you from?" asked the miller in amazement.

"Haymana," I said.

"May God keep it so!" [48] he said. "You are a good Haymana man. You have drowned the bey's camel and killed his horse."

"What could I do?" I demanded. "I couldn't help it. You saw what happened."

The miller ground the dry wheat and we spread the wet wheat on some carpets to dry. When that had been dried and ground, it was time for lunch. My bread had been lost in the stream, so I took some of the flour to make more bread for myself. I poured some water on the flour, but I used too much water, so I poured some more flour in. Then I used more water, more flour, more water, more flour, until finally I had a huge trough full of dough. We made a fire, placed a large griddle over it, and started baking the bread.

"Which of us is going to eat this?" asked the miller.

"When it is ready, we shall both eat it," I said.

"No, no," said the miller. "Let us tell tales, and the one who tells the best tale will eat all of the bread."

"I don't know many tales," I said, "so you start." He began and told the following tale.

"Once upon a time, when there wasn't such a time, it was forbidden to talk too much. God had many people, but it was a sin to say so. In that former time we had a hive of bees. One day one of the bees did not return to the hive, and my grandmother said to me, 'The lame bee has not returned to the hive. Go and find it.' I went to the vegetable garden and there I saw many bees but not our lame bee. After a while I grew tired of looking for him, and so I lay down on the grass and fell asleep.

"When I awoke next morning I discovered that a man had caught our lame bee and had forced it to pull a plow until it was completely exhausted. I examined the poor bee and found that its neck and shoulders had been rubbed raw by the yoke, so I smeared some mud on the injured places. After a while a sycamore tree started to grow from that mud on the bee's shoulders, and this tree prevented it from climbing back into the hive. The children of the village had a habit of throwing

168

mud clods at the birds that perched in that sycamore tree, and after three or four years, a whole field had been built up around it."

I interrupted the miller at this point and asked him, "What was the bee doing under all this?"

"Oh, he just kept chewing his cud to pass the time away," [49] said the miller, and then he continued with his story.

"As I was saying, there was a field now at the foot of that sycamore tree. I sowed barley in the field, and when it was ripe, I went back to the field to reap it."

I interrupted the miller again and asked, "And what was the bee doing then?"

"Oh, it was still chewing the cud," said the miller, and then he went on with his tale.

"Before I started reaping, I thought I might as well smoke a cigarette, so I sat down and smoked for a while. When I finished smoking, I looked around and saw a hound chasing a fox round and around the field, and the grain was swaying back and forth in the breeze they made. As the fox ran past me, his bushy tail caught the sickle and pulled it from my hand. As he ran around the field, with the tool in his tail, he cut the barley wherever he went. In no time at all he had finished reaping that whole field of barley."

Again I stopped the miller to ask, "What about the bee all this time?"

"Oh, he just kept on chewing the cud," said the miller. "After that I got my barley together, loaded it on my donkey, and took it home. They gave me some copper money for it."

Now it was my turn to tell a story, and so I began at once:

"Where I come from there is a large river called the Kizilirmak.[50] I planted a hill of watermelons on one side of that river and a hill of pumpkins [51] on the other side. The vines from the plants that sprang from these hills grew very fast and hung over the banks of the river. They grew so fast that in a short time they met, and they were so thick that they formed a wide mat across the river that a man could walk on. After a while people started to use this as a bridge across the river.

"There were only two pumpkins on the pumpkin vine, and only one wartermelon on the other side of the river, but each was very large. One pumpkin grew so large that I had to use two horses, two oxen, and two water buffaloes to drag it from the field. I got a long pole and stuck it into the pumpkin to serve as a wagon tongue, and then with the six animals I dragged it to a mine where there were many men working. After splitting the pumpkin with a great crashing sound, I sold half of it to the miners for one day's food supply and the other half for the next day's supply. Then somebody bought the empty rind and made a shop for himself with it. When the other pumpkin was ripe, we planned a feast. We had to get an enormous caldron in which to cook it, and when we couldn't find one large enough, we ordered one made. Two men came and measured the pumpkin and started to make a special caldron, but they had to send to several villages to collect enough copper for it. It was such a big caldron that when one coppersmith was hammering on one side of it, the other coppersmith, working on the opposite side, could not even hear the clanging of his hammer.

"But the pumpkins were not nearly as large as the watermelon that grew on the opposite side of the river. It was so large that I knew we could never move it, and so when it was ripe I decided to cut it up right in the field where it grew. I made a cut into it with my knife, but, unfortunately, I let the knife slip out of my hand, and it fell down inside the melon, 'Plunk!' I took off my hat, put it under my arm, and dived into the melon to try to find my knife. I searched and searched for my knife for a long time but couldn't find it. After a while I met an old woman who had helped us cook the second pumpkin, and I asked her for a drink of water.

"She asked me, 'What are you looking for, my son?'

" 'I am looking for my knife,' I said. 'I have lost it somewhere in this watermelon.'

" 'How do you expect to find something as small as a knife?' she asked. 'We lost seven camels in this very melon over a week ago, and we are still searching for them. Here is some water.'

"She poured me a cup of water from a jug that she carried with her, and I lifted it to my lips. As I was about to take a swallow, I noticed a hair on the brim. I took hold of this hair and began pulling it. I pulled and I pulled, and the seven camels that the woman had lost came out, all of them tied in a row along that hair. And with them was still one more camel, a creature with one blind eye. I gave that extra camel to my son, and it is now about five years old — but it was quite a long time ago when all these things happened to me."

At that point the miller interrupted me saying, "Stop, friend; you surpass me in telling tales, and you have won."

I started eating the bread, while the miller watched me sadly, looking at my eyes. After I had finished eating the bread, he said to me, "What are you going to tell Ali Bey when you reach home?"

"I really do not know what to say to him," I answered.

"Why don't you tell him that I borrowed his horse for a day? Then, if you like, you can run away from there," said the miller.

I returned to the village with the two camels. Ali Bey asked me, "Where is the other camel?"

"It hurt its foot and is coming along behind," I said.

"What about my horse?"

"Well, the miller borrowed it for a day, but he will return it to you in the morning," I said. I think he was not pleased with what I told him, because he reached for his book, turned the pages, and found my name in it: Sorsavush of Haymana.

He paid me one nickel coin and two copper coins, and then he said to me, "Get out of here. Let my eyes not see you again in this village."

After that I walked and walked and finally reached the plain just north of here. When I went to the fountain there to drink, I saw approaching someone that I knew. It was Hasan Uyar. (You knew Hasan. He is dead now.) Hasan did not remember me — I had been away so long — and he suspected that I was a thief. When I reached for my handkerchief, he thought I was reaching for a pistol. He shouted, and soon a whole group of people came and surrounded me. When I told them who I was, they were amazed. They all thought I had been killed by the Greeks, and when they saw that I was still alive, they all invited me to come and drink coffee with them. It took me a whole week to visit everyone.

PART IV

Moralistic Tales

In a broad sense, almost all folktales can be considered moralistic, with types as different as *märchen* and outlaw sagas developing their respective patterns of value for human behavior. In the more restricted sense understood here, moralistic is meant to suggest a didactic motive. Even this restriction does not set the tales of this section entirely apart, for clearly many of the anecdotes of Part VII are also instructive. The following six tales, however, have as their primary function the imparting of one or another kind of folk wisdom.

In the version here presented, "Do Not Do Anything Without Considering Its End" includes Nasreddin Khoja, Turkey's most cherished comic character and the subject of several anecdotes in Part VII. Both the Khoja and his alleged relationship to Tamerlane, the Mongol conqueror, are discussed in that section of the book. Usually the actors in this tale are not specific historical personages.

I.

Lazy Ahmet and the Padishah's Daughter [1]

There was once a padishah who was in the habit of looking out of his window every morning to enjoy the view. The only thing that spoiled the view for him were the many poor people, shabbily dressed or wearing tatters, who used to sleep on the pavements of the town. "Oh, God's poor people! I am sorry for you," he would say. But the padishah's daughter, looking out of her bedroom window, used to say, "Oh, wives' poor men!"

This went on for several days, the padishah saying, "Oh, God's poor people!" and his daughter saying, "Oh, wives' poor men!" until at last he overheard her and asked her the meaning of her remark. "Oh, Father," she said, "those people are not turned poor by God. They are made poor by their own wives."

The padishah thought about this explanation for a while, and then he decided to test the truth of his daughter's observation. He called his chief crier [2] to him and said, "Go and make known to my people that I will give my daughter to the laziest man that can be found in my realm."

The chief crier called out all the assistant criers, and they set out in all directions shouting, "The padishah seeks the laziest man in the realm to marry his daughter!" In a village they found sleeping in a small hut a man who was reported by all the people of that area to be the laziest man in the realm. His name was Lazy Ahmet. He slept for forty days on one side, and then he rolled over and slept for forty days on the other side. The criers who found him reported to the padishah that his laziest subject had been found.

The padishah was pleased with the news, and he announced that his daughter would be given in marriage to Lazy Ahmet. But Lazy Ahmet was not even aware of this for some days. He just kept on sleeping until his friends awakened him to tell him the news. Even then, he did not rouse himself very much but took the news quite casually.

At the appointed day the padishah's daughter was brought to the hut of Lazy Ahmet and presented to him as his wife. He was not even awake when she arrived, and she was greeted by Lazy Ahmet's old mother, who lived in the hut with him. When the padishah's daughter entered her new home, she saw that the fireplace was so filled with ashes that it was heaped right up to the chimney. She took out the ashes, and then she asked her mother-in-law to go out and buy some reed canes. While the old woman was away, she got ready a pail of water, and when the canes arrived, she soaked the canes in water to make them more flexible, and then she poured water on Lazy Ahmet and beat him. She did this several times, first pouring on water and then beating him. [3] She beat as hard and as fast as she could, but at first, Lazy Ahmet didn't even feel the blows striking his body. But after she had broken four or five

173

canes on him, he finally stood up and said to the girl, "Yes, master. What can I do for you?"

"From now on," said the girl, "you are under my command."

"Yes, master," said Lazy Ahmet, "it shall be so."

"Well, now get out of the house," said the girl. "Go down to the marketplace and walk about there and observe what happens there."

When Lazy Ahmet went out to fulfill this order, she cleaned the house and put it in order. Then she cooked a good meal and fed Lazy Ahmet when he came home that night.

After Lazy Ahmet had walked around the town for several days, coming home only in the evenings, he began to change, and after a while he was completely changed. He could not even enjoy lying down during the day now but became a very active person. One day as he was walking down the main street of the town, he met two porters who were discussing how much they had earned that day. When Lazy Ahmet heard them telling about their earnings, he said to himself, "Why don't I work? I can also earn a few liras a day, but before I decide on this, let me first go and consult my master."

He went home and said to his wife, "Master, with your permission I'll go to work. I shall become a porter."

"All right," said his wife, "I give you my consent. Take this money and buy a rope for yourself with it so that you will not be ropeless." [4] Lazy Ahmet bought a rope and began to work as a porter, carrying wood from the forest to the town. He earned two or three liras a day, enough to buy food for his household.

One day Lazy Ahmet became acquainted with another porter. He said to this new friend, "We get our backs sore by carrying such heavy loads of wood. Why don't we buy a donkey to help us carry our loads of wood?"

His companion said, "It is a good idea." And they went to consult with Lazy Ahmet's wife about this plan. She gave her consent, and a donkey and all necessary harnesses were purchased.

After working three or four months with the help of their donkey, his friend suggested to Lazy Ahmet that they let the donkey rest for a day while they each cut enough wood to make four trips in one day instead of the usual two. After consulting his wife, Lazy Ahmet accepted this proposal, and the two porters went to the forest to cut wood. Lazy Ahmet had now become a very good wood cutter, and he cut so much wood that day that his companion became jealous of his ability. He decided to play a trick on Lazy Ahmet. As they were going home, he sent Lazy Ahmet on an errand, and then he went back and set fire to Ahmet's pile of wood.

When Lazy Ahmet arrived home, his wife said to him, "Well, what did you do today?"

"Oh, I cut four donkey loads of wood today, and tomorrow I shall bring it all to town and sell it."

But next day when Lazy Ahmet went to the forest with the donkey, he found that all the wood he had cut had been burned to ashes. As he was walking around the spot where his wood had been burned, he noticed several pieces of flint lying on the ground. He picked these up to take them home as backgammon counters for his master. When he got home he reported to his master that all his wood had been burned.

"It doesn't matter," she said. "It must have become charcoal. You can load the charcoal on the donkey and bring that to the town market to sell."

"Yes, master," he said, and then he remembered the flints which he had found. "Here are some pieces of flint which I have brought for you for backgammon counters. I found them by the pile of ashes."

These pieces were in fact made of gold and not flint, and since his wife was a padishah's daughter, she was quick to recognize this. She asked her husband, "Is there more of this where your wood pile was?"

"Oh, yes, any amount of it," he replied. Apparently a treasure of gold had been buried once on the spot where he had piled his wood. When the wood was burned it melted some of the gold, and pieces were scattered about. Lazy Ahmet went back to the forest and brought back a load of what he thought was flint.

His wife took pieces of this gold to a goldsmith and exchanged them for money. She bought furniture for their house, and she also bought quantities of grain and sold them for higher prices. One day she hired a crier and said to him, "Go and announce that I want pack mules to carry rice to the city of Sivas." Lazy Ahmet no longer had to work, but when he heard the crier making this announcement, he went to his wife and said, "Master, let us join the caravan, too."

The request was approved, but before he left he was given all kinds of useful advice by his wife. Among other things, she said to him, "Whenever the group camps for the night, they will try to find level ground for sleeping, but you be sure to sleep on high ground."

The next day the caravan set out, and the drivers stopped that night to rest by a stream, but Lazy Ahmet climbed up on a rock to rest. The others laughed at him for staying in such a strange place. But during the night it rained and the stream overflowed, soaking the other drivers and spoiling their beds. In the morning Lazy Ahmet said, "Hey, you drivers. You thought that I was a fool, but you were the fools."

Now we go back to Lazy Ahmet's wife. As soon as the caravan left, she hired workers to build a large palace. She had a palace built which was exactly like that of her father.[5]

The caravan had now reached a wide plain where they traveled for a long time without finding any water. The animals were thirsty, and the men were tired. At last they came to a well, but they were warned away from it by a shepherd who said that no one who descended it ever came out again. All the drivers asked, "Who will go down the well and get water for us?" Lazy Ahmet was not very smart, and so he said at once, "I will!"

Lazy Ahmet was lowered down the well on a rope. When he reached the bottom, he saw a giant lying there asleep. Near the giant was imprisoned a boy who said to Lazy Ahmet, "You are fortunate, for you have come during one of the forty-day sleeping periods of this giant."

"Who are you?" asked Lazy Ahmet.

"I am the son of the sultan of Sivas," [6] said the boy. "What are you doing here?"

"Well, I was sent here to get some water," said Lazy Ahmet, and he filled all his buckets and skins with water. These were pulled up by his companions, and when enough water was raised, Lazy Ahmet was also pulled up out of the well. The caravan then moved on toward Sivas.

When they reached the city, they delivered their load of rice. When the sultan of Sivas heard of the arrival of a caravan, he had criers announce among the drivers that he was seeking news of his lost son. "The sultan will give farms and cattle and many other things to anyone who can bring him news of the whereabouts of his lost son," the criers announced.

As soon as he heard this announcement by the criers, Lazy Ahmet came forth and said, "Tell his majesty that I have news of his son."

His fellow drivers all tried to quiet him: "Be silent, you fool! How could you have seen the sultan's son? You have been with us all the time."

Lazy Ahmet spoke with great assurance and insisted that he had seen the sultan's son. When he appeared before the sultan, he said, "Your majesty, if you will provide me with men and enough rope, I can pull your son from the well in which he is imprisoned." He was given the rope he requested and a number of men to help him.

He and the men left Sivas, and he led them to the well where the sultan's son was imprisoned. Lazy Ahmet was lowered into the well, where the giant was still sleeping and where the boy was still a captive. The boy said to Lazy Ahmet, "There is a magic sword on that wall. It belongs to the giant. If you say the Kulhuvallahi [7] prayer to God, you will be able to draw that sword from its sheath, and with that magic sword you will be able to kill the giant." Lazy Ahmet did as he was directed. He said the Kulhuvallahi prayer to God, drew the magic sword, and killed the giant. He then freed the sultan's son, and they were both pulled from the well.

When they returned to Sivas, there was great rejoicing. The sultan called Lazy Ahmet to him and said this to him: "Ask for anything that you would like from me."

But Lazy Ahmet answered, "I cannot say anything without consulting my master first."

"Where is your master?" asked the sultan.

"Oh, she is very far from here," said Lazy Ahmet. But finally he said, "I don't really want anything from you."

Hearing this, the sultan's son said, "Father, he does not want anything, but please load his mules with pearls and precious stones and let him go wherever he wishes."

The sultan loaded the mules with pearls and precious stones, and then Lazy Ahmet left Sivas. After traveling for several days, he reached his own town, but he went around and around in the streets and could not find his own home. Finally, after several days, he was observed by his wife, who saw him one morning as she looked out of her palace window. She asked him, "What is all this?" pointing to the heavy loads on the mules.

"I don't know what it is," answered Lazy Ahmet. "It just followed me."

His wife opened up the saddlebags and found the pearls and precious stones, and she took these out and sold them for a great amount of money. She then sent a message to the owner of the local Turkish bath: "Wash my husband well and shave his beard. Burn his old clothes and dress him in new ones." Lazy Ahmet was taken to the bath and washed and shaved. When this was completed, he looked for his clothes. "Where are my clothes?" he asked.

"They are gone," said the owner of the bath. "But you are to wear these new clothes."

Upon reaching home, Lazy Ahmet had his pockets filled with money by his wife. "Go about the town," she said, "and spend this money carelessly."

"Yes, master," he said. He went to the marketplace and bought various things, but always he neglected to wait for his change. He gave a lira for something worth only fifty kurus. His wife had ordered him to behave this way in order to attract the attention of the padishah, and in time just this did happen. The secret agents of the padishah noticed this lavish spending and reported it to the padishah. "A strange man has come to your town," they said, "and this man spends great quantities of money very carelessly." The sultan ordered them to have this stranger brought into his presence.

The next day the agents found Lazy Ahmet again spending his money in the marketplace, and they said to him, "You are invited to the palace by the padishah."

"I cannot accept any invitation until I have consulted my master," he said.

Lazy Ahmet went and told his wife that he had been invited to the palace of the padishah. He asked her for permission to make the visit. She consented, but she told him many things to do and many things not to do. "See that you don't behave foolishly. Watch your talk. Use polite language. Don't speak before you are spoken to. Eat and drink whatever you wish. When you leave the palace, say to the padishah, 'I hope that your majesty will soon honor our humble dwelling with your presence.' If he asks where you live, just give him the number of our house." [8]

Lazy Ahmet went to visit the padishah, and he got along well with him. As he left the padishah's palace, he extended the invitation for the sultan to return the visit. "I hope that your majesty will soon honor our humble dwelling with your presence," he said, just as his wife had directed him.

The padishah accepted this invitation, and he visited Lazy Ahmet's house the very next day. He was amazed to find that Lazy Ahmet lived in a house exactly like his own. For a moment he wondered if he had come to the right place, but he was soon greeted by his host, who led him to the dining room. Three servings of food were brought in, one placed before the padishah, one placed before the host, and one placed before an empty seat. The sultan said, "Let the person for whom this dish is set come forth." At that moment, Lazy Ahmet's wife entered the room.

When she sat down, she pulled back her veil and asked, "Do you recognize me, father?" The padishah immediately recognized his daughter. "Well, father," she continued, "you can now see that those men who came before your palace were poor because of their wives. If their wives had been frugal and industrious, they would not have been so poor. A husband is like a bird. He gathers and brings what he has gathered to his nest, and if the wife doesn't use what he has brought her wisely, that home cannot prosper."

In the end, Lazy Ahmet said, "Well done, my master. You will be my mate, and I shall be your lady, and, by the permission of God,[9] let us get married." And they were now married with a regular wedding, in the palace of the padishah, and they lived happily ever after.

2.

Do Not Do Anything Without Considering Its End [10]

One day Nasreddin Khoja's wife went to a bath. She sat down by a trough,[11] but when she was getting ready to wash herself, a bath attendant came to her and asked her to move. The bath attendant said to her, "Move along from here! The wife of merchant Hasan Agha is going to wash here."

When Nasreddin Khoja's wife heard this, she got up from where she was and moved, and found another place for herself. She prepared to take her bath by another trough, but when she started to wash herself, some other bath attendants came along and said to her, "Mehmet Agha's daughter is going to wash here. Will you please find another place for yourself?"

Nasreddin Khoja's wife got up from that place and went to still another place and sat down. When she was about ready to start washing there, she was again called to get up and go elsewhere. "Ahmet Agha's wife wants to wash here. Will you please get up and find some other place?" The poor woman realized that she would not be able to wash herself anywhere in the bath, and so she took her belongings and went home.

Nasreddin Khoja that day decided to ask his wife how she felt, but when he looked at her face, he saw that she was sulking and looked very angry. He passed a few jokes at her, but she didn't respond and continued to sulk.

After a time, she began to talk. She said to Khoja, "From tomorrow on, I want you to be a merchant."

"Please don't say that," said the Khoja. "How can I be a merchant? You cannot be a merchant simply by saying so. You need cash to become a merchant."

"I don't care how you become one," said the wife. "If you can't be a merchant, I shall divorce you!"

Khoja was quite concerned by this. He said to his wife, "Please give me twenty-four hours to think about it."

Khoja went to bed that night, but he couldn't sleep. He kept thinking all of the time. He realized that he could not possibly be a merchant just by his wife's saying so. He finally remembered that he had a donkey that he could possibly sell to raise some money with which to open a shop. In the morning Nasreddin Khoja took his donkey to the marketplace and sold it there for twenty liras. As there were many empty shops in those days, he rented a shop for twenty liras a month. But as the Khoja gave all of the money that he had for the rent, he had no capital left with which to buy merchandise. Khoja didn't mind that, however. He opened his shop in the morning and closed it in the evening, though there was absolutely no business in it. His wife, on the other hand, was very proud that her husband had, after all, become a merchant. Whenever she went to the bath she washed wherever she pleased.

This empty business of Khoja's went on for some time. One day Tamerlane came to take part in the Friday noon service [12] in the Mosque of Akshehir. After the service was over, Tamerlane decided to inspect the market. During his walk through the marketplace, he saw that Nasreddin Khoja was just sitting and doing nothing in his shop. He asked Khoja, "What are you selling?"

"I am selling wisdom, your majesty," answered Khoja.

"How much do you charge for it?" asked Tamerlane.

Pointing to an earthenware pot near him, Nasreddin Khoja said, "One pot full of wisdom is worth one gold lira."

Tamerlane then said, "All right, sell me some."

Nasreddin Khoja said, "The wisdom that I give you is this: Do not do anything without considering its end."

Tamerlane said, "Well, Khoja, this piece of wisdom cost me a lot. Do you think it is worth it?"

Nasreddin Khoja said, "Of course it is, your majesty. It is even cheaper than it should be. You will realize its value afterwards."

One day, a little while after this, Tamerlane's vezirs plotted to assassinate him. They wanted to get rid of him and then make someone else their leader. But who could kill Tamerlane? They thought that perhaps Tamerlane's private barber could do it most easily. They then decided to make the barber the grand vezir if he could do this job for them. They called the barber to them and explained to him what it was that was to be done. They promised to make him the grand vezir if he would cut Tamerlane's throat while he was shaving him. "Can you do this?" they asked him.

"Of course I can do that," said the barber.

"Well, the day you do it, you will become grand vezir."

A little while later Tamerlane called his barber to him in order to be shaved. In the room where Tamerlane met such people, he had framed and placed on the wall the words which Nasreddin Khoja had said to him: "Do not do anything without considering its end." Tamerlane had liked this expression, and he had made a habit of reading it aloud whenever he was about to do anything. When the barber was shaving him, he was just at the point where he was going to cut Tamerlane's throat. Tamerlane's eye at that moment caught the writing on the wall, and, as it was his custom, he read it aloud. He said, "Do not do anything without considering its end."

When the barber heard this, he thought that the ruler was speaking to him. He suddenly felt that Tamerlane knew all along that he was going to cut his throat. He was terrified. He dropped the razor from his hand and fell to the feet of the great despot, saying, "Your majesty, it is not my fault! I was entrusted by your vezirs to do this terrible thing. I was told by them to cut your throat, but you knew this all of the time."

After this confession, Tamerlane had the barber and his fellow conspirators punished. He then had Nasreddin Khoja brought to his presence and he said to him, "The wisdom that you sold me was really very cheap. As a matter of fact, it saved my life today." Then turning to his attendants he said, "Give the Khoja another piece of gold. I have decided to make this wise man the *müdür* of a *nahiye*." [13]

3.

Solomon and the Vulture [14]

One day Allah sent Azrail [15] to the Emperor Solomon [16] telling him that he had come to take his life. Solomon was a ruler who had great power and also the ability to understand a great many things about life. When Azrail told him that he had come for his life, Solomon said, "Very well, but who is going to rule after I am dead? Will the ruler who comes after me be a good one or a bad one? I have lived for five hundred years. How can I leave my realm without knowing what the world will be like after I die? I am entitled to know this."

Azrail thought him right and went back to Allah and repeated to him what Solomon had said. Allah listened to Azrail's report and said this: "I shall give him forty more days of life. Go and tell him that in that time he must find out what has happened in the past. Why should he want to live longer? When he sees what has happened in the past, maybe he will change his mind."

Azrail returned to Solomon and told him that he had been given forty more days by Allah. "During these forty days, you are to travel around the world to find out what has happened in all of the past."

Solomon consulted with his wise men about which creature had the longest life span in the world. He was told that the Ak Baba,[17] the vulture, was the creature that lived longest. Solomon went out and found a vulture that was fifteen hundred years old. Solomon said to the vulture, "I have lived five hundred years and Allah has given me forty more days of life. During this time, I must find out what has happened during the past. Can you tell me this?"

To this the vulture said, "I have lived only fifteen hundred years. Go and talk to my brother, who is two thousand years old and lives on the other side of yonder mountain."

Solomon went around the mountain and there he found the vulture that he was looking for. He asked the vulture about the past, but this vulture said to him, "I am only two thousand years old, but I have a friend who is a vulture who lives at the river here who is two thousand and five hundred years old. Go and talk to him."

Solomon went to the place where the vulture of two thousand and five hundred years lived and explained to him his mission. "O vulture, tell me what remarkable experiences you have had in your life."

The bird said, "In my long life I had a series of memorable experiences and I will tell you of the most important of these. Once I was caught up in a terrible winter during which I almost starved to death. During this winter I landed one day on top of a minaret which was made of gold. When I looked down, I saw that there was a service in progress in the mosque to which the minaret was attached.[18] Men with white beards were sitting in the front row. Ones with black beards were standing behind them in a row, and the shaven men were in the rear. When they finished praying, the congregation looked up and saw me standing on the minaret. One of them said, 'Poor bird. He is perhaps hungry. Let us kill an ox and give it to him to eat.' They killed an ox and gave it to me to eat. After eating it I was happy and I flew away.

"One hundred years later there was another terrible winter. I flew to a strange country during that winter and I landed on the silver minaret of a mosque, and there I looked down and saw that a service was in progress. Black-bearded men were standing in the front row. White-bearded men were behind them, and the shaven ones were at the rear. When the service was over they looked up and saw me, and one of them said, 'This poor bird must be hungry. Let us kill a sheep and give it to him.' They killed the sheep and gave it to me. I ate it and flew away.

"One hundred years later there was another long and terrible winter. This time I found a mosque with a minaret that had a bronze top. I landed on the top of the minaret and looked down. I saw a service in progress. Shaven men were in the front; black-bearded ones were behind them; and the white-bearded men were at the rear. When the service was over the people saw me there on the minaret. In great excitement they said, one to another, 'Look, there is a bird on the minaret. Bring a gun and let us shoot it.' Everyone went home for his gun. When I realized that I was in danger, I flew away and thus saved my life.

"As you can see from this, the world does not get any better.[19] After you die it will be a worse place than when you lived in it. Go back to your kingdom and accept Allah's will."

4.

The Wise Old Weaver [20]

One day the padishah was watching his capital from the balcony of his palace. As he looked around the city, his eye was caught by a flag which was waving above a house. This flag was unlike any that was known to the padishah. He ordered one of his attendants to go to that house and find out what the flag was. One of his attendants found the house with the strange flag, and knocked on its door. When the door was opened for him, he asked if he could be allowed to come in and sit down for a few minutes to discuss some business. He was shown into the house by an old man with white hair and a sparse beard, and he was asked to sit in a chair.

The old man then went back to his loom, sat down again, and began to weave. The palace attendant noticed that the old weaver's trousers were muddy. He wondered why they were muddy and he asked him, "Why don't you clean the mud off your trousers?"

The old man explained as follows: "You see, there are many rat holes in the walls of my house. To stop them I mix mud with my feet while I sit here working the loom with my hands, and because of this I get my trousers soiled with mud."

"Very well," said the palace attendant. "But what about this pole that goes straight up through the ceiling?"

"That pole has a flag on the end of it, and by waving the flag I am able to keep the birds away from the washed wheat that my wife has spread on the roof to dry. The pole is attached to the loom here, and by moving from side to side while I work I am able to shake it enough to frighten the birds away."

The palace attendant was amazed at this and he said to the old man, "But what about the string that is tied to your finger?"

"Ah," said the old man, "that is attached to the child's hammock. My wife goes to the bath at this time of the day, and she leaves the baby for me to attend. This is how I rock the baby to sleep by pulling on the string."

"Well," said the padishah's attendant, "who are the children with the books in their hands sitting over in the corner?"

"They are the neighbors' children whom I am teaching while I work here," said the old man.

The palace attendant was greatly impressed with this old man who could carry on five activities at the same time. He thanked him for his hospitality, and left his house. He returned to the palace and reported to the padishah what he had seen.

The padishah said to the attendant, "Take a note to that man. I want him here with me in the palace. We may need such an ingenious man in the future." The attendant did as he was told, and the old man was given a job in the palace.

Some time later a stranger came to the palace, drew a circle in the courtyard, and then sat in the middle of the circle. This man disregarded all questions asked of him, and no one was able to find out who he was, or what it was that he wanted. He just sat in the middle of the circle and kept quiet. Many people tried to make the stranger talk, but they all failed. Upon this, the padishah asked one of his attendants to bring the old weaver to him.

The weaver was brought from his home, and the padishah explained to him that this stranger had come to the palace, had drawn a circle, and was sitting in the middle of this circle without saying a word. The padishah asked the weaver if he would make the man talk and explain what it was that he wanted, or what it was that he meant.

The weaver thereupon went to his henhouse, caught a cock, and put it under his arm. Then he took two walnuts and put them in his pocket. Then he went to the garden of the palace where the stranger was sitting. By this time the padishah had had his throne moved to the garden of the palace too so that he could watch the weaver try to make the stranger explain his purpose.

When the weaver arrived, he took a stick and drew a circle inside the circle that had been drawn by the stranger and then he sat in that inner circle. Everyone was watching what the weaver was doing in great amazement. The stranger took a handful of millet from his pocket, at that point, and scattered it on the ground. Upon this, the weaver let loose of the cock which he had hidden under his gown, and the cock began to pick up the grains of millet from the ground. When the stranger saw this, he said, "But there will be blood shed!" Upon this the weaver took out of his pocket the two walnuts which he had brought and he threw these upon the ground. When the stranger saw this, he shouldered his bag and left, and since the weaver's work was over, he put the walnuts back in his pocket, put the cock under his arm again, and went back to his own house.

The padishah, like everybody else, was greatly surprised and puzzled with the things that they had seen. They could not understand how the two men had communicated with each other, and so the padishah ordered that the weaver be recalled to the palace. The weaver returned and was taken to the presence of the padishah. When the padishah asked him to explain all that had happened, the weaver said this: "Your majesty, this man is an infidel Muscovite.[21] By drawing a circle and sitting in the middle of it he meant that the world was his. But then I drew a little circle in his and sat in it, by which I meant to say that we are also a nation and that we had a right to occupy part of that world. When he scattered a handful of millet on the ground he meant that he had many soldiers. I let the cock loose, which ate the millet which he had scattered, and that meant that we had many heroes who could defeat those soldiers of his. Then he said, 'But there will be blood shed!' Upon this, I threw the two walnuts upon the ground. By this I meant that I was willing to venture my testicles on the outcome."

Very impressed with the weaver's explanation, the padishah said this to him: "In this city of mine, where dwell over a million and a half people, nobody but you was able to solve this problem. Therefore, you may ask of me whatever you wish, and I will grant it to you."

"Your majesty," said the weaver, "I want nothing but health for you for the rest of your life. I am a weaver, and I can manage to get along that way, especially with the additional job which you have given me in the palace."

"No," said the padishah, "padishahs should give gifts to those who render service to them."

"Well, then, your majesty," said the weaver, "here is my wish. Give me a charter in which it will be written, 'This man will receive one kurus from anyone who is a weaver and two kurus from anyone whose name is Hasan, one kurus from anyone who is bald, and one kurus from anyone who has two wives.' "

"There is nothing easier than that, my man," said the padishah, and he ordered that a charter be drawn up for the weaver with these stipulations in it. The padishah then stamped it with his seal. The weaver put the charter in his pocket and went down to the marketplace.

When he reached the marketplace he saw a weaver there who was selling some sheets that he had woven. "You must pay me one kurus," said the old man to the person selling the sheets. When the man asked him why, he said, "Because you are a weaver."

"Why do you want me to pay one kurus?" asked the man. "I have children, and two wives to support."

"Well, in that case," said the old man, "you will have to pay me another kurus for that."

"For what?" shouted the younger man.

"For the fact that you have two wives," said the old man.

When the man selling the sheets refused to pay the money, the two began to quarrel. The clever old man hit the other weaver's fez and knocked it down. When this happened he saw that the younger man was also bald, and he said to him, "Now you must pay me another kurus. That will make three kurus that you must pay me."

"Why is this?" asked the younger weaver, in great anger.

"This is because your head is bald," said the older man.

Now there were many weavers in the land, and there were many men that had two wives, and many of these men were bald, especially since there was very little sanitation in those days.[22] It was also the case that there were a great many men named Hasan, just as there are today. As a result of this, the old man became rich very soon. As a matter of fact, the problem that he caused soon became a national problem. One day the padishah discovered that there was a large crowd of people in front of the palace shouting, "We want you to take the taxing charter away from the weaver! We want you to take the taxing charter away from the weaver!"

When the padishah realized what was happening, he called the weaver to his presence. When the old man came, the padishah asked him, "What sort of trouble is this that you are causing me? Is it true that you are collecting so much money from my subjects that they are ready to rebel in this way?"

"Yes, your majesty, that is true," said the old man.

"Well, then, why do you persist in this? Have I not treated you very well in the past?"

"Yes, your majesty," said the old man, "you have. I have done this, however, to give you a lesson. There are certain evils in this world which are discovered quickly, and there are others which take a long time to discover."

The padishah at first was very angry with the old man for this arrogance, and he had him thrown in jail. He took the charter away from him, and so the clamor of his subjects ceased; but the padishah was a good man, and he realized, after a while, that the old man was indeed a wise person, and he released him from the jail again. After this, the old man became one of his most trusted vezirs.

5.

The Ugly Padishah and the Wise Vezir [25]

Once upon a time, there was a padishah with no children. As he was very wealthy, and held extensive territories, he was very unhappy at the thought of dying without an heir. One day he gathered together all the soothsayers in his kingdom, and these men prayed for him. Some of them also wrote various kinds of amulets.[24] With the help of the prayers and the charms, the queen eventually gave birth to a male child. As it turned out, however, the boy was an ugly child. The padishah, nevertheless, was pleased to have a son, though he was somewhat unhappy at the fact that he was so ugly. He celebrated the event on a large scale, and felt that he would now be succeeded on the throne by a child of his own.

The grand vezir of that realm was a very wise man, and so in order to protect the child, he had removed from the palace all the mirrors. This made it impossible for the boy to see how ugly he really was. When his father died, he became the padishah. He married many beautiful women, and these women all had mirrors. One day, when he was in the library, he found a piece of mirror among the books. When he looked in the mirror, he saw his own face, and he was horrified. He began to cry and sob.

The grand vezir was informed of the situation and he ran to the library. "Why are you crying, your majesty? What is bothering you?"

"I didn't know that I was such an ugly man until now. I just saw my face in the mirror today," said the young padishah. "Why am I so ugly? What is my sin?"

When the grand vezir heard this, he began to cry also. The young padishah said to him, "I am crying because I have discovered that I am so very ugly. But why are you crying?"

"Yes, your majesty," said the grand vezir. "You saw your face just once in your life, and look how you are crying. But we, your people, have seen your face all our lives. That is why I am crying."

6.

The Two Hunchbacks and the Wednesday Witches [25]

There was once a hunchback named Ali who fired a furnace in a Turkish bath. The heat felt good on his back, and the owner of the bath permitted him to live in the furnace room. He worked at this job for many years.

One night, long after all the customers of the day had gone home, Ali heard a noise upstairs in the bath. Going upstairs quietly, he saw a number of little people, only a hand high, dancing around in a circle on the floor of the bath and singing, "Charshambadir, Charshamba!" — "It's Wednesday! It's Wednesday!" The hunchback also began to sing with them, "Charshambadir, Charshamba!" and he danced in the circle with them, and everything that they did, he did, too. The little people were very pleased with him, and as a reward, they took the hump off his back and hung it up on the wall of the bath.

The next day Ali met one of his friends, another hunchback. The friend was surprised to see that Ali no longer was deformed, and he asked him how he had been cured. Ali told him about the little folk and how they had taken off his hump. The friend begged Ali to let him tend the furnace for a few days and perhaps the little people would come again and take off his hump too. Ali agreed to let his friend fire the furnace for several days and live in the furnace room at night.

One night, a short while after this, the friend was awakened by a noise upstairs in the bath. He went up the stairs quietly, and he saw there the little people, just as Ali had seen them, dancing around in a circle and singing, "Charshambadir, Charshamba!" But it wasn't Charshamba that day; it was Pershembe — Thursday. So the friend shouted loudly, "Yok! Yok! Pershembedir, Pershembe!" — "No! No! It's Thursday! It's Thursday!" The little people were so annoyed at this that they took down from the wall Ali's hump and put it on the back of his rude friend. And always after that, this friend had two humps on his back.

PART V

Köroghlu

Apart from the other character types in Turkey's vast folklore stands one larger-than-life figure, the chivalrous outlaw. Among a people mindful of their recent heroic past, the image of the outlaw appeals to deep sentiments unstirred by a Keloghlan or a Karagöz or a Nasreddin Khoja. Bandits still pose frequent threats to life and property in the mountainous regions of Turkey, and outlaw heroes are by no means cultural fossils,[1] though most of those who appear in folktales today have passed at least partly from the historical into the legendary world. Like Robin Hood, the Turkish outlaw appeals to folk sympathy because of his defiance of an unjust agent of government. Like Robin Hood and Rob Roy, he often robs from the rich in order to give to the poor. Like the former, he is the subject of folk songs and ballads; like the latter, he is a folktale hero.

Of greatest stature among Turkey's many celebrated outlaws is Köroghlu (literally, the Son of the Blind Man). His adventures are recounted throughout all Anatolia, with greatest frequency in the eastern and southeastern provinces. Many of these recitals are in the *cante fable* form, lengthy accounts of love and war, with much of the dialogue sung, evidence that they may well be, as Eberhard claims,[2] the productions of folk minstrels. Supposedly Köroghlu was himself a saz poet who improvised and sang and accompanied his own simple arias, but such spontaneous creation, credited to many of the outlaws, is probably no more than a convention.

For more than a century now Köroghlu songs and tales have been collected and discussed by both Turkish and foreign students of folk-

190

lore and literature, with the result that a considerable body of scholarship is available. Sources, texts, social and political implications, possible historicity of characters and incidents, cruxes within the cycle — these and other problems have been examined at length, especially by Eberhard and Boratav in their respective volumes. It is not the purpose of this survey to review or analyze such studies except as they contribute to a better understanding of those episodes of the Köroghlu story that follow.

In barest outline the Köroghlu story has a simple plot line. One Rushan (or Rushen) is renamed Köroghlu after his father, a groom, has been blinded in punishment for selecting two apparently worthless colts for a nobleman's stable. Köroghlu then departs with his disabled father and one of the colts, which eventually develops into a superior gray horse (Kirat) with magical qualities. When he grows up, Köroghlu gathers about him five hundred warriors, several of great distinction themselves, and builds a fortress at Chamlibel, a name which means mountain pass with pine trees. From this base he avenges his father's mistreatment, robs caravans, raids the holdings of wealthy landlords, goes on hunting expeditions, and engages in amorous pursuits. After experiencing numerous adventures and performing many feats of strength and courage, Köroghlu feels his death approaching, bids his companions farewell, bequeaths his estate and his authority to his son, Hasan Bey, and goes off to join the Forty Saints.[3] With this general pattern[4] most of the texts agree fairly well, but the cycle is sufficiently old and so widely distributed that as soon as one becomes more specific, variants occur not only in major episodes but in almost all of the details comprising them.

How old the Köroghlu story is no one knows for certain. There is evidence of a historical Köroghlu whose given name was Rushen at the end of the sixteenth and the beginning of the seventeenth centuries. Several imperial decrees for the arrest of a bandit of that name were sent to the governor of Anatolia.[5] His stronghold was first listed in these documents as Gerede in the province of Bolu, and the folk tradition supports this official statement, for several place names in that area attest to his reputation there; these same names appear in the tales. (A number of peasants near Köroghlu Mountain pointed out to us sites associated with the outlaw.) He then, apparently, moved to east-central Turkey and preyed upon caravans using the then important trade route between Tokat and Sivas; a mountain pass between those two cities also retains a cluster of place names from the legend. This was the period of the protracted disturbances in rural Turkey that were known as the Jelali Revolts,[6] uprisings led by various brigand chieftains beginning with one Bozuklu Jelal. Although it is impossible to be certain, it seems likely that the historical Köroghlu was one of the Jelali leaders and that topical factors helped shape the legendary figure. As Eberhard observes, both the Köroghlu cycle and the Jelali movement "expressed the reactions of the common people against an oppressive government." [7] (Indeed, it seems a safe assumption that much of the continuing folk interest in the tales of Köroghlu and other outlaws is a veiled expression of protest against not only the government but, perhaps more strongly, against the powerful landlords, the agas, who still hold large areas of Turkey in a semifeudal arrangement.) By the time that Chodzko made the first careful attempt to collect Köroghlu material (1830–1840),[8] some of these tales were known to be already more than a century old.

A varying number of episodes are ascribed to the "biography" of Köroghlu. Chodzko divided the material into twelve episodes; Boratav claims that there are twenty-four.[9] Eberhard, who has used the Chodzko text as a base and collated with it seventeen other full or partial texts, concludes that there are fifteen distinct episodes, and it is his text letters and episode numbers that we have used as reference points in our notes.

"How Köroghlu Became an Outlaw" was narrated by Tellal Mehmet Chavush (Crier Mehmet the Sergeant) of the town of Nallihan, not far from Köroghlu Mountain. Town crier of Nallihan for many years, Mehmet Bey finally retired to the less strenuous job of chief cowherd. (He was seventy years old when we collected tales from him in April 1962.) We encountered him in the fields, at the end of a day in early April, bringing home, with the help of several small boys, the combined herds of a number of Nallihan farmers. While the cattle cropped the sparse spring grass, he spent an hour and a half with us, filling two small reels of tape with four folktales, including fragments of the Köroghlu story.

Throughout much of "The Early Life of Hasan Bey," Köroghlu remains in the background, for the tale is concerned primarily with some of the adventures of his son. Just as the Arthurian cycle contains sequences of tales about individual members of the Round Table, so too the exploits of several of Köroghlu's band are recounted at some length. Those of Hasan Bey, Ayvaz (his adopted son), and Demirjioghlu (Son of the Blacksmith) are the most popular. The following story of Hasan

Bey was narrated by Mustafa Uchar at Omerlanli (new name: Tav-shanchali), near the caza city of Cihanbeyli, on the Plains of Konya. Although eighty years old when he told the tale, in February 1962, Mustafa Bey was a vigorous, alert man, a shepherd, who spoke easily and sang the verse dialogue in a clear tenor voice. He was an excellent raconteur, as attested by the large and respectful audience that gathered to hear him outside the home of the muhtar. Though a Turk, he spoke a heavily dialectal Turkish, studded with Kurdish words and delivered in the unmistakable singsong Kurdish speech tune. We did not have to be told that he had spent most of his long life in the extreme south-eastern section of Turkey.

1.

How Köroghlu Became an Outlaw [10]

Köroghlu's father was a groom in the household of Bolu Bey. One day some wealthy beys came to Bolu with thousands of fine horses, and Bolu Bey asked them to give him one. The visiting beys told Bolu Bey's groom to come and select from their pack whatever horse he wished and then take it to his master. The groom went and selected a horse that looked very weak and poor. He mounted this horse, took it to Bolu Bey, and showed it to him.[11]

Bolu Bey was furious. "Is that the best horse you could choose out of all those thousands of horses?" he demanded. He was so angry that he had his servants poke out the eyes of the groom with a hot rod. Then he was put on the poor horse and headed for his home.

When Köroghlu's father reached home, he said to his son, "Build four walls here." After Köroghlu had built the four walls, his father said, "Now cover these four walls with a roof so that not even a single ray of sunshine can penetrate it."

The horse was put in this dark stable, and there it was groomed for six months. After that time had passed, Köroghlu's father ordered that a field be plowed twelve times and watered after each plowing. After this was done, he ordered Köroghlu to mount the horse and ride through the plowed field. When Köroghlu had done this and returned, his father felt the horse's hoofs with his hands, but he was not satisfied with what he felt there.

"There must be a leak in some corner of the stable," he said to Köroghlu. "This horse must be kept in complete darkness in the stable for another six months." Köroghlu found the place in the roof where a small amount of light leaked in and fixed it.[12] Then he cared for the horse for another six months.

At the end of that time, his father ordered that the field be again plowed and watered twelve times. Köroghlu then mounted the horse and rode around the field several times, jumped over a high wall, and returned to his father, who again felt the horse's hoofs with his hands. This time he was satisfied, for he found some dry earth on the hoofs and knew that the horse had been able to reach down through the mud to the firm earth.

"As long as you have this horse," he told Köroghlu, "nobody can defeat you. Now I want you to go and take my revenge against Bolu Bey."

2.

The Early Life of Hasan Bey [13]

One day Köroghlu went hunting. He met an old woman along the road, all alone, and he asked her, "Why are you wandering about here, grandmother?"

"I was with a party of pilgrims going to Mecca," she said, "but they have gone on and left me behind. Who are you?"

"I am Köroghlu. Suppose I put you on my horse behind me and we ride until we overtake your companions. What would you give me for doing this?"

"What can I give you?" she asked. "Suppose that I tell you where there is a very beautiful girl whom you could probably win for yourself?"

"Grandmother," said Köroghlu, "that is just what I am looking for. Come — let me take you up behind me on my horse."

Köroghlu rode until they overtook the pilgrims, but on the way the old woman had said to him, "Go to Daghistan [14] where Pilgrim [15] Ahmet lived before he died at Mecca. His wife, Gülnigar, is a widow now, but she is the most beautiful woman in the world. She is the paragon of beauty, intelligence, and virtue. Go and win her."

After leaving the old woman with the pilgrims, Köroghlu returned to Chamlibel where he had five hundred men. "Oh, my gallant friends," he said to them, "I am going to Daghistan, for I have some business there. I shall see you again when I return. If it happens that I do not return, see that you live here like brothers, in peace with one another." Then he said farewell personally to each of his five hundred clever men, all of them as strong as wrestlers, and departed for Daghistan.

He reached that place in twenty-one days, and when he arrived there he asked for the house of Pilgrim Ahmet. When he found it, he was attended by the servants of the house, as Gülnigar had directed. When evening came, the servants returned to their homes, and Köroghlu said to Gülnigar, "I have come all this distance to take you as my wife."

"You have come to the wrong place," said Gülnigar.

"No, I don't think that I have come to the wrong place," said Köroghlu. "I have come here for you."

"But this is not the proper way in which to ask a lady to marry," she said.[16]

"In my opinion, it is the best way," said Köroghlu. Then they spent some time arguing about this, but after a while Gülnigar accepted Köroghlu's proposal. In the end, the two were married.

After that Köroghlu spent forty days with Gülnigar in her house there in Daghistan.[17] By that time Gülnigar had become pregnant. Köroghlu came to her one day and said, "It is time for me to go. I have business elsewhere to attend to now."

"Yes, but you married me and now you are leaving me in this condition," said Gülnigar. "What will now become of me?"

"I shall leave you a saddlebag full of gold and also an arm band. If the child is a girl, the money I leave you will take care of you both until the day you die. May you spend it and live happily. If the child is a boy, strap this arm band on him, and when he is old enough, let him search for me."

Saying this, Köroghlu left his pregnant wife in Daghistan and returned to Chamlibel, near Sivas.[18] When the time was ripe, a son was born to Gülnigar, but he was given no name until after he was three years old. One day Gülnigar invited to her home all of the neighborhood women and bade them sit down to a feast that she had prepared.

"Why are you giving such a feast?" they asked Gülnigar.

"I am giving this on the occasion of naming my son," said Gülnigar. "What do you suggest that I name him?"

Some of the women present suggested Ahmet. Others suggested Mehmet. Some said this and some said that, and in the middle of their discussion a dervish appeared out of nowhere and said to Gülnigar, "What is going on here? What is the matter?"

"We are trying to find a suitable name for my son," Gülnigar said, "but so far we have not succeeded."

"Why don't you call him Hasan Bey?" asked the dervish, and then he disappeared as he had come. The people present were all sorry that he had gone before they had received his blessing, for they thought him the prophet Hizir himself. The boy was named Hasan Bey.

Pilgrim Ahmet had had a mare, and it was still in the stable at the time Köroghlu had visited. Köroghlu's horse had mated with this mare, and when a colt was born, they named it Kamber Tay.[19]

One day when Hasan Bey was seven years old, he was playing with the children of the neighborhood. He was so strong that when he wrestled, he threw every other boy to the ground. He was so powerful that he made anyone whom he gripped cry aloud. On that one day, he tore the ear of one of the other children, and the child went home crying. "The son of Gülnigar has torn my ear," he said to his mother.

The woman hunted through the streets until she found Hasan Bey. She slapped his face several times and then she said to him, "You bastard! If you are the son of Pilgrim Ahmet, we shall respect you. If you are not, then God knows where she got you! You offspring of adultery!"

Hasan Bey went home to Gülnigar crying, and he said to her, "Mother, tell me who my father is."

"Your father was Pilgrim Ahmet," said Gülnigar. "He went to Mecca and died there."

Hasan Bey thereupon drew his dagger, held it at his mother's breast, and said to her, "Tell me the truth or I shall kill you!"

Then his mother said, "My son, your father is Köroghlu. He dwells at Chamlibel with five hundred loyal friends. You are still too young to go to him. When you have grown up a little more, then you can go and find him. In the meantime, I shall send you to live with your uncles, so that people here cannot insult you."

Hasan Bey went to live with his uncles, and he stayed with them for seven years. By the end of that time he had become such a capable young man that he was directing most of their business for them.

He returned to his mother now that he was fourteen years old. She granted her permission for him to go and seek his father, and so he mounted Kamber Tay and set out for Chamlibel. He reached there after traveling for twenty-four days.

As he drew near to Chamlibel, he stopped at a fountain [20] at the end of a level pasture. From there he could see Köroghlu's mansion across the fields. As he was standing there at the fountain, Hasan Bey saw a traveling peddler approaching with a long string of horses and mules loaded with his wares. After watering all his animals, the peddler started to turn off the main road to take a roundabout way past Köroghlu's mansion, for he feared him. He went along a side road toward the forested mountains. Hasan Bey got on Kamber Tay again, rode up to the peddler, and said to him, "You have watered your animals here. Why are you now leaving the main road and heading toward the mountains?"

"Who are you?" asked the peddler.

"What is that to you?" said Hasan Bey.

"I do not want to go through Köroghlu's territory," said the peddler. "If I drive my animals through his lands, he will surely catch me, cut off my ear, and confiscate my goods."

"Who could that damned Köroghlu be?" asked Hasan Bey, pretending that he did not know. "Why are you afraid of him? Unfasten your horses and mules and let them graze for a while in this fine pasture." But Hasan Bey did not himself dismount from his horse.

Köroghlu had been watching, with his binoculars,[21] the strange men at the fountain and the strange animals grazing in his pasture. With him was one of his companions, Son of the Blacksmith, whom Köroghlu had found in Nallihan.[22] (Köroghlu had gone to Nallihan to have his horse shod. At the blacksmith shop, he did not like any of the horseshoes that the apprentice, the son of the blacksmith, showed him. Köroghlu took them one by one, broke them in half, and threw them in a corner. As he was about to leave the shop, he handed the apprentice some coins, but the young man broke each of the coins in half, threw them on the ground, and said that they were not good money. Köroghlu was so impressed with this strong boy that he took him as one of his followers, and he was called Son of the Blacksmith. You know that Köroghlu got Ayvaz from his father's butcher shop in Usküdar and adopted him as his own son.)

Köroghlu was still looking through the binoculars. He called Ayvaz to him and said, "Look, there are strange horses on my land. Go and see if they belong to a poor man or to a peddler. If they are a peddler's, we shall go and plunder his goods."

Ayvaz went to where Hasan Bey was sitting on his horse and asked him who he was. Instead of answering, Hasan Bey galloped up to him and his servant and knocked them both off their horses with his mace.

He then bound them both hand and foot, tied them to the fountain, and turned their horses loose to graze in the pasture with those of the peddler.

Köroghlu, who was watching this scene through his binoculars, was amazed to see Ayvaz and his man bound hand and foot and their horses grazing with those of the strangers. He wondered if some powerful person was going to cause him serious trouble. Köroghlu said to Son of the Blacksmith, "Let us go and find out who that is."

As they approached the pasture, they saw a handsome young man riding back and forth on his horse. Let us listen to what Köroghlu said to the young man: [23]

> Look, yonder a wealthy peddler has come,
> Has come here and settled in my pasture.
> "Why are you grazing your animals in this pasture?
> Wait — I shall be there in a moment,
> Throw my lance at your neck, tie your head on my saddle."

Now let us hear what the young man answered to that:

> "Now don't be rash, oh gentlemen!
> I am in a bad mood today,
> And my sword has long been rusty.
> I come from a noble family,
> And your lance will not cut me."

Here is what Köroghlu replied:

> Our lances can be oiled,
> And their tips can be dipped in blood.
> Heads can be tied to saddles.
> Let me have the peddler.

After this Köroghlu and Hasan Bey started wrestling, and their feet plowed up the earth. Hasan Bey felt certain, after a while, that he could throw Köroghlu down and defeat him, but he decided not to do this, for he wanted to show the respect that is due to a father. Instead, he relaxed his hold on his father so that Köroghlu could defeat him. When Köroghlu had thrown Hasan Bey on the ground, he saw the arm band which he had left with Gülnigar, and he then recognized the boy as his own son. They embraced each other, and after releasing Ayvaz, Köroghlu took Hasan Bey to his mansion. He placed him in the care of Ayvaz, saying to him, "I have two sons in this world: you and Hasan Bey."

Shortly after his arrival at Chamlibel, Hasan Bey said to Ayvaz, "I am going to look around my father's mansion." It was a large mansion with forty-one rooms.

KÖROGHLU

When Hasan Bey began examining the mansion, Köroghlu said to Ayvaz, "Let him look in all of the first forty rooms, but don't you dare let him look into the forty-first, because Telli Hanim's picture is in there. If he sees her picture and falls in love with her, he may go after her and waste himself trying to get her." [24] Once Köroghlu had fallen in love with Telli Hanim, who lived in Akshehir. He had pursued her for seven years but had been unable to win her. After that, Köroghlu bought a picture of Telli Hanim and hung it in the forty-first room of his mansion. Whenever he thought about her, he would go and look at her picture and in that way find relief. Later he put Ayvaz in charge of that picture.

Hasan Bey looked through all the rooms in his father's mansion except that last one. He said to Ayvaz, "What is in that room?"

"Nothing but horsehoes, nails, saddles, harnesses, and such things," replied Ayvaz.

But Hasan Bey was determined to see what was in the room, and when Ayvaz refused to unlock the door, Hasan Bey kicked with all his might, and the door flew open. Hasan Bey walked in, came face to face with the picture of Telli Hanim, and fainted, falling flat on his back.

Ayvaz ran to Köroghlu and told him how Hasan Bey had come to see the picture of Telli Hanim. Köroghlu went to the forty-first room and threw a pail of water on Hasan Bey, who then got up from the floor. Let us hear what Hasan Bey said to his father:

> These rooms of my father's house
> Were possessed at the cost of his blood.
> But these rooms of his house are all dusty,
> Though if I speak thus he will be offended.

Köroghlu knew what Hasan Bey was thinking, and this is what he said to him:

> "Don't go, Hasan; don't go all the way to Akshehir.
> The castle of Akshehir is seven-storeyed;
> It is made of steel and marble and tile;
> Everyone there, young and old, will defend it."

Hasan Bey now sang:

> "She has a jeweled belt round her waist
> And she glitters in sunlight or in moonlight.
> If I don't go to get her, a stranger may.
> Then my heart would be so deeply wounded."

Köroghlu now:

> "Don't go, Hasan Bey; don't go, my son.
> I'll send Ayvaz to try to bring her here.

I have tried night and day myself. But perhaps
In this way can my broken heart be eased."
But Hasan Bey persisted:
"I left my mother to come here to you,
And that made a wound in my heart.
I cannot survive now a double wound —
By God! I shall go and pursue her."
Köroghlu:
"Don't go, Hasan Bey; don't go, dear son.
If you must, then let me come with you.
I shall find her, and then when I've found her,
I shall win her or give up my head."

When Köroghlu could not persuade Hasan Bey to forget Telli Hanim, he filled his saddlebag with gold and said to him, "Listen, Hasan Bey. I have a friend in Akshehir named The Pilgrim Veterinarian.[25] Let me write a letter to him, and when you get there, let him help you solve your problem."

Hasan Bey took the letter and put it in his pocket, mounted his horse with the saddlebag full of gold, and rode to Akshehir. Someone showed him the home of The Pilgrim Veterinarian, and he was received there.[26] The people of that house saw that this stranger was a handsome young man who gleamed as brightly as an oil lamp. The Pilgrim's wife sent a messenger to The Pilgrim Veterinarian, who was now the keeper of several government supply houses,[27] saying that he should lock up, come home, and there see the man who had come to visit him. "Tell him to come and talk with the visitor," she said, "and find out what it is that he wants."

The Pilgrim Veterinarian locked up his storehouses, came home, and greeted Hasan Bey: "Oh, visitor, pardon my asking, but where do you come from and where do you go?"

"I came from Chamlibel," said Hasan Bey.

"Whose son are you?" asked his host.

"I am the son of Köroghlu," said Hasan Bey.

"Are you truly the son of Köroghlu?" asked his host.

"By God, I am," said Hasan Bey.

"Well, then, welcome to my home," said The Pilgrim Veterinarian. "I am pleased to see you here."

After Hasan Bey had stayed in that house for three days, The Pilgrim Veterinarian said to him, "I have several government supply houses to attend to, but you may stay here as long as you wish. Here is

200

my wife. Regard her as your sister, and use this home as your own. If you should become tired of living here, just let me know the cause, and I shall then do whatever I can to help you."

The Pilgrim Veterinarian went to his business then, and Hasan Bey filled his pockets with gold and walked out into the streets of Akshehir. After a while he became hungry and so went to a bakery shop to get some bread, but he arrived there just as the baker was locking up his shop. "Oh, baker," he said, "open your shop again, for I am hungry."

When the baker ignored his request, Hasan Bey kicked open the iron door.[28] Taking the long wooden spatula that is used to put bread into the oven, he hit the baker at the base of the skull with this tool, and the man collapsed like a March bull.[29] "Please don't kill me," he said.

"You unpleasant man!" said Hasan Bey. "Why did you close your shop against me? I only wanted to buy some bread."

"I was closing my shop because I wanted to go and see Telli Hanim and her forty attendants," said the baker. "They can now be seen in the pleasure garden [30] of the palace, and everyone has gone there to look at them. I did not want to miss the sight. That is why I closed my shop."

After getting some bread to eat, Hasan Bey went with the baker to the pleasure garden. When he arrived there, he went to the chief gardener and his assistant and said to them, "What are you doing here?"

"We are guarding this garden right now," the chief gardener said.

"What is there in it to guard?" asked Hasan Bey.

"Telli Hanim and her forty palace girls," said the gardener.

"What is your monthly salary?" asked Hasan Bey.

"I receive twenty liras a month," said the gardener.

"Well, I shall count sixty liras into your hand if you will let me stay in the garden until evening," said Hasan Bey.

The chief gardener was about to agree to this bargain, but his assistant said, "We cannot do this. If Telli Hanim does not like this man, she will dismiss both him and us."

To this the chief gardener replied, "But if she should like him, then let her do whatever she likes with him." And so finally Hasan Bey counted sixty liras into the hand of the chief gardener and sixty liras into the hand of his assistant, and then they let him through the gate.

The chief gardener said to Hasan Bey, "In the middle of the garden there is a pool, and over the pool hangs a sycamore tree. Climb into the tree and wait until Telli Hanim and her girls come that way. They will come, wash their faces at the poolside, eat a lunch there, and then go for a walk around the garden. Telli Hanim's father is the ruler of this city, and in the evening he will send carriages to the garden to take all the ladies home. Telli Hanim does not live with her father's household but in a palace of her own."

From the sycamore tree where he had hidden himself, Hasan Bey saw Telli Hanim coming with her forty girls. Let us hear what he said to Telli Hanim:

> "Oh, look at the lovely flamingoes.
> I wish they would land on our lakes.
> I wonder if she can tell
> That the singer of these verses loves her."

Telli Hanim said to Bright-Faced Girl,[31] the most beautiful of all her forty attendants, "Go and bring a saz for me." And now let us hear what she sang in reply to Hasan Bey's verse:

> "I'll have you hanged by my brothers;
> I'll have your teeth and mouth battered in.
> Go away now from my garden,
> For you're no lover of mine."

Hasan Bey sang:

> "I've come all the way here for your sake.
> My origin stems from the beys round Köroghlu,
> Known through the land for their hospitality.
> Will you still throw me out of your garden?"

Telli Hanim answered:

> "If you have come here from Chamlibel;
> If you are both foolish and mad;
> If you have killed many a man;
> Pack up and go home from my garden."

Hasan Bey now:

> "Yes, I have come here from Chamlibel;
> And I am both foolish and mad.
> I have risked my life many a time.
> Will you still throw me out of your garden?"

Bright-Faced Girl said to Telli Hanim, "If you do not care for this brave young man, at least let me marry him."

After hearing Bright-Faced Girl say this, Telli Hanim sang to Hasan Bey in this way:

> "Oh, Hasan Bey's beautiful words
> Have set all of us here on fire.
> There are many fair girls in Akshehir —
> Come and take one and then go away."

Hasan Bey said to himself, "I have come here for her, and now she is throwing me into the arms of another girl." But to Telli Hanim he said:

"Her head is adorned like a royal throne,
From which she directs all the beauties.
The passion of her in my heart I must seize:
Send me not from your garden, oh Telli!"

Bright-Faced Girl then said to Telli Hanim, "It is clear that Hasan Bey wants to marry none of us but you."

Telli Hanim now sang in this different way to Hasan Bey:

"Go away from this palace, oh, Hasan Bey,
Where I cannot pay heed to your lament.
But come to my palace at night, if you will;
There are too many people around us here."

Hasan Bey sang:

"How can I enter your house at night?
If you give me your word, give it fully.
Make the way of my going clear to me
So that I can believe the promise you give."

Upon this, Telli Hanim said to him, "Do not worry, for I shall take you there myself."

Her attendants decorated Telli Hanim with flowers and jewels, and as she stood in her gorgeous dress, they said to Hasan Bey, "Do not sit silent in front of her."

Let us hear what Hasan Bey sang:

"Telli, the bride among forty girls,
Don't think these the words of an enemy.
Telli, I swear you can trust me,
And I'll do all the things you request of me."

Telli Hanim then went and sat with Hasan Bey. In the evening when the carriages came, Hasan Bey was dressed in the clothes of a lady and taken with the girls to the palace of Telli Hanim. When they entered her palace, Telli Hanim said to the chief of her drivers, "I shall not be visiting the garden again for forty days. Go and find something else to do."

Hasan Bey spent twenty-eight days happily with Telli Hanim, but on the twenty-ninth day, she said to him, "We cannot keep this secret any longer. What way do you have of traveling? If you have your father's immortal horse,[32] I shall go with you."

"No, I have Kamber Tay with me," answered Hasan Bey.

Hearing this, Telli Hanim said to him, "Your father tried for seven years to take me away from here, but he couldn't do it. Do you think you can get me away from here on Kamber Tay?" Then, in anger, she said to her seravnts, "Throw this man out of my house!"

The servants caught Hasan Bey by the arm and threw him out of the palace, but after they had done this, Telli Hanim said, "Open the door again! I have something more to say to him." When they opened the door, she said, "Hasan Bey, there is a bey here in this city who has a famous bay horse which he never lets out. My father gave him that horse once, and he has kept it ever since. If you can get the bay horse and bring it here, I shall go with you on it. If you cannot bring it, I shall stay here." After she had finished saying this, the door was closed again and locked.

Hasan Bey then returned to the home of The Pilgrim Veterinarian in a very sad mood. He did nothing but sit and brood. They brought him water, but he wouldn't drink it. They brought him food, but he wouldn't touch it.

When The Pilgrim Veterinarian came home, he asked Hasan Bey, "Son, why are you not eating? What do you want me to do for you? Tell me what it is. I shall see that it is done, and then you can go home."

Hasan Bey took out of his pocket his father's letter and handed it to The Pilgrim Veterinarian. After reading the letter, his host said to Hasan Bey, "Son, Köroghlu has written about a horse. He says, 'If Hasan Bey comes to see you, it will be about a horse.' "

The Pilgrim Veterinarian took Hasan Bey to the horse market next morning. They went to a horse dealer and examined one of his horses. The Pilgrim Veterinarian grasped the horse by the head, pulled it toward himself a little, and then pushed it back. As he pushed it back, the horse collapsed on its rump. He went to another horse, pressed steadily on its back with his hands, and soon the horse's belly dragged on the ground.

Hasan Bey then said to him, "Such horses are of no use to us. Köroghlu has so many fine horses grazing at Chamlibel! But there is in this city a bay horse called Ashkardor which was once owned by Telli Hanim's father. If you could bring me Ashkardor, it would be welcome."

When The Pilgrim Veterinarian heard the word Ashkardor, he was greatly surprised. He wondered where Hasan Bey could have heard of Ashkardor, that horse which Telli Hanim had tried for so long to recover.

The Pilgrim Veterinarian's wife said to him, "If you cannot deliver Ashkardor to Hasan Bey, Köroghlu will probably kill both of us."

The Pilgrim Veterinarian thought that the end of his life was near. He went to one of his government supply houses and left there his good clothes, so that they would not be lost too when the bey killed him. He wore only his vest and his long underdrawers, tied at the ankles. As he mounted his horse and set out for the home of the bey who had Ashkardor, he took with him only his sword, his mace, and, under his arm, his burial shroud.[33]

Before The Pilgrim Veterinarian reached the mansion of the bey, the bey's attendants reported to him, "There is a barefooted, bareheaded man coming, wearing only long underdrawers, and carrying a sword, a mace, and his burial shroud."

The bey ordered his men, "Go and bring that man here. Let us see why he is going about bareheaded." [34] When he was brought into the mansion, the bey said, "Oh, it is The Pilgrim Veterinarian! What is the matter, Pilgrim? I have seven sons, and I shall sacrifice all of them for your sake if you need their help. If that is not enough, I have much property, all of which I shall sell to give you as much money as you need. Tell me — what is your problem?"

The Pilgrim Veterinarian said to him, "Let your sons and your property be yours. I don't want you to sacrifice either for me, but I want Ashkardor."

Greatly surprised, the bey was silent for a minute, and then he said, "All right. You may have Ashkardor." He ordered that Ashkardor be taken from the stable and saddled, but after that no man among his servants dared to touch the horse with his hands. Instead, they pulled Ashkardor by the reins to the mounting stone where The Pilgrim Veterinarian mounted him and rode rapidly to Akshehir.

When he arrived home, the Pilgrim said to Hasan Bey, "Here is Ashkardor. I am giving him to you. As I rode him back to Akshehir, he galloped so fast that he kicked up great clouds of dust, covering everyone along the way."

Ashkardor was put in The Pilgrim Veterinarian's stable, and then Hasan Bey said to the Pilgrim's wife, "Go to Telli Hanim and tell her that I have Ashkardor here. If she wishes to go away with me tonight, let her come here; otherwise, I shall go there after her."

The woman went to Telli Hanim's palace and knocked on the door. "Who is it?" asked Telli Hanim.

"It is I, The Pilgrim Veterinarian's wife," she answered. When the servants opened the door and admitted her, she said to Telli Hanim, "Hasan Bey is at our house now, and he has there Ashkardor. If you wish to go away with him tonight, come to our house; if you do not, he will come here and take you away with him."

Telli Hanim said to the Pilgrim's wife, "I cannot come now. Go home and tell Hasan Bey to meet me in front of my mansion seven hours from this time."

Hasan Bey had Ashkardor groomed and saddled, and then sat down with a watch in his hand to wait for the appointed time. About midnight, riding Kamber Tay and leading Ashkardor, he approached Telli Hanim's mansion. He looked and saw there, riding back and forth on horseback, a person dressed all in black like a Circassian [35] warrior and wearing a calpac. [36] Upon seeing this horseman, Hasan Bey thought at first that he was being beset by the palace guard, and so he prepared to escape, but Telli Hanim shouted from behind, "Don't be afraid! It is I, Telli Hanim."

The two of them rode together out of Akshehir into the country toward Chamlibel. After they had gone for some distance, Hasan Bey said to Telli Hanim, "I cannot wait longer to be close to you. I am going to ride on Ashkardor with you." Saying this, he jumped from Kamber Tay to Ashkardor and rode along behind her, embracing her and kissing her. But unnoticed by Telli Hanim, Hasan Bey was directing their horses in a large circle, so that when morning arrived, they had returned again to Telli Hanim's mansion.

When Telli Hanim realized what had happened, she said to Hasan Bey, "Why did you return? For what? I have already divided all my jewelry among my forty attendants and told them to inform my father of my departure with you."

Hasan Bey replied, "I cannot leave Akshehir without fighting a battle with your father. It would be dishonorable of me to steal you without facing him. If I carry you home without a fight, the five hundred friends of my father at Chamlibel would taunt me about this disgrace for the rest of my life."

"But what is the reason for a fight?" asked Telli Hanim. "I loved you and you loved me."

"No," said Hasan Bey. "I cannot take you like this without a fight."

Thus they returned to Akshehir, and there Hasan Bey rode around until everyone could see that he had abducted Telli Hanim. Then he rode away from the town for three hours and stopped at a fountain and waited.

KÖROGHLU

In the household of Telli Hanim's father there was an Arab servant who had worked for that ruler for seven years. This Arab, who was very fond of Telli Hanim, became furious when he saw her riding on a horse with a strange man.

Bright-Faced Girl went to Telli Hanim's father in the morning and said to him, "Your daughter has eloped with the son of Köroghlu."

When Telli Hanim's seven brothers heard this, they were very angry and wanted to set out after Hasan Bey. But their father said to them, "I don't want you to pursue him. We were going to give her to a dog anyway. What difference does it make? Let that dog be Köroghlu's son!" When they heard their father say this, the brothers remained silent.

The Arab, on the other hand, had mounted his horse and was busy spreading the news in the marketplace that Hasan Bey had run off with Telli Hanim. He said to the townspeople, "If you are going to permit this without trying to do anything about it, you are all dishonorable cowards. I am going after Telli Hanim."

The seven brothers were thus forced to go in pursuit of Hasan Bey, too, and their father had to take action as well. After his sons had followed the Arab, the ruler had town criers announce, "Telli Hanim has been stolen. Let everyone from the ages of seven to seventy take up arms and join the army to recover her."

Hasan Bey was asleep by the fountain when Telli Hanim saw the Arab and her seven brothers approaching. The Arab was so angry that his mouth was open and foaming, like that of a runaway wolf. Behind the seven brothers was a large army made up of children and adults. Let us hear what Telli Hanim sang to Hasan Bey:
> "Wake up, wake up, my lover from Daghistan;
> The mountains are covered with marching troops.
> They have planted their banners, side by side,
> For they see you are sleeping. Wake up, my love!"

When Hasan Bey heard this, he arose and said to Telli Hanim, "If you do not want to remain with me, then go over to your father's side. There is the way."

The Arab charged first and attacked Hasan Bey, who was riding Kamber Tay. He ran up to Hasan Bey, threw his lance at him, swung his mace, and shot his arrows at him, but he could not hit Hasan Bey with any of them.

"Now it is my turn," [37] said Hasan Bey. The Arab started darting to left and right in front of Hasan Bey in an effort to get away from him. Hasan Bey hurled his mace at him so violently that when it hit him, his eyes popped out of his head and he fell down from his horse dead.

Telli Hanim's seven brothers now attacked Hasan Bey, and they were so angry that their eyes were fiery. But Hasan Bey killed all of them, too. Telli Hanim was so saddened at seeing her brothers killed in that way that she cried, "Let my father's troops come and kill Hasan Bey!"

The whole army now attacked Hasan Bey, and he fought with them until noon, receiving ninety wounds in the battle. As the fighting went on, Telli Hanim reasoned to herself in this way: "The Arab is dead, my seven brothers are all dead, and many of my father's troops are also dead. It would be a great disgrace for me to go back to Akshehir now. What can I do? Hasan Bey is lying with ninety wounds in his body. If he should die, what could I then do in Akshehir?"

Under the circumstances, Telli Hanim decided to help Hasan Bey. She took Hasan Bey's sword, mounted Ashkardor, and began fighting with the rest of her father's army. When Hasan Bey saw her fighting, he managed to get up again and join her in the battle. Between them they killed so many soldiers that the blood shed there was enough to float away many of the corpses. Fighting together, they pushed the rest of the army all the way back to Akshehir. When the battle was over, Hasan Bey lay on the ground among the dead troops, tired and bleeding. Let us hear now what Telli Hanim said to him:

"Where are you, Hasan Bey? Let me come near,
And let me take your hand in mine.
Let us go to your country; let us go home.
Let me hear you speak, so I'll know where you are."

When Hasan Bey heard Telli Hanim singing this, he said to her, "Don't worry, Telli Hanim. I am alive. Come here to me."

She went to Hasan Bey and carried him to a fountain where she washed his wounds. She sprinkled salt in all his wounds and then covered them with cotton. Telli Hanim had also received many wounds and she was very tired.

Before Hasan Bey had left his father's house Köroghlu had said to him, "Whenever you are in great difficulty and need me, just wish strongly for me to be near you. I shall then come to your assistance." During the night, as Hasan Bey lay near the fountain, his wounds became even more painful, and he cried out three times in his sleep, "Father! Father! Father!"

At Chamlibel, in the meantime, Köroghlu lay in bed that night with Gülnigar, whom he had just brought from Daghistan. He had a terrible dream, and he jumped up, throwing the blankets from the bed.

"What is the matter, Köroghlu?" asked Gülnigar.

"I dreamed that Hasan Bey was in great distress," he said. He dressed himself, rang a bell, and called together his five hundred friends in the square before his mansion.[38] They all then rode from Chamlibel toward Akshehir.

When Telli Hanim arose in the morning she saw that Hasan Bey lay near her unconscious. Suddenly, out of nowhere, a dervish appeared and said to her, "What is the matter, Telli Hanim? I see here Hasan Bey lying as if he were dead. Let us go to the woods and pick certain herbs and flowers. I will show you how to boil them, and then we shall dress his wounds with them." She went to the edge of the nearby forest with the dervish to pick herbs and flowers.

While they were gone, it became very hot, and the flies disturbed Hasan Bey so much that he woke up and rose to his feet. Looking around him, he could not at first see Telli Hanim, but then he saw her at a distance gathering something by the side of the forest. At the same moment, he saw riding toward him Köroghlu with his five hundred gallant men.

Let us hear now what Hasan Bey sang to Telli Hanim:
"Look, daughter of the vezir,[39] look there!
My father is coming from Chamlibel,
My father whose fires continue to burn,
With all of his friends to his left and right.
Oh, daughter of the vezir, he comes!"

But Telli Hanim could not hear clearly the song which Hasan Bey sang to her, and she thought that the approaching troops were a new army which her father had sent to kill Hasan Bey. She had nothing on her head, and her clothes were torn, but she came forward to meet the army. Seing her approach, Son of the Blacksmith charged toward her, but Köroghlu threw his lance into the ground between them as a sign to stop. "Why are you charging toward a woman?" he asked Son of the Blacksmith. "Let us at least ask first who she is."

Now let us hear what Telli Hanim answered when they asked her this:
"Allah has sent you along this road,
And written this fate on my forehead.
I am angry with what you have done.
Don't come near me or I will kill you, Father."

Köroghlu turned to Ayvaz and said, "This woman calls me father, Ayvaz, but as far as I can remember, I have no daughters in this world. I must find out who she is."

Let us hear now how he speaks to her:
"I am Köroghlu, with no fixed home in this world.
I have many more foes than friends.
And I know that no daughters were sired by me.
Whose sweetheart are you? You're no daughter of mine."
Telli Hanim said to herself, "Oh, how mistaken I was! I remember
him now. He is Köroghlu, who once wanted to marry me."
This is the way she answered him:
"I'm the snow that is found on the mountain tops,
The fruit from the Garden of Paradise,
Who loves Hasan Pasha of Daghistan.[40]
Oh, welcome, in peace, dear sir, now welcome!"
But then, fearing that Köroghlu might kill Hasan Bey in order that he
could possess her himself, she said to him, "There is the road. You can
go. But don't dare to attempt any treachery, or I shall kill you with
this sword."

When Köroghlu saw Hasan Bey lying on the ground, covered with
blood, he went to him and tried to help him. As he examined his wounds,
crying, "Oh, my dear son! What has happened to you?" she knew for
certain that no harm would come to Hasan Bey from Köroghlu.

"While I was gathering flowers and herbs to treat his wounds, Hasan
Bey sang to me about your arrival," she said to Köroghlu, "but I misunderstood what he meant." Then she told him how the dervish had
appeared out of nowhere.

"That dervish who told you to gather these flowers must have drunk
of the Abu-Hayat," [41] said Köroghlu. "I am sure that they will help my
son's wounds to heal."

They applied the boiled juices of the flowers and herbs to Hasan Bey's
wounds, and within a week he had recovered. When he was well again,
Köroghlu took him and Telli Hanim to Chamlibel, where their wedding
lasted for seven days and seven nights. They ate and drank, and we hope
that you will do the same and live happily.

PART VI

Anticlerical Tales

In every culture there is an accepted and delimited area
for verbal sacrilege, a zone within which it is fair game
to throw dead cats into sanctuaries. The *fabliaux* of Continental Europe
during the Middle Ages, the limerick of the British Isles in more recent
times, and the "preacher stories" of the modern American South — these
are often typical products of this psychological escape from the rigid
lines of religious conformity. In the Moslem tradition their counter-
parts include jibes at the expense of the sufi and other mystics — perhaps Omar Khayyám exploited this vein of humor most effectively —
undercutting of the dignity of the Caliphate (even that of the great
Haroun al Raschid), the countless Bektashi stories (discussed in Part
VII), the genial jokes at the expense of the beloved Nasreddin Khoja
(also represented in Part VII), and the common accounts of evil men
in sacred offices.

The three tales selected for this section are primarily of this last type.
The first two concern immoral Moslem khojas, but the third, "Crazy
Mehmet and the Three Priests," is aimed at the clergy of one of the
Christian minority groups in Turkey, probably Greek or Armenian. It
is of interest to note that the folktale type which provides the base for
this story (Aarne-Thompson no. 1536 B, The Three Hunchback Brothers Drowned) is not in itself anticlerical; nor is our narrator sufficiently
familiar with Catholicism to make his victims more than hypocrites
subject to venial sins. An anti-Christian bias has here found expression
in a tale common to the people of many different religions.

One suspects that since the secularization of Turkey under the Republic, anticlerical tales have declined both in number and in therapeutic value. Not only did the Atatürk reform movement include a policy of laicism, completely separating the state from church control, but it also abolished some of the religious organizations most likely to provoke humorous, cynical, or satirical stories: the Caliphate, the dervish brotherhoods, and the many fanatical sects.

I.

Piety in Excess [1]

There was once a man whose wife did not like him very much, but she did not say anything about this. One day in the yard of their house the man noticed that his wife turned her face to the wall when a rooster walked past her.

"Why did you turn your face to the wall then?" he asked her.

"Well," she said, "the rooster is a male creature, after all." By doing this, she was trying to make her husband believe that she was an exceptionally chaste woman, but really she was not. [2]

This woman, in fact, had a secret lover who used to visit her when her husband was away from home. He did not go away often enough to suit her, however, and she wished to have more time with her lover. One day she told her husband that she had heard a report that in a nearby town pups were being sold at a very high price. The husband thereupon collected all the stray dogs he could find in their town, tied them together in a long string, and led them to that town where they were in such demand.

When he reached the town, he met an old friend who said to him, "What are you doing with all of those dogs?"

"I have brought them here to sell them," said the man. "I have been told that they sell here for a very high price."

"Who told you that?" asked the friend.

"My wife did," said the man.

"Your wife is not a good woman, then," said the friend.

"Oh, yes, she is," said the man. "She is an exceptionally good woman. She is so chaste that she avoids looking at any man or any male creature — even a rooster."

"No, I think your wife is not a good woman, and I suspect that she has a lover. Let me sell this load of grapes, and I shall show you."

The husband tried to sell some of the dogs he had brought, but no one would buy them. People laughed at him, and he wondered if the friend might perhaps be right about his wife.

When the friend had sold his large basket of grapes, he told the husband to climb inside the basket. He then carried the husband to his own home, knocked on the door, and, when the wife came, said to her, "I am selling grapes. Would you like some?"

"Yes, I would like some. Won't you come inside?"

The friend unloaded the basket from his back and set it down in the front room of the house. The friend then sat down on a cushion, and the wife began to entertain him. She sang for him, danced for him, and was becoming very familiar with him. The husband, who was hidden in the basket, listened to everything that was going on, and he concluded that his wife was really not the good woman she pretended to be. After the friend had carried him away from his house, still in the basket, they went to a coffee house together. There he thanked the friend and went home discouraged.

Shortly after this, the husband pretended to go away on business for a week. At the end of the first day, at sunset, he returned, however, and found the lover visiting his wife. He killed both of them, gathered a bundle of food, and went into a nearby woods to live in a cave.

In the meantime, a great robbery had taken place at the palace of the sultan. The sultan's treasury had been broken into, and the thieves were being hunted all over the country. One day while searching for the thieves, the sultan's men found the husband in the cave, and they accused him of the theft.

When he was brought before the sultan, the man tried to explain that he had nothing whatever to do with the robbery. But they still suspected him and refused to release him. Finally he said to the sultan, "Efendi, allow me forty days in which to find the real culprits. If I have not found both them and the treasure within that time, I shall return to you for whatever punishment is in store for me."

The sultan agreed to this and released him for forty days. The husband thought and thought about how he was to proceed to catch the real thieves, but he could not decide upon any plan. One day as he was sitting in the marketplace, he saw a khoja coming toward him wearing bells on his shoes that tinkled as he walked.

"Who is that?" the husband asked a bystander.

"Oh, that is the famous Khoja with Bells," [3] the man said.

"Why does he wear those bells on his shoes?" asked the husband.

"He is such a holy man that he warns all the insects and little creatures on the ground of his approach so that he does not step on any of them. He has such a reputation for holiness that the sultan made him the grand vezir a short while ago."

As soon as the husband heard this, he arose and went immediately to the sultan. "Your majesty," he said, "I have found the thief. It is the Khoja with Bells, your grand vezir. If you do not believe this, ask him to lend you his prayer beads for a while. Then you will be able to discover it for yourself."

When the Khoja with Bells came to attend the sultan that day, the sultan said, "Khoja, let me borrow your prayer beads for a while." The khoja did as the sultan requested, and afterwards the sultan gave the beads to the husband. "Here are the prayer beads. Now you must prove to me something that seems impossible. How could that good man be the thief?"

The husband said nothing, but, taking the beads, he went to the khoja's home while he was still at court. When the khoja's daughter opened the door, the husband showed her her father's prayer beads as a token of his friendship. "Take me to the sultan's treasure. Your father wants a certain piece of it brought to him." The husband took a ring and went with it to the sultan. "Was this ring part of your treasure, Efendi?" he asked.

"Yes, it was," said the sultan.

"Come with me, then, and I shall show you the rest," said the husband, and he took the sultan to the home of the Khoja with Bells.

When the sultan saw the entire treasure heaped on the floor in a room of the khoja's house, he was greatly surprised. "How did you discover this?" he asked.

"Your majesty," said the husband, "I had a wife once who pretended she was so chaste that she would not even face a rooster when it approached her. But later I discovered that she was a bad woman. I killed her and her lover and then I hid myself in a cave. Your soldiers found me there and accused me of this offense. I discovered the guilt of the Khoja with Bells because of my experience with my wife."

2.

The Immoral Khoja and the Daughter of the Aga [4]

There was once a rich man in a village, an aga,[5] who had a son and a daughter. One day the aga said to his son, "What are we going to do with all of the money that we have? Let us spend some of it by making a pilgrimage to Mecca."

"Very well," said the son, "but who will look after my sister while we are gone?"

The village khoja was a very good friend of the aga and had eaten bread at his house many times, and so the aga suggested that they leave the girl with him. "Surely, the khoja would not mind looking after her for a couple of months," he said. And so they left the girl with that khoja and they started on their journey to Mecca.

The very first day they were gone, the khoja winked at the girl and tried to win her affection. The next day he said to her, "Fatma, you and I will go to the market and buy some nice things." After they had made several purchases in the market, the khoja said, "Fatma, while we are here in town, we might as well go and have a bath at the bathhouse." [6]

They went to the bathhouse together, and the khoja said to the owner, "Whatever the daily income for this bathhouse is, I shall pay it to you, but we must have the bath to ourselves. You will not admit any other customers while we are here."

After they had entered, the doors of the bathhouse were locked, and the khoja and the girl began to take their baths. Soon the khoja said to the girl, "Fatma, let us be united."

Quite surprised at this improper suggestion, the girl said, "But, Khoja, efendi, you are not only a close friend of my father, but you are the khoja of the village. How dare you suggest such a thing to me?"

"Well," said the khoja, "such things do happen from time to time. There is nothing wrong with it."

"Before we do such a thing, then," said the girl to the khoja, "let me wash you properly."

The khoja agreed to this suggestion, and the girl took a cake of soap and started to wash him. She produced a great pile of lather on the khoja's head, and when his face was covered with this lather, she took off a clog [7] and started beating the khoja with it. She beat him on the head and face, without regard to where she struck him, and the khoja

215

was soon covered with blood. The owner of the bathhouse heard the noise, and wondering what was going on inside, knocked on the door. When he heard the khoja shout, "Open! Open!" he unlocked the door and entered, and as he did so, the girl slipped out.

The owner of the bathhouse washed the blood off the khoja, and as he did this, he asked, "What happened, Khoja?" Upon this, the khoja gave him a full account of what had happened.

That night the girl returned to the khoja's house as if nothing had happened. But the khoja was very angry with her, and he decided to write to the aga, telling him that his daughter had become familiar with a number of men since his departure for Mecca. She has been running around with Ahmet and Mehmet,[8] the khoja wrote.

When the aga received this letter, he was furious. He sent his son back to the village with orders to find his sister, cut her throat, and bring her blood-stained shirt back to him. The aga's son proceeded to their village with this in mind, but when he again saw his sister, who was a very beautiful girl, he could not help pitying her. Taking her to a mountain, he gave her a supply of money and told her not to return home. Then he killed a puppy and dipped one of her shirts in its blood. After several days of travel, he arrived back at Mecca and gave his father the bloody shirt. "Well done," said the aga. The two then completed their prayers at Mecca and returned home again.

In the mountains, meanwhile, the girl lived with shepherds who had brought their flocks up to the summer pastures. One day she bought a sheep from one of these shepherds. She killed the sheep and removed its stomach. She cleaned this stomach very carefully and then, cutting it to the right shape, pulled it over her head to make it look as if she were a keloghlan. Disguised now as a boy, she went to a nearby town and found work as a waiter in a coffee house.[9]

The manager of the coffee house was well pleased with the work of the new waiter. He worked hard, and he was such a handsome young man that he soon became known as The Coffee House Beauty. Everyone talked about this handsome waiter, and many people came to the coffee house just to see him.[10] His reputation finally spread beyond that town, and eventually it reached the attention of the aga, the waiter's father, back in his village.

The aga suggested to the khoja one day that they travel to the town and see for themselves this Coffee House Beauty about whom everyone talked. So the aga, the khoja, and the aga's son all traveled there one day, and they all agreed that the waiter was indeed very handsome. The girl recognized them at once and asked them to come back that evening as her guests. When they returned, they exchanged all of the customary greetings, and then the aga asked the keloghlan to tell them about his adventures in life. But the keloghlan turned politely to the khoja and said, "Khojas are men of great experience, and they have much more to tell than I. Khoja why don't you tell us about your most exciting adventure?"

The khoja then told this story: "I once had living in my house a girl who was very beautiful. I wanted her badly, but she was a good girl and refused me every time that I tried to make love to her. Finally, I hired a bathhouse and planned to make love to her there before we left, for we were to be the only ones using the bath at that time. But she was smarter than I thought, for when she had my head and face covered with soap, and I could not see her, she beat me with a clog until I was covered with blood from the cuts that she made. When the bathhouse owner heard my cries and unlocked the door, she escaped, and I never succeeded in making love to that girl."

They all laughed at this story, and now the aga again asked the keloghlan to tell a story. This time the Coffee House Beauty agreed, and she said she would also tell a story about a girl.

"Once there was a girl who was the daughter of an aga. Her father and brother decided to take a pilgrimage to Mecca, and while they were gone, they left the girl in the care of a khoja whom they trusted. He was their friend, but, as it turned out, he was an immoral man. He tried to seduce this girl on the very first day that her father and brother had left for Mecca. When he could not succeed at this, he took her to a bathhouse which he had rented for his private use, and when they were locked inside together, he suggested that they be united. The girl was quite amazed at this suggestion and asked him how he dare do this. 'You are a close friend of my father,' she said, 'and besides you are the khoja of this village.' The khoja said to her, 'Well, such things do happen from time to time. There is nothing wrong with it.' The girl then said, 'Before we do such a thing, let me wash you properly.' The khoja agreed to this, and the girl proceeded to wash him. She made a great pile of lather on his head, and when his head and face were so covered with lather that he could not see, she took off a clog and beat him with it. He was soon covered with blood, and he called to the bathhouse owner, 'Open! Open!' When the bathhouse keeper unlocked the door and went to help the khoja, the girl slipped out and escaped.

"The girl stayed away from the khoja's house for the rest of that day,

217

but at night she returned to it, for her father had ordered her to remain there while he was away. The khoja was so annoyed and angry at her that he wrote a letter to her father saying that she had become familiar with several men during his absence. The father believed the khoja, and sent his son back to kill the girl, ordering that he bring him her blood-soaked shirt. But the son was sorry for his sister and killed a puppy instead, soaking one of her shirts in its blood and taking this shirt to his father as evidence. The girl was left in the mountains by her brother, who gave her a handful of money, and she lived with shepherds there. One day she bought a sheep from one of these shepherds, killed the sheep, and cleaned its stomach carefully. Then she put the lining of the stomach on her head to make herself look like a keloghlan, and, coming to this town, took a job as waiter in a large coffee house."

The keloghlan then turned to the aga and said, "This is the coffee house where she worked. I am she. You are my father. This is my brother. And that is the immoral khoja." After saying this, she pulled the casing of the sheep's stomach from her head, and her long, beautiful hair fell down on her shoulders.

All who heard this story of the Coffee House Beauty were amazed. Her father and brother killed the khoja on the spot, and the daughter of the aga was reunited with her family.[11] They lived happily, as they had before, and so now let us go climb the Mountains of Kaf.[12]

3.

Crazy Mehmet and the Three Priests [13]

Once there was and once there wasn't, when God's creatures were many but it was a sin to talk too much — in those olden times there was a rich infidel merchant,[14] and this faithless merchant had a very pretty wife.

One day his wife said to the merchant, "Please give me some money so that I can go to the church and be absolved of my sins and purified." As soon as she got the money, she went to a church and she said to one of the priests there, "Oh, good priest, absolve me of my sins and I shall pay you whatever you want for this."

The priest looked at her and thought to himself about what a pretty woman she was. Then he said to her, "All right. I shall absolve you of your sins." After he had absolved her — God knows how he did it — he said shamelessly, "May I come to visit you at your home at your convenience tonight?"

The woman became very angry. "Go on, you dog!" she scolded the priest, and then she rushed out of the church. To herself she thought, "God knows — probably my sins were not really absolved by such a man. I had better go to another church."

At the second church to which she went she offered money to another priest, and she said, "Here is money for you, oh priest. Absolve me of my sins."

After he had absolved her of her sins — God knows how he did this — he winked at her and said, "Hey there! Come on!"

The woman answered, "You dog! Whatever do you mean? I shall tell my husband of this, and he will show you the light of day!"

The poor woman went to still a third church and there, as she had done before, she offered the priest money: "Here is money for you, priest, efendi, for which you are to absolve me of my sins."

"Very well," said the priest, "but tell me first — when may I come to see you at your home?"

"What kind of talk is this?" she asked. "I am a married woman. Don't you have any shame?" Then she returned home.

That night, when her husband came home, she complained to him at length. "You should have come to the church with me. I went to three different churches and talked with three priests, and if you had heard what they said, you would have been amazed."

"Well, what did they say?" asked the merchant curiously.

"The first asked if he could come to visit me tonight. The second one winked at me and said, 'Hey there! Come on!' And the third, like the first, asked when he could come to my home to visit me."

The merchant thought for a minute, and then he said, "Very well. Tomorrow send your servant to those three churches and have her invite the three priests to visit you at home. The first should come at one o'clock the next morning; the second should come at two o'clock; and the third should come at three o'clock."

Who wouldn't be surprised at hearing this? "What sort of talk is this? What do you mean?" asked the woman of her husband.

But his answer was, "Don't ask too many questions. Do as I tell you."

The next day the servant of the woman knocked on the door of the first priest and said to him, "The lady who was with you yesterday for the absolution of her sins sends greetings. She says that her husband will

219

not be at home at one o'clock tonight and that she will be waiting for you." She then went to the second priest and said, "The lady who was with you yesterday for the absolution of her sins sends greetings. She says that her husband will not be home at two o'clock tonight and that she will be waiting for your arrival." She then went to the third priest and repeated the same thing: "The lady who came to you yesterday to be absolved of her sins sends her greetings. She says that her husband will not be home at three o'clock tonight and that you should come to see her then."

While this was going on, the merchant at home had finished preparations for their coming. He placed food and drinks in the bedroom, and after midnight he hid himself under the bed.

At one o'clock there was a knock on the door, and the first priest came. The wife, dressed very attractively and wearing make-up, went downstairs, opened the door, and welcomed him in: "Welcome, priest, efendi! My husband is not at home tonight, and that is the reason I invited you." So the priest went up to the bedroom with the woman.

They ate and they drank and they talked. As it neared two o'clock and she realized that the second priest was coming, she said, "My husband will be coming home any time now."

"All right, then," said the first priest, "let us go to bed as soon as possible."

"You sit on the edge of the bed and start getting undressed," she said, "and I shall go downstairs and check the doors." She took the lamp and went downstairs.

As the priest was sitting there, waiting in the dark, the merchant crawled from beneath the bed, jumped on the man, and strangled him. Then he pushed the body over in a corner and covered it with a blanket.

"What have you done with the priest?" asked the woman when she returned to the room.

"Don't interfere with my work," answered the merchant. "Do as I told you to do."

Soon there was a knock at the door again, "Tok! tok! tok!" The second priest had come. The wife opened the door and said, "Come in! Come in! My husband is not home now, and I invited you to come so that we might eat and drink together and enjoy ourselves."

She took him upstairs to the bedroom. After the second priest had drunk much wine, he insisted, "Let us go to bed now."

"You sit on the edge of the bed and get undressed. I shall take the lamp, go downstairs, and be sure that all of the doors and windows are locked. I shall be right back."

As soon as the woman had left the room, the merchant crawled out from under the bed, jumped on the second priest, strangled him, and sent him to the other world. Then he placed him in the corner too and covered him with the blanket.

"What have you done?" asked the wife when she returned, but she got the same answer as she had before.

They again rearranged the table and replenished the drinks on it, and by then it was three o'clock. "Tok! tok! tok!" The third priest had arrived, and the woman went down to let him in. "Come in! Come in! Welcome! My husband is not at home tonight, and that is why I invited you."

They went upstairs together to the bedroom. After they had eaten and drunk for a while, the third priest made the same request: "Let us go to bed now."

"Then you sit on the edge of the bed and start getting undressed. I shall take the lamp and go downstairs to check the doors and windows. I shall be right back."

As the priest was sitting there, ready, waiting for her return, the merchant crawled out from under the bed, jumped on him, strangled him, and placed him by the side of the other two priests.

When the woman realized what her husband had done, she said to him, "What are we going to do with these three dead bodies?"

He said, "I know what I am going to do with them. Don't interfere with my work." He tied a rope around the waist of the first priest and dragged him to the door of a tavern.[15] He knocked on the door, "Tok! tok! tok!"

The tavernkeeper was tired, and so he called his apprentice and said, "It could only be Crazy Mehmet at this time of the night. Go down and open the door."

The merchant had propped the dead priest against the door and had run away. When the apprentice came and opened the door — flop! — the priest fell on the floor. "Master! Master!" cried the apprentice, "this drunk fell dead on the stone floor. What shall we do with him now?"

What could the tavernkeeper say? "Drag him over behind that barrel of raki.[16] When Crazy Mehmet arrives, he will take care of him."

By the time that the tavernkeeper had gone back to bed and had just put his head on his pillow, the merchant arrived with the second priest. "Tok! tok! tok!" he knocked on the tavern door, and he propped the second priest up against one wing of the door in the same way that he had the first. When the tavernkeeper heard the knocking, he sent his apprentice down again, thinking it must be Crazy Mehmet now.

Of course, as soon as the apprentice turned the knob — flop! — the second priest fell on the floor. "Master! Master!" cried the poor apprentice, "this drunk also fell on his head on the stone floor and died. What shall we do with him now?"

"Put him behind the raki barrel, too," said the tavernkeeper, "and we shall have Crazy Mehmet take care of him too when he comes."

They had hardly gotten back to bed when the merchant arrived with the third priest and knocked, "Tok! tok! tok!" When the apprentice opened the door a third time, the body again fell into the tavern, dead. They dragged this body behind the raki barrel also, and then they went back to bed again.

Almost at daybreak there was another "Tok! tok! tok!" on the tavern door. This time it was Crazy Mehmet, as the tavernkeeper hoped it would be. He was already drunk, but, as always, he wanted still more to drink. The tavernkeeper took a body from behind the barrel and said to Crazy Mehmet, "If you take this body out of here and throw it in the bottomless lake, you may have this whole barrel of raki free."

Crazy Mehmet tied a rope around the priest and dragged him to the bottomless lake. He hurled the body into the lake and then returned to the tavern for his raki. But the tavernkeeper met him at the door and said, "What is the matter with you? The priest you took to the lake came back again!"

"It is impossible, for I threw him into the middle of the lake," said Crazy Mehmet.

"I don't know about that," said the tavernkeeper, "but if you don't believe it, come in and see for yourself," and he showed him the body of the second priest.

"Very well, then," said Crazy Mehmet, and he picked up the second priest, dragged him to the lake, and threw him in. "Don't you dare come back this time," he said. He hurried back only to find the tavernkeeper at the door with a body.

"What have you done, Mehmet?" he asked. "Look — he is back again."

"How can that be when I threw him into the middle of the bottomless lake?"

"I don't know," said the tavernkeeper, "but, as you can see with your own eyes, here he is, back again."

So, once more Crazy Mehmet dragged a body to the bottomless lake and threw it into the water. In this way the tavernkeeper got rid of the three corpses.

As Crazy Mehmet was on his way back to the tavern, with a raki bottle in his hand, he met a priest, riding his donkey,[17] on the way to his church. The priest rode along rapidly, "Tekker, tekker, tekker."

Crazy Mehmet lost his wits completely when he saw this, and he said, "Oho! So that is how you do it! I throw you into the middle of the bottomless lake, and you ride this donkey to beat me back to the tavern each time!" As he said this, he grabbed the bridle of the donkey and led it to the lake where he threw both the priest and the donkey into the water.

Relieved at last, Crazy Mehmet ran all the way back to the tavern and said, "I have just thrown him into the middle of the lake for the fourth time, and this time he won't come back, for I threw his donkey in along with him."

The tavernkeeper could not understand this, but rather than be too curious, he simply said, "All right, here is your barrel of raki. It is all yours." And then he put the whole thing out of his mind. And Crazy Mehmet had all the raki he had yearned for for so long!

PART VII

Anecdotes

In marked contrast to the long and often elaborate tale
of Part I stands the anecdote known in Turkish as a
fikra.[1] This is a short tale, set in the real world, based on a humorous
situation, and informed by the shrewd insight and sometimes cynical attitude of the peasant mind. There is a fikra for almost every occasion. They
are used to illustrate a truth, to point a moral, to satirize a vice, or just
to laugh at human folly. How many of these might be collected in Turkey, for a definitive study of the type, there is no way of knowing, for
they are legion.

A majority of Turkish anecdotes center on the activities and observations of five characters. Two of them are types, without names: the kadi
or judge (usually understood to be a judge of Moslem canonical law),
and the Bektashi, a member of the dervish order of that name. The other
three appear to have had originals in real life, though most of their identity has been lost to the transmuting effects of time and the folk imagination. To Nasreddin Khoja, Bekri Mustafa, and Incili Chavush are assigned specific times and places, but, as with so many other folk figures,
they have also been incorporated into the numerous anecdotes common
to many peoples.

Nasreddin Khoja. By far the largest single group of anecdotes are
those told about Nasreddin Khoja, the Turks' favorite comic figure, and
several volumes of tales about him have been published in various lan-
guages. His rotund figure, turbaned and riding on a donkey, has for
centuries been an element of Turkish design, an emblem that has appeared on art objects, mementos, souvenirs, and greeting cards. Alter-
nately stupid and shrewd, naïve and wise, Khoja is, by turns, both

224

noodlehead and trickster, like Jack, Joe Miller, and Till Eulenspiegel. Compounding his potential as a comic figure is his profession. A khoja in pre-Republican Turkey, he served as both preacher and teacher and was automatically the butt of humor everywhere aimed at both those occupations.

About the man behind the legend there is disagreement. Where he lived, and when, are moot points among scholars, and there are some who go so far as to deny his actual existence; among those who doubt his authenticity is Albert Wesselski, whose two-volume study *Der Hodscha Nasreddin* [2] is still the most authoritative work on the tales themselves. By those who believe in his historicity, Khoja has been assigned to four different periods: (1) to the time of Haroun al Raschid, at the end of the eighth and the beginning of the ninth centuries; (2) to the middle of the Seljuk era, the time of Saladin, the end of the twelfth century; (3) to the middle of the thirteenth century; (4) to the time of Bayazid I and Tamerlane, the late fourteenth and early fifteenth centuries. For the first two hypotheses very little real evidence has been adduced, and they can probably be discarded. A number of the most widely distributed Khoja tales are set at the court of Tamerlane, a figure who left a lasting impression on the Turkish folk mind, and if one were to rely on oral history for the solution, one could assume the fourth hypothesis to be tenable. Today, however, the balance of scholarly opinion inclines to the third hypothesis, and the "official" version of the Khoja story published by the Turkish government (through its Ministry of Press, Broadcasting, and Tourism [3]) accepts this view. It was supposedly at the village of Hortu, attached to the town of Sivrihisar, that Nasreddin Khoja was born; and in a cemetery at Akshehir [4] is a tombstone for him dated 683, a year on the old Moslem calendar which converts to 1284 on the modern calendar. The stone lies behind an iron grate fastened with a huge lock, but with humor befitting the occupant, there was long no wall or fence attached to the locked entrance. Recently, because of its attraction for tourists, the tomb has been fenced in. [5]

Besides the Khoja anecdotes of this section, there are longer tales into which the name and character of Nasreddin Khoja have been inserted. A good example is "Do Not Do Anything Without Considering Its End" in Part IV.

Bekri Mustafa. Bekri Mustafa, Injili Chavush, and the Bektashi have in common their flagrant disrespect for tradition. Obvious rascals whom no one could openly condone, they are secretly cherished for their uninhibited behavior, their religious unorthodoxy, and their near blasphemous remarks. Laughing at their improprieties constituted, in former times, a therapeutic release from the strictness of Moslem principles.

Bekri Mustafa, also known as Bekri Mustafa Agha, was a drunkard who lived during the reign of Sultan Murad IV (1623–1640). Tradition says that his conviviality was so contagious that it led Murad himself into bad habits. He has become the alcoholic type in Turkey, and ever since his time the name Bekri has had a connotation of drunkard; he is always pictured starry-eyed, brandishing a flask or a jug. Inasmuch as alcohol is forbidden by Islam, Bekri Mustafa is automatically a ne'er-do-well, but his ludicrous escapades make him a comic rather than an evil character. Besides his role in folktales, Bekri occasionally appears also in puppet plays as a Bohemian figure with a sharp and ready wit.[6]

The most frequently recurring story about Bekri Mustafa in our archive is a variant of the Aarne-Thompson Type 1531, The Man Thinks He Has Been in Heaven. Before the sultan departs for a brief trip, he has Bekri picked up, while drunk in a tavern, and carried to his palace. When Bekri becomes sober, he is told that he is the sultan, and he is treated accordingly by all of the palace personnel. For three days he rules in splendor. Then, at the return of the real sultan, he is carried back drunk to the tavern where he was first found and subsequently becomes the butt of humor as he tries in vain to persuade relatives and friends that he was once their ruler. We have not included the tale here because it lacks the speed and succinctness that characterize the other anecdotes.

Bekri Mustafa and Injili Chavush were both personalities of the court juxtaposed, in almost all cases, with the figure of the sultan. As such they are, like most of the characters of the Karagöz theater, urban types, and even further limited in that their stage is always Istanbul and its environs. In view of this, their popularity throughout all of Turkey is remarkable.

Injili Chavush. Injili Chavush — his name means Pearl Sergeant — was a member of the Corps of Janissaries,[7] the best-known and eventually the most notorious military organization in Turkish history. Founded as a palace guard early in the fourteenth century, they also provided the sultan with a private, highly disciplined army of his own. To establish an esprit de corps among them, the Janissaries were granted special privileges and exemptions from the law. Because many of them were from Christian backgrounds, captured as prisoners or taken in tribute as children, they were not required to observe all Moslem religious practices. As years passed and their power grew, they became a distinct class of their own, an elite group, respected and feared, a vested interest and a political entity. At times they even went so far as to make the sultan their virtual hostage and impose their terms upon his government; one of their favorite gestures of discontent was to set fire to Istanbul, a prank they perpetrated more than a hundred times during the reign of Sultan Ahmet III (1703–1730). Finally, in 1826, they were destroyed in their Istanbul barracks by a coalition of regular troops and citizen volunteers, but their 500-year-long role in the Ottoman Empire has made them an enduring part of Turkish folklore. Like Bekri Mustafa, Injili Chavush appears both in folktales and, occasionally, in puppet plays; in the latter medium he is often the loud soldier, the bully, but one representing law and order after his own arbitrary fashion. Because he is a court favorite, Injili Chavush often has the license of a clown to address the sultan and behave toward the sultan's retainers in an outrageous manner.

The Bektashi. The Bektashis form one of the two distinctly Turkish orders of dervishes, along with the Mevlevi, the "Whirling Dervishes." Sometime after their founding, they were, apparently, named after the Moslem saint Haji Bektash Veli (d. 1516), and their headquarters during their heyday was a monastery built over his tomb, about halfway between Kirshehir and Kayseri.[8] Although their beginnings are obscure, it is clear that they had a well-established organization by the fourteenth century, and since then they have played an active political as well as religious role in Turkish life.

Religiously they stand apart from the majority of Turks in being closer to the Shiites than to the Sunnites, placing Ali, the fourth caliph (656–661), at the center of their worship. They have always disregarded much of the Moslem ritual and worship, including the salat, the special prayer to Mohammed. By some they are considered semi-Christian, partly, perhaps, because of their serving bread and wine at initiation ceremonies in the manner of the Eucharist. Patrons of the Janissaries (another semi-infidel association), they became closely affiliated with that military group, and they participated in several of the Janissary revolts. At the destruction of the Janissaries in 1826, the Bektashis suffered a severe setback, but a century later, just before the dissolution of all dervish orders by the Republic, they had regained much of their former strength. It was estimated that there were still 30,000 Bektashis in Turkey in 1950,[9] continuing their operations in clandestine fashion, and they are still quite strong in parts of the Balkans, especially Albania. It is in that country, at Tirana, that their chief monastery is now located.

In our archive we have over two hundred Bektashi tales, but this is a mere handful. Scholars with whom we have consulted estimate that there may be as many as five thousand in the oral tradition. A high proportion of those we have heard are, like numbers 17 and 18 below, extremely brief: retorts of Bektashis to accusations that they have broken Moslem canon laws on prayer, fasting, and abstinence from alcohol.

The Kadi. In a land where, until recently, both secular and canon law existed, it is not surprising to find an extensive body of lore about courts and judges. The magistrate closest to the common people in the days of the Empire was the kadi, the dispenser of justice according to canon law in the provincial town. Consequently, the judge in Turkish folktales, regardless of the nature of the case, is always a kadi.

Sometimes he is a virtuous and wise man beset by curious dilemmas of justice; sometimes he is an immoral grafter who exemplifies the peasant concept of the corrupt government official of pre-Republican days; at other times he is more a referee or an arbiter than a judge in the ordinary sense. In folktales he is appealed to for the settlement of a great variety of problems: civil cases, criminal cases, love spats, and conflicts over questions so academic that they could never actually become matters of litigation.

1.

How to Behave in Heaven [10]

One day Nasreddin Khoja [11] climbed on his donkey and left Akshehir, traveling toward Yalvach. On the way he met a man who stopped him and said, "Khoja, when am I going to die?"

"How could I know that?" responded Khoja.

"Well, I can tell when you are going to die."

"When?" asked the Khoja in surprise.

"You will die when your donkey brays three times in a row," said the man.

"Amazing!" said Nasreddin Khoja. He continued on his way toward Yalvach, and about an hour later, his donkey started to bray. Khoja counted the brays, and after the third consecutive bray, he dismounted from his donkey, lay on the ground, and said, "Now I am dead." As he lay there on the ground Khoja saw a wolf come along and eat his donkey. "Oh, my poor donkey," he said, "your death and mine have coincided."

When Nasreddin Khoja did not return that night, his wife and their servant went in search of him. They found him lying by the side of the road, and his wife asked, "Khoja, why don't you come home?"

"I cannot, dear wife, for I am dead. You must take me home and give me a decent burial."

They tried to reason with Khoja, but it was useless. He insisted that he was dead and that he should be buried. So, his wife and the servant carried him home, washed him, and wrapped him in his shroud. Then she called in the neighbors and announced Khoja's death. After prayers and the customary ceremonies, Khoja was taken to the cemetery and laid in a grave. His wife requested, however, that he not be buried until the following day, hoping that he would come to his senses before that.

After Khoja had lain in his grave a couple of hours, he heard a tinkling sound approaching. It was a peddler whose donkey was loaded with glassware and dishes. Khoja raised his head from the grave to see what was making the noise, and this frightened the donkey terribly. It jumped and ran about wildly, throwing off its back the peddler's load of wares and smashing it. The peddler was furious with Khoja and started beating him.

"Why are you beating me? I am dead, and you should not beat a dead man."

But the peddler paid no attention to this and gave Khoja a good beating. Afterwards he felt so sore that he dragged himself home. His neighbors were surprised to see him alive again, and one of them said to him, "You have been in the next world, Khoja. Tell us what it is like in heaven."

"It is very pleasant there," said Nasreddin Khoja, "just as long as you do not frighten any donkeys loaded with glassware and dishes."

2.

Nasreddin Khoja and Tamerlane [12]

When Tamerlane invaded Anatolia, he heard about a man named Nasreddin Khoja who lived at Akshehir. Tamerlane went to Akshehir, set up his camp there, and then sent a platoon of soldiers to invite Khoja to come to his tent. "Come, Khoja," one of them said. "The emperor is here and he wants to see you."

The Khoja thought that since the emperor killed almost everyone who was called before him, there was no point in his hurrying. He stayed for a while longer at his home. When Tamerlane realized that Khoja was not coming immediately, he sent another platoon to invite him again. Khoja said to them, "All right, I shall not be long."

But when Khoja still did not come to his tent, Tamerlane became very impatient. He ordered his horse brought, mounted it, and set out at once for Nasreddin Khoja's village on the outskirts of Akshehir. In that village some of the peasants crowded around Tamerlane, and some crowded around the house of Khoja saying, "Khoja, quick!"

Nasreddin Khoja put on a gown and his large turban [18] and started to go in the direction of Tamerlane. They met in the middle of a narrow street, and Tamerlane's horse was so frightened by the appearance of Khoja that it jumped and threw the emperor off its back. Tamerlane was so angry that he ordered his men to seize Khoja and hang him.

After he had been captured by Tamerlane's men, Khoja asked them, "Where are you taking me?"

"To be hanged," they said.

"Go and tell that rascal," said Khoja, "that I want to know what my offense is."

The soldiers went to Tamerlane and told him what Nasreddin Khoja had said. Upon hearing this, Tamerlane said, "Bring him here before me."

Nasreddin Khoja was brought before Tamerlane, and he said to the emperor, "What is the offense that causes me to hang?"

"You brought bad luck to me," said Tamerlane.

"Who has brought bad luck? Is it you or I?" asked Khoja. "You are the bringer of bad luck, for I am about to be hanged. If I had been the bringer of bad luck, you would have fallen off your horse on your head and died — and then there would have been reason to hang me."

Tamerlane saw the justice of his observation and decided to forgive him, but he said that he wanted to ask him a question. "Am I a tyrant or a learned man?" he asked Khoja.

"Your majesty," said Khoja, "you are neither a tyrant nor a learned man. It is we who have been such cruel tyrants that God has sent you to scourge us."

Tamerlane was again pleased with the answer he had received from

Nasreddin Khoja, and so he said to him, "All right, you may go in peace."

Sometime later Tamerlane began to impose very heavy taxes upon all of the towns and villages of that part of Turkey. Very concerned with this situation, all of Nasreddin Khoja's neighbors came to him, and one of them said, "Oh, Khoja, you have formed a friendship with Tamerlane. Go and beg him to reduce a little the taxes on our village."

Nasreddin Khoja went to the tent of Tamerlane, and the emperor said to him, "Welcome, Khoja! I am pleased to see you again."

After they had talked for a while, Khoja said to Tamerlane, "Your majesty, the people of my village are very poor. Will you please reduce their taxes a little?"

After thinking a moment, Tamerlane said to Khoja, "Very well. Take the elephant [14] that is tied outside my tent, and let your people feed it instead of paying taxes."

When Khoja returned with the elephant, the people of his village were all pleased with this new arrangement. In about fifteen days' time, however, the elephant had eaten all the crops of the villagers, and they realized that he was a greater burden than the taxes. They all came to Khoja and said, "Khoja, efendi, please take this elephant back to Tamerlane, and let him impose on us whatever taxes he wishes."

Khoja thought for a while about this dangerous mission, and then he suggested that all of the people of the village go with him to see Tamerlane. They agreed to this proposal, and they all followed him as he approached the emperor's tent. But when Khoja was about to go through the entrance of the tent, he looked around and saw that all of the villagers had deserted him for fear of the despot. He had to go before Tamerlane alone.

"What is the matter, Khoja?" asked Tamerlane.

"Your majesty," said Khoja, "I have come to tell you that the elephant you gave us is lonely. We wish that you would give us a female elephant too."

But Tamerlane had been informed about how the villagers had deserted Khoja, and he said to him, "I know what they have done to you, Khoja. If they had come with you to see me, I should have granted their request, but because they played this trick on you, I am going to have them all impaled. Khoja, depart in peace." [15]

Sometime later, when all the fruit was getting ripe, Khoja said to his wife, "Let us go and gather some ripe figs, and I shall take them to the emperor as a gift."

They went to the orchard and began to gather figs, but soon his wife said, "Look, Khoja, the pears are also ripe. Let us gather some pears for the emperor too."

"No," answered Khoja, "you gather only what I tell you to gather. Pick only ripe figs."

A little while later his wife said, "Look, Khoja, apples and peaches are also ripe. Perhaps the emperor likes them too."

"No, no, woman," said Khoja. "You gather just what I tell you to gather — ripe figs."

They filled their basket with ripe figs, and Khoja took it to Tamerlane's tent and placed it before the seat of the emperor. "Sit down, Khoja," said Tamerlane, opening the basket. He took out a fig and threw it in Khoja's face. He took out a second fig and threw that in Khoja's face too. Then, one by one, he took all of the figs from the basket and smashed them against Khoja's face.

After the basket was completely empty, Khoja looked up to the sky and said, "Thank you, oh my God!"

"Why did you say that?" demanded Tamerlane.

"Your majesty," answered Nasreddin Khoja, "if I had picked the fruit that my wife had suggested, I should have neither head nor eye left. I thanked God that I followed my own judgment and gathered only soft, ripe figs to present to you." [16]

3.

How Long Will It Take? [17]

One day Nasreddin Khoja was chopping wood close to the road a few kilometers from Akshehir. After a while a man came along the road, walking toward Akshehir, and he called to Khoja, "Can you tell me how long it will take me to get to Akshehir?"

Khoja heard him and looked up from his work, but he said nothing. So the man called again, louder this time, "How long will it take me to get to Akshehir?"

Still Khoja said nothing, and this time the man roared like a lion, "How long will it take me to get to Akshehir?"

When Khoja did not answer even then, the man decided he must be deaf, and so he started walking rapidly toward the city. Nasreddin

Khoja watched him for a moment, and then he shouted, "It will take you about an hour!"

"Well, why didn't you say so before?" demanded the man angrily.

"First I had to know how fast you were going to walk," answered the Khoja.

4.

Nasreddin Khoja Dividing Five Eggs [18]

During the invasion of Turkey by Tamerlane,[19] the great despot came to Akshehir, where Nasreddin Khoja lived. As Tamerlane entered the city, he saw Nasreddin Khoja sitting by the side of the road watching the procession. Khoja was wearing a blanket wrapped around his head as a turban,[20] and this called Tamerlane's attention to him. Tamerlane ordered that the man be brought before him.

"Who are you?" he asked Khoja.

"I am the god of the earth," answered Khoja.

"Since you are the god of the earth, perhaps you can enlarge the eyes of this attendant of mine. See what very small eyes he has."

"I wonder," answered Khoja, "whether I did not make it plain to you or whether you just did not understand me. I am not the god of the heavens who can do such things. If you want something done above the waist, ask him; anything below the waist is in my sphere."

Tamerlane talked for a good while with Nasreddin Khoja, and he was very pleased with his wit. He sent him away finally, but a few days later he ordered him brought back for his amusement. One of the emperor's wives had cooked five eggs, and he invited Khoja to join them in a meal. He said to Nasreddin Khoja, "I want you to divide these five eggs fairly among the three of us."

Without hesitating, Khoja took the five eggs and said, "Here is one for you, your majesty, and since you have two below your waist, that makes a total of three eggs for you. This one is mine, and that makes three for me too. And the other three are for your wife, for she has none below the waist."

5.

Nasreddin Khoja and the Overcrowded Bed [21]

After Nasreddin Khoja's first wife died, he married again. The woman he married had also been married previously. One night as they lay in bed, Khoja's second wife started to talk about her first husband, telling Khoja what a wonderful man he was. Khoja then started to talk about his first wife, saying that she was the most wonderful woman he had ever known. But this second wife could talk faster than Khoja, and so she was winning the discussion. Khoja finally became so angry at her that he kicked her out of bed, and she fell on the floor.

The next day the woman went to a kadi and made a complaint against Khoja. When the trial started, she told the court that Khoja had kicked her out of bed onto the floor.

"Did you really do that, Khoja?" asked the kadi.

"No, I didn't, efendi," said Khoja. "It was this way. We were in bed together when a friend of hers came along and got into bed with us. Then a friend of mine came along and got into bed too. With four of us in the bed together, it became very crowded, and she fell out."

6.

Nasreddin Khoja and God's Son-in-Law [22]

A hafiz [23] once came to Akshehir and asked for the home of Nasreddin Khoja. The way was shown to him, and the hafiz went to Khoja's house after the evening service in the mosque. When the stranger knocked at the door, Khoja looked out the window and asked, "Who is it?"

"I," said the hafiz.

"Yes, but who are you?" asked Khoja.

"I am God's son-in-law. Will you accept me as your guest?"

"Just a minute," said Khoja. He came downstairs, put on his gown and shoes, and walked to the mosque, with the hafiz following him. When he arrived at the mosque, he opened the door and said to the hafiz, "Walk right in! This is your father-in-law's house."

7.

Nasreddin Khoja in God's Watermelon Patch [24]

One day Nasreddin Khoja planted watermelon seeds in his garden. He said to his wife, "I am going to plant two patches of watermelons, one for myself and one for God."

Khoja planted his own patch of melons in good soil, but he planted God's in very poor soil. When the watermelons grew, however, it happened that the melons he had planted for God grew large while his own did not thrive at all. Each melon in God's patch grew as large as a barrel.

When the watermelons were ripe, Khoja decided one night to steal some from God's patch. Taking a bag, he went to the garden and stole several large melons from God's patch. But as Khoja was carrying the melons home, some villagers sneaked up behind him in the darkness and quietly took his bag away from him. Terrified, Nasreddin Khoja rushed home and cried to his wife, "He caught me! He caught me!"

8.

Nasreddin Khoja Does What a Human Being Should [25]

One day Nasreddin Khoja and a group of his neighbors were going somewhere together. They all rode upon their donkeys. When they came to a hill, Khoja noticed that his donkey was sweating. He got down from its back and whispered into its ear, "I am sorry that you are working so hard that you are sweating."

His neighbors noticed Khoja get down from his donkey's back and whisper into its ear, and they were curious about this. "Khoja, what did you whisper to your donkey?" one of them asked.

"I told my donkey I was sorry he had to work so hard that he sweated," answered Khoja.

All of his neighbors laughed, and one of them said, "Why did you do that? Donkeys do not understand human speech. They are not at all human."

"What *I* have to do is what concerns me. I did what is expected of a human being, and I do not care whether or not he understood what I said."

9.

Nasreddin Khoja as Witness in Court [26]

Once there were two friends who left their village and went to a town to try to find work there. When they arrived in the town they were hungry, and so they went to a restaurant and ordered two boiled eggs apiece. After eating their eggs, they waited for an opportunity to sneak out, and when the manager's back was turned, they left without paying for their meal. They did this because they had no money at all.

They found work in that town, and after ten months they went again to that restaurant where they had got the free meal when they arrived. They ate a meal there and paid for it, and then they told the manager that they wished to pay for the meal that they had had on their first day in town. They handed him twenty kurus [27] apiece.

"What did you eat on that day?" asked the manager.

"We ate two boiled eggs apiece," said one of the friends.

"Ah, then I cannot take this money from you. It is not enough," said the manager.

The two friends were surprised at this answer. "Is that not the correct price for eggs?" one of them asked.

"You had that meal here ten months ago. Don't you realize that those four eggs would by this time have hatched into four chickens, and those four chickens, in turn, could have laid enough eggs to hatch twenty or thirty more chickens. No, you each owe me twenty liras apiece."

The two friends refused to pay this amount, and so the manager of the restaurant went to a kadi and entered a complaint against them. The kadi listened to his complaint and then he set a date for the trial.

On their way home the two friends met Nasreddin Khoja. He saw at once that there was something troubling them. "Why do you look so sad?" Khoja asked them.

"We are in great trouble, Khoja, efendi," one of them said.

"What is the trouble?" asked the Khoja.

"Ten months ago we came to town and we went to a restaurant because we were hungry. It was the restaurant near the mosque. We ate two boiled eggs each, but we didn't have any money to pay for what we ate."

"And today," said the other friend, "when we went to pay the manager of the restaurant the twenty kurus apiece that we owed him, he would not accept the money."

236

"Why not?" asked Khoja.

"He said that those four eggs would have become chickens and laid eggs that would also have become chickens, and by now there would be twenty or thirty chickens. These, he said, would be worth forty liras, and so he asked us each for twenty liras. Khoja, efendi, we do not have twenty liras apiece."

Nasreddin Khoja thought about this for a few minutes, and then he said to the two friends, "On the day of the trial, enter my name as a witness for you." The two friends agreed to do this, and then they went home and waited for the day of the trial.

When that day arrived, they went to the court and asked the kadi to enter the name of Nasreddin Khoja as a witness for them. The hearing progressed, but when Nasreddin Khoja's name was called, he did not appear. The judge sent two gendarmes to bring Khoja to court. When the gendarmes knocked at Khoja's door, he told them that he was too busy right then to come to court, but he said that he would come when he had finished his work. The gendarmes paid no attention to his protests, however, and they carried him off to the court by force.

"Why didn't you come on time?" demanded the kadi.

"I was too busy," said the Khoja.

"What business was so important that you could not come to court when you were supposed to?" asked the kadi.

"Kadi, efendi," said the Khoja respectfully, "tomorrow I shall begin to sow wheat, and today I have to boil enough wheat to sow all my fields."

"Sow boiled wheat!" exclaimed the kadi. "How do you expect boiled wheat to grow?"

"As easily as boiled eggs could hatch into chickens, efendi," answered Nasreddin Khoja.

Upon this evidence the kadi gave a judgment in favor of the two defendants and dismissed the court.

10.

Bekri Mustafa as Ferryman [28]

Once during his life Bekri Mustafa was a ferryman on the Bosporus. He took people back and forth from Istanbul to Kadikoy on the Anatolian side, and he always served raki to his passengers during the crossing.

One day Sultan Murad and his vezir went traveling in disguise, as they often did, and they decided to ride across the Bosporus in Bekri Mustafa's boat. They agreed on a price, and then Bekri started rowing toward Kadikoy. After he had rowed for a few minutes, he took in his oars and got out a bottle of raki and three glasses. The sultan said, "It is against Moslem law to drink raki, but if you must drink it, we shall not."

"Yes, you must," said Bekri Mustafa. "In my boat everyone drinks raki when I do. If they do not, then I refuse to row them back to shore."

So the sultan and the vezir had no choice. They had to drink several glasses of raki, for Bekri stopped every few minutes as he rowed his boat. When they finally reached Kadikoy and they were climbing out of the boat, the sultan said to his companion, "Now you can tell Bekri Mustafa that I am the sultan and you are my vezir."

When Bekri Mustafa heard this, he laughed loudly and said, "What? I have been drinking raki for forty years and I was never able to be either sultan or vezir. If you should drink with me on this return trip, you will think one of you is God and the other the Prophet!"

II.

Bekri Mustafa as Muezzin [29]

One day in the time of Sultan Mahmut [30] Bekri Mustafa was appointed muezzin to Saint Sophia Mosque.[31] He helped conduct funerals there,[32] standing in front of the congregation for the part of the service held in the mosque yard. At one of these funerals, he lifted up the lid of the coffin and whispered something into the ear of the corpse, "Fis, fis, fis." [33]

Someone from among the congregation asked, "Mustafa, what did you talk about with the deceased?"

"Only God and the deceased and I know that," answered Bekri Mustafa.

"Yes, but we want to know too," insisted the man, and all of the congregation agreed with him.

"Well, if you must know, then, I shall tell you. The deceased is on his way to the next world. I have father, mother, relatives, and friends there, and they are certain to ask him how things are back here on earth.

I told him simply to say to them, 'Bekri Mustafa became muezzin for Saint Sophia Mosque during the reign of Sultan Mahmut.' From that fact alone they will understand how corrupt the times have become."

12.

Bekri Mustafa Forgives His Enemy [34]

All his life Bekri Mustafa drank raki and wine. Whenever he wanted something to drink, he always asked for one of these two things. When he lay dying, however, he called for water.

One of his friends asked, "Bekri Mustafa, why do you want water now?"

Bekri Mustafa replied, "The holy Koran says that before we die we should forgive our enemies. I have hated water all my life as my worst enemy, and now I wish to forgive it."

13.

Injili Chavush and the Distant Fire [35]

One day Sultan Mahmut asked Injili Chavush to come into his presence, and when he arrived, the sultan said, "You will climb up the minaret, you will remain there until tomorrow morning, and then you will report to me whatever you have observed."

"But, your majesty, it is winter," said Injili Chavush. "I shall be frozen up there."

"I cannot help that. I want you to report to me in the morning what you have seen from the minaret during the night."

There was nothing for Injili Chavush to do but obey this command, and so he dressed as warmly as he could and then climbed the minaret. It was a cold night, and the wind was blowing hard, and so Injili Chavush walked round and round the balcony in an effort to keep warm. Toward morning, he observed a fire burning at a great distance but he did not know what caused it. Finally morning arrived and Injili, half-frozen, climbed down from the minaret and went to the presence of the sultan.

"What did you observe from the minaret last night?" the sultan asked.

"I was very cold up there and almost froze to death, your majesty. All I saw during the whole night was a great fire in the distance, but it was so far away I could not tell what caused it."

"Aren't you ashamed to say that you were cold when you had a great fire like that to warm yourself?"

Injili Chavush said nothing, but he put the sultan's comment in his pocket. Sometime later, after the warm weather had returned, Injili Chavush invited Sultan Mahmut and his vezirs to his house for a feast, and the sultan accepted the invitation.

When the day of the feast arrived, Sultan Mahmut and all his vezirs made a procession to Injili Chavush's house where they were received with great respect. Injili Chavush led them to the garden where they all sat talking. They sat there for two or three hours, and the company began to grow more and more hungry. Finally, one of the vezirs asked Injili Chavush, "Are we not going to eat tonight?"

"Yes," said Injili Chavush, "the cook is preparing dinner but he says it is not ready yet."

They talked further and walked about the garden until it was very late. By this time everyone was extremely hungry, and the same vezir said to Injili Chavush, "Let us go to the kitchen and see how the dinner is being made ready."

"Very well," said Injili Chavush, and he led the vezir to the kitchen. There the vezir was amazed at what he saw. Injili Chavush had ordered his cook to place the food to be cooked in a large caldron, to hoist the caldron up to the ceiling, and then to place a lighted candle beneath it on the floor.

"What is the meaning of this?" demanded the vezir. "How will the dinner ever get cooked in that way?"

"You wouldn't understand this," said Injili Chavush, "but Sultan Mahmut would."

The vezir went to Sultan Mahmut and told him what he had seen and what Injili Chavush had said. "What does he mean by this, your majesty?"

"I don't know," said the sultan, and he called Injili Chavush to him. "How can a candle ever cook a caldron of food several meters away?"

"Why, I thought you would understand this, your majesty. It can be done as easily as I could warm myself by the distant fire during the night I spent on the minaret."

14.

Neither in Heaven Nor on Earth [86]

One day while Injili Chavush was serving in the palace, he came upon a room where the padishah was making love to one of his wives. Instead of going away, Injili Chavush watched through a crack in the door. Afterwards his wife told the padishah that Injili Chavush had been looking at them, and he asked, "How do you know this?"

"I saw him watching through a crack in the door," she said.

"If he did, I shall learn of it," said the ruler, "and I shall punish him." Later that day the padishah said to Injili Chavush, "Injili, go out to the market and buy my wife Fatma a pair of shoes."

Injili Chavush went to the market and he bought a beautiful pair of shoes with paper soles. When he returned with them, the padishah looked at them and then said, "Injili, how long do you think paper-soled shoes will last my wife?"

"Your majesty," said Injili Chavush, "if your wife always keeps her feet in the position I saw them earlier today, she could wear these shoes all the rest of her life!"

The padishah was very angry with Injili Chavush and to punish him, he ordered, "You will be seen neither in heaven nor on earth, and you will be found neither among the faithful nor among the infidels."

"Yes, efendi," said Injili, and he left the padishah's presence. To carry out the padishah's orders, he climbed a nearby mountain and found a Yürük [37] tribe, and near them he had his tent put up. The ends of the tent were open to allow ropes tied to two trees to pass through, and from these ropes Injili had a hammock slung. At night he slept in that hammock, and during the day he sat on it.

After several days the padishah said to some of his attendants, "Go and search for Injili Chavush, and when you find him, bring him to me." It took the attendants many days to find Injili Chavush, but at last they searched the mountain slopes and found him near the Yürük camp. They took him back to the palace, and there the padishah questioned him: "Didn't I tell you to be seen neither in heaven nor on earth? Didn't I tell you not to be found either among the faithful or among the infidels? Why didn't you obey my orders?"

"Your majesty, I did obey your orders. I was staying with Yürüks, who are not faithful Moslems, for they have no mosque; neither are they infidels, for they have no church or cross. I slung my hammock between two trees, and I lived in that hammock day and night. In that way I was not on the earth, but neither was I in heaven."

When the padishah heard this explanation, he was greatly pleased, and so he pardoned Injili Chavush.

15.

The Offensive Excuse [38]

Because of his many offenses, Injili Chavush was one day condemned to death. Just before the hour of the execution, the padishah called him into his presence and said to him, "I shall pardon you on one condition: You will commit another offense and then you will beg to be excused for it, but the excuse must be more offensive than the offense."

"Very well, your majesty," said Injili Chavush.

As they were leaving the room, Injili Chavush goosed the padishah. The padishah looked at Injili Chavush in surprise and asked, "What did you do that for?"

"Excuse me, your majesty," said Injili Chavush, "I thought it was your wife."

Everyone agreed that this had met the padishah's condition for a pardon, and so Injili Chavush was released.

16.

The Horse's Kick [39]

One day Injili Chavush had some business in a law court, and he rode to the court on a very beautiful horse. The kadi admired this horse and wanted it for himself. He sent his clerk to tell Injili

Chavush that he would take care of his business well if Injili would make him a present of that horse. The kadi did not know at that time that Injili Chavush had great influence in the palace.

Injili Chavush was furious at the kadi's request, but he said nothing. Instead he rode immediately to the palace and asked that the kadi be dismissed from his position. The sultan immediately sent a letter of dismissal to the kadi, without giving any explanation for his action.

Sometime later the former kadi was sitting in a coffee house talking to his friends. It happened that Injili Chavush was also in that coffee house at the same time. Injili listened to them discussing the former kadi's dismissal from office without any explanation. "Well, friends," said the former kadi, "somebody kicked me, but I do not know who it was."

Then Injili Chavush spoke. "My horse kicked you, kadi, efendi," he said. "It was nobody but my horse."

17.

The Bektashi in the Mosque [40]

One day a Bektashi sat in the mosque, and there he started to drink raki. A man passing by looked in and saw the dervish desecrating the mosque in this way, and he became very angry with him. He walked into the mosque, spat on the dervish, and said to him, "Aren't you ashamed of yourself? It is bad enough to drink raki, but it is an unforgivable thing to drink it here in the mosque!"

The groggy Bektashi looked up at him and said, "If I weren't so busy, I should teach you what a sinful thing it is to spit in a mosque!"

18.

The Traveling Bektashi [41]

One day during the Ramazan a Bektashi was caught eating during the fasting hours. He was seized and taken before a kadi to be tried.

243

"O man!" said the kadi. "Why do you eat during the hours of the fast?"

"I eat because I am a traveler."

"You have lived here for forty years, and I have never seen you travel once in all that time."

"Is there evidence that I shall live for another day in this world? All my life I have been traveling toward the other world." [42]

19.

Haroun's Creatures and God's [43]

There was once a Bektashi who lived during the reign of Haroun al Raschid.[44] This dervish went once to visit the land of that ruler. While he was walking along the street in the chief city of that land, he saw some servants, magnificently dressed, coming toward him. Turning to a person near him, the dervish asked, "Who are these people approaching us?"

"They are the creatures of Haroun," his companion answered him.

As the Bektashi was very shabbily dressed, he opened his hands,[45] turned his face up to the sky, and said, "O God, first take a look at Haroun's creatures and then take a look at me, your own creature!" [46]

20.

The Bektashi and the Beggar [47]

Once there was a Bektashi who went to a bath. He spent several hours in the bath and was treated well there, but when he was leaving, he discovered that he had no money with which to pay the owner. The price for a bath in those days was one kurus.

Just before the Bektashi reached the cashier, sitting at the door, he asked God, "O, my God, pull down this bathhouse so that I will not be put to shame for not being able to pay for my bath."

Right then the dome of the bathhouse did fall crashing down, and the Bektashi rushed out just in time to save himself. Outside the bath he came face to face with a beggar who begged one kurus from him. The Bektashi said to the beggar, "What are you talking about? Even God hasn't one kurus, for if he had, he wouldnt' have had to pull down this huge dome."

21.

Allah Gives a Thousand for One Through a Bektashi [48]

Once there was a man who carried in his pocket a gold coin, all the money he had in the world. As he was walking along the street one day, he heard a town crier calling, "Allah gives a thousand to the man who gives only one."

When the crier approached the man, the man said to him, "All right, here you are. Take this money," and he gave the crier his golden coin. Then he began to count the days, waiting for Allah to give him the thousand gold liras for his one.[49] After waiting for a considerable length of time, however, the man became impatient, and so he decided to go and look for Allah in order to collect his money from him.

One day at sunset he reached the edge of a forest, and because there were no houses there where he might request lodging, he prepared to spend the night in the best way he could manage. He climbed a tall tree in order to be out of the reach of animals, but just as he was ready to go to sleep, he looked down and saw that another man was coming toward the tree. This second man, who was a Bektashi, came to the foot of the tree, placed his saddlebag there, and then sat down beside it. The man in the tree watched to see what he would do.

The Bektashi took from his saddlebag a piece of dough which he began to squeeze and shape with his hands. Finally he placed it on the ground before him saying, "This is Allah." Then he took another piece of dough, pressed it hard, and finally shaped it into a second figure. He placed this alongside the first figure and said, "This is Mohammed." Taking still another piece of dough from the bag, he shaped this into a third figure which he placed with the others, saying, "And this is the Caliph Ali." [50]

The Bektashi looked at the three figures for a while, and then he picked up the piece of dough representing Ali. "All of my life I have begged you to help me," he said, "but I cannot remember that you ever helped me with anything. I think I shall eat you."

After eating Ali, the Bektashi turned to Mohammed next. "Ah, Mohammed! I asked a lot from you at different times in my life, but you gave me nothing. I think that I shall eat you too." Thereupon he ate the second piece of dough.

Then he took up the third piece of dough, which represented Allah. He said, "O Allah, why do you give others things in great abundance and your humble servant nothing whatever? I am going to eat you too."

Hearing this, the man up in the tree shouted down at the dervish, "Wait! Wait! Don't eat him! He owes me a thousand gold liras!" Then he jumped down out of the tree and landed right alongside the Bektashi, frightening him to death. Afterwards he examined the Bektashi's clothes, and he found there a purse containing a thousand gold coins.

22.

The Bektashi and the Khoja [51]

One day a Bektashi was sitting under a huge sycamore tree, near a fountain, eating bread and cheese and drinking raki. It was just a few days before Ramazan, and the kadi of that place had forbidden the drinking of all alcoholic beverages. He had had criers announce that anyone who disobeyed this ruling would be thrown into jail.

A khoja, going to preach at a village mosque, happened along and saw the Bektashi. "Selamünaleyküm," he said.

"Aleykümselam," answered the Bektashi.

Seeing the Bektashi drinking raki, the khoja asked, "Aren't you ashamed to drink raki on such a blessed day?"

"Sit down, khoja," said the Bektashi. The khoja was rather tired from walking, and the place was cool and inviting, and so he accepted the Bektashi's suggestion and sat down. He took bread and olives from his bag and began to eat. The Bektashi addressed him, saying, "Khoja, look at this natural beauty given to us by God. If we people do not benefit from the wealth of such beauty, given to us by God, then tomorrow, in the next world it may accuse us of ingratitude. God will demand their right from us. Look at this beautiful tree, its cool shade, and that fine fountain. Shouldn't one drink this excellent raki in such beautiful surroundings?"

"What you say may be true," answered the khoja, "but the Ramazan is very close. Wouldn't it be better to do this after Ramazan?"

"Ah, khoja, the Ramazan comes every year, again and again, but once we go, we shall never return.[52] Come — have a drink!"

The khoja could not resist the temptation, and so he took a swallow of raki. But once he had taken a swallow, he wanted another, and so he began drinking with the Bektashi. At night when the night watchman saw them there, quite drunk, he arrested them and took them before the kadi.

The kadi was surprised to see a khoja, wearing his large turban and black gown, brought before him in the company of a Bektashi. Addressing the Bektashi, he said, "What is your name?"

"Yorgi," [53] answered the Bektashi.

"You are not one of the faithful anyway, then," said the kadi. Turning to the khoja, he said, "But you, you shameless fellow! Aren't you embarrassed for your turban and your gown? I am told that you preach in mosques. How could you do such a disgraceful thing on such a blessed day? The Bektashi observes neither prayers nor fastings and is more Christian than Moslem. But you — why did you do this?"

Then the kadi ordered the khoja carried off to jail and the Bektashi released. "You are not a true Moslem and your customs are different from ours. It may not be a sin for you to drink raki."

As the Bektashi was leaving the court, he felt sorry for the khoja. He asked the guard if he might speak to the kadi again, and when he had been granted permission, he said to the kadi, "Kadi, efendi, would you like to convert an unbeliever to Islam?"

"Of course I would," answered the kadi.

"Then I should like to become a regular Moslem," said the Bektashi, "but I have one condition: you will set the khoja free."

The kadi thought about this proposal for a minute, and he came to the conclusion that converting a Christian to Islam was a greater act of piety than imprisoning a sinner. "All right, I shall set the khoja free, but now repeat after me, 'There is only one God and Mohammed is his Prophet.'"

After the Bektashi had repeated this, he left the court with the khoja. As they were walking down the street, the Bektashi said, "How wonderful religion can be!"

The khoja was ashamed of his disgrace and angry at the Bektashi. "How can a person like you say that?" he demanded. "What do you mean?"

"Well, first I became a Christian and saved myself," said the Bektashi, "and then I became a Moslem and saved you."

23

The Kadi and Karabash [54]

Once upon a time there was a shepherd who had a beautiful dog named Karabash. Karabash was such a good sheep dog! No matter whether the shepherd was present or not, he would protect the flock from all kinds of danger. He would never allow wolves to get near the sheep. If a wolf even approached the flock, he would catch it and strangle it. He was such a strong dog! [55]

One day, however, Karabash became ill, and soon after that he died. The shepherd loved him so much that he gave Karabash a fine funeral, just as if he had been a human being. He had him washed and wrapped in a white linen shroud, and then he had him buried in a Moslem cemetery.

As there are busybodies all over the world, so there was one in this village too. He went to the kadi and complained that the shepherd had held a Moslem funeral for his dog and that he had buried him in a grave among those of the faithful. "It is a sacrilegious act," said this busybody, "and I demand that he be punished."

The shepherd was summoned to court, and the kadi asked him, "How is it that you give an unclean creature a Moslem burial and place him in a grave among the faithful? Don't you know that this is a blasphemous thing to do?"

In his own defense the shepherd said, "Efendi, so great was the service of this dog to me that during his life I presented him with thirty sheep as a token of my appreciation. When the dog was about to die, he said to me, 'When I am dead, kill ten of my sheep and spend the money from them on my funeral expenses; kill ten more and give the money they bring to the poor.'" [56]

"That makes twenty sheep," said the kadi. "What about the rest?"

"Well," said the shepherd, "he placed the remaining ten at the disposal of the kadi of this area and said that he should do whatever he thinks appropriate with them."

Very pleased with this arrangement, the kadi inquired, "What was the name of the deceased?" When the shepherd told him it was Karabash, the kadi opened his hands toward heaven and addressing all those present, he said, "Join me, O faithful, in a prayer for the soul of Karabash."

24.

The Kadi and the Forty Witnesses [57]

Once a rich aga decided to take a case to court. Wanting badly to win this case, the aga sent a large tray of baklava [58] to the kadi. There were forty pieces of baklava on the tray, and beneath each piece was a gold coin.

The kadi's clerk took the tray of baklava from the servant of the aga and carried it upstairs to the kadi. On the way up, the clerk was so tempted by the delicious aroma of the pastry that he could not resist eating a piece of it. Of course, he discovered the gold piece beneath the pastry, and he put this in his pocket. In all, he ate four pieces of baklava and pocketed the four coins placed beneath them.

The next day was the hearing for the aga's case, and the judge summoned the witnesses for both sides. When he saw no witnesses for the aga, he asked, "Aga, where are your witnesses?"

"Efendi, I sent forty witnesses to you yesterday to be examined."

"Ah, yes, I remember now," said the kadi, "but you are mistaken about the number. There were only thirty-six."

The clerk, who had been listening to this conversation, realized that his theft had been discovered. He said, "I beg your pardon, kadi, efendi, but the other four witnesses were too old and feeble to climb the stairs. I took their evidence downstairs, and I shall account to you for them afterwards."

25.

Let Us Not Go Too Deeply into That [59]

Once a farmer went to a kadi to have a contract signed. The kadi said that he did not have time to sign it just then, but that he would sign it on the following day. When the farmer appeared at court on the following day, however, the clerk told him that the kadi was still too busy and that he should return again on the next day. After this had continued for some time, the farmer finally realized that the kadi wanted a bribe.

This angered the farmer, but he needed the kadi's signature on his contract, and so he decided to give him a present. He took a large jar and filled it most of the way with ox dung. Then on top of this he spread a layer of white cheese. Taking this jar to the court, he presented it to the kadi with his compliments. At once the kadi found time to sign the contract. After the farmer had the contract safely in his hands, he could not resist asking, "Kadi, efendi, do you think it was proper for you to take that jar of cheese for signing this paper?"

The kadi smiled at him and said, "My friend, let us not go too deeply into that." Then he scooped some cheese from the jar and put it into his mouth. "What a fine jar of cheese."

"Well, as you said, let us not go too deeply into that," answered the farmer and left the court.[60]

BIBLIOGRAPHY
NOTES
INDEX

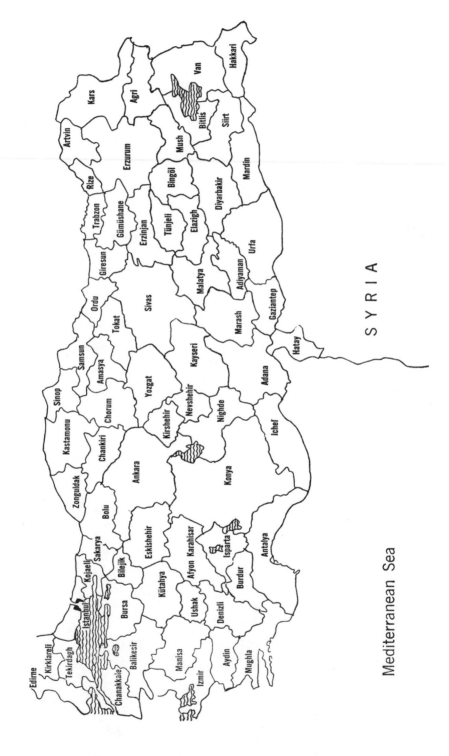

Black Sea

Mediterranean Sea

S Y R I A

Hakkari
Van
Kars
Agri
Bitlis
Artvin
Siirt
Erzurum
Musth
Mardin
Rize
Bingöl
Diyarbakir
Trabzon
Gümüshane
Tünjeli
Elazigh
Giresun
Erzinjan
Urfa
Ordu
Sivas
Malatya
Adiyaman
Tokat
Gaziantep
Samsun
Amasya
Marash
Sinop
Yozgat
Kayseri
Hatay
Kastamonu
Chorum
Kirshehir
Nevshehir
Adana
Chankiri
Nighde
Zonguldak
Ankara
Ichel
Bolu
Konya
Sakarya
Eskishehir
Kojaeli
Bilejik
Afyon Karahisar
Antalya
Istanbul
Kütahya
Isparta
Kirklareli
Bursa
Ushak
Denizli
Burdur
Edirne
Tekirdagh
Balikesir
Manisa
Aydin
Mughla
Chanakkaie
Izmir

Bibliography

Aarne, Antti, and Stith Thompson. *The Types of the Folktale: A Classification and Bibliography*, second rev. Helsinki, 1961.

Ajipayamli, Orhan. *Doghumla Ilgili Adet ve Inanmalarin*. Erzurum, 1961.

Akdagh, Mustafa. "Der Beginn der Celaliden Aufstande," *Dil ve Tarih-Coghrafya Fakultesi Dergisi*, IV, i (1946), 23–50.

Ali, Maulana Muhammad, ed. *The Holy Qu'ran*, fourth edition. Lahore, 1951.

And, Metin. "Dances of Anatolian Turkey," *Dance Perspectives* 3 (Summer, 1959), pp. 1–76.

——— *A History of Theatre and Popular Entertainment in Turkey*. Ankara, 1964.

Arberry, A. J. *More Tales from the Masnavi*. London, 1963.

——— *Tales from the Masnavi*. London, 1961.

Bain, Nisbet, ed. *Turkish Fairy Tales and Folk Tales Collected by Dr. Ignacz Kunos*. London, 1901.

Barnham, Henry D., ed. *The Khoja: Tales of Nasr-ed-Din*. New York, 1924.

Birge, John Kingsley. *The Bektashi Order of Dervishes*. Hartford, 1937.

——— *A Guide to Turkish Area Study*. Washington, 1949.

Boratav, Pertev Naili. "Anadoluda ve Türkmenler arasinda Köroghlu destaninin izlerine dair yeni notlar," *Türkiyat Mejmuas*, 5 (1935): 79–86.

——— ed. *Contes Turcs*. Paris, 1955.

——— *Halk Edebiyati Dersleri*. Ankara, 1942.

——— *Köroghlu Destani*. Istanbul, 1931.

——— ed. *Zaman Zaman Ichinde*. Istanbul, 1958.

Boratav, Pertev Naili, and H. V. Firatli. *Izahli Halk Shiiri Antolojisi*. Ankara, 1943.

Chodzko, Alexander. *Specimens of the Popular Poetry of Persia, As Found in the Adventures and Improvisations of Kurroglou, The Bandit Minstrel of Northern Persia, and in the Songs of the People Inhabiting the Shores of the Caspian Sea; Orally Collected and Translated, with Philological and Historical Notes*. London, 1842.

Eberhard, Wolfram. *Minstrel Tales from Southern Turkey*. Berkeley, 1955.

Eberhard, Wolfram, and Pertev Naili Boratav. "Sechzig türkische Tiermärchen," *Annales de L'Université D'Ankara*, 1 (1947): 246–303.

Eberhard, Wolfram, and Pertev Naili Boratav. *Typen Türkischer Volksmärchen.* Wiesbaden, 1953.

Ekrem, Selma *Turkish Fairy Tales.* Princeton, 1964 (juvenile).

Encyclopaedia of Islam, 4 vols. and Supplement. Leiden, 1913–1938; new ed., I——. Leyden, 1960—— (in progress).

Frazer, Sir James George. *The Golden Bough: A Study in Magic and Religion,* abridged ed. New York, 1922.

Gerhardt, Mia L. *The Art of Story-Telling: A Literary Study of the Thousand and One Nights.* Leiden, 1963.

Gibb, E. J. W., ed. and trans. *The History of the Forty Vezirs or The Story of the Forty Morns and Eves by Sheykh-Zada.* London, 1886.

Golpinarli, Abdülbaki. *Alevi-Bektashi Nefesleri.* Istanbul, 1963.

——— *Vilayetname, Manaib-i Hunkar Haci Bektas-i Veli.* Istanbul, 1958.

Güney, Eflatun Jem. *Gökten Uch Elma Düstü.* Istanbul, 1960.

——— *Nasrettin Hoca Fikralari.* Istanbul, 1962.

Hemden, Ibn. *Turkish Evening Entertainments: The Wonders of Remarkable Incidents,* trans. John P. Brown. New York, 1850.

Hikmet, Murat. *One Day the Hodja.* Ankara, 1959.

Jansen, William H. "Turkish Folklore: An Introduction," *Journal of American Folklore,* 74 (1961): 354–361.

Kelsey, Alice Geer. *Once the Hodja.* London, 1943.

——— *Once the Mullah.* London, 1954.

Kent, Margery, ed. *Fairy Tales from Turkey.* London, 1946 (juvenile).

Kinross, Lord (Patrick Balfour). *Atatürk: A Biography of Mustafa Kemal, Father of Modern Turkey.* New York, 1965.

——— *Within the Taurus.* London, 1954.

Kunos, Ignaz. *Nasreddin Hodsa Tréfái.* Budapest, 1899.

Lane, Edward William. *The Arabian Nights' Entertainment,* ed. and rev. by Stanley Lane-Poole. 4 vols. New York, 1882.

Lerner, Daniel. *The Passing of Traditional Society.* New York, 1958.

Lewis, Bernard. *The Emergence of Modern Turkey.* London, 1961.

Makal, Mahmoud. *A Village in Anatolia.* London, 1954.

Montagu, Mary Wortley. *Letters.* London, 1934.

Nicholson, Reynold A. *Rumi: Poet and Mystic, 1207–1273.* London, 1950.

Oktay, Emiz. *Tarih: Yeni ve Yakinchaghlar,* III. Istanbul, 1958.

Onder, Ali Riza. *Yashayan Anadolu Efsaneleri.* Kayseri, 1955.

Pierce, Joe E. *Life in a Turkish Village.* New York, 1964.

Planhol, Xavier de, ed. *Contes et Légendes des Peuples Turcs.* Paris, 1958.

Ramsay, Allan, and Francis McCullagh. *Tales from Turkey.* London, 1914.

Remer, Theodore G. *Serendipity and the Three Princes.* Norman, Okla., 1965.

Rescher, O. "Einige nachträgliche Bemerkungen zur Zahl 40 in Arabischen, Türkischen und Persischen," *Der Islam* 4 (1913): 157–159.

Ritter, Hellmut. *Karagös, türkische Schattenspiele,* 3 vols. I, Hanover, 1924; II, Istanbul, 1941; III (with Andreas Tietze), Wiesbaden, 1953.

BIBLIOGRAPHY

Sinor, Denis, ed. *Aspects of Altaic Civilization.* Bloomington, Ind., 1963.

Siyavushgil, Sabri Esat. *Karagöz: Its History, Its Characters, Its Mythical and Satirical Spirit.* Istanbul, 1961.

Smithers, Leonard C., ed. *The Thousand and One Quarters of an Hour (Tartarian Tales).* London, 1897.

Tezel, Naki. *Keloghlan.* Ankara, 1945.

Thompson, Stith. *The Folktale.* New York, 1946.

———— *Motif-Index of Folk Literature,* 6 vols. Bloomington, Ind., 1955–1957.

Walker, Barbara K. *Just Say Hic!* Chicago, 1965 (juvenile).

Walker, Barbara K., and Ahmet Uysal. "Folk Tales in Turkey," *Horn Book,* 40 (1964): 42–46.

Walpole, Horace. *Horace Walpole's Correspondence,* XX, ed. W. S. Lewis. New Haven, 1960.

Wesselski, Albert. *Der Hodscha Nasreddin,* 2 vols. Weimar, 1911.

Winner, Thomas G. *The Oral Art and Literature of the Kazakhs of Russian Central Asia.* Durham, 1958.

Yasa, Ibrahim. *Hasanoghlan: Socio-Economic Structure of a Turkish Village.* Ankara, 1957.

Yasharoghlu, Ahmet Halit, ed. *Hakiki Bektashi: Fikra ve Nükteleri.* Annotated by Mehmet Ali Nurbaba. Istanbul, 1957.

Yurdatap, Selami Mümür. *Keloghlanin Merakli Masallari.* Istanbul, 1960.

Notes

Introduction

1. Metin And is the most articulate authority on folk dance in Turkey, and, fortunately for Western readers, he writes in English. He provides a good introduction to the subject in "Dances of Anatolian Turkey," *Dance Perspectives 3* (Summer 1959). Photographs of some of the principal folk dance movements appear in his *A History of the Theatre and Popular Entertainment in Turkey* (Ankara, 1964), plates 103–117.

2. The folk poet is referred to as a saz poet (*saz shair*), or, more often, as a lover poet (*ashik shair*), or, simply, lover (*ashik*). Ordinarily the folk poet in Turkey finds his career through an idealized love affair. He becomes enamored of an inaccessible woman, a high-born lady or perhaps a distant beauty whose picture he has seen, whose charms he has heard described, or whose face he has seen in a dream. She will be the object of his earliest compositions, and throughout his life he will continue to devote pieces to her occasionally. It is a tradition that suggests Petrarch, the Troubadours, and the conventions of courtly love, and, before that, the Neo-Platonists; but it may well antedate anything of the type in the West.

Some authorities attribute the travels of *ashiks* to their searchings for the beloved, romantic quests: "Traditionally speaking, these journeys are necessary: the singer must try to find his love, the girl whom a saint has shown him in a dream and with whom he has drunk the love potion. He may have other adventures, he may even marry, but his ideal remains the same and forces him to travel eternally, because he knows only her face but not the place where she lives. Practically speaking, these journeys bring the minstrel to audiences interested in his songs and willing to pay him." Wolfram Eberhard, *Minstrel Tales from Southeastern Turkey* (Berkeley, 1955), p. 9.

3. *Zaman Zaman Ichinde* (Istanbul, 1958), pp. 14–15.

4. See Part III of this volume for commentary on Karagöz both in drama and folktale.

5. Hatay, formerly the sanjak of Alexandretta, is the southernmost province in Turkey and includes her only deep-water port on the Mediterranean. Placed under French control, along with Syria, after World War I, it was restored to Turkey again in 1939.

6. For observations on the *teķerleme* see Barbara K. Walker and Ahmet Uysal, "Folk Tales in Turkey," *Horn Book,* 40 (February 1964): 42–46.

For some examples of *teķerlemeler* see the twenty-one composites that Boratav gives in *Zaman Zaman Ichinde* — the title of which is itself the opening expression ("Time within time") of a very popular *teķerleme*. One should be cautious about these involved jingles, however, for Boratav clearly indicates that they were never uttered by individual informants. They are composites of many variants of these twenty-one formulas. His rationale is that all of the elements are genuinely folk, and so there is no harm done and much good accomplished by combining motifs to make composites. For purposes of art, this is, of course, a perfectly legitimate procedure, but it would seem to be open to some question as a scholarly practice. It is an easy step from this to sorting out "desirable" motifs from variants of a folktale to construct the most colorful and impressive tale that was never told.

7. Well known to everyone interested in the folktale is *The Types of the Folktale* (Helsinki, 1961), compiled by Antti Aarne and Stith Thompson. The work by Wolfram Eberhard and Pertev Naili Boratav may be less familiar. Filling a great gap in our knowledge about folktales of the world, *Typen Türkischer Volksmärchen* was welcomed as a milestone of scholarship. See William Hugh Jansen's excellent review in *Journal of American Folklore,* 68 (1955): 231–235. It is to be hoped that, subsequently, more comprehensive editions of this valuable work will be published as additional collections of current Turkish tales become available in print.

Stith Thompson originally published his six-volume *Motif-Index of Folk Literature* (Bloomington, Ind.) during the years 1932–1936; it was the revised edition (Bloomington, Ind., 1955–1957) that was used for this study.

8. *The Folktale* (Bloomington, Ind., 1946), p. 8.

Part I. Tales of the Supernatural

1. With good and justifiable reasons of their own, Eberhard and Boratav do not index anecdotes, so very numerous in Turkey; consequently, it is impossible to make any valid statistical comparisons between the tales in their sources and those in our archive.

2. One minuscule bit of evidence to indicate how much the supernatural still preoccupies the folk mind in Turkey is the frequency with which the word *dev* (monster, giant, demon) occurs. It is the sixty-fifth most commonly used word in rural spoken Turkish, according to Frequency List IV developed for teaching vocabulary in the army literacy program.

3. *Zaman Zaman Ichinde* (Istanbul, 1958), pp. 30–31.

4. Keloghlan stories in inexpensive editions have a steady market in Turkey today, and in popularity they are second only to tales about Nasreddin Khoja (Part VII). Among the most available collections are Naki Tezel's *Keloghlan* (Ankara, 1945) and Selami Mümür Yurdatap's *Keloghlanin Merakli Masallari* (Istanbul, 1960), which sell for 150 kurus (roughly 15¢) and 100 kurus respectively. In his excellent section "Prolegomena zum Türkischen Märchen" of the Introduction to *Typen Türkischer Volksmärchen* Boratav indicated his intention to undertake a detailed study of Keloghlan stories.

5. Beards and moustaches have been valued more in Moslem countries than in most

other areas of the world. The beard of the Prophet was considered sacred, and oaths were, and are, sworn in its name. At the chief shrine of the Mevlevi (The Whirling Dervishes), in Konya, there is said to be a hair of Mohammed's beard, wrapped in a hundred folds of silk, inside a small silver casket that one can view in the glass case that stands in the center of the main chamber. (One suspects that there may be in Moslem sanctuaries as many hairs of the Prophet's beard as there are drops of Christ's blood or pieces of "the true cross" in Christian shrines.)

During the Ottoman era a beard and moustache were necessary parts of a government official's makeup. Military men wore at least a moustache as an inviolable symbol of their honor. Its importance is illustrated by an episode in the tales told about Jakirjal Mehmet Efe, a chivalrous outlaw, apparently of the eighteenth century. He became so notorious for some of his exploits that at length the Sultan dispatched a group of thirty crack troops, Albanian hussars, to capture him. Mehmet managed to surprise them, however, and with his band surrounded them in a coffee house in Izmir. In retribution against his pursuers and in defiance of Istanbul, Mehmet made a single gesture: he cut off the moustaches of the thirty soldiers and sent them in a silk bag to the Sultan.

Most of the religious community continue to wear whiskers. A man preparing to make a pilgrimage to Mecca allows his beard to grow, sometimes for as long as a year in advance, as a token of his dedication. He is referred to as a *haji,* and, if an older man, as a *haji baba* (pilgrim, and pilgrim father). After his return he enjoys a certain prestige for having gone on this holy mission, and if he wishes to retain this social advantage permanently, he may place the title *Haji* before his name, and he may also continue to wear his beard, chest length, as a status symbol for the remainder of his life.

In Turkish cities men shave daily, but in the villages, beards are still very common. The average villager shaves weekly, a few only monthly.

6. *Narrator:* Sukru Dariji, a native of Kavshit, who works as custodian at the Language and History-Geography Faculty (College of Liberal Arts) of Ankara University.

Site of recording: Kavshit village of the caza of Sungurlu of the province of Chorum.

Date collected: August 1964.

Types: Aarne-Thompson 301, The Three Stolen Princesses. Eberhard-Boratav 72, *Der Phönix.*

Motifs: B11.10, Sacrifice of human being to dragon. D1505, Magic object cures blindness. K1935, Impostors steal princess. K1931.2, Impostors abandon hero in lower world. F101.3, Return from lower world on eagle. B322.1, Hero feeds own flesh to helpful animal.

7. Most of the ridiculous elements of this *tekerleme* are obvious. The expression the "sieve was in the straw" is a comic inversion. It refers to the final winnowing of wheat when the chopped straw is placed in a sieve and the wheat sifted out. *Tingir, mingir* is the onomatopoetic expression for the sound produced by a rocking cradle.

8. The Turkish word *Kismet* means fate or destiny, often thought to be written on one's forehead and visible to those with religious insight.

9. Engagement palaver, usually carried on between the bride's parents and a matchmaker representing the groom, is a protracted and highly stylized social event. It often includes ritualistic eating and drinking. The word sherbet here is used in the Turkish and British senses to denote a cold fruit drink, rather than in the American sense of a frozen dessert.

10. The khoja is a Moslem priest, formerly both priest and teacher. Sometimes the women in the family of a khoja acquire his title, informally, among friends and ac-

quaintances. The daughter of a khoja is sometimes called Khoja Kiz (Khoja Daughter or Khoja Girl), and the wife, Khoja Hanim (Khoja Lady). One of our informants at Tashköprü, whose husband had been a khoja and whose father had been a hafiz (a religious person who can recite the entire Koran by heart), is known by everyone as Nuriye Khoja. This is a title of respect, however, and she has no religious function whatever.

There is another dimension to the term khoja girl as it is used in this tale, however, for the person involved here does have a religious quality, and with her curative powers and her gifts of magic objects plays the role of a typical Moslem saint. Actually, there are no female khojas, and except among the minority Shiite (Alevi) sect, women do not participate in the regular religious services in the mosque; in those orthodox Sunnite mosques, where women are occasionally admitted, they are restricted to a balcony in the rear of the mosque where they are apart from the male congregation and not seen by them. Occasionally in folktales, however, there is a toying with the notion of a female religious leader in Islam, an idea characterized by the same attraction-repulsion syndrome that informed the Pope Joan legend in the West.

11. Before each of the prayer services a devout Moslem performs ritual ablutions, and for this purpose several faucets or free-flowing taps are mounted in a stone panel in front of every mosque. Hands, elbows, face, mouth, nose, ears, and feet are all washed three times before religious cleanliness is attained. One becomes aware of the rigorous Spartan element of Islam when one sees even aged men making these protracted, cold-water ablutions before mosques in severe winter weather.

12. Throughout this volume we have frequently used the untranslated form of the initial greetings between strangers in all Moslem countries: *Selamünaleyküm*, meaning "I give you my greetings"; and *Aleykümselam*, "I return the greetings."

13. *Bismillah* is the common shortened form of *Bismillahirrahmanirrahim*, meaning "in the name of the most merciful God." It is a word used, audibly or silently, by many devout Moslems before starting any undertaking, great or small, and it then signifies "I begin this act by mentioning the name of God as a sign of respect."

14. The *ezan* is the call to prayer chanted from the minaret of a mosque by a religious crier known in Turkish as a *meyzin*, though the word often appears in English as transliterated from the Arabic, muezzin. Because Friday was the Sabbath prior to the Atatürk Reforms, the Friday services were once considered more important than those on other days. The reference here, as the tale subsequently discloses, is to the main service of the day, the *öghle namazi*, which occurs around noon.

Throughout this volume reference will frequently be made to one or another of the five daily services of the Moslem faith, and so their names and hours are here listed: *Sabah namazi*, morning service, at sunrise; *Oghle namazi*, noon service, usually between 12 and 1 o'clock; *Ikinde namazi*, mid-afternoon service, roughly 3 or 4 o'clock; *Aksham namazi*, evening service, about sunset; *Yatsi namazi*, night service, at dusk, around 9 o'clock. The Moslem religious calendar indicates the exact hour of each day when these services are to be performed. The precise hours, varying from year to year, are computed by a priest-astronomer known as a *müftü* (English, mufti) in each caza town. All of these caza-level muftis come under the jurisdiction of an official of the national government, the Director of Religious Affairs, formerly known as the Grand Mufti. This is, incidentally, one of the few remaining links between Church and State since the secularization of modern Turkey.

15. Both Keloghlan and the audience here were well versed in giant lore. According

to many folktales one must not cut off all of the heads of a multiheaded monster. With six heads gone, the giant will weaken and bleed to death. But if one cuts off the seventh, he undoes all his work, for immediately all seven will be restored to the giant, and all of his original strength will be renewed. One wonders whether this is simply a magic formula or whether there may also be an element of hubris in this taboo. During the narration of this episode the audience indicated its approval of Keloghlan's conduct.

16. The precise words of the narrator here were: "Men like me sold their fields." Inasmuch as the narrator does not elsewhere enter this tale personally, we have, in this one sentence, departed from the literal transcription.

17. Pilaf (*pilav*) is a very common buttered rice dish, sometimes flavored with bits of meat and pieces of pine nuts. The expression "to fall like a heap of pilav" means to collapse in a shapeless mass.

18. The *Zümrüdü Anka* Bird is often identified with the Phoenix, as it is by Eberhard and Boratav in their Type 72, *Der Phönix*. Though these fabulous birds have certain features in common, it is an oversimplification to equate the two completely. The Phoenix, for example, was almost always represented as male; the Anka is often female.

The Anka has been more accurately associated with the Roc (Rok, Rukk, Rukh), the gigantic bird that appears in *The Arabian Nights*. The Roc is mentioned by Marco Polo as traditionally inhabiting Madagascar, and one of its feathers was supposedly taken to the Great Khan. One Moslem legend places the Roc's home on a distant island in the Circumambient Ocean and attributes the bird's exile there to a crime it once committed in carrying off a bride. Supposedly it lives to be 1700 years old, though its life may be terminated before that if one of its young, of the same sex, comes to maturity. If such a replacement does appear, the parent vanishes, sometimes (like the Phoenix) in flames.

In this tale the Anka is a benevolent creature, but this is not always the case. In a variant of this tale, collected in 1962 at Karahamzali (a village 90 kilometers south of Ankara on the Konya road) the Anka is an oppressive bird that with spread wings shuts out the light of the sun from a whole kingdom. The hero, equipped with a magic horse and a magic sword, eventually kills the Anka and thus redeems the land from darkness.

Obviously a product of fantasy, the Anka may, nevertheless, have been suggested originally by one or another of the species of huge, long-lived vultures that inhabit the Middle East. Some of these have been reported to have wingspreads of twelve and thirteen feet, and some are known definitely to live for a great span of time. Several centenarians are housed at the Atatürk Zoo, just outside Ankara, the oldest of them credited with an age of 165 years.

19. See above, note 14.

20. Neither the peasant narrator nor the audience saw any inconsistency in the Anka's speech here being limited to common bird sounds, "gok" and "guk," after it had just carried on an intelligible conversation with Keloghlan. This shift to bird calls occurred in every single variant of the tale we collected or encountered.

It should be noted here that the Turkish peasant imitates and enjoys others' imitations of common sounds: bird cries, animal calls, and a wide variety of noises made by domestic and agricultural equipment. While collecting in Izmir among migrant workers from Konya, for example, we used as "bait" in their coffee house a set of subtly varied partridge calls taped from the lips of a professional hunter on the Plain of

Konya. Whenever our narrators wearied or the audience started to drift away — a good Turkish raconteur requires a minimal audience of eight or ten — we revived the partridge. Frivolous as this might seem, the success of our all-night sessions at that particular site was due in part to this device.

21. Musicians are available for hire in every town of caza size in Turkey, and they are still used to add an air of festivity to social occasions of all kinds: weddings (often week-long), circumcisions (ceremonies of three or four days' duration), holidays, and public events of all kinds. Quite often an ensemble will consist simply of two or three *zurnas* (cracked pipes) and a drum.

22. Several days before a wedding, the hands of the village bride and her attendants are dyed with henna (a reddish-orange color) as a public token of the approaching marriage.

23. This is a literal translation. There is a custom in Turkey that the bearer of good tidings must be rewarded. Sometimes in Turkish folktales when a messenger announces to the padishah that he has good news, he is rewarded even before he reports the facts. *Müjde vermek* means "to give good news," but implicit in the expression is the understanding, on the part of all who use or hear it, that a gift is involved.

24. *Jirit* is a game played on horseback, usually by a whole field of contestants, similar to the collective tournaments of the Middle Ages. Like the tournaments, jirit games were supposed to be friendly contests, and usually blunted javelins were used. Occasionally, however, as in the West, encounters were fatal.

25. *Efendi* was an Ottoman title for civil and religious officials, in contrast to military leaders, and it was often a term of respect applied to intellectuals. In the later days of the Empire it was used to honor any man of consequence, including the businessman. Today it carries no class distinction at all, and it is roughly equivalent to sir when that word is used deferentially after a man's name: "Mr. Smith, sir." Efendi always follows the person's name when the two are used together: "Ahmet, Efendi." Like sir, however, it can be used alone.

26. The black and red horses and the matching black and red suits are here more decorative than functional. In one of the common variants of the story, however, Keloghlan, in his Male Cinderella role, performs prodigious feats in three successive athletic contests, each time dressed in a suit of the same color as his horse. After each contest there is widespread talk and speculation about the identity of the black, or brown, or gray champion, and, in some versions, searches are made for him. Among those who talk about the unknown hero so brightly accoutered are the elder brothers of Keloghlan who come home and report to the Male Cinderella what marvels they have witnessed.

27. To indicate a small number, the Turkish peasants rarely say one or two, a couple, two or three, a handful, or half a dozen. Throughout Anatolia the expression used is three or five: three or five kinds of foods, three or five days. This expression recurs throughout this volume.

28. Although Turkish weddings are lengthy — they are still frequently a week long in villages — it is doubtful that they ever actually lasted for forty days and forty nights. Forty is an extremely popular number in Turkey (and to a degree in other Moslem lands, too), and the first common stopping place in numbers above twelve is at forty. Hence, there are Forty Saints as well as Forty Thieves, Forty Sons, Forty Daughters, forty units of all kinds of merchandise, and weddings that last for forty days and forty nights.

29. *Narrator:* Bulduk Ozel, farmer, 38.

Site of recording: Chorja village of the caza of Cihanbeyli of the province of Konya. (New name designated by Ministry of Interior, 1965: Damlakuyu.)

Date collected: March 1962.

Types: Aarne-Thompson 560, The Magic Ring; 566, The Three Magic Objects and the Wonderful Fruits. Eberhard-Boratav 58, *Der Dank von Katze und Hund;* 157, *Das Zauberportemonnaie.*

Motifs: L114, Hero of unpromising habits. D810, Magic object a gift. B505, Magic object received from animal. D1131.1, Castle produced by magic. D860, Loss of magic object. D861.5, Magic object stolen by hero's wife. D881, Magic object recovered by use of second magic object. K2213, Treacherous wife. D992.1, Magic horns grow on forehead. D1375.1, Magic object (fruit) causes horns to grow. D1375.2, Magic object (fruit) causes horns to be removed. D881.1, Recovery of magic object by use of magic apples. D895, Magic object returned in payment for removal of horns.

30. There is nothing especially Egyptian about this tale, and one should not expect to find Egyptian themes, characters, settings, or stage properties. This is simply a conventional opening for a tale. Usually Turkish narrators confine the locales of their tales to the Near and Middle East, but within that general area, almost anything can occur almost anywhere.

31. There are a great many Turkish folk remedies for female sterility, most of them religious. Intercession by khojas and dervishes was once very common. For the most comprehensive and authoritative treatment of the subject see Orhan Ajipayamli's study of childbirth lore, *Doghumla Ilgili Adet ve Inanmalarin* (Erzurum, 1961).

32. At one time women wore the family fortunes in necklaces of gold coins. This practice still continues among some groups, most noticeably among the Shiites (Alevi) of southern Turkey. In Hatay Province one often sees women with rows of gold coins across their foreheads.

33. Snake men, snake women, serpents with human heads, lamias, and serpentine creatures endowed with human speech are common in the oral traditions of many countries, and numerous studies have been made of them. Judging from linguistic evidence, one would have to conclude that those appearing in Turkish folktales are often of Persian origin.

34. This is a standard *tekerleme* used both to indicate long journeys and to keep the listeners from being bored with the details of the trip itself.

35. This is the polite response to make when one is asked to name his wish. It is usually repeated three times before proper reticence is rendered, just as one refuses a proffered gift or an invitation three times before accepting.

36. The Turkish night watchman blows upon a shrill police whistle as he makes his rounds. Pairs of watchmen often patrol parallel streets and keep each other apprised of their whereabouts by sounding these whistles.

37. The word *bey* is now commonly used after a man's first name as a sign of respect (Hasan Bey), much as Mr. is used before a surname in English. Until recently, however, it was a status label, roughly equivalent to lord, and at one time it indicated a political position.

38. This is a proverbial expression which means "to the end of the earth."

39. To appreciate the humor of this expression, one must be acquainted with Turkish street cries. Often as nonsensical as the *tekerleme*, they rarely name the object being sold but refer to it as something entirely different. One peddler we encountered was hawk-

ing, "Fish! Fresh fish!" but he was actually selling strawberries. The insulting exchange between peddler and customer here is also part of this humorous tradition.

40. This is a good instance of the intrusive image of the keloghlan. Mehmet is not a keloghlan, nor is he even disguised as one, but because of his general shabbiness, he is associated with the type.

41. The pilgrim to Mecca, the *haji,* is an esteemed person, sometimes thought to have acquired special insight.

42. Lokman (Luqman) was a legendary figure cast in different roles in each of the periods with which he was associated. In pre-Islamic Arab tradition he was viewed as hero and sage. In the Koran (Sura XXXI) he was pictured as a contemporary of King David and the author of proverbs; numerous collections of Moslem proverbs are attributed to Lokman. To the Middle Ages he was a doctor and creator of fables, and because most of these moralistic pieces have parallels in the works of Aesop, Lokman was often identified with that shadowy Greek figure; as with Aesop, his original nationality was often listed as Egyptian, Ethiopian, or Nubian, and like Aesop, he was at different times described as a deformed slave, a shepherd, a carpenter, and a tailor. Tale 37 of Jalal al-Din Rumi's *Tales from the Masnavi* (London, 1961) is based on an episode in his life. For additional notes on this little-known figure, see Edward Lane's edition of *The Arabian Nights' Entertainment* (New York, 1882), II, 439, and *The Shorter Encyclopaedia of Islam* (Leiden, 1953), pp. 289–290.

43. *Narrator:* Mehmet Anli.

Site of recording: Mehmet Anli was born and reared in Samsun, but the tale was collected from him at Sinop Penitentiary, where he is serving a life sentence for murder. The tale was narrated in the prison yard before an audience of two hundred men imprisoned for life.

Date: August 1964.

Types: Aarne-Thompson 302 B, Hero with Life Dependent upon His Sword. Eberhard-Boratav 215, *Dem Helden helfen übernatürliche Wesen.*

Motifs: T511.1.1, Conception from eating apple. E761, Life token; object has mystic connection with life of a person, so that changes in life token indicate changes in the person, usually disaster or death. F574.1, Resplendent beauty [usually face, here hair] lights up dark. F601, Extraordinary companions. D810, Magic object a gift. D812, Received from supernatural being [here a saint]. D1080, Magic sword. H1301, Quest for the most beautiful of women. H1213.1, Quest for princess caused by sight of one of her hairs dropped by bird (or floating on river).

44. *Hüsnügüzel* could have different meanings though it is commonly translated "beautiful of soul."

45. Hizir, known in Arabic as Al-Khadir or El-Khidr, is probably the most frequently mentioned Moslem saint. A guardian of the virtuous and deserving, he often appears on the scene suddenly to save them from disaster after all other help has failed, and in folktales Hizir is the most commonly employed *deus ex machina.* He is usually represented as being an old man with a white beard, often dressed as a dervish.

Probably no figure is more deeply embedded in Near Eastern lore than is Hizir. Often thought to be a contemporary of Abraham, he is probably of earlier origin, and he may well have been an ancient vegetation god. Al-Khadir is an epithet meaning "The Green Man," and he is often associated with the Abu-Hayat, the Spring of life from which flows the Water of Immortality. At least three accounts of this water and its god appear before its mention in the Koran (Sura XVIII, 59–81): in the Gilgamesh epic, in the Romance of Alexander (Episode I), and in the Jewish legend of Rabbi Joshua ben Levi. See *The Encyclopaedia of Islam*, ed. T. Houtsma, *et al.* (Leiden, 1927), II, 862–864; and *The Arabian Nights' Entertainment*, ed. Edward W. Lane, rev. Stanley Lane-Poole (New York, 1882), I, 23–40.

In Turkey and in several Arab lands Hizir is either identified with or associated with Ilyas (the Biblical Elias or Elijah) who was also supposed to have drunk of the Water of Life. When the two appear as associated saints, Hizir is sometimes credited with being the patron of seafarers while Ilyas protects desert travelers, keeping them from going astray. The two are said to meet annually to travel together to Mecca, and the time of this pilgrimage is thought to coincide with the festival of Hidrellez (a word that combines the names Hizir and Ilyas or Elyas), which falls during the first week in May. Probably a festival for fertility rites at one time, Hidrellez is still recognized, however vaguely, as a day of ritual throughout Turkey. Among some urbanites wish-fulfillment pantomimes are carried out, in complete silence, just at the break of dawn. Among rural Turks' observances there remain motifs of fertility rites, including the throwing of green-clad youths into the water, as is done in the "Green George" ceremonies in the Balkans. See Sir James Frazer's *The Golden Bough*, abridged ed. (New York, 1922), pp. 125–129.

46. Aghabey, composed of two titles, *agha* and *bey*, is defined as "older brother." It is also often applied to a person of social status superior to that of the speaker to indicate deference or respect.

47. The quest, physical or spiritual, for a beautiful woman — often the most beautiful in the world, often one seen first in a dream — is a very common motif in Turkish lore. As mentioned earlier, it animates folk poets (lover poets). The quest is undertaken by the heroes of folktales, especially young men of noble birth. In real life the notion sometimes so captivates the imagination of a young man that it may be the cause (or result?) of mental derangement; we knew of one such person so beset by this obsession that he gnawed away most of his upper lip in his frustration at not being able to find again the girl glimpsed in his dream. Eventually this person recovered his mental stability.

Contributing to the persistence of this motif may well be the institution of the family-arranged marriage, still common in Turkey. Often a man does not view his prospective bride at close range until the time of the wedding; he may remember her from their childhood days, or he may see her from a distance, or he may be shown a picture of her, or he may know of her beauty only by reputation.

48. The word *jadi,* used here, means "witch" or "hag." In Turkish folktales a witch may have supernatural powers (as does another witch later in this same tale), but more often she is simply a meddling or malicious old woman, frequently an accomplice of the villain in his efforts to abduct a girl.

49. This is a figure of speech used commonly in tales. Whether it was formerly applied to armies on the march, which might generate smoke as well as dust, we do not know.

50. A common expression.

51. "Ya Allah!" was once a Turkish battle cry.

52. The witch asks for a *küp*, a large amphora-shaped earthenware vase used for storing water. This is the most common airborne vehicle for Turkish witches.

53. The Turkish exclamation *Ay! Vay!* is here translated "Oh! Oh!"

54. Animals' instinctive awareness of the presence of an evil person is a very common belief.

55. The epithet "donkey and the son of a donkey," usually contracted to *esh' oghul eshek*, is one of the most offensive of Turkish insults.

56. *Narrator:* Shahismail Teckchan, farmer.

Site of recording: Chorja village of the caza of Cihanbeyli of the province of Konya. (New name designated by Ministry of Interior, 1965: Damlakuyu.)

Date collected: March 1962.

Types: Aarne-Thompson 465, Man Persecuted Because of Beautiful Wife; 513, The Helpers. Eberhard-Boratav, 86, *Das Froschmädchen;* 207, *Die Elefantzähne.* The tale incorporates more elements of the Aarne-Thompson types than it does of those in the Eberhard-Boratav index.

Motifs: B16.1.3.1, Wild, man-eating mare. H1154.3.1, Bridling a wild horse. F574.1, Resplendent beauty (usually face). H931.1, Envious king covets the wife. H911, On advice of evil counselor. H1211, Hero given impossible tasks. H1233.2.1, He accomplishes these with help of wife. F601, Extraordinary companions. F632, Mighty eater. F633, Mighty drinker. H1114, Task: eating enormous amount. H1142, Task: drinking enormous amount. H1135, Task: annihilating army single-handed. Z71.5.1, Seven brothers and one sister.

57. To define *pasha* simply as general, as the term is used in Turkey today, is to miss the full implication here. In former times a pasha was a general or the governor of a province, though in a militaristic society the qualifications for these two positions were very similar if not identical. In either case, the pasha of Ottoman times had greater status and wealth than does either a general or governor today. Pashas appear in a great many Turkish folktales — how many Anglo-American tales include generals or governors? — and so we have used the word pasha, in an effort to retain its real cultural significance.

58. A favorite simile in Turkish folktales to describe surpassing beauty. In the lunar month of twenty-nine and a half days, the moon would be full on the fifteenth day. It is thought to be most attractive just before its fullness, that is, on the fourteenth day.

59. In Turkish folktales houses, castles, and palaces are often sealed to keep the occupants from escaping. In Turkish life today people are not sealed inside buildings, but the practice of sealing houses or apartments for legal purposes is common. If a will is contested, for example, the home of the deceased may be sealed (not just locked) by the authorities until the case has been settled. If the home of the deceased happens to be a rented apartment, this works a hardship on the owner, for while it is sealed — perhaps six months — he is unable to draw income from the tenantless rooms.

60. In folklore, nuts are frequently repositories of all sorts of magical objects. Although several kinds of nuts are grown in Turkey, including almonds, pecans, and walnuts, most lore of this kind revolves around the hazelnut. Hazelnuts are a primary money crop along the Black Sea coast all the way from Sinop to Trabzon, tons of them being exported annually to countries of Western Europe.

61. Giving one's guests parting gifts was an old Turkish custom. Sometimes it was simply leftover food, but in affluent circles it might be a gold piece. To justify such an additional largesse and to assuage the guests' pride, the host said, "This is for the rental of your teeth."

62. A legendary creature about whom little seems to be known.

63. At this point the narrator paused, addressed the collectors specifically, and said,

"Oh, we know thousands of such stories, but we do not tell them to strangers because we think they are not worth anything."

64. The Orpheus theme here is obvious.

65. Chairs to which special meanings are attached are common in Turkish folktales. Often a particular chair is occupied by a person who comes to ask for the hand of a girl. Both the host and the guest understand the gesture as a stage in the stylized matchmaking ritual. Sometimes it is the color of the chair that distinguishes it, sometimes its position in the room.

66. *Narrator:* Muharrem Choban, day laborer, aged 40.

Site of recording: Ashagh Chavundur village of the caza of Chubuk of the province of Ankara.

Date collected: December 1961.

Types: Aarne-Thompson 408, The Three Oranges. Eberhard-Boratav 89, *Die drei Zitronmädchen.*

Motifs: D211.1, Transformation: woman to orange. D721.5, Disenchantment from fruit by opening it. S375, Old woman's maledictions inform hero of his future. B350, Grateful animals. D1658.11, River grateful for being praised even when ugly. D1658.3, Bitter water grateful for being praised even when ill-tasting. Q40, Kindness rewarded. E710, External soul. A person (often a giant or ogre) keeps his soul or life separate from the rest of his body. E765, Life dependent on external object. J1791.6.1, Ugly woman sees beautiful woman reflected in water and thinks it is herself. K1911, The false bride (substituted bride). K1911.1.3, False bride takes true bride's place at fountain. D610, Repeated transformation. D1868.1, Broken-down nag becomes magnificent horse. K1911.3, Reinstatement of true bride.

67. More often it is an "orange girl," one who, under a spell, is held captive in an orange.

68. In a variant collected in the Province of Konya three sons are all responsible for breaking the woman's pitcher, and the curse is not on any of the young men but on the lovely flower garden of their father. She declares that the garden will dry up until the *Hazaran* Nightingales (legendary birds sometimes deglamorized by the corruption of their name to *Haziran* or June Nightingales) sing within its walls. Instead of seeking an enchanted girl, then, the sons undertake the equally arduous task of finding the magic birds and bringing them back to restore the garden. After the two older sons fail, the youngest captures the nightingales and starts back with them; the jealous brothers intercept him, steal the birds, and throw him into a well. After many adventures, the hero returns, and at his appearance the nightingales burst into song and the garden comes to life again.

What we consider simply a variant is set apart by Eberhard and Boratav as a separate type, number 206, *Die Hazaran-Nachtigall.* Whether variant or type, this tale does suggest parallels to the Grail legend and its Wasteland.

69. Both the appearance and the omniscience of the old man indicate that he is Hizir, though he is never so named in the tale.

70. This is clearly a recent addition to the tale.

71. In numerous variants of this tale in our archive the hero performs acts of kindness or courtesy to people, animals, or objects that he encounters. When he finds a cow with meat set before it for food and a lion with hay, he ingratiates himself with both by switching their foods. He closes (or opens) a gate that has been left open (or shut) for years, and thus endears himself to it. The beneficiaries of these acts of kindness later

reward the hero by refusing to catch or stop him when ordered to do so by the giant or ogre or jinn of the area.

Here the fountain flowing with blood and pus is praised and its filthy water drunk, in humility, by the hero, but the motif (D1658.1.1 or D1658.1.3, listed above) has lost entirely its real function in the tale: the fountain never has an opportunity to show its gratitude.

72. In different tales in our archive, the life force, life secret, or external soul resides in a hairpin, a sword, a small box inside the belly of a yellow deer, and, in twelve equal parts, in twelve captive fish.

73. This is a recurrent pattern of motifs in Turkish folktales: a horse, sick or starving, eats grass that springs up miraculously where a girl has walked; the horse recovers his health by eating this grass; thereafter, it cannot be managed, or even approached, by anyone but the girl. A good example of this pattern can be found in a tale entitled "Pearls and Corals" stored in the collection of folklore on tape in the Milli Kütüphane (National Library) at Ankara.

74. Offering a choice of types of execution is common in Turkish folktales. The unlucky person is often given the choice between forty swords and forty horses. Knowing that the swords can mean only death but thinking that the horses may provide a means of escape, the victim invariably chooses the horses. He chooses the worse death, however, for he then has forty ropes attached to his body, each rope tied to one horse. When the horses are whipped, they run off wildly, and the victim is torn into small parts. The choice given the victim is phrased in the form of a *tekerleme:* "Kirk satir mi? Kirk katir mi?" In this tale the *tekerleme* is not used, and the execution is somewhat different, but the basic pattern is the same.

75. *Narrator:* Mevlut Unal, shopkeeper, 35.
Site of recording: Karahamzali village of the caza of Bala of the province of Ankara.
Date collected: March 1962.
Types: Aarne-Thompson 1000, Bargain Not to Become Angry; 1003, Plowing; 1007, Other Means of Killing or Maiming Livestock; 1009, Guarding the Storeroom Door; 1011, Tearing up Vineyard or Orchard; 1012, Cleaning the Children; 1120, Ogre's Wife Thrown into Water. Eberhard-Boratav 357, *Keloghlan und der böse Köse.*
Motifs: Each of the Aarne-Thompson types listed above is also assigned a Motif number, Type 1000, for example, being the same as Motif K172, Anger Bargain.

76. Sandal is the closest word in English to the Turkish *charik.* This is like a moccasin, but with turned-up toes and walked-down heels — the latter feature to make them easier to slip off and on as one enters or leaves a house. They are ordinarily made of the hide of a cow, an ox, or a donkey. Until recently they were the standard footwear of the Turkish peasants, but within the present generation they have been largely replaced by a laceless, thick rubber shoe made of reconstituted latex from old automobile tires.

77. Yogurt is, along with rice, wheat, and lamb, one of the peasants' four most common foods.

78. *Yufka* is a kind of bread made without yeast. The dough is rolled to paper thinness and placed on a circular, slightly convex, steel sheet about two feet in diameter and then baked for only a few seconds. While it is still hot, it is flexible and can be folded down into an easily manageable bundle that looks like a handkerchief. When it cools it becomes very brittle, like soda crackers. It is a whole yufka, unfolded, that is referred to here.

79. It is a general belief in Turkey among peasants that farm animals can be encour-

aged to drink by whistling. Whenever cows, horses, or donkeys are watered — it is usually a matter of taking them to the public fountain — their drinking is accompanied by constant whistling.

80. A pastry kneaded with butter, ground nuts, and yeast.

81. The Turkish word for burst is *patlamak* or *patlatmak*. In the area where this tale was collected it has a dialectal meaning: to take a child to toilet. We have been unable to discover whether there is a similar root meaning to urinate, or whether *patlamak* is simply a regional circumlocution. Often in this tale the order is to clean the child — we have such a version from the Silifke area — an order which is deliberately misinterpreted to eviscerate him.

82. The very thick and heavy felt coat is a distinctive feature of the shepherd's attire. It serves as both coat and sleeping bag into which he huddles on cold, rainy, and snowy days.

83. *Kirk* is the word for forty, a special number in Turkey and other Middle Eastern countries. See above, note 28.

84. *Narrator:* Muharrem Choban.

Site of recording: Ashagh Chavundur village of the caza of Chubuk of the province of Ankara.

Date collected: December 1961.

Types: Aarne-Thompson 554, The Grateful Animals; 302, Ogre's Heart in an Egg. Eberhard-Boratav 213, *Das Amulett des Geistes.* Actually, these types comprise only small sections of this tale.

Motifs: F102.1, Hero shoots monster and follows it into lower world. N773, Adventure from following monster into lower world. R11.1, Princess abducted by monster. R11.2.1, Princess rescued from lower world. K975.2, Secret of external soul learned by deception. H310, Suitor test: suitor is put to severe test by prospective bride or father-in-law. S110.3, Princess builds tower of skulls of unsuccessful suitors. G530.1, Help from ogre's wife (mistress). E710, External soul; a person (often giant or ogre) keeps his soul or life separate from the rest of his body. E715, Separable soul kept in animal. E765, Life dependent on external object or event. K956, Murder by destroying external soul. R111.1, Princess rescued from captor. B481.1, Helpful ant.

85. As mentioned in note 65 above, chairs often serve emblematic functions in the sign language connected with marriage. Sign language of various kinds is common in Near and Middle Eastern tales, especially tales about love. A lover may send a set of objects to his beloved, and either from suggestiveness of the objects themselves or from some connotation or double entendre of the roots of the words from which the objects are named, the receiver deduces their meaning.

Edward Lane, in his edition of *The Arabian Nights,* has a note (II, 115–116) entitled "Conversing and Corresponding by Means of Signs, Emblems, Metaphors, Etc." Lane cites as the first thorough introduction of the subject for Western readers M. Du Vigneau's *Secretaire Turc, contenant l'art d'exprimer ses pensées sans se parler, et sans s'écrire* (Paris, 1688).

Writing from Istanbul in 1718, Lady Mary Wortley Montagu sent to a friend in England an account of a Turkish "love letter" of objects that included a pearl, various flowers, spices and fruits, and a golden thread. *Letters* (London, 1906), pp. 158–161.

86. This is a modern Turkish peasant's conception of where a king might live. So great is the culture gap between rural and urban Turkey that the ultramodern apartment houses of Ankara seem little short of fabulous to the Anatolian farmer.

87. Here and in the tale entitled "The Many Dilemmas of the Padishah's Three Sons"

(Part II) mounds of skulls are mentioned. There is evidence to indicate that the frequency of this image in Turkish folktales is part of the heritage of Tamerlane. Judging from the number of times he is mentioned in tales, one would have to conclude that this Mongol conqueror left an indelible impression on the folk mind in Turkey. And among his infamous achievements were the massacres (70,000 at Isfahan, Persia, in 1386; 80,000 at Delhi, India, in 1398; 50,000 at Izmir in 1402) from which pyramids of skulls were built.

88. Again this is the peasant psychology applied to the behavior of a prince. When peasants in Turkey travel — particularly migrant workers and those seeking employment — they always carry their beds with them, usually in the form of a mattress roll and blanket. This is true even of the thousands of peasants who come to Ankara seeking work. Obviously a sultan's son and king's son-in-law could afford to pay for or could commandeer suitable lodgings en route.

89. *Narrator:* Habibullah Sömez.
Site of recording: Azizli village of the caza of Ceyhan of the province of Adana.
Date collected: March 1962.
Types: Aarne-Thompson 938, Placidas (Eustacius); 938 B, Better in Youth. Eberhard-Boratav 136, *Das Unglück.*
Motifs: J214, Choice of hardship in youth or old age. N251, Person pursued by misfortune. His goods are destroyed, his wife carried off by a ship captain and his children by animals. N370, Accidental reunion of families. H171.2, Election by having bird land on one's head.

90. A *bezirgan* is an itinerant trader. He may be a simple pack peddler, or he may have greater resources: beasts of burden, servants, and so forth. Because Turks did not engage in such menial occupations in the past, businessmen, especially those who traveled, were usually members of minority groups (often Jews, Armenians, or Greeks) and hence objects of prejudice and even abuse. Partly because of his social position and partly because the traveling salesman seems everywhere to be both a nexus and a transmitter of the oral tradition, the bezirgan is frequently an object of conversation and the subject of tales — all quite unsympathetic. He is clearly a folk type, and for that reason we have retained the Turkish term bezirgan.

91. Eau de cologne is obviously a substitution for some medicine or other liquid. Possibly the Turkish liquid of an earlier version of the tale also had an erotic as well as a medicinal connotation. The expression eau de cologne is used very loosely and may be applied to any aromatic spirits, including the alcohol-base freshening fluid forever being shaken into the hands of passengers on Turkish buses, trains, and airplanes.

92. Padishahs were not, of course, elected, nor did they live in villages. To the extent that this element derives from the peasants' own experiences, the reference is to the village leader, the only administrative officer who is actually elected in the whole hierarchy of local government from village through caza to vilayet. In the larger context of the folk tradition in which the narrator is working there is precedent for the choice of a ruler by a bird in this manner (Motif H171.2).

93. Here again, though the protagonist is not a real keloghlan, this intrusive type is inferred by the folk mind from his shabby and unpromising appearance.

94. The presence of a gendarme — at least of the word gendarme — is another anachronism in this story. In modern Turkey all young men must serve two years in military service. Some of the draftees are transferred from the regular army to the Department of Interior, which is responsible for internal security. A city will have its own regular

police system; villages and towns will have a few night watchmen, but law and order is maintained by the *jandarma*. Because their training in police methods and crime detection is minimal, and because their tenure is brief, members of the gendarmerie are far less effective than are Turkey's municipal policemen.

95. *Narrator:* Osman Tan, 10.
Site of recording: Azizli village of the caza of Ceyhan of the province of Adana.
Date collected: February 1962.
Types: Aarne-Thompson 315 A, The Cannibal Sister. Eberhard-Boratav 148, *Das Hexenmädchen.*
Motifs: K2212, Treacherous sister. G33, Child born as cannibal. E761, Life token. Object (animal, person) has mystic connection with the life of a person, so that changes in the token indicate changes in the person, usually death or disaster. B520, Animals save life. R251, Hero climbs tree and when it is gnawed down escapes to next tree. B524.1.2, Hero calls dogs and they kill sister. D992.5, Magic tongue.

96. Although the Turkish government has encouraged peasants to tile their roofs, many of the rural homes in Central Anatolia still have the traditional clay-and-straw roofing surfaces. After a rain such a roof is rolled with a heavy concrete roller in order to seal up any cracks made by the latest watering. The roller is left up on the roof and is a familiar object against the skyline.

97. Common to many types is the sequence of events in the escape: flight to trees previously planted by the hero; their attempt to protect him; the calling of the hero's animals; and their destruction of his adversary just as the last tree is being cut down. Although they are date palms here and cypresses in the next tale, the trees are usually poplar trees; not only are poplars common in Turkey but they are trees that grow so rapidly that one could, in fact, plant them and relatively soon afterwards have fully grown trees. The truth of this is illustrated by one of the customs of rural Turkey. When a girl is born in a village, the family will often plant a row of poplar trees for her dowry fifteen or twenty years later. By then the trees will be sufficiently grown to provide several cords of salable firewood.

98. *Narrator:* Tahir Ruzgar, alias "Yamyam" ("The Cannibal").
Site of recording: The tale was collected at Sinop Penitentiary, but the narrator was originally a resident of the caza town of Germenjik in the province of Aydin.
Date collected: August 1964.
Types: Aarne-Thompson 315, The Faithless Sister; 315 A, The Cannibal Sister; 550, Search for the Golden (or Wonderful) Bird. Eberhard-Boratav 76, *Der Rat des Fuchses.*
Motifs: H1331.1, Quest for marvelous bird. H1324, Quest for miraculous remedy. H1241, Series of quests; one accomplished when second finished, etc. K2212.0.2, Treacherous sister as mistress of robber (giant) plots against brother. G11.4, Negro cannibal. H1211, Quests assigned to get rid of hero. H1212, Quests assigned because of feigned illness. H1361, Quest for lion's milk. F615.2.1, Strong man sent to milk lions; brings lions back with him. B431.2, Helpful lion. B520, Animals save life. B391, Animal grateful for food. B435.1, Helpful fox. B313, Helpful animal an enchanted person. D711, Disenchantment by decapitation.

99. The "jeweled" or "priceless" cage (*jahveri kafes*) is a recurrent motif, though usually its occupant has the curative power sought and is the real object of the quest.

100. The Kulhuvallahi is one of the most important prayers in Islam. It comes from Chapter CXII of the Koran, entitled "The Declaration of God's Unity." The prayer reads: "In the name of the Most Merciful God. Say, 'God is one God, the eternal God;

he begetteth not, neither is he begotten, and there is not anyone like unto him.'" This prayer is credited with having special potency, and in folktales it is often recited as a kind of incantation when magic formulas or miracles are being worked.

101. This is a gesture of deep respect shown to older women in Turkey.

102. In Turkish tales the word Arab usually denotes a Negro or a dark-skinned person. Many Arabs are, of course, quite light-skinned, while others, especially from Africa, are dark. At one time people from the southern parts of the Ottoman Empire were often mistakenly thought of as being universally black Arabs. For various social and historical reasons — not the least the Arab role in World War I — relations between Arabs and Turks have been strained. Among some groups in Turkey today Arab is an epithet comparable to nigger in the United States.

103. It is at this point that the tale shows a greater similarity to Type 315, The Faithless Sister (married to an ogre), than to Type 315 A, The Cannibal Sister, of the previous tale. The cannibalism here is attributed not to the sister herself but to her lover.

104. Otherwise unrelated children may become "milk brothers" or "milk sisters" by being nursed by the same woman. They are committed to undying loyalty and support for each other, almost as if they were actual siblings. Nursing mothers often deliberately establish this relationship by exchanging children for a feeding; at other times it occurs simply through a wet nurse. In just such a way the hero of this tale protects himself by becoming a "milk brother" of the nine giants and a "milk son" of their mother.

105. *Bulgur* is made from wheat. Whole kernels of wheat are boiled and allowed to dry in the sunlight. The husks are then removed and the wheat is coarsely ground, sometimes by pounding in a large mortar. It is then ready to be recooked as a hot cereal.

106. At one point in the Moslem service the worshiper looks over his right shoulder and then over his left, each time saying, "Peace be on you and the mercy of God." Some authorities say that on each shoulder is an angel or guardian spirit to whom he is paying his respect; others claim that it is a social gesture, in part, to unite the members of the congregation; still others, attributing it to the strong militaristic tradition of Islam, feel that it began as a "dressing right and left," a means of restoring the originally straight rows of worshipers after their ranks had been broken by the body movements required by the service.

107. Here the actual decapitation of the fox does not occur, as it ordinarily does at the end of Type 550, but instead the sword is simply waved over his head in order to break the enchantment.

108. Mustafa Sinan, formerly an officer of the gendarmerie, who kindly arranged for our collecting at the Sinop Penitentiary.

109. *Narrator:* Sukru Dariji.
Site of recording: Kavshit village of the caza of Sungurlu of the province of Chorum.
Date collected: August 1964.
Types: Aarne-Thompson 432, The Prince as Bird; 432*, Bird Prince Disenchanted; 400*, The Swan Maiden; 425 D, Vanished Husband Learned of By Keeping Inn (or Bathhouse). Eberhard-Boratav 93, *Der Taubenmann.*
Motifs: H11.1.1, Heroine sets up inn or bathhouse where all must tell stories; she thus hears of [future] husband. N825.3, Old woman helper. H1233.1.1, Old woman helps on quest. D150, Transformation: man to bird. B642, Marriage to person in bird form. D620, Periodic transformation. D641.1, Lover as bird visits mistress. D721.3, Disenchantment by destroying skin (covering).

110. The hospital is clearly a recent addition to this tale.

111. The name Shemsi Bani means literally Life-Giving Sun or Life-Creating Sun. *Bani* is an adjective derived from the verb *bina etmek,* to build or to create.

112. This was undoubtedly a *cante fable* originally, recited and sung by a "lover poet" to the accompaniment of a saz. The concentrated euphony, the verbal echoes, and the incremental repetition of folk poetry were retained in the dialogue as it was narrated by our informant.

Part II. Perplexities and Ingenious Deductions

1. This is parallel to Eberhard-Boratav Type 312, *Die Zeichensprache.*

2. With the number of Turkish folktales now archived and the large body of riddles in print, it should be possible to determine whether there exists any geographical or cultural correlation between the distribution of tales of this type and the frequency of riddles.

3. *Narrator:* Ekrem Gench.
Site of recording: caza town of Iskenderun in Hatay province.
Date collected: February 1962.
Motifs: H700, Riddles of numbers. J1230, Clever dividing.

4. This puzzle is common in many other countries as well as throughout Turkey. The wise man who solves the riddle is usually not a specific person; the presence of Caliph Ali here is a regional variant. The minority Alevi (Shiite) branch of Islam is strong in southern Turkey, especially in the region where this tale was collected. Although they also differ from the dominant Sunnite group in matters of theology, ritual, and morality, their primary distinction is their emphasis on Ali as second to (sometimes almost the equal of) Mohammed. They deny the legality and sanctity of the first three caliphs (Abubekir, Omer, and Osman), claiming that Ali, the Prophet's son-in-law, was his rightful immediate successor. Besides the purely religious material on Ali there exists a large body of "Aliana."

5. *Narrator:* Abdurraham Boyaji.
Site of recording: village of Kazimkarabekir of the caza of Karaman of the province of Konya.
Date collected: February 1962.
Types: Aarne-Thompson 655, The Wise Brothers; 655 A, The Strayed Camel and the Clever Deduction; 976, Which Was the Noblest Act? Eberhard-Boratav 348, *Die Detektive II.*

The Aarne-Thompson Types 655 and 655 A are fairly common among Turkish tales both oral and written. One version appears in Ibn Hemden's *Turkish Evening Entertainments: The Wonders of Remarkable Incidents,* trans. John P. Brown (New York: Putnam, 1850), pp. 14-17.

In the West this story is known, in various versions, as "The Three Princes of Serendip" (Ceylon). It was from this tale that Horace Walpole coined the word serendipity, which he defined as "the gift for discovery by accident and sagacity of things . . . not in quest of." *Horace Walpole's Correspondence,* XX, ed. W. S. Lewis (New Haven: Yale University Press, 1960), pp. 407-408.

The first printing of this tale in Europe appeared in Michele Tramezzino's *Peregrinaggio di tre figliuoli del re di Serendippo; tradotto dalla lingua persiana in lingua italiana da M. Christoforo Armenno.* Venice, 1557. Le Chevalier De Mailly translated this into French (1719), and it was the Amsterdam edition (1721) that Walpole read. Voltaire also picked up the tale from De Mailly and included it in his *Zadig* (1750), in his story entitled, "Le Chien et le cheval." The best modern version of "The Three Princes of Serendip" is that translated directly from the Italian of Tramezzino by Augusto and Theresa Borselli for *Serendipity and the Three Princes,* ed. Theodore G. Remer (Norman: University of Oklahoma Press, 1965), pp. 56–87.

Motifs: J1661.1, Deduction from observation. J1661.1.2, Deduction that the king [judge] is a bastard. F647, Marvelous sensitiveness: wine tastes like corpse. F647.5.1, Marvelous sensitiveness: meat tastes of foreign matter. F1661.1.1, Deduction: one-eyed camel.

6. The kadi was the judge of Moslem canonical law in pre-Republican Turkey, though in folktales any judge, religious or secular, past or contemporary, may be called kadi.

7. The Yürüks are nomadic Turks, many of whom have wandered into Anatolia from Central Asia only recently — within the past three centuries. They live in mohair tents and move north and south with their flocks as the seasons change. Because they have been, traditionally, graziers of flocks, the stereotype is pictured as a herdsman wearing the very heavy felt coat that serves both as garment and as sleeping bag. The Yürüks form one of Turkey's most colorful cultural groups.

8. Although *kebab* (*kebap*) means, generally, any roasted or broiled meat, the word usually refers to lamb in Turkey. There are many different kebab dishes and several different kebab cooking processes, some of them used throughout Turkey, others limited to one section or even one province.

9. *Pekmez* is grape juice boiled down until it has the consistency of heavy syrup.

10. The dilemma here is similar to that at the end of Chaucer's "Franklin's Tale," except that here the problem posed is not an academic question; the answers determine who are the rightful heirs and who should be dispossessed.

The more serious application of the dilemma is also present in one of the earliest versions written in Turkish — a manuscript probably dating from the early fifteenth century. See "The Lady's Eighth Tale," in *The History of the Forty Vezirs, or The Story of the Forty Morns and Eves,* trans. E. J. W. Gibb (London, 1886), pp. 105–111.

11. *Narrator:* Suzan Koraltürk.

Site of recording: Trabzon, capital city of province of Trabzon.

Date collected: May 1962.

Types: Aarne-Thompson 924 B, Sign Language Misunderstood. Eberhard-Boratav 312, *Die Zeichensprache.*

Motifs: D1812.3.3, Future revealed in dreams.

12. "Stuck to some great door" is a figurative expression meaning to find a patron or to get a steady job.

13. The word used was *saray,* a palace or government building. The *saray* in Istanbul is probably the palace of the sultan, and so the padishah who lives in it is no less a ruler than the head of the empire.

14. In his successive tasks Keloghlan proves to be a fool. Accordingly, this tale could also be placed in Part III, Tales of Humor, which includes adventures of both clever and stupid people.

15. In real life wars are often waged for ridiculous reasons; in folktales these ridiculous reasons often involve riddle solving. Type 312, *Die Zeichensprache,* listed above,

has a variant, in the Eberhard-Boratav index, in which war can be averted by the correct responses in sign language. Our own archive suggests that in Turkey the basic type involves the threat of war and only an occasional variant does not.

16. "To lay some eggs about it" is a slang expression which may be equated with "to produce some answers right out of the blue," or "to come up with something," in American slang.

17. *Narrator:* Nuri Konuralp.
Site of recording: Iskenderun, caza city in province of Hatay.
Date collected: February 1962.
Types: Aarne-Thompson 945, Luck and Intelligence [it is only the second part of this type that is in our tale]; 653 A, The Rarest Thing in the World. Eberhard-Boratav 290, *Zimmermann, Schneider, und Imam;* 291, *Das geheilte Mädchen.*
Motifs: T68.1, A princess is offered to the one bringing the rarest thing in the world. D1323.15, A telescope that shows all that is happening in the world (or some other similar device). D1520.18, A carpet which transports one at will. D1500.1.5.1, An apple (or other object) which heals or resuscitates. H620, The unsolved problem: enigmatic ending of a tale. H621, Companions create woman. To whom does she belong? F954.2.1, Suitor test: bringing dumb princess to speak. S110.3, Princess builds tower of skulls of unsuccessful suitors.

18. This is a proverbial expression. When one borrows a bit of flour, he carries it home in a dish, and inevitably some of it is blown into the air.

19. See note 87 of Part I of this volume.

20. It is a widespread belief in Turkey that one's fate, or kismet, is written on his forehead. Seers can see this writing and parents pretend to, often extracting truth from children by threatening to read it instead from their foreheads.

21. For a brief account of how such contracts are reached, see Joe E. Pierce's *Life in a Turkish Village* (New York, 1964), pp. 14–19.

22. Women were, in fact, sometimes left to rule when sultans were away on military expeditions or other business.

23. All Moslem prayer and religious activity — not only service in a mosque — is preceded by ablutions.

24. Nightingales are not among the birds taught to talk. They are thought to sing continuously throughout the night, however, and this common figure of speech suggests ceaseless vocalizing.

25. This is a very common folktale type. The riddling dilemma (Who deserves the girl most?) is a question sometimes thrown open to the audience, and there are often several answers suggested. Although it is usually the third suitor who is awarded the girl, the reasons for this decision vary. In a variant from Ovajik (Gülnar caza, province of Ichel), in which the curative object is a lemon, one listener awarded the girl to the third suitor because he had been motivated by humanitarian interests, purchasing the magic fruit to help the sick. Another member of the audience gave him the decision because his purchase was expendable: once he had squeezed the juice of the lemon to cure the patient, he had sacrificed his entire investment.

26. *Narrator:* Kalayji Mehmet. (Although this man must have had a last name — the surname law went into effect in 1935 — he went under this name only; translated it means Mehmet the Tinsmith.)
Site of recording: Deghirmendere village of the caza of Silifke of the province of Ichel.

Date collected: February 1962.

Types: Aarne-Thompson 725, The Dream. Eberhard-Boratav 197, *Der Traum des Jungen.*

Motifs: L114, Hero of unpromising habits. D1812.3.3, Future revealed in dream. L425, Dream of future greatness causes punishment. H506.10, Test of resourcefulness: to find relation among three sticks. Placed in water; degree of sinking shows what part of tree they come from. H506.11, Test of resourcefulness: to discover how old, respectively, three horses are.

27. It is a belief in Turkey that if one does tell his dream before his auditor has extended this courtesy, then the event foretold in the dream may end in disaster. Besides serving a function in the narrative here, this custom provides a good example of the ritualistic quality of much Turkish discourse. As in many non-Western countries, a fairly high percentage of statements, actions, and situations require specific traditional responses. Even an event as commonplace as a haircut or the purchase of a garment evokes a stylized response from well-wishers.

28. After a meal in a home in rural Turkey there is a practical and ritual washing of the hands. Two people appear, one with a large basin, and the other with a pitcher of water. One of them also carries over his arm a towel. Water is poured over the hands of each guest beginning with the eldest.

29. The word *ay* in Turkish means moon; the word *günesh* means sun.

30. *Narrator:* Gülsüm Yüchel, a lady of 86 years.

Site of recording: caza town of Tashköprü in Kastamonu province.

Date collected: August 1964.

Types: Aarne-Thompson 875, The Clever Peasant Girl; 875 A, A Girl's Riddling Answer Betrays a Theft. Our tale is not exactly parallel to either of these types but incorporates elements of each.

Motifs: H580, Enigmatic statements: Apparently senseless remarks or acts interpreted figuratively prove wise. H600, Symbolic interpretations. H607, Discussion by symbolic sign language. L162, Lowly heroine marries prince (king). J1111.4, Clever peasant daughter.

31. See note 85 of Part I.

Part III. Humorous Tales

1. Kayseri (ancient Caesarea), a city of some 70,000 inhabitants, lies at almost the exact center of Turkey.

2. Among the numerous commentaries on these Kayseri traditions is that of Patrick Balfour (Lord Kinross) in his *Within the Taurus* (London, 1954).

3. Karagöz plays are performed behind a fine silk screen, sufficiently translucent to permit the shapes and colors of the puppets to show through. The whole performance may be a one-man show, or the production may include one or more assistants and musicians. The camel-skin puppets, flat and two-dimensional, twelve to fifteen inches in height, are brightly painted figures which represent a cross-section of society in a city *mahalle* or district.

The two leading characters are Karagöz, the poor man, the country bumpkin, good-natured, naïve, spontaneous, long-suffering, and devout; and Hajivad, well-placed socially and financially, intellectual, sophisticated, the embodiment of gentility. To a degree, Hajivad represents the privileged upper class just as Karagöz stands for the peasantry. About a dozen other characters play supporting roles: Chelebi, the dandy, the fop; Teryaki, the dope addict; Zenna, the strumpet (dancer, sorceress, prostitute, procuress); Beberuhi, the dwarfed, simple-minded hunchback; Tuzsuz, the *miles gloriosus,* reminiscent of the Janissary; and such ethnic types as the Persian, the Arab, the Albanian, the Armenian, and the Levantine. Setting is suggested by a few simple stage properties, also camel skin: a divan, a house, a tree.

The performance may begin with introductory music by the orchestra, or with songs by Hajivad, but always before the play proper starts, there is a slapstick dialogue between Hajivad and Karagöz, which ends when Karagöz, out of patience, drives his opponent from the stage. The play that follows, highly stylized, is usually based upon one of about forty standard plots. In days past each performer had a repertoire of at least twenty-nine plays, one for each night of Ramazan, the season of the year when he was most in demand. With other forms of entertainment becoming available, he shadow theater is on the decline, and today there are very few authentic Karagöz operators left. The best-known puppeteer in the old tradition is Küchük Ali (Little Ali) whom we saw perform at the Turkish-American Association in December 1961.

The best introduction to the Karagöz theater is *Karagöz: Its History, Its Characters, Its Mystic and Satiric Spirit* by Professor Sabri Esat Siyavushgil. It appeared first in Turkish (Istanbul, 1941), and was then translated into French (Istanbul, 1951), and into English (Ankara, 1955); to provide an inexpensive edition in English, the publisher (Ministry of Press, Broadcasting, and Tourism) reduced the large album format to ordinary book size. Printed on glossy paper and graced with numerous color prints, it is a beautiful work in any edition.

For an excellent select bibliography on the subject, see Metin And's *A History of Theatre and Popular Entertainment in Turkey* (Ankara, 1964), pp. 139–144.

4. In more recent times Karagöz has moved into the written tradition too. He has become a staple of cartoon, souvenir, and greeting card art. Intermittently for the past two decades a tabloid newspaper has borne his name. A political organ that purports to speak to and for the common man, it is filled with genial satire and homespun philosophy.

5. During World War I the father of Ahmet Uysal fought in the Dardanelles Campaign, and then, after the British withdrawal, was transferred to the Eastern Front. At the end of the war he returned from the province of Mush to Bursa, in Western Turkey, traveling some 1400 miles of the trip on foot. The hardship, hunger, and disease that he suffered, along with thousands of others, are almost beyond credibility. Time has obliterated the horror of it, and in the folktales that draw upon this common experience, only the humor remains.

6. *Narrator:* Agah Selchuk.
Site of recording: caza town of Ceyhan of the province of Adana.
Date collected: February 1962.
Types: Aarne-Thompson 1565, Agreement Not to Scratch. Eberhard-Boratav 321, *Die drei Leidenden.*

7. *Narrator:* Nuri Gench.
Site of recording: Iskenderun, caza city of Hatay province.
Date collected: February 1962.

8. The verb *yalamak* means to lick. A *yalama* is a lip-licker, usually suffering from a type of dermatitis that causes him to moisten his lips frequently.

9. *Narrator:* Muharrem Choban.

Site of recording: Ashagh Chavundur village of the caza of Chubuk of the province of Ankara.

Date collected: March 1962.

Types: Aarne-Thompson 1654, The Robbers in the Death Chamber. Eberhard-Boratav 353, *Der Geizige im Grab.*

10. The kurus is a very small amount of money today, 1/100 of a lira, roughly 1/10 of an American cent. A few years ago, however, this would have amounted to more, for the kurus — a silver coin when first minted in the 1620's — was divided into 100 *paras,* and the para was the standard small coin. The word para is still used in Turkish, even though there are no longer para coins in circulation. The expression *Kach para?* means "How much money?" or "How much does it cost?"

11. When a Moslem dies, his body is given a ritual washing with soap and water; this is usually done by the village khoja, though it may be done by anyone. The body is then wrapped in a piece of white linen about thirty feet long and five feet wide. The shroud thus formed is tied at the top and bottom, though the knots are untied again when the body is laid in the grave. In order to assure themselves of this treatment, many old people in Turkey keep on hand a bolt of linen (or other cloth) with a bar of soap wrapped inside it.

12. In poor villages, where peasants may not be able to afford individual coffins, there is a community coffin called *Dört Kollu* (The Four-Armed One), stored at the mosque. It is used to carry the body to the cemetery; after the body is buried, the coffin is returned to the mosque for the next funeral. The village in which this tale was collected had such a community coffin.

13. The *mimber* is the staircase, usually rather ornate, that leads up to the pulpit in a mosque. The khoja performs some parts of the prayer service from the mimber rather than from the pulpit proper.

14. *Narrator:* Ekrem Gench.

Site of recording: caza city of Iskenderun of the province of Hatay.

Date collected: February 1962.

15. *Narrator:* Agah Selchuk.

Site of recording: Ceyhan, caza town in the province of Adana.

Date collected: February 1962.

16. *Narrator:* Agah Selchuk.

Site of recording: caza town of Ceyhan of the province of Adana.

Date collected: February 1962.

17. *Narrator:* Agah Selchuk.

Site of recording: Ceyhan, caza town in the province of Adana.

Date collected: February 1962.

Types: Aarne-Thompson 1591, The Three Joint Depositors. Not listed in Eberhard-Boratav.

18. This seems to be a well-known and fully appreciated story in southern Turkey. In 1961 an attendant in a bus depot from which luggage had been stolen used the innkeeper's argument to defend himself in an actual lawsuit similar to that brought by the two friends against the owner of the inn at Kayseri. The court, at Iskenderun, acquitted the attendant.

19. *Narrator:* Muharrem Choban.

Site of recording: Ashagh Chavundur village of the caza of Chubuk of the province of Ankara.

Date collected: December 1961.

Types: Aarne-Thompson 1535, The Rich and the Poor Peasant; 1542, The Clever Boy with the Fooling Sticks; 1542 A, The Trickster Pretends to Return Home for Tools to Perform His Tricks, Steals Horses to Go. Eberhard-Boratav 351, *Das Vieh im Meer.* Although our tale incorporates elements of both this type and the Aarne-Thompson types, it lacks some of the motifs which the types in the two indexes have in common.

Motifs: K143, Sale of dung. K121, Lime (or other worthless material), said to be gold, is sold or exchanged. K941.1, Trickster reports price his cowhide brings; enemies kill all their cows to sell hides.

Aarne-Thompson lists this as a prank of a clever boy; in our tale the protagonist is a köse, not the sympathetic type that the clever boy is.

20. One can appreciate several levels of dramatic irony in this tale. The duped villagers seem uninformed about the outside world, but so too are the raconteurs who transmit this tale. Bursa, Edirne, and Istanbul were the Ottoman capitals, and Konya was the most notable Seljuk capital. Ankara, however, was not the capital at any time before the creation of the Republic, and so there was no sultan of Ankara. Nor, of course, did sultans live in apartment houses, wherever their capital was located.

21. An *oda* is any room; the oda in a village is the public meeting place. It may be part of the muhtar's house; it may be attached to it; it may merely be nearby. It is not his, however, for it is furnished by and used by the community at large.

22. The *muhtar* is the lowest executive in the Turkish administrative hierarchy and the only one who is elected directly by a constituency of voters. In rural areas he is the head man or leader of a village; in a city he is the executive officer of a *mahalle* or ward.

23. In the "standard" version, the trickster borrows a horse. There are few horses owned by peasants in central Anatolian villages, the ox being the common beast of burden.

24. Chubuk is the town to which Ashagah Chavunder is attached. It would be the place to which one would go to buy or sell anything.

25. Being beardless, the köse could impersonate a woman more easily than other men.

26. *Narrator:* Muharrem Choban.

Site of recording: village of Ashagh Chavundur of the caza of Chubuk of the province of Ankara.

Date collected: December 1961.

Types: Aarne-Thompson 1358 C, Trickster Discovers Adultery: Food Goes to Husband Instead of Paramour. Eberhard-Boratav 359, *Keloghlan und der Ehebrecher.*

27. According to Moslem belief, at some point between death and the moment of final Judgment, every person is queried, by an angel, about his behavior on earth. Some think that this interrogation comes after burial; others think it occurs before burial during the final part of the funeral service when the coffined body rests on a marble slab in the yard of the mosque. It is apparently the latter notion to which reference is made here.

28. In one of our variants the son drops several apples along the path as he returns

from "inviting" the khoja to dine; as here, he has not invited him but told him that the father will seek vengeance against him. When the boy reports that the khoja has declined the invitation, the father, rather than the mother, then goes to extend the offer. As he goes, the father picks up the apples dropped by the son. The khoja, supposing that he is picking up rocks, flees. To save the khoja, the wife actually goes to the authorities to report a fight, but the reason for her going to the police station is misrepresented to the father, when he returns, as her intention to accuse him of sodomy.

29. *Narrator:* Ibrahim Bozkaya.
Site of recording: village of Akdere of the caza of Gülnar of the province of Ichel.
Date collected: February 1962.
Types: Aarne-Thompson 1536, Disposing of the Corpse; 1536 C, The Murdered Lover; 1537, The Corpse Killed Five Times [here three]. Eberhard-Boratav 351, *Das Vieh im Meer.* It is only the last part of *Das Vieh im Meer,* a very common tale in Turkey, that appears in this narrative.
Motifs: K2151, The corpse handed around. K941.1, Trickster reports high price his cowhide has brought; his enemies kill all their cows to sell hides. K842, Trickster caught, put in cask, exchanges place with a shepherd.

30. The nub of this story depends upon a play on words in Turkish. *Kirk* means forty. The gurgling noise in the throat of a drowning person, "Kuk! kuk! kuk!" is here made to sound like "Kirk! Kirk! Kirk!" as it is told orally. In some versions, the köse interprets the gurgling noises for bystanders, who might otherwise rescue the drowning men: "Forty! Forty! They are saying 'Forty sheep'!"

31. *Narrator:* Neriman Hizir.
Site of recording: Ankara.
Date collected: May 1962.
Types: Aarne-Thompson 1696, "What Should I Have Said?" Eberhard-Boratav 328, **Hich.**
In *Zaman Zaman Ichinde* (Istanbul, 1958) Boratav also includes a widely known variant of this not among the tales of that volume but among the humorous introductions, the *tekerlemeler.* We have not yet collected it as a *tekerleme.* Another variant of this tale, collected in Istanbul, was adapted by Barbara K. Walker for her juvenile *Just Say Hic!*
Motifs: J2461.2, Literal following of instructions about greetings. Numskull gives wrong greeting and is told how to give the correct one. When he tries it, however, the conditions are wrong.

32. A flat, unleavened bread, usually fifteen to twenty inches in diameter and about an inch thick. It is eaten all year round but is especially popular during Ramazan.

33. The holiday following Ramazan is *Sheker Bayram,* the Sugar or Sweetmeat Holiday. It is a three-day visiting period during which one visits everyone of his acquaintance within the immediate area. At each ten- or fifteen-minute stop, some sweet is served. Candy is given to children who call at the door.

34. This is a figurative way of saying, "May the children outlive the clothes." Several of the expressions Hajivad tries to teach Karagöz are the proper polite responses he should make in these situations.

35. *Narrator:* Hidayet Akjan, age 12.
Site of recording: Aghabeyli village of the caza of Cihanbeyli of the province of Konya.
Date collected: May 1962.

Types: Aarne-Thompson 1642, The Good Bargain. Eberhard-Boratav 323, *Der kluge und der dumme Bruder.* The Aarne-Thompson type is similar to this tale only in the sale of goods to frogs; the Eberhard-Boratav type has more elements in common with the tale, including the humor; with neither type, however, is our tale completely consistent.

Motifs: J1852, Goods sold to animals.

36. *Bekchi* is the term used for a night watchman in cities and towns; in rural areas the word *koruju* is more common. The humorous play on words of the climax, however, requires the choice of *bekchi,* similar in sound to and understandably confused with *kechi,* the word for goat.

37. *Narrator:* Hayrettin Kimyon.
Site of recording: Antakya, capital city of Hatay province.
Date collected: March 1962.

Types: Aarne-Thompson 1655, The Profitable Exchange. Eberhard-Boratav 19, *Der Vogel mit dem Splitter.* In the Eberhard-Boratav type the protagonist is not a person but a bird, usually a crow. At the end of a fantasy, in which the bird behaves as a human being, the tale takes a sudden realistic turn: the bird cannot very well marry the girl he has won, and so he trades her for a flute! For a good example of this type see Boratav's *Contes Turcs* (Paris, 1955), pp. 41–45.

Motifs: Z47.1, Series of trick exchanges. K251.1, The eaten grain and the cock as damages [here neither cock nor grain, but precisely the same sequence].

38. To have some winds blowing through one's head is to be in a capricious mood. To have poplar winds blowing through one's head is taken to mean that one is interested in a member of the opposite sex.

39. Bald people, *kels* and others, are sometimes thought to be stubborn. This is the meaning suggested here when Keloghlan is said to have his baldness about him.

40. This is a rattling noise, a rhythmic sound often used in nonsense jingles and in the *tekerlemeler* that introduce folktales. It is similar to such English nonsense noises as clippity-clop or bumpity-bump.

41. To have one's head swollen is to be at the breaking point. A slang equivalent in English might be "ready to blow up."

42. *Narrator:* Abdullah Aslan.
Site of recording: Karahamzali village of the caza of Bala of the province of Ankara.
Date collected: February 1962.

Types: Aarne-Thompson 1960 D, The Great Vegetable; 1960 F, The Great Kettle; 1920, Contest in Lying. Eberhard-Boratav 358, *Keloghlan und der Müller.*

Motifs: X1401, Lie: The Great Vegetable. X1030.1.1, The Great Kettle. X1411.1.1, Lie: Large Watermelon. X1411.3, Lie: Large Pumpkin Vine.

43. Haymana and Chemishgezek are Turkish towns thought to be inhabited by dull-witted people. The names of these two towns have a comic sound to most Turkish ears, just as Keokuk, Kankakee, and Kalamazoo do to many American ears.

44. This is the peasant's riddling description of a goad, a harness, and a plow.

45. Turkish sheep dogs are huge, fierce creatures, their collars bristling with long steel spikes to protect them from wolves. It is customary to approach these dogs cautiously, usually with club or stones in hand.

46. See Part II, note 9.

47. Sorsavush is a humorous name that means "Ask, then go away!"

48 The Turkish expression *Mashallah* was used here with double entendre: a wish

for God's protection for Sorsavush but also a wish that God would keep a man of his type at Haymana.

49. The miller's answer drew a loud laugh from the audience, about fifty peasants, and Abdullah Aslan, being a sensitive raconteur, used the line several times again, with the same effect each time.

50. *Kizilirmak* means Red River. The longest river in Turkey, it winds about for 715 miles in central Anatolia. It is the subject of one of Turkey's most widely distributed folk songs, a ballad about a wedding party drowned when a bridge over the river collapsed.

51. Pumpkins are an important source of food in Turkey. They are prepared in a great variety of dishes.

Part IV. Moralistic Tales

1. *Narrator:* Mevlut Unal.
Site of recording: village of Karahamzali of the caza of Bala of the province of Ankara.
Date collected: March 1962.
Types: Aarne-Thompson 923 B, The Princess Who Was Responsible for Her Own Fortune; 986, The Lazy Husband. Eberhard-Boratav 256, *Der faule Mehmet.*
Motifs: H592, Princess responsible for her own fortune. W111.4, Lazy husband. D1081, Magic sword.

2. In some parts of Turkey there are still town criers. One of our informants had long been the official crier of Nallihan, announcing on all streets all matters of public interest.

3. Wetting a person's clothing before beating him apparently inflicts more pain. This motif recurs in a number of the tales in our archive.

4. The narrator here used the word *ipsiz,* ropeless. In this instance the meaning is literal: a porter ordinarily carries a length of rope with which to secure his load. If the load is bulky, he coils his rope about it, and then, placing the two free ends over his shoulders, hoists the burden on his back. Those who carry very heavy loads (even refrigerators and pianos) wear a special saddle on their backs, a heavy pad, thin at the shoulders but about a foot thick at hip level. The laborer reduced to being a porter and so poor that he does not even have a porter's rope is called *ipsiz.* In its figurative use the word can be applied to anyone and means utterly destitute.

5. The narrator used here the word *apartman,* meaning a block of flats or an apartment house. Again this is a clue to the great gulf between the world of the village peasant and that of the urbanite. The peasant's grandest vision of a home suitable for a sultan is an *apartman.*

6. On several trade routes to the East, Sivas has been an important city since Roman days and was among the first strongholds taken by the westering Seljuk Turks. It was never, however, the capital of the Empire, and hence never the seat of a sultan.

7. See note 100 of Part I.

8. In Turkish villages great importance is attached to the numbering of houses. A house number, officially recorded, is a status symbol, though it often serves no practical purpose. Seldom are houses in villages built along planned streets; they are built wher-

ever the owner's fancy dictates. Regularized numbering is, therefore, almost impossible. Furthermore, in most villages there is no need for numbering: few peasants ever receive any mail; visitors who seek anyone in a village go first to the muhtar and are directed to the appropriate house by him. Nevertheless, the numbering of houses receives great attention and is solemnly supervised by the muhtar.

9. Lazy Ahmet is obviously a comic character. Frequent reference to his wife as Master underscores this as does his echoing here of the opening speech of a regular matchmaker, "In the name of the Prophet and with the will of God."

10. *Narrator:* Omer Uysal.
Site of recording: Adana, provincial capital of the province of Adana.
Date collected: February 1962.
Types: Aarne-Thompson 910 C, Think Carefully before You Begin a Task. Eberhard-Boratav 308, *Die drei Ratschläge;* 313, *Die zwei Herten.*

There are two tales involving advice of this sort in the juvenile collection *Fairy Tales from Turkey,* edited by Margery Kent (London, 1946). "Good Advice" (pp. 119-121) is close to the Eberhard-Boratav Type 308; it is similar to our tale here only in sale of advice. "Mustapha and Mehmet" (pp. 162-165) similarly has the sale of advice, though, again, little other parallel to our tale.

Eberhard and Boratav note that the tale is found in China and Mongolia. They cite a reference to it, which we have not seen, in Antoine Mostaert. *Folklore Ordos* (Peking: Catholic University, 1947), no. 54, end.

Motifs: J21.1, Barber drops razor and confesses.

11. In a Turkish bath there is a series of large steam rooms, progressively hotter, which one shares with the other customers. The actual bathing, however, is done in a private cubicle where there is a marble tub or trough. Beside these troughs are hot and cold water taps.

12. Until the time of the Atatürk Reforms, Friday was the Sabbath in Turkey. The Friday noon service at the mosques was the one at which almost everyone was present, and political leaders often made quite a show of their attendance at that time. They would attend with a procession, wearing their finest clothes, and often would distribute money or goods to the poor along the way. Whether or not Tamerlane attended Moslem services is a moot point, but to the peasant mind it seems quite logical that he would.

13. The *müdür* has the lowest administrative rank in the Turkish civil service. He is the executive officer of a *nahiye,* a large town at the center of several villages; he is appointed to his position by the Ministry of Interior. In the administrative table of organization there is not often a *nahiye* between the village and the district or county; it occurs more often in larger cazas where residents may be many miles from the county seat.

14. *Narrator:* Hasan Hazir.
Site of recording: Chamalan village of the caza of Tarsus of the province of Ichel.
Date collected: February 1962.
Although a number of tale types include Solomon, and a number include vultures or similar birds, none, to our knowledge, combines the elements found here.

15. Azrail is the Angel of Death in Islamic mythology. He is comparable to the Grim Reaper in Western tradition. Frequently he is pictured as an old man carrying a scythe.

16. Occasionally in Turkish tales there seems to be a merging of two widely sepa-

rated figures, the Biblical King Solomon and the sixteenth-century Ottoman Emperor, Suleiman the Magnificent, both referred to as Süleyman. Here the ability to talk with birds is a clear reference to the Hebrew king; the Islamic elements and the title emperor would seem to refer to the Turkish sultan.

17. Ak Baba means, literally, White Father, a common sobriquet for the vulture. The lore on vultures here may be of mixed origins, from factual and imaginative sources. There are a number of large birds of the vulture family in the Middle East. Although they do not live for 2500 years, some of those in captivity are known to have considerable longevity; the oldest at the Atatürk Farm Zoo, in Ankara, was listed as being 165 years old in 1964. When the ancient sage Lokman (Luqman) was offered a long life by the gods, he chose to live through the life span of seven generations of vultures. (For additional information on Lokman, see note 42, Part I.)

Legendary material comes from tales about the Anka bird, associated sometimes with the rok (rukk), sometimes with the Phoenix. The Anka was exiled to an island in the Circumambient Ocean for carrying off a princess to prevent her from marrying a certain prince; Fate brought the couple back together, however, and the Anka was punished. (This element only is similar to the Eberhard-Boratav Type 140, *Salomon und der Phönix.*) Its successive descendants live yet in exile, each reaching the age of 1700 years, if nothing causes it to die earlier.

For additional and possibly pertinent information on large, fabulous birds and on real vultures, see note 18, Part I.

18. Whether the Solomon referred to was the Hebrew King or the Ottoman Emperor, there is a great anachronism here to which the peasant narrator was quite oblivious.

19. The decline of civilization is suggested in three ways by this allegory: (1) by the cheapening of the materials used for the roofs of the minarets — from gold to silver to bronze; (2) by the loss of charity — from giving an ox to giving a ram to threatening the suppliant's life; and (3) by the loss of prestige and position suffered by the old and white-bearded men who were in the forefront in the golden age. The Turkish audience, well aware of Islam's emphasis on charity and its respect for age, easily inferred the meaning of this tale.

20. *Narrator:* Nuri Konuralp.
Location: Iskenderun, caza city in the province of Hatay.
Date collected: February 1962.
Types: Aarne-Thompson 924, Discussion by Sign Language; 1661, The Triple Tax. Eberhard-Boratav 312, *Die Zeichensprache.* There is no reference to the triple tax in the Eberhard-Boratav type. It does appear in Wesselski's *Der Hodscha Nasreddin* (Weimar, 1911), II, 194, no. 382.

21. *Moskof gavuru* was the expression used here by the narrator, meaning the non-Moslem from Moscow.

22. The reference here is to *kel*, the dermatitis similar to ringworm, which is spread by uncleanliness.

23. *Narrator:* Nuri Gench.
Site of recording: Iskenderun, caza city of Hatay province.
Date collected: February 1962.

24. An amulet for this purpose is called a *muska*. It is a piece of paper on which a religious expression or a quotation from the Koran is written. This is blessed, read to from the Koran, or prayed over by a khoja. It is then folded into a small triangle, an

inch or two across the base, wrapped in oilskin, and hung about the neck of the person to whom it is supposed to bring good luck.

25. *Narrator:* Agah Selchuk.
Site of recording: caza town of Ceyhan in the province of Adana.
Date collected: February 1962.
Types: Aarne-Thompson 503, Gifts of the Little People. Eberhard-Boratav 118, *Die Buckligen.*
Motifs: F261, Fairies dance. F340, Gifts from fairies. F331.1, Mortals win fairies' gratitude by joining their dance. F331.3, Mortals win fairies' gratitude by joining their dance and completing it by adding names of days of week. F344.1, Fairies remove hunchback's hump.

The Turkish bath is almost inevitably haunted or inhabited by supernatural beings of the lesser orders — not giants or monsters or jinns. The fact that most baths are not used after sunset by human beings explains in part its attraction for otherworldly creatures.

In Turkish folklore there is frequent reference to the Wednesday Witches, *Charshamba Jadilar.* They are reputed to be wild-looking creatures with disheveled hair, and so a Turkish child running about with his hair askew may be asked if he thinks he is a Wednesday Witch.

Part V. Köroghlu

1. On December 29, 1961, Ankara newspapers gave front-page notice to the defeat and death of the notorious "Ismo" and his band of outlaws at the hands of gendarmes in Eastern Turkey, near the city of Siirt.

The July 24, 1964, issue of *Time* carried an account of the death of Mehmet Ihsan Kilit, alias Kojero, in a gun battle with police. Before his final defeat Kojero had eluded gendarmes of the Department of Interior so long and so successfully that the Minister of Interior, Sahir Kurutluoghlu, had been forced to resign. It is still too early to know whether this daring bandit's exploits will be immortalized in ballad and tale, but his memory is being preserved in Turkish minds by sympathetic youth of Adana organized under the title Kojero Admirers' Club.

While we were collecting in the Province of Kastamonu, a bus load of people bound for the provincial capital of the same name were robbed, on August 25, 1964, as they were crossing the Ilgaz Mountains. The incident received more attention than usual because the bandits stole not only the valuables in the bus but the passengers' outer garments as well. Among the victims who reported in their underwear to the authorities in the next town were a federal judge and the district attorney of his area.

On September 2, 1964, in the extreme southwestern province of Mughla, a whole line of vehicles was stopped, and between 300 and 400 people were robbed by a large, heavily armed band. Troops were dispatched to pursue the bandits and a few were taken. Opposition newspapers exploited the incident for political purposes. See, for example, *Milliyet,* September 3, 1964, p. 1.

2. Wolfram Eberhard, *Minstrel Tales from Southeastern Turkey* (Berkeley, 1955). This is an excellent introduction to tales about Köroghlu and three other outlaws. Still

perhaps the most authoritative study of Köroghlu is Pertev Naili Boratav's *Köroghlu Destani* (Istanbul, 1931). The word *destan* is roughly equivalent to epic, and the Köroghlu cycle is often referred to (mistakenly, we think) as a folk epic.

3. In Islamic mysticism, largely the product of the Bektashi dervishes (see Part VII), there is a pyramidal hierarchy of saints and angels known as The Three Hundred, The Forty, The Seven, The Four, and The Three. At all times there is one person or being in the world who is aware of the primary quality of Allah, self-knowledge. This person is called *Kutup,* that is, "The Pole." The universe is likened to a mold or pattern, and its soul is Man collectively; in terms of individual units, the Kutup is the pattern for the human being; and the Kutup is subject only to what comes from within. There are two persons near the Kutup, and, all together, they constitute The Three. The two persons near the Kutup are called the *imaman,* that is, persons to follow, to imitate, to agree with. The one on the right of the Kutup is called *imam-i yemin,* and the one on the left is called the *imam-i yesar.* Because the human heart is on the left side of the body, it is the *imam-i yesar* who replaces the Kutup when he dies. The *imam-i yemin* then becomes the *imam-i yesar,* and his place, in turn, is filled by the extreme left member of The Four, on the level just below the level of The Three; everyone in the hierarchy moves up one position. The universe is ruled by these beings who have greater knowledge of things than ordinary mortals. No explanation is given as to why Köroghlu joined The Forty, rather than the lowest level, The Three Hundred. Because forty is a favorite number in folktales, it may have been the influence of the oral tradition rather than any religious reason that placed him at that level immediately after his death. For further information on this element of Islamic mysticism, see Abdülbaki Gölpinarli, *Alevi-Bektashi Nefesleri* (Istanbul, 1963), pp. 331f; also his *Vilayetname, Manaib-i Hünkar Haci Bektash-i Veli* (Istanbul, 1958), p. 139; and John Kingsley Birge, *The Bektashi Order of Dervishes* (Hartford, 1937), pp. 251, 266.

4. For a more comprehensive summary, see Pertev Naili Boratav and H. V. Firatli, *Izahli Halk Shiiri Antolojisi* (Ankara, 1943), pp. 215–216.

5. For the earliest references to Köroghlu in official records, see the *Mühimme Defteri,* which contains the decrees of the various sultans of this period: XLII, 75; XLIII, 302; XLVI, 310. These are accessible at the State Archives at Istanbul. For copies of these and for their translation into modern Turkish, we are indebted to Professor Faruk Sümer of the History Department of Ankara University. See also Boratav's *Halk Edebiyati Dersleri* (Ankara, 1942), pp. 103–104; and Boratav and Firatli, pp. 24–34.

6. For an introductory discussion of the Jelali Revolts, see the chapter so labeled in Emiz Oktay, *Tarih: Yeni ve Yakinchaghlar,* III (Istanbul, 1958); for a more scholarly treatment, see Mustafa Akdagh, "Der Beginn der Celaliden Aufstände," *Dil ve Tarih-Coghrafya Fakultesi Dergisi,* IV, i (1946), 23–50.

7. Eberhard, *Minstrel Tales,* p. 30.

8. Alexander Chodzko, *Specimens of the Popular Poetry of Persia* (London, 1842). Chodzko collected from Turkish tribesmen living in northern Persia. Besides variations in the names of people and places, his version has one major difference from any of the Anatolian texts: Köroghlu and his father are both avid Shiites (Alevi), the Shiite branch of Islam being stronger in Iran than in Turkey where the larger Sunnite group prevails.

9. Boratav and Firatli, *Izahli Halk Shiiri Antolojisi,* p. 215.

10. *Narrator:* Tellal Mehmet Chavush.

KÖROGHLU

Site of recording: caza town of Nallihan of the province of Ankara.

Date collected: April 1962.

11. In many accounts the groom chooses two horses of unpromising appearance, and often the rationale for his choice is elaborated upon. In some versions he watches horses drinking and decides upon their quality in that way; in some, he observes them crossing a stream, noting their behavior in the water; in still others, he chooses colts that he knows have been sired by a river stallion, wild and unearthly. The horse — the better one if there are two — is always named Kirat, The Gray Horse.

12. More often the horse is to be walled in for forty days before he is tested. The tests vary, as do the reasons for his failure to pass the test at the end of the first prescribed period. In the Chodzko text the initial failure is Köroghlu's fault: out of curiosity he removed a chink from the horse's sealed pen in order to peek at Kirat, on the thirty-ninth day, and the single ray of light entering in this way destroyed the charm.

13. *Narrator:* Mustafa Uchar.

Site of recording: village of Omerlanli of the caza of Cihanbeyli of the province of Konya (new name designated by Ministry of Interior, 1965: Tavshanchali).

Date collected: February 1962.

14. Daghistan — the word means the place of mountains — is an area in the Caucasus Mountains just west of the Caspian Sea. It is inhabited by the following Turkic peoples: Karachai, Balkar, and Azeri, as well as by the Caucasian peoples: Circassian, Chechen, Ingush, and Georgian. Daghistan is now part of Soviet Russia.

15. The regular Turkish title of respect, *Haji,* is used here. Inasmuch as the title before the name appears to English-speaking readers like a given name, we have translated it as Pilgrim.

16. Gülnigar is here referring to the stylized discourse of the matchmaker.

17. At this point in the narration, someone from the audience called, "Grandfather, do not hurry! Tell everything slowly so that you do not miss anything."

18. Because this was the first time during our collecting that reference was made to the Chamlibel near Sivas, we asked the narrator if he had ever seen Köroghlu's castle there. "Yes," he replied. "It has a large square in front of it, and there is also a trough, made of stone, where his horse fed. They are still there, and you can see them even today."

19. Kamber is a proper name; *tay* means foal, but it may be used here simply as a diminutive: Little Kamber.

20. A *chesme,* the word used here, is, in fact, a very special kind of fountain. It consists of a slablike section of wall, usually 5–8 feet high, 6–12 feet long, and 1–2 feet thick. Pipes project from this wall, and from the pipes water flows continuously into a stone trough or tub below. The trough may hold 100 gallons, and hence serves as a reservoir for wash water. Because they are supplied by "gravity feed," they are usually in a low spot.

21. It is unlikely that an outlaw in Köroghlu's time would have anything resembling binoculars. Because of Turkey's long and strong military tradition — there is still a universal draft — a number of modern army elements have been superimposed upon the older heroic patterns of the folktale.

22. Although the narrator has heard Köroghlu tales from eastern Turkey, having placed Chamlibel near Sivas, he has also been influenced by versions from the Bolu region. Nallihan — literally, the inn of the blacksmith — is a town not far from Bolu. In Nallihan is a huge, rusted horseshoe fastened to a stone wall, said to have been that of

Köroghlu's horse. Nearby too is Köroghlu Mountain. Köroghlu's going to Nallihan to have his horse shod argues for placing Chamlibel in the nearby Bolu region, perhaps on Köroghlu Mountain. He would hardly have traveled the 600 kilometers from Sivas to Nallihan to have his horse shod!

How Köroghlu collected his band of followers is often recounted in great detail. Here the meeting with Son of the Blacksmith (Demcircioghlu) is summarized very briefly; the abduction of Ayvaz from his father's butcher shop, a lengthy episode in itself, is merely alluded to. Usküdar, near Istanbul, may be better known to Western readers as Scutari.

23. All passages in verse were sung by the narrator. The verse suffers from translation generally — lost, for example, is the beautiful vowel euphony of the Turkish — and, more specifically, from the necessity we felt to translate it literally in order to make its content clear.

24. The motifs of the forbidden chamber (C611) and the youth smitten with love for a woman whose picture he has seen (H1381.3.1.2.1) are common in folktales. Among the previously recorded texts, however, only Text O, collected at Elazigh, contains these motifs; they occur in Episode 3. See Eberhard, *Minstrel Tales,* p. 79, note 35.

25. The man's name in Turkish was Haji Baytar, *Haji* meaning Pilgrim, and *Baytar,* Veterinarian. Although the name rendered into English is awkward, we have retained the literal meaning that the Turkish listener would understand.

26. This sentence summarizes an incident rather too quickly for the usual pace of the folktale. Because the narrator felt under pressure to complete his tale, as he subsequently revealed, there was undoubtedly telescoping here.

27. The context of the story suggests that The Pilgrim Veterinarian was in fact an animal doctor, for his function in the tale is limited to selecting or securing a horse. His role as manager of a government commissary is a late addition.

28. This also is probably an anachronism. The corrugated iron doors rolled down at night to protect shops are of more recent times.

29. During winters of the past, as many as 25–30 percent of Turkey's cattle died of starvation and cold, and the survivors were often weak and unsteady on their feet in the spring. "To collapse like a March bull," or "To fall like a March bull," has become proverbial in Turkey.

30. The expression used here is *Has Bahche,* which means, literally, special garden; but to Turks it suggests paradisiacal qualities: beauty, peace, plenty. It is comparable to the Garden of Eden.

31. In Turkish the girl was called Akcha Kiz, whitish girl, literally.

32. All accounts of Kirat credit him with special abilities, though all do not cite him as immortal. In Chodzko's text, for example, he dies before Köroghlu does. The suggestion here of his immortality may be a reference to one of the incidents appearing in several of the texts. Köroghlu was sent by his father to a certain spot along a stream where, at a prescribed time, the *Abu-Hayat,* the Spring of Life, would rise in bubbles to the surface; this was the magic fluid which would cure the father's blindness. On the way home with the jug of elixir, Köroghlu drank some of it, unwittingly assuring thereby his own immortality, and then accidentally spilled the rest on his horse, thus making Kirat also deathless. The Abu-Hayat is discussed at greater length in note 45 of Part I.

33. In preparation for death, many Turks have their shrouds — sometimes even their coffins — made while they are still alive. Old people often keep on hand a roll of white

linen, to be used for their shroud, and a cake of soap to be used for the ritual washing before burial.

34. Until the present century it was thought disgraceful in Turkey for a man to go about in public bareheaded. Note that it is not the long underwear but the bare head that disturbs the bey.

35. Caucasians and for a long while Christianized, the Circassians were converted to Islam in the seventeenth century. Located north of the Black Sea, their territory was once incorporated in the Ottoman Empire, later (1829) ceded to Russia. Although their fair-skinned women were legendary for beauty — many were sold or given to Turkish sultans for their harems — the Circassians as a people were fierce and untractable. To avoid Russian rule several hundred thousand migrated to Anatolia in the nineteenth century, and there are still several sizable communities in Turkey today, one of about 25,000 centered at Pinarbashi, in central Anatolia, and another in the Adapazari area of western Turkey. At present they are considered by many intellectual Turks to be the only remaining minority with reasonable claims to nationhood.

36. The high, wedge-shaped hat, made of caracul fur, worn in winter in several Eastern European and Asiatic countries.

37. In the Turkish chivalric tradition there was a practice of permitting each combatant to take turns at attacking and defending. During his offensive period, the combatant might use all the weapons in his possession. This is quite different from the more familiar image of medieval combat in which each participant was involved simultaneously in attack and defense.

38. There is a song omitted here: Köroghlu's exhortation to his men. At this point in the tale, the narrator looked at his watch and saw that the afternoon prayer time was approaching. "I must go to prayers soon," he said, "and besides, my sheep and goats are probably starving by now."

39. Telli Hanim's father was supposedly the ruler of Akshehir in this tale. He is sometimes referred to as padishah, but at this point as vezir. Although a vezir was usually a minister assisting the sultan or one of his advisers, the word would sometimes be applied to any government official on a high administrative level.

40. She is immodestly acknowledging how rare and sweet she is. Snow brought from the mountains in summer is considered one of nature's wonders. The fruit — the narrator actually specified the pomegranate — of the Garden of Eden is, of course, of a superior kind. It is also interesting that she here calls him not Lord Hasan (Hasan Bey) but General Hasan (Hasan Pasha).

41. The inference here is that the dervish was Hizir who, in such eleventh-hour rescues, often appeared in that guise.

Part VI. Anticlerical Tales

1. *Narrator:* Mehmet Chatal.
Site of recording: village of Chamalan in the caza of Tarsus in Ichel province.
Date collected: February 1962.
Types: Aarne-Thompson 1360 C, Old Hildebrand. Eberhard-Boratav 273, *Der dumme Kaufman.* Both of these types concern only the first part of our tale, the disabusing of the husband about his faithless wife. Interestingly, although the denouement of our tale

is anticlerical, it fails to utilize the anticlerical element of these types that form its initial episode; in Old Hildebrand the wife's lover is a priest.

Motifs: K2058, Pretended piety.

2. Despite the fact that the veil has been outlawed now for four decades, there is still the feeling in some parts of rural Turkey that women should not expose their faces to the gaze of men. Peasant women invariably wear shawls which they clutch about their faces. In some areas a woman will turn her face to the wall when a man approaches. The wife in this tale is affecting such virtue when she faces the wall in the presence of any male creature.

3. The narrator spoke of the Khoja with Bells (*Zilli Khoja*) as if he had been a historical personage. We know of no specific individual with whom he could be identified.

4. *Narrator:* Muharrem Choban.

Site of recording: village of Ashagh Chavundur in the caza of Chubuk of the province of Ankara.

Date collected: March 1962.

Types: Aarne-Thompson 883 A, The Innocent Slandered Maiden. Eberhard-Boratav 245, *Die schöne Helva-Verkäuferin*. In the Eberhard-Boratav type the would-be seducer is not a khoja but a lesser religious figure, a muezzin. Both the Aarne-Thompson and the Eberhard-Boratav types are longer than our tale and are similar in some ways to the variant in our archive described in note 11 below.

5. Aga is the unofficial title of respect given to a wealthy landlord in Turkey. Comparable to an English squire or a Scottish laird, he is the chief personage in a village, often ruling it in an arbitrary and almost feudal manner.

6. Ordinarily men and women do not use the bathhouse at the same time. For women, whose social lives are strictly circumscribed, a day at the bath is a cherished occasion; they may spend six to eight hours there, having their lunch sent in to them by prearrangement.

For a good brief introduction to the physical and social aspects of the Turkish bath in rural Turkey, see chapter X of Pierce's *Life in a Turkish Village*.

7. The *nalin* is a very thick (three or four inches) clog or patten worn in Turkish baths. It is much heavier than the average clog worn in shower stalls by American bathers. After one comes out of the steam rooms and the bath proper, one rests on benches in the lounge, where tea and coffee may be served; for use in the lounge, cloth or leather bedroom slippers are issued.

8. The expression Ahmet and Mehmet used in this way is equivalent to every Tom, Dick, and Harry.

9. The Turkish coffee house is not like a European or American cafe or restaurant. Only coffee and tea are served — no food. Customers are all male. In order to work in a coffee house, the aga's daughter had to pass as a man, hence the skin over her hair to make her look like a bald boy, a keloghlan. This method of disguise is a regular motif in Turkish folktales.

10. The fact that the Coffee House Beauty is understood to be a man suggests a male interest in male beauty that has homosexual overtones.

11. In a variant of this tale collected at the village of Chamalan, in southern Turkey (Ichel province), the exiled daughter marries a poor, nomadic Yürük tribesman, with the proviso that she be allowed to name her children as she sees fit. She names her three sons What Have We Become? What Shall We Become? and What Shall We In-

herit? In the recognition scene it is the suggestiveness of these names that leads the father to identify his wronged daughter. This is also listed as 883 C, a variant of the Aarne-Thompson type. Interestingly, both the texts cited by Aarne-Thompson, one Greek and the other Turkish, were recorded in Anatolia.

12. This is a regular formula for the ending of a Turkish folktale. The imaginary Mountains of Kaf are part of Moslem mythology, thought to form the rim of the world around the edges of the Circumambient Ocean.

13. *Narrator:* Saliha Arel.
Site of recording: Sivas, provincial capital of the province of Sivas.
Date collected: November 1961.
Types: Aarne-Thompson 1536 B, The Three Hunchback Brothers Drowned. Eberhard-Boratav 264, *Die drei Buckeligen.*

14. In earlier times Turks did not often participate in the business life of their country. The peasants tilled the land and the upper class Ottomans were engaged mainly in government administration, military service, and religion (which then included teaching on all levels of education). Commerce and industry were carried on by minority groups, primarily Greeks and Armenians, who were Christians. It was almost a foregone conclusion that a merchant would be an "infidel," and it is thus that he appears in most folktales.

15. Although alcoholic beverages can be bought throughout Turkey, and although there are taverns in major cities, taverns are rare elsewhere. Devout Moslems do not drink, and in most parts of rural Turkey consumption of alcohol is low. As a defense against the growing custom of drinking in the more secularized cities, a prohibitionist society known as The Green Crescent (*Yeshilay*) has been organized; both the crescent and the sacred color of green emphasize the religious motivation of the society.

16. Raki is a liquor made from rice, molasses, or grain. In Arab lands it is known as arrack. Turkish raki has an anise flavor. Mixed with water it becomes milky in appearance, and it is often referred to as lion's milk. The most popular hard liquor native to Turkey, it is now produced by a state-operated distillery.

17. The village khoja commonly rides a donkey, and so his parallel, the priest, is also given a donkey. Nasreddin Khoja, who provides the principal khoja image in Turkey, had a donkey which figures in countless tales about him. On postcards, greeting cards, souvenirs, and various decorations Nasreddin Khoja is pictured riding his donkey, usually seated on it backwards.

Part VII. Anecdotes

1. The anecdote dependent upon a play on words for its humor or wit is known as a *nükte.*

2. Weimar, 1911.

3. *Nasreddin Hoca,* selected and translated by Mübin Manyasig (Istanbul, 1960). Since the publication of this booklet, tourism has been upgraded to the status of a separate ministry.

4. The fact that Tamerlane stayed at Akshehir for some time — Bayazid I, the captive Ottoman Sultan died in his camp there in 1403 — may have merged with local legend to initiate hypothesis number 4.

5. A good summary of the information available about Nasreddin Khoja along with a bibliography of studies, can be found in *The Encyclopaedia of Islam,* III (Leiden, 1936).

Many of the Nasreddin Khoja tales appear in the folklore of other Near and Middle Eastern countries. The Arabs have similar tales about one Djuha, and the Berbers about Djeha. Sicilian tales about the fool Giufa (Giuca) seem to be related, and those in Persia about the Mullah clearly are, in many instances, parallel, as a quick survey of Alice Geer Kelsey's *Once the Mullah* (London, 1954) will reveal. Khoja tales practically identical with those current in Turkey are common in Romania, Bulgaria, Greece, Albania, and Yugoslavia, not only as vestiges of the Turkish occupation but also as the continuing lore of the many Turks still living in the Balkans; the same is true of the Armenian, Georgian, and Ukrainian Soviet Socialist Republics.

The oldest known (1625) European manuscript (Leiden, no. 2715) about Nasreddin Khoja contained 76 tales. A chapbook in Arabic script appeared in Istanbul in 1837 with 125 tales. In 1883 Mehmed Tewfik published a selection of 71 tales from this chapbook, omitting all of those that were considered coarse. The first really important edition is that of Ignaz Kunos, *Nasreddin Hodsa Tréfái* (Budapest, 1899), containing 166 tales collected between Aydin and Konya. The fullest edition in Turkish is that of Weled Chelebi, the fourth edition of which (Istanbul, 1926) contains nearly 400 tales. Albert Wesselski's *Der Hodscha Nasreddin* (Weimar, 1911), with over 500 tales in two volumes, is still the most complete collection in print. For an English text of some of the tales, Henry D. Barnham provides a fair sampling in his *Nasr-ed-din Khoja* (London, 1923; New York, 1924), though the foreword by Valentine Chirol is not reliable. Other editions in Turkish and in English are listed in the Bibliography.

6. For this particular aspect of the subject, see Hellmut Ritter, *Karagös, türkische Schattenspiele,* 3 vols. (I, Hanover, 1924; II, Istanbul, 1941; III, Wiesbaden, 1953).

7. Janissary is the form used in Western Europe. The Turkish is *yeni cheri* for new troops, as this body of soldiery was always called.

8. In his book *The Bektashi Order of Dervishes* (Hartford, 1937) John Kingsley Birge posits a founder named Haji Bektash at the inception of the movement: "It would seem to be reasonably clear that a man named Haji Bektash came to Asia Minor in the thirteenth century; settled in the neighbourhood of *Kir Shehir* in the village later called by his name; was himself a part of a general movement of *Türkmen Babas* carrying on under a guise of fairly orthodox Islam both social and religious practices of earlier Turkish life, combined with a system of mysticism influenced by the Central Asian Sufi, Ahmet Yesevi; gradually won for himself a general recognition among these Türkmen tribes as the leading saint of the times; won and initiated definite followers; taught the beginnings of a simple ritual including the use of the candle, and a ceremonial meal and dance; wore himself and gave his followers a characteristic headpiece; and before he died appointed and sent into areas in different directions apostles who were to carry on his teachings" (pp. 50–51). Although not all scholars concur with this hypothesis, most would agree that Birge has produced a valuable study of the sect. He not only worked, over a long period, with the pertinent historical documents, but he also was on friendly terms with a number of Bektashi leaders in the Balkans and in Turkish Thrace.

9. *Encyclopaedia of Islam,* I, new ed. (1960).

10. *Narrator:* Darbaz Ozel, a Turkish Kurd, 80.

Site of recording: village of Chorja in the caza of Cihanbeyli in the province of Konya (new name designated by Ministry of Interior, 1965: Damlakuyu).

Date collected: March 1962.

Types: Aarne-Thompson 1313 A, The Man Who Takes Seriously the Prediction of Death.

Motifs: J2311.1, Numskull to die when horse breaks wind three times.

This is probably the Nasreddin Khoja tale with the widest distribution in Turkey. Seemingly it is known to every Turk.

11. In these anecdotes about Nasreddin Khoja the word Khoja is used almost as if it were a name. We have, accordingly, capitalized it.

12. *Narrator:* Tellal Mehmet Chavush.

Site of recording: Nallihan, caza town in the province of Ankara.

Date collected: April 1962.

Types: Aarne-Thompson 1689, Thank God They Weren't Peaches!

13. Throughout its history Turkey has honored various types of headgear as upper class status symbols. The much discussed fez, abolished by Atatürk despite the furious protests of Moslem orthodoxy, was not wholly acceptable attire until the clothing reform law of 1829. This statute then restricted the sacred turban to high-ranking religious officials. This was the "small turban" which, in turn, had replaced the billowing "large turban" in which most sultans, through the eighteenth century, were pictured. It is the older, oversize turban to which reference is here made. There is an early miniature, probably sixteenth-century, of Nasreddin Khoja wearing such a turban in the Hazine Library of the Topkapi Palace in Istanbul.

14. Tamerlane did use elephants in his campaigns. Legend says that his victory over Bayazid I and the Ottoman forces, just west of Ankara, was facilitated by panic that spread among the Turks when they first encountered these huge beasts.

15. In a variant of this tale in our archive Nasreddin Khoja returns to his village with the female elephant. The angry villagers assemble and their spokesman demands, "Khoja, what did you do at Tamerlane's court?" To this Khoja simply replies, "And where were you when I was at Tamerlane's court?"

16. This tale is actually a combination of three separate Nasreddin Khoja anecdotes. Nowhere else in our archive are they joined in this sequence, though Tamerlane, the element common to all three, appears in many separate Khoja tales.

17. *Narrator:* Ahmet Kiygi.

Site of recording: Ankara.

Date collected: May 1962.

Although this is a tale with fairly wide distribution in rural Turkey, the version we have included was collected in Ankara. It is one of the few in our archive not collected on tape, for it was told by the family doctor of the two editors in the course of an ordinary conversation. Asked when the seriously ill member of the family would be well enough to travel, Dr. Kiygi responded that that would depend upon the patient's rate of recovery. Then to illustrate the point he told this Nasreddin Khoja story.

18. *Narrator:* Ahmet Uyar.

Site of recording: village of Zir of the caza of Yenimahalle (a suburb of Ankara) of the province of Ankara (new name designated by Ministry of Interior, 1965: Uluköy).

Date collected: January 1962.

Types: Aarne-Thompson 1663, Dividing Five Eggs Equally between Two Men and One Woman.

Motifs: J1249.1, Dividing five eggs equally between two men and a woman.

19. Outside Turkey Tamerlane does not, to our knowledge, appear in this tale. In some Turkish versions he is not present either, but after his frequent appearance in

variants that we collected, we came to think of this tale as one of the "Tamerlane Group" among Nasreddin Khoja anecdotes.

20. This is Khoja's comic attempt to acquire status by appearing to be in the large turban group.

21. *Narrator:* Hasan Kachar, muhtar.

Site of recording: village of Emrem Sultan of the caza of Beypazari of the province of Ankara.

Date collected: April 1962.

Emrem Sultan, after whom was named the village where this tale was collected, was the teacher of Turkey's great folk poet of the Middle Ages, Yunus Emre (1250?-1307). Unorthodox, mystic, and in many ways Romantic, Yunus Emre was "folk" primarily in his use of colloquial Turkish rather than the Persian of the court poets and of his contemporary Mevlana.

This Khoja tale and several legends of Yunus Emre were collected in the village guest house which is attached to the tomb of Emrem Sultan. Although the thousands of tombs of Moslem saints, considered shrines, were closed at the time of the Atatürk reforms — they were condemned as breeders of pernicious superstitions — this one was allowed to remain open, partly because of its historical value, partly because Yunus Emre and everything associated with him had become objects of a nationalist literary cult of the twentieth century. A typical central Anatolian village of 300 people, Emrem Sultan has probably changed very little since the time of Yunus Emre.

22. *Narrator:* Mehmet Otach.

Site of recording: Chorja village of the caza of Cihanbeyli in the province of Konya (new name designated by Ministry of Interior, 1965: Damlakuyu).

Date collected: March 1962.

Barnham's *Nasr-ed-din Khoja* includes a similar tale. There the mendicant claims that he is "God's guest," and so Khoja takes him to "God's house," the mosque.

23. A hafiz is a person who has committed to memory the entire Koran. Such an achievement earns respect from the community, and here the hafiz in question was trying to exploit his status to get a night's lodging from Nasreddin Khoja.

24. *Narrator:* Darbaz Ozel.

Site of recording: village of Chorja in the caza of Cihanbeyli in the province of Konya (new name designated by Ministry of Interior, 1965: Damlakuyu).

Date collected: March 1962.

25. *Narrator:* Mehmet Otach.

Site of recording: village of Chorja in the caza of Cihanbeyli in the province of Konya (new name designated by Ministry of Interior, 1965: Damlakuyu).

Date collected: March 1962.

26. *Narrator:* Ahmet Uyar.

Site of recording: village of Zir of the caza of Yenimahalle (a suburb of Ankara) of the province of Ankara (new name designated by the Ministry of Interior, 1965: Uluköy).

Date collected: January 1962.

Types: Aarne-Thompson 821 B, Chickens from Boiled Eggs. Eberhard-Boratav 295, *Die Aufrechnung.* In their Type 295 Eberhard and Boratav do not cite this as a well-known Nasreddin Khoja story — perhaps because they consistently exclude anecdotes from their index and Nasreddin Khoja is always considered a fikra character.

Motifs: J1191.2, Advocate suggests cooking peas for planting to point a moral.

27. There are 100 kurus to the lira, and the Turkish lira is currently worth about ten cents in American funds. The purchasing power of the kurus here might well indicate the date of this variant of the tale.

28. *Narrator:* Mehmet Altach.

Site of recording: collected at Sinop Penitentiary, but the informant was a resident of the village of Yukara Asma of the caza of Bor of the province of Nighde.

Data collected: August 1964.

29. *Narrator:* Mehmet Genishgen.

Site of recording: caza city of Tashköprü of the province of Kastamonu.

Date collected: August 1964.

30. It is often pointless to try to establish the historicity of rulers mentioned in Turkish folktales. Peasant narrators have little knowledge of and less regard for dates, and Sultan Mahmut might be any one of the six Ottoman emperors so named. If Bekri Mustafa did live during the reign of Murad IV (1623–1640), then the Mahmut referred to might be Mahmut (Mehmet, Mohammed) IV who reigned from 1648 to 1687. Murad IV was succeeded by his brother Ibrahim, and Ibrahim was succeeded by his son Mahmut IV.

31. The Church of Saint Sophia (Hagia Sophia) became a mosque in 1453, with the conquest of Constantinople, and remained one until Atatürk converted it into a museum in 1935. Even while serving as a mosque, it retained the title Aya Sofia.

32. The muezzin probably did little more than chant or recite parts of the ritual, the imam or priest being in charge of the service. There are two parts to the Moslem funeral service at the mosque, one inside the building and one outside, in the mosque yard. There there is always a raised marble slab on which the coffin rests for this part of the service.

33. This is the Turkish onomatopoetic representation for the sound made by whispering.

34. *Narrator:* Ahmet Oztürk, muhtar.

Site of recording: village of Ejirli in the caza of Denizli, capital city of the province of Denizli.

Date collected: May 1962.

35. *Narrator:* Mehmet Genishgen.

Site of recording: caza city of Tashköprü of the province of Kastamonu.

Date collected: August 1964.

Types: Aarne-Thompson 1262, Roasting the Meat. There is no Eberhard-Boratav entry for this type, although it is a very common tale in Turkey. A variant of it is one of the best-known Nasreddin Khoja stories. See, for example, Wesselski's *Hodscha Nasreddin,* II, 212, no. 434.

Motifs: J1191.7, Rice pan on hole, fire far away. As easy to cook rice thus as to warm man at distance from a lamp in a balcony. J1945, Warming hands across the river.

36. *Narrator:* Mehmet Altach.

Site of recording: collected at Sinop Penitentiary, but the informant was a resident of the village of Yukara Asma of the caza of Bor of the province of Nighde.

Date collected: August 1964.

37. The Yürüks, many of them latecomers to Anatolia, are still largely nomadic. In the summer they graze their flocks high in the Taurus Mountains; in the winter they move south, often to the Mediterranean coast. Because they are nomadic, they do not, of course, have mosques, and might be considered faithless for that reason; living

largely in southern Turkey, they are often under the influence of the minority Shiite branch of Islam and the related Kizilbash sect, and so are considered unorthodox.

Not all Yürüks are nomadic; we collected tales in several Yürük villages, including Ejirli, on the Plains of Denizli. Nor are all nomadic groups Yürüks, as is often implied when the words Yürük and nomad are used interchangeably.

38. *Narrator:* Ibrahim Shafak.
Site of recording: Kastamonu, capital of the province of Kastamonu.
Date collected: August 1964.

39. *Narrator:* Omer Chatal.
Site of recording: caza town of Ayvalik of the province of Izmir.
Date collected: May 1962.

40. *Narrator:* Hasan Otach.
Site of recording: village of Chorja of the caza of Cihanbeyli of the province of Konya (new name designated by Ministry of Interior, 1965: Damlakuyu).
Date collected: March 1962.

41. *Narrator:* Kemal Tashchioghlu.
Site of recording: village of Gökchedere of the caza of Yalova of the province of Kojaeli.
Date collected: May 1962.

42. During the daylight hours of the month of Ramazan faithful Moslems, with certain exceptions, are supposed to fast, eating and drinking absolutely nothing. Those excepted from this strict self-denial are children (girls under nine years of age, boys under twelve), invalids, pregnant women, and travelers.

43. *Narrator:* Omer Uysal.
Site of recording: Adana, capital city of the province of Adana.
Date collected: February 1962.

44. This is an anachronism, of course, for the Bektashi sect was not founded until at least four centuries after the time of Haroun al Raschid. The fifth and most famous of the Abbasid caliphs (786–809), he brought Baghdad to its highest point culturally. Best known in folk literature for his appearance in *The Thousand and One Nights,* Haroun is a character in many other folktales too. Of especial interest is a large group of tales, told throughout Turkey but with greatest frequency in the extreme eastern provinces, in which the character of Haroun is undercut by that of his brother or son, Behlül Dane. In most of them Behlül Dane, supposedly a simpleton but actually very wise, demonstrates intellectual and spiritual superiority to the caliph. Although the holdings in our archive are limited for this area, they are adequate to suggest the need for a separate study of Behlül Dane tales.

45. Opening of the hands, with palms upward, is a gesture of respect to the Deity used by Moslems in prayer.

46. Rebuking God in this manner is, of course, blasphemous, but this is typical of the behavior attributed to the members of the Bektashi order.

There is a parallel to this tale in the *Masnavi* of Jalal al-Din Rumi, the thirteenth-century mystic who founded the Mevlevi order of dervishes, centered at Konya. In the *Masnavi* the tale is entitled "The Bold Dervish of Herta," though nothing is said of his particular order.

The *Masnavi* version (like all of the exempla of that great religious work) has a clear-cut moral at the end. After making his protest to God that he is not as well off as the slaves of a certain nobleman, the dervish is taught a lesson, or perhaps exhorted to devotion, by a voice from heaven. It so happened that the nobleman fell into disfavor with the king of that land and was imprisoned for embezzlement. Then his slaves were put to the rack and tortured to death, but not one of them would reveal the secrets of his master. In a dream the dervish heard a voice out of heaven: "You too learn to be a slave, sirrah, and then come to Me." A. J. Arberry, ed., *More Tales from the Masnavi* (London, 1963), p. 157.

47. *Narrator:* Omer Uysal.
Site of recording: Adana, capital city of the province of Adana.
Date collected: February 1962.

48. *Narrator:* Omer Uysal.
Site of recording: Adana, capital city of the province of Adana.
Date collected: February 1962.

49. In the seventeenth century when the kurus, the hundredth part of a lira, was silver, the lira itself could logically have been golden.

50. See note 4 of Part II.

51. *Narrator:* Hasan Ozgürbüz.
Site of recording: collected in the caza town of Unye in Ordu province; the informant, however, had spent most of his life at Kula, a caza town in the province of Manisa.
Date collected: September 1964.

52. This is a common remark made, throughout Turkey, by those who do not fast during Ramazan.

53. Probably for George, but certainly non-Turkish and hence, by implication, non-Moslem.

54. *Narrator:* Nuri Gench.
Site of recording: Iskenderun, caza city in the province of Hatay.
Date collected: February 1962.

55. There are still great packs of wolves in Turkey, and the large, powerful dogs of shepherds are indispensable aids. They are fitted with steel-spiked collars to protect their throats against wolves. Dogs are, however, considered unclean creatures and for this reason are not permitted inside Moslem homes.

56. Great emphasis is placed on charity in Moslem lands. Almost inevitably a will reserves at least some small portion of the estate for the poor of the area.

57. *Narrator:* Kemal Tashchioghlu.
Site of recording: village of Gökchedere of the caza of Yalova of the province of Kojaeli.
Date collected: May 1962.

58. One of the most popular desserts in Turkey, *baklava* is made from light, flaky pastry, baked thoroughly, and then soaked in honey.

59. *Narrator:* Hasan Ozgürbüz.
Site of recording: collected in the caza town of Unye in Ordu province, but the informant had spent most of his life in Kula, a caza town in the province of Manisa.
Date collected: September 1964.
Type: Aarne-Thompson 1861, Jokes on Judges.
Motif: J1192.2, Error was in the honey.

60. There are many variants of this tale in Turkey. Often it is told with Nasreddin Khoja as protagonist. See, for example, Barnham's *The Khoja: Tales of Nasr-ed-Din*, pp. 224–226. Almost always ending with a witticism, this anecdote qualifies as a fikra of the kind known as a *nükte*. In some variants the witty rejoinder is not made at the

time of the bribe but later, after the judge has discovered the joke played upon him. He sends his clerk to the protagonist requesting to have the contract returned because there was an error in it. Refusing this request, the protagonist says, "Tell the kadi that the error was in the jar, not in the contract." Close to this is the version in Wesselski's *Hodscha Nasreddin,* I, nos. 170, 252.

Index

INDEX

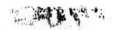